Spirit

of an

Eagle

By

Steven S. Foster

Spirit of an Eagle
Copyright © 2018 by Steven S. Foster

WWW.SPIRITOFANEAGLE.COM

Cover design by Scott Foster

www.sfislandmana.com

ISBN 978-0-578-43977-8

Dedication

I dedicate this novel to my lovely wife, Sandi, who has been my muse, confidant and best friend for more than 50 years of marriage. Her support and advice helped me to write the Spirit of an Eagle, as a work of love, and it is a fulfillment of my dream.

Acknowledgements

I am grateful for the following people, who helped me. First, I thank my son, Scott Foster, who designed the cover of my novel. Second, Amanda Rau, my editor provided the guidance and clarity to make this novel a reality. Third, I thank Sam Cudney, author of How to Publish Your Book for Free. He patiently guided and assisted me in the final formatting for publishing. Also, I appreciate the advice and support I received from D.F. Dempster, author of Chapel on the Moor.

Table of Contents

1 Live or Die

I cy wind howled and swirled around Anthony's frost-covered face. He stood knee-deep in snow, with wet sneakers, and his flesh shivered under a light denim jacket. Never had he felt so cold, lost and hopeless. Anthony squinted through frozen eyelids but he only saw a blur of white, like a veil over a dead man. It would be over soon.

Perhaps it was better this way--to die in an unforgiving wilderness alone. Existence had been bitterly cruel since his wife, Amy's death. How could he go on living with himself? It was his fault that she died. Heartbroken, he no longer had the strength to face the agony of sorrow, shame and grief. He must die.

Anthony plopped his rear into the snow, and he held up shaky hands to surrender. What a strange sensation, he thought. It had only been a couple of weeks ago when he longed to live, to feel, to taste.

Now, he just wanted to sleep and not wake up, so he laid back in the soft, cold, damp snow. Tiny flakes tickled his eyelids, and he blinked, as white flurries blanketed his face. The only sound he heard was the slight ruffling of his leather gloves settling across his chest. He waited in deep silence, closed his eyes and felt no pain.

Just as he was about to drift off, something jerked him awake. In that thick haze of his tortured mind, ghostly images of his past flashed and tormented him without mercy. Anthony's heart raced, and he gasped. "No! Please God!" He sobbed uncontrollably, "Not again!

Anthony's gut wrenched in agony. He tried to vomit but only had dry heaves, and he curled up in a fetal position. He felt so small, and he shook his head from side to side. "No! You can't make me go back!"

May 9, 1969: Village firefight, Vietnam.

Yet, his demons forced him to live it all over again. Flames swirled around a burning village and shots ricocheted from every direction. Mutilated bodies strewn everywhere, and Army medic, Anthony Lorenzo, was on his knees. He cradled a naked Vietnamese baby girl in his arms, and she had to be no more than a year old. Heartbroken for a child he did not know, he tried to wipe the bloody hair away from her tiny face. Amidst all this hellish madness, he knew she was dying.

If only he could save her. Suddenly, a sergeant grabbed his shoulder. "Let's go! Move it!"

Lorenzo ignored the order and frantically tried to breath life-giving air into her lungs. Her lips were cold. "No!" Tears streamed down his cheeks, "Come on!" He blew air into her tiny mouth and nostrils. Nothing. She was dead. He gasped and cried. She was gone. Slowly he laid her body on ashen, burned-out ground.

Shots fired, "Tat-a-tat! Tat-a-tat!"

"Doc!" A soldier cried out, "I'm hit!"

Lorenzo had no time to grieve, to feel. Instead, he ran and knelt at the side of a young soldier with a severe wound to his chest. Blood oozed, and the medic held the dying soldier's hand. "Hang on, Benny!"

"Doc!" Benny wheezed, "I don't want to die!"

"Hey! Look at me. We'll get you out of here."

The dying soldier gazed into his eyes. "Doc! Tell my mom I…" The kid gasped his last breath.

Lorenzo felt a bloody hand go limp. That fatal image seared into his mind.

December 9, 1969: Back in the states.

Instantly, Lorenzo's memory flashed to his San Diego home after his discharge, and his demons followed him there. He desperately tried to forget. So, he drank heavily with his buddies every night after work. Loud music, insane laughter and all the sickening booze could not quiet his tortured mind.

Nothing helped...except his wife, Amy, the most important person in his life. They had only been married a month before he was shipped out for over a year, and he returned just a few weeks ago. In that hellish bar, Lorenzo remembered her, staggered toward the parking lot and somehow drove home.

When he slammed the door of his 1968 Ford pick-up truck, he noticed Amy at the entryway of their apartment. Ashamed and embarrassed, he could not look at her angry expression. Instead, he plopped on the living room couch.

"Anthony! How could you?" Amy's voice snapped like a whip.

Dizzy, he tried to see through a drunken haze. He saw the hurt and disappointment in her sweet hazel eyes, and it was like a branding iron, which seared into his heart. Anthony Lorenzo lowered his head in shame, stared at his shoes and felt like the barroom scum he tracked in.

Amy shook her head with disgust. "You promised me that you wouldn't drink anymore, Anthony!"

He bobbed his head and tried to focus, while he sat up as straight as his inebriated mind would allow. It pained him to see the tears in her eyes. "Ah, come on, baby." He waved his right hand in a clumsy attempt to make an oath. "I swear this is the last time. No more booze from now on."

Amy plopped on the couch next to him and sighed, "I've heard that too many times." She folded her arms across her chest and angrily fumed. "Besides, you were supposed to take me out to dinner tonight. You promised me, Anthony."

"Hey babe," Anthony leaned forward and slapped his knees, "We can still go. Come on honey," he pleaded and stood up, "Let's have some fun."

"No, Anthony," she sat firmly on the couch with her arms crossed.

Without warning, Anthony grabbed Amy's hand and yanked her hard off the couch. "I said, let's go!" Surprised by his own rough behavior, he released his grip. "Oh! Sorry, babe, I didn't mean to do that," He sighed and gazed into her teary eyes.

Amy cried softly and rubbed her right wrist. "What's gotten into you? Ever since you got back from Vietnam, you've been acting crazy!" Amy stroked his cheek and hugged him. "Please, honey, talk to me. I love you." The warmth of his wife's hand soothed his heated face.

"Hey!" He tried to smile as though nothing had happened. "Come on, let's go out! I'll take you some place special." He wobbled and straightened himself up as best as he could.

For the first time, Amy giggled and tried to make the best of it. "Okay," she shook her head and sighed, "I must be crazy, too."

"Alright! That's my girl!" Anthony held her hand. When they walked to her car, Amy took the keys from her purse and smiled, "I'll drive."

Suddenly, Anthony grabbed her keys and laughed playfully, "No, I got this." He ran awkwardly to the passenger side and opened the door. "Come, my Lady."

A few drops of rain splattered the windshield. Amy frowned warily and sighed. "Oh well, at least it's nice to see you smile. Alright, honey, I'll get in…but, you better be careful."

With Amy in the passenger seat, he had a false sense of confidence, and he sincerely believed that he could handle the driving. That is, until he drove into heavy traffic and raindrops pelted the windshield. He squinted from blinding on-coming headlights, but he convinced himself that it was okay.

Wiping his eyes, he suddenly realized that he drove into the wrong lane of cars heading right at him. In a panic, Anthony swerved back to the right, while the car instantly hydroplaned, and it was airborne.

The car flipped over several times, and Anthony bounced around like a rag doll in a tin can. Yet, he felt no pain. Metal scratched, creaked and crunched brutally in his ears. Amy let out an eerie scream that seemed far away. Deadly silence crept into his foggy mind. Nothing moved. What happened, he wondered? Groggy and disoriented, Anthony realized that he was upside down, with his head on the roof, and his legs were curled oddly on the passenger side.

A siren screamed out from somewhere. When he tried to move, he discovered his wife was missing. "Amy!" Dazed and confused, Anthony twisted and struggled until he crawled out onto the cold, wet pavement. He staggered to his feet, tried to orient himself, and he felt something wet on his forehead. In the glare of head lights, rain drops dribbled down into his eyes. He blinked and tasted blood on his lips.

Anthony Lorenzo's heart raced, and he frantically looked in all directions. People gawked like vultures, and he heard their voices, but he stumbled to the other side of the car. Bright lights beamed down at the puddles of heavy rain, and, with wobbly knees, he managed to get closer to Amy's crumpled body on the road.

"Amy!" Lorenzo rushed and knelt at her side. When he touched her mangled face, blood oozed between his fingers, and he knew that his once beautiful wife was dead. Bitterly cold raindrops streamed down his cheeks, and he turned away.

Anthony's legs buckled, then he fell flat onto the pavement, and he sobbed. His gut wretched, and he puked. He had seen the blood and gore of war, but this was more than he could take. That horribly disfigured body beside him was his wife, Amy.

December 12, 1969: Amy is laid to rest.

Memories raced ahead. At Amy's funeral, he kept his head down because he could not bear to see the accusing looks of people's faces. Yet, no one said what he already knew—Anthony Lorenzo was a drunkard, who had his wife's blood on his hands. He should pay for his tragic mistake. Oddly, no one came to arrest him, nor did he have to spend any time in the hospital. Why was he even alive? This made no sense.

Gradually, people said brief condolences and left. Alone, he stayed until men started piling dirt onto a lowered coffin. When Anthony heard the first thud that was thrown from a shovel, he could take it no longer. Nauseous, he drove off in his pickup truck and never looked back.

Soon, he headed north and left his home in San Diego, California. While he drove, Anthony felt numb until he heard the song, Sugar Shack, on the radio. Once their favorite tune, now it brought streams of tears down his cheeks. So, he turned it off and gripped the steering wheel in silence. A steel-gray sky reflected his dark mood.

Endless miles of black pavement flowed under the truck's tires, and buildings gave way to farmlands. Oblivious of his surroundings, he drove up a winding mountain road in an unknown wilderness.

Somewhere on that rugged terrain, Lorenzo snapped out of his grief-stricken trance, and he noticed raindrops on the windshield. Lightening flashed, thunder cracked and roared. Marble-sized hail violently pelted the truck's hood, and, for a split second, he was not sure, if he was still in Vietnam.

Yet, the war vet remembered he was back in the states and cursed himself for not paying attention to the weather or his surroundings. It did not matter, however, where he was going, so he continued up the mountain, and he white-knuckled the steering wheel even more.

Several thousand feet higher, the weather changed drastically, and it snowed heavily. Lush green foliage turned to cold, wintry white. Windshield wipers hypnotically sloshed back and forth. Fatigued, Anthony's mind clouded up. His eyelids fluttered, and he tried to stay awake. For a brief moment, he lost consciousness.

Before he realized what was happening, the truck slowed down, lazily meandered up the steep road and rolled into a ditch. This sudden jerking motion awoke Anthony to the realization that his truck rested on its side, as though it, too, just wanted to sleep. Startled by his predicament, he pushed hard on the driver's side door, which faced upward while gravity pulled back to close it.

Finally, Anthony scrambled out and landed ankle-deep into an ice-cold, roaring stream. Immediately. he groaned by the shock, leaped onto a snow bank, then clambered on hands and knees. After a long struggle, he made it to a narrow road where reality struck him. Shivering and wet, he was stranded in a wilderness without hope of survival.

Disgusted with his stupidity, Anthony swore, grabbed a handful of snow and threw it against a tree. "You idiot! Now, look what you did!"

As if to confirm Anthony's foolishness, gusts of icy wind howled ever stronger, and snow flurries whipped up ghostly swirls. Even nature seemed to mock his existence. Shaking, he glanced at where he had been and discovered that the wreckage was completely hidden from view of the road. Furious, Anthony left his truck behind and trekked into the wild. For hours, he wandered in an unforgiving blizzard.

December 14, 1969: Lost in the Sierra Nevada Mountains of California.

These bitter memories emotionally drained Anthony's spirit. Now a violent storm beat him down into a snowdrift on a mountainside far from home. Lying face up, his frozen body left him paralyzed, and he waited to die.

In a brief moment of clarity, he whispered, "God, I know it's been a long time since we had a talk, but I just want to ask you to have mercy on me. I made a horrible mistake, and now Amy is dead because of me. Please forgive me." His throat froze up, and he coughed. Weakened, he could say no more.

A dark cloud swept into his weary mind, but he fought the temptation to give up. Anthony lifted his hand in a last attempt to reach out to his creator.

Just as he moved, something warm and heavy pressed hard on his chest, and sharp, knife-like claws sliced into his jacket. "Uh…what is that?" Anthony lifted his head and gasped, "This can't be happening!"

2 Follow the Eagle

Anthony Lorenzo was flat on his back in a blizzard. Brutal wind howled in his ears. Weary, he was about to die in a bed of snow. He felt something heavy on his chest. Barely able to lift his head, he blinked his frozen eyelids and saw a three-foot tall bald eagle sitting on his chest.

"I remember you!" His voice cracked like ice.

The eagle just stared with intense interest.

Lorenzo tried to move but felt weak, and he lowered his head again. "What's happening to me?"

Suddenly, the great eagle took flight, called out and disappeared. Anthony reached up in alarm and yelled, "Wait! Don't go!"

Unforgiving icy wind howled again. Lorenzo dropped his arms in despair. Perhaps this was just another hallucination that his weary, disturbed mind had played on him. Feeling tired and weak, all he wanted to do was sleep. He began to drift off, but noticed that something brushed against his side, and he looked up. There, he saw a grizzled, old mountain man, who knelt before him. It was the same powerful figure he had seen once as a 12-year-old boy, and all he could do was stare in disbelief. First the eagle, now this.

The ancient man towered over him and appeared to be from a distant past, with his knee-length bear skin coat, buckskin pants and moccasin shoes. His long, scruffy white hair blew wildly in the fierce wind, and he smiled reassuringly through a thick, unkempt beard. Anthony watched in amazement while the tall figure knelt at his side. Several eagle feathers fluttered from his coonskin cap, and he uttered strange words that the young man could not understand.

Anthony coughed and tried to clear his throat. "Thought I'd never see you again," he said weakly... "Been a long time."

The mountain man began to rub and warm up Anthony's hands. "You were a boy, then." His voice sounded deep, low, soothing and began to make sense.

Anthony raised his head and coughed again. "Am I dead?"

"Not your time yet," the mountain man placed his thumb directly over Anthony's heart.

Instantly, the young man felt a jolt, like an electrical charge. Heat radiated through his body. This gave Anthony a strange sensation, as his blood began to flow in his veins, and he had renewed energy. The ancient one rubbed his palm on Anthony's forehead, which cleared his tormented mind.

Then, the mountain man took his hand, and the beaten war vet rose up like nothing happened. The blizzard raged all around him, but he felt so peaceful and warm, as though he was in a protective bubble. "What's happening?"

"You get a second chance to live. Now, you must not waste it."

Anthony lowered his head. "I'm not worthy."

The wise one placed his big hands on Anthony's shoulders. "It is a gift."

"But...I have blood on my hands. I'm no good. See?" Anthony Lorenzo could not make eye contact and held up his palms.

"You see different." The ancient wise one placed his soothing hand upon Anthony's chest. "God sees here."

Anthony looked up at this towering sagacious being and said, "I don't know if I can go on."

"You are wounded bad." The man touched Anthony's chest again, "Here…deep in your soul. You will need time and help to heal. He placed a hand on Anthony's forehead. Your worst enemy is in here. Stay alert. Now, go, follow the Eagle. He will lead you to others. The wise one turned and vanished in the wind.

"Wait!" Anthony shivered and anxiously glanced around but could not find the eagle anywhere in sight. Somehow, he had to go on, for deep within his soul was the renewed will to live. So, he trekked on, but each knee-deep step was slow and treacherous. Yet, the storm mercilessly raged on.

Blindly, Anthony groped with his hands in the air while the relentless force of the blizzard swirled like a tormenting ghost without mercy. Just several feet ahead, he barely saw something. He squinted and tried to wipe the snow off his eyelids with swollen, bare hands. It was the eagle perched on a bright red object partially buried in a snow bank.

The desperate young man struggled to get closer. He reached out to the great raptor, but it flew off. At that moment, Anthony's hand brushed up against cold, hard metal, and he recognized it as a stop sign on a two-lane intersection. Although he saw no structures amidst a thick forest, he had renewed hope to find shelter.

Stomping his feet to get a grip on the slick, icy road, Anthony muttered to himself, "Okay, Tony, you can make it." He inhaled deeply and was amazed by how energetic he felt, then exhaled as a frosty mist blew from his mouth. Unsure of his direction, he looked from left to right and noticed that the pavement must have been recently plowed. "Which way do I go?"

Something zipped past him to the left, and he saw the eagle flying low through the blizzard, and it seemed oblivious to the bitter wind. Encouraged by this strange sight, he loudly said to himself, "Go that way! Move it!"

Slowly, Anthony trekked up a steep incline in the road, which made his breathing heavy, and his pulse raced. He gasped for air, but he kept going, although he could not see a leveling of the road.

After what seemed like hours, Anthony paused and realized that the oxygen was thinner high up in these mountains. While he tried to catch his breath, he took a step and felt his foot slip and down he fell on his rear.

Stunned and weary, he sat there on the icy pavement. Suddenly, the eagle swooped down, grabbed the back of his jacket collar, shrieked in his ear and jerked him hard. The eagle wildly flapped its wings until Anthony struggled to his feet.

"Okay! I get the hint! I'm going!" He shook himself angrily and stumbled forward, until the eagle let go. With it off his back, he looked, but the great bird had vanished again.

"I don't know why you bother!" He yelled in the wind with increased irritation.

Further up the road, Anthony felt his leg muscles cramp up, and he remembered the image of the Tin Man in the Wizard of Oz film. He chuckled to himself, "Great, now I'm about to freeze up solid. Somebody's going to find a human popsicle, and it'll be me."

Realizing how goofy he sounded, Anthony slapped his forehead. "Come on, Tony, Get a grip on yourself. You're okay. You can do this." He rubbed his leg muscles and hiked further up the road.

Another hour passed, and he struggled to keep going around a steep curve. Freezing wind slapped him even harder, and he could not see past his outstretched arms. Each slippery step wore him down.

Floating through his foggy consciousness were memories of his wife, Amy. At first, he had joyful images filled with laughter and cuddling together. Then, his mind grew dark, and he saw Amy's lifeless body on the side of the road. Tormented by guilt and shame, he began to have an overwhelming sense of paranoia. Voices shouted in his head. Loud explosions rang out, and somehow, he knew he was about to die.

Disoriented, his mind flashed into a memory of the jungle, and he tried to make out the terrain. He saw the enemy at the top of a ridge, and they waited to cut him down. It felt so hot and sticky. Fetor of death filled his nostrils. Corporal Lorenzo ran and dove off the road and rolled several feet in the dirt. Flat on his stomach, he waited and listened. Mad with fear, he wiped the sweat from his face with his sleeve.

Lorenzo heard a loud rumbling sound. He slowly looked up and there was something large, like a tank over on the ridge. It grew louder and seemed to be heading toward him. More shadowy figures appeared, and they came for him. Gripped in hysteria, he knew that he deserved to die but was terrified of the inevitable. Lorenzo stood up, started to run, but tripped on a tree branch and fell face down.

Jolted back to the present moment and lost in an unforgiving wilderness, he felt no steamy jungle-like world. Instead, he shivered in bitter cold.

Aware that he just had another bizarre mind trip, Anthony felt a sharp nudge on his shoulder. When he turned and looked up, there before him was the eagle perched on a nearby conifer branch.

"This is becoming a habit with you! Isn't it?"

Just as he spoke, the raptor pecked his right hand. "Ouch! Why did you do that?" Anthony rubbed his skin and glared with increased annoyance.

The great bird just stared back at him with an omniscient look of superiority. Wearily, the fatigued war vet sighed and frowned, "Why don't you just let me die?"

Lorenzo heard that loud roar again, and he squinted his eyes to see through the flurries. There, up on a ridge, he spotted a snowplow and it scooped up a mound of snow. He shook his head and chuckled with amusement at the sight. So, that was the tank he thought was real in his crazy hallucination.

"Get with it man!" Anthony lectured himself out loud. He turned and faced the eagle. "See that! I'm a hopeless case!"

The eagle seemed to look right through him. In his mind, Anthony heard the mountain man's words again. 'Your worst enemy is here. Stay alert.' The eagle took flight. Anthony watched in amazement while the majestic bird flew and circled hundreds of feet above him, then it nose-dived and landed on a snowy-covered roof. Encouraged by this sight, Anthony ran up the road and noticed a neon sign that blinked, "Jenny's Place," in bright red letters. He smiled in relief and looked toward the rooftop, but the eagle was gone.

Anthony brushed off the snow and walked past several parked cars to the front entrance. When he opened the café's glass door, warm, dry air caressed his weather-beaten face. He could not wait to plop his weary body down, but where? It was so crowded, and the only spot available happened to be near the door. Unable to take another step, he slid into that cushioned booth and rested his weary arms on the table. His eye-lids felt heavy, and his wet, cold feet were like bricks.

Slowly, his mind began to thaw, and he sniffed the irresistible aroma of steak that sizzled on a skillet. Alert, he noticed that the room was abruptly quiet. Nothing moved. Anthony glanced around to see people staring at him, and, as he looked, they turned away. Normal chitchat continued again. So, he lowered his head with a strange sense of déjà vu, but he could not remember being here before.

Confused by this, Anthony rubbed his hands together, and he was amazed that his fingers did not appear to be frostbitten. He wiped his damp forehead with a sleeve, which caused little chunks of ice to fall from his eyebrows to the table. Melted streams flowed down his beard and dribbled into tiny puddles in front of him.

Anthony took napkins from a dispenser and was shocked to see his haggard reflection in the stainless-steel container. That had to be someone else: some crazy, homeless derelict, not him. Yet, it was Anthony Lorenzo, who squinted back at him with puffy eyes, red swollen skin, and long wildly tangled hair just below his ears. Embarrassed, he sank a little lower in his seat. No wonder people stared at him.

In spite of this, he was still grateful to be in the warmth of a shelter. At least he could rest for a while and figure out what to do next. Just in that second, a blast of bitterly cold air stunned the back of his neck. Someone had flung the door wide open, brushed past him, and white flakes splattered down his shoulders.

Anthony realized why this booth near the door had been vacant, so he quickly scanned the coffee shop for another spot. The only possible location for him was a table on the far side where a 60ish-looking bearded man sat alone. The stranger wore a black Stetson cowboy hat and a heavy brown wool jacket with a beige sheepskin collar.

While Anthony pondered that booth as an alternative, an icy gust rattled the door, and he felt a wisp of freezing air on his neck again.

"That does it!" He whispered in frustration. Desperate to keep warm, and irritably hungry, he trudged past rows of tables and people seemed to stare at him. This made him feel unclean and not fit to be in their presence. Wary, but determined, he took one stiff, heavy step after another until he finally arrived at the stranger's booth. Anthony started to speak, but he felt unsure of how to present himself.

The elder man did not look up. Instead, he slowly forked a small portion of scrambled eggs into his mouth and chewed in silence. His face had a tough, rawhide appearance, well-aged by winter winds. Thick bushy eyebrows and a grizzled one-inch curly grayish beard along solid cheekbones gave a hint of Celtic ancestry. A chiseled hawk-like nose and distinctive three-pronged wrinkles on the sides of his eyes added to the first impression of gruffness.

Anthony stood just six feet away from that booth, fidgeted his thawing fingers, and wondered why he felt so shy about approaching the man. What could be so intriguing and intimidating about this rough-hewn cowboy? He would soon find out.

3 Great Thaw

The elder man took a sip of coffee, set his cup down, looked up, and he smiled. A lone gold eyetooth shined in the light of a small candle. Disarmed by that friendly expression, Anthony immediately felt welcome. He also discovered a youthful spark in the man's penetrating blue eyes that seemed to defy his weather-hardened features. Oddly, it was as though the young man had found a long-lost friend.

Mystified, Anthony cleared his throat and asked, "Mind if I sit here?" He gestured to the empty space across the table.

"Have a seat, young fella," the elder man nodded. A rugged, hardy voice projected out of that warm smile with a hint of southern hospitality in his tone.

"Thanks." Anthony slid into the bench and faced the man. For the first time, he noticed a silver band with interconnected shapes of eagles in flight that flowed around the rim of the gentleman's cowboy hat.

The elder man bit into some wheat toast, chewed slowly, and stared out a side window. Heavy snow flurries blew almost horizontally against the glass, and moisture dribbled down the surface. Anthony shivered, "Looks like it's getting worse out there."

"Yep," the man responded in between his chewing.

A sudden burst of laughter echoed from the other side as people talked. Anthony glanced around and rubbed his hands together. He unbuttoned his wet denim jacket and felt warmer. "Kind of cozy in here."

"Compared to all that ruckus out there," the elder man smiled and waved a thumb at the frost-covered window and added, "I'd say it's right nice."

Encouraged by the fellow's warmth, he leaned forward and reached out a hand, "My name is Anthony Lorenzo."

The stranger wiped his leathery hands on a napkin and squeezed Anthony in a vice-like grip. "Friends call me Bolt."

When the younger man's hand was released, he rubbed it to relieve the pain and get back circulation. In all his 22 years, he never experienced such a powerful handshake, and, coming from an older man, it was especially disconcerting.

"Bolt, you say. Interesting name."

"Yep," Bolt laughed, "Got tagged with it when I was helping my Pa mending fences on our ranch. About 10-years-old, I reckon, when lightening zapped a post. Knocked me clear out of my boots."

Bolt paused and stared ahead, as though he could still see it in his mind. "Strange thing is…when I came out of it, I saw an eagle circling directly overhead. My Pa looked down at me, and I asked him what had happened. He said, 'A lightning bolt got you, son.'" The elder man chuckled at the memory and grinned, "After that, folks called me, Bolt. It darned stuck with me ever since."

Just then, an attractive waitress in her early 40's came over and said, "Oh, there you go again, boring people with your stories." She smiled warmly and placed a hand on Bolt's shoulder.

He grinned, "Ah, Jenny, you're always spoiling our fun."

Jenny turned to Anthony, and her eyes widened. "Oh, my goodness, young man. You look like you've been in the snow too long."

"Young folks call that being cool," Bolt teased with a playful grin.

Anthony laughed and found it easy to go along with this light-hearted couple. "Well, I call it almost freezing to death."

Jenny patted Anthony's shoulder. "We better do something about that." She handed him a menu. "What can I get to warm you up?"

"Coffee, please. Make it black and steaming hot."

"Sure, dear." Jenny looked as though she had all the time in the world, although the café was packed. "Anything else?"

"Um…" Anthony felt the warmth of her hand on his shoulder, and his stomach growled. Embarrassed, he patted his waistline and grinned awkwardly. "Uh…I'll take the biggest meal you got, and don't hold back."

"Honey, I'll make sure you get our Mountaineer's Special, and I'll even add a tall glass of fresh orange juice, too. How's that?" She paused with an endearing smile.

"Thanks." Anthony nodded affirmatively and watched her write down his order. He felt as though the warmth of her hand was still there, as he gazed upon her features.

A long, raven ponytail with several fine streaks of gray flowed elegantly down to the back of her apron strings. She wore a lovely turquoise necklace with an eagle, which appeared to be in flight. Her light brown eyes were soft and pleasing to look at, and her pupils seemed like gems perfectly set by a master jeweler. An oval face, high cheekbones, and subtle wrinkles that lined a rich caramel skin gave her an air of Native American nobility.

Jenny tapped the pencil on her notepad, smiled graciously and said, "Be right back." She glanced at Bolt. "I'll bring more coffee." She turned and walked away with such poise, that the young man was awestruck, as he watched her leave.

Suddenly realizing that he was staring, Anthony looked over at Bolt, who grinned knowingly and sighed, "She does have a way about her, doesn't she?"

Anthony lowered his gaze to the glass of water and took a sip. "Well...I..."

"Where you from?" Bolt quickly changed the subject.

"San Diego...my truck slid off the road." Anthony took another sip, paused and added, "Had to walk a long way to get here." He looked out the window and shivered, as he noticed that the blizzard continued to rage. "Truth is...I should've frozen to death out there."

Bolt studied the almost horizontal icy winds shaking the parked cars outside. "Judging by that storm, and the looks of you, young fella, I'd say it's a miracle you are here right now."

Anthony shrugged and looked down at his hands resting on the table. "Well, all I know is that miracles ought to be saved for people who deserve them."

The elder man leaned back, rested his arm on the top edge of his seat, and he stared out the window in silence for a moment. Finally, he turned and sighed, "Miracles are for anyone in need." He narrowed his eyes, leaned forward and asked, "What do you need, young fella?"

Before Anthony could answer, Jenny returned and set down a steaming plate with a glove. "Careful, it's hot." She poured more coffee in Bolt's cup, smiled and left.

Anthony sniffed and stared at his massive, simmering late afternoon meal. It was piled with luscious yellow scrambled eggs, waffles with little melted squares of butter on top, and he sighed.

Circling like covered wagons were the logs of fried sausages and wheels of bright red sliced tomatoes. To the side of the plate, four crisp bacon strips were laid out in tempting planks, while steam rose to the young man's red nostrils. He inhaled deeply and greeted the aroma with delight.

"Can you handle all that?" Bolt nodded at all that food.

Anthony grabbed a fork, stabbed a whole piece of sausage, held it and said, "Watch me." He stuffed the whole two-inch log of pork into his mouth and proceeded to savor every chew that squeezed the sizzling juices onto his tongue.

Without a word, Anthony delved into the mounds of all this wonderful sustenance with the vigor of an athlete preparing for a great race. Oh, to relish such palatable splendors after feeling dead inside, he wanted to live more than ever.

At least another 10 minutes passed, while Bolt silently watched in amazement. "Well, I'd say you haven't eaten in quite a spell, young fella."

Anthony chewed, swallowed, and then washed it down with the tall glass of orange juice. He gulped, burped happily and looked up. "Yep," he nodded toward the window, "This storm nearly killed me."

"That reminds me…" Bolt leaned forward and rested his elbows on the table, "We were talking about miracles, and you mentioned something interesting. You said that miracles are for people who deserve them, right?"

Anthony nodded, just as Jenny came over and poured more coffee into their cups. When she walked away, the young man watched her for a second, then turned back to face the elder man. "Yep," he looked at his hands in shame again.

"Okay…then, I said miracles are for anyone in need, correct?"

Anthony looked up from the coffee cup that poised at his lips, took a sip, and he set it down slowly.

With an odd sense of being interrogated, he nodded and stared at his swollen fingers.

"I don't mean to pry into your personal affairs, young fella," Bolt leaned a little closer, "But you got that look. I've seen it many times before." His voice lowered to a whisper, "In fact, I've been there myself."

Anthony looked up and their eyes met. "Yeah…how do you know what I've been through?"

Bolt tapped the young man's right open palm. "You keep looking at your hands, young fella. You got the face of a vet that's been through a lot." For a moment, Bolt stared out the frost-covered window, then turned and studied the young man again. "Now, ya see, it's like this, I fought in World War II, and I reckon you just came back from Vietnam. Right?"

Without waiting for an answer, he said, "But, we can still relate to a common cause like brothers, and that makes it my business. You just survived a miracle, so I'm asking you again. What do you need?"

The young vet fidgeted, took another sip from the coffee mug, and pondered this question with a sense of unease. Intrigued by the elder vet's tone that was firm, gritty and honest, he hesitated. It was like Bolt's voice had been sandblasted with the winds of time, and buttressed by ancient, rough-textured Sequoias.

The elder veteran watched in silence, and he seemed to have the patience to wait out any change in weather. Anthony glanced at him and turned away. It was difficult to focus directly into his eyes, which had such glaring brilliance of sky blue, with a hint of tranquil green that seemed to flow right through to his wounded soul. He tried to look again, but quickly faced the window, only to see his own distorted reflection, and he frowned.

"Take your time, young fella." Bolt leaned back and rested his arm on the edge of his seat in a gesture of opening up more safe space for the weary vet to talk.

Anthony turned, looked directly into those penetrating eyes and thought of what he needed the most. It was as though the elder veteran could reach in, see, feel, and touch all of his deep, dark, painful secrets. Finally, he firmly said, "A hot shower, dry shoes and fresh clothes."

Bolt slapped his hand on the table and grinned, "Now you're thinking about survival. Now!" He hit the table so hard, it shook. "That's it! No use letting the past kill you! Your worst enemy is here." He tapped his own forehead. "What else?"

"A place to sleep." The young vet lowered his head and stared at his coffee mug. "If they're open all night, maybe I'll just stay here...keep warm."

"Not a chance," Bolt's tone was firm, direct, and the quality of a seasoned master sergeant. His voice softened again, as he added, "Jenny's got to go home sometime." He looked out the window and sighed with relief. "Well, it seems to be letting up."

Anthony nodded, "Yep, the wind's calmed way down and, it stopped snowing."

"All right, here's the plan. I'll take you to my place for the night. You can sleep in the spare room. Got some extra clothes and all." He slapped the table again. "And, you can get that hot shower you talked about."

"Well...I don't want to be a bother."

Bolt waved a hand in the air. "Forget it, I've had hard times myself and it was always nice to have a helping hand."

The thought of all that much-needed comfort made the young vet smile. "Okay."

"By the way," the elder vet grinned with a look of satisfaction, "I got a hoist. When the weather clears tomorrow, we'll get that truck of yours out of the ditch in no time."

"Thanks."

"Glad to help." Bolt nodded and leaned back, "Like I said, I've been in need myself, many times." He had a far-off look and added, "Once my car got stuck up against a boulder. A flash flood pushed me right off the road. Water gushed in, and I thought I was going to drown. I must've been about 16, I reckon."

"What happened?"

Bolt stared out the window, as though he relived the experience. "Well, along came this farmer on a wagon pulled by a team of four horses, and he hitched up a chain on the back of the rig. Next thing I knew, my old Ford got pulled backward, and, all of a sudden, I was up on dry land."

Bolt paused with a thoughtful gaze, "You know, I was so grateful, I offered to pay the fella. But he just grinned through yellow, crooked teeth, spat out a wad of chew, and he said something that changed my life."

Anthony leaned in with interest. "What did he say?"

"The farmer tilted his dusty straw hat back on his balding head and looked at me real intent like. Then, he said, 'Sonny…If you really want to pay me, here's what I want you to do. Whenever you see folks in need, you just pass on a good turn to them.'"

Anthony was so intrigued, he asked, "How did that change your life?"

Bolt grinned and put his right hand over his heart. "When I was a young fella, I used to be cocky. I had no time for anyone else, and I sure didn't think they cared much about me." He gestured with his arms out wide.

"That ole farmer made me realize I needed to be open and caring about others. From then on, I tried to pass on a good turn whenever I could. Now, I reckon it's a way of life."

The war-weary vet shook his head and frowned cynically, "I've seen a lot of people that are just in it for themselves."

"Maybe you haven't met the right people." Bolt glanced out the window, "Sky's clearing." He opened a wallet that revealed an eagle embossed on the leather, spread a wad of cash on the table and stood up. "Let's go while the weather's good. It'll be dark soon."

"But...I need to pay for my..."

"I got it." Bolt kept walking toward the entrance but turned and smiled reassuringly, "Meet me out front." The elder man said something to Jenny, gave her a quick hug, and closed the door behind him.

Anthony shrugged, waved to Jenny, and he rushed outside the Chalet-style café but did not see Bolt anywhere. Suddenly, an old beat-up Jeep swerved from around the back, and it skidded to an abrupt halt in front of him with a loud screech of the brakes. Bolt was at the controls, and he yelled, "Let's go! Looks like clouds are dark up the mountain. We better hurry!"

When the young vet slid into the passenger seat, the vehicle jerked forward, raced out of the parking lot, and he had to hang on tight. Bolt skillfully drove along treacherous mountain roads, with such precision, it was obvious that he knew the terrain well. Just as he turned sharply into a narrow curve, an icy gust blasted the windshield, and the elder vet maneuvered around one fallen branch after another on the slick pavement.

Anthony braced himself while it began to snow again, and the wind swooped wildly down the mountain. He glanced at Bolt and admired the confident, highly-skilled way the elder vet handled every twist and turn. For the first time since Anthony became stranded in this wilderness, he felt more relaxed and at ease. He had no idea where they were headed, nor how long it would take, but he knew he was in good hands.

Just as the Jeep swerved around a narrow bend in the road, Anthony spotted the great eagle perched on a branch, and he felt even more assured. "Did you see that?"

Bolt kept his eyes on the road, and he gripped the steering wheel. "What?"

"Nothing." Anthony noticed the eagle flying low along a ridge, and he spotted a brick structure. "Is that your place?"

"You'll see."

4 The Refuge

Monstrous clouds grew darker, and the wind blew horizontally, as Bolt drove up a steep driveway and parked next to a stonewalled cabin. Thick, storm shutters battened-up four front windows, which gave the appearance of a sturdy, well-built structure. Giant pine trees stood sentry around a 200-foot-wide clearing, and a lone ancient oak tree was firmly anchored in the center.

A flatbed truck sat near a large metal building that looked like some kind of warehouse or workshop. The Jeep's headlights revealed a sign that hung above a roll-up garage door, and Anthony made it out as, "Woodcrafts by Bolt Mac Arthur."

"Come on," Bolt yelled through the bluster, "Let's get inside."

Without a word, the men stumbled up the redwood porch, and a powerful gust propelled them forward. When Bolt opened the front door, snow flurries spewed wildly into the room, and biting wind stung their ears. Both men struggled to push the door closed, and Bolt reached for the wall switch, but an eerie darkness prevailed.

Flashlight in hand, he shot a beam across the blackened stillness. Shadows danced and flickered on the walls, then a spot light settled on a stone fireplace.

"Hold this," Bolt ordered, as he handed over the flashlight. A match was struck on dry kindling wood, and, gradually, yellow, red flames flickered and illuminated the hearth.

With the fire going, Bolt stood and nodded to his guest, "You keep warm by the fire. I'll get you a change of clothes."

When he returned from a back bedroom, Bolt reached out, "Here, put these on."

Anthony quickly changed into dry pants, a long-sleeved shirt and a heavy wool coat. Bolt hung up the young man's wet clothes on the back of chair near the fire, then glanced at Anthony's bare feet. "That's odd."

"What?" The young vet looked up as he was about to put on dry socks.

Bolt scratched his whiskers and commanded, "Let me see your feet."

Anthony lifted his trouser legs, and the elder man examined them carefully. "Strange…I don't see any sign of frostbite." His piercing blue eyes studied him. "All you've been through…I expected at the very least that you would have some swelling. Don't you reckon?"

"Yeah…" Anthony stared at his toes, "I don't get it."

"Most men would be in bad shape by now," Bolt paused with hands resting on his narrow hips. "Unless…"

"Unless, what?"

Bolt knelt and stoked the fire. "Never mind, I'm just glad you are okay, young fella." He stood up and smiled reassuringly, "Let's get some coffee on."

Moments later, wood crackled in the fireplace, and the men huddled near flickering red flames to keep warm. Anthony sipped his hot coffee while Bolt added more wood to the fire. What was it about his host that captivated him? Never had he felt so relaxed with someone he hardly knew. Strange, he thought. It was like sitting with a long-lost father. He had been orphaned as a boy, and he was passed from one foster home to another. As far as he knew, no relatives existed. Besides, the guy had to be old enough to be his grandfather.

Bolt quietly stoked the flames with an iron poke. Anthony stood up to stretch his exhausted body and noticed several framed pictures dimly lit by candlelight on a brick mantel. One faded black and white photo revealed a man and woman with six children in a background of what appeared to be a barn. Names were scrawled in ink below the people, and Bolt was shown as an infant in his mother's arms.

Anthony leaned closer and felt as though a story was unfolding before him. He looked at a wrinkled, well-worn photo of Bolt at the age of 10 in 1919. Another picture displayed a master sergeant with Bolt's name scribbled above his head, and he sat with several noncommissioned officers at a beach-side café. On the bottom right hand corner, it had the words, Honolulu, Hawaii, August 29, 1945.

Anthony glanced at Bolt. "I see you have a lot of memories here."

"Yep," Bolt jabbed the flames and sparks flew.

Anthony picked up the photo of 1945. "So, you fought in the South Pacific?"

Bolt clanked the poker back on the metal rack and let out a deep sigh, "Yep, I enlisted two days after Pearl Harbor, and I fought to the end of it." He waved a hand toward the pictures, "Some folks want to forget. I keep them to remember."

"Remember what?" Anthony was intrigued.

The old veteran just stared at the photos for a moment. Then, he said, "Freedom is precious. A man should never forget the sacrifices of those who didn't make it." Bolt gazed into the young man's eyes. "If he remembers long enough and tells the truth about history…maybe the next generation won't make the same mistakes."

Anthony Lorenzo turned away, stared at the raging fire and blurted out, "I spent 11 months, 28 days in Nam." He stood rigid and tense while the wood crackled. "Been back just a month. I wish I could forget!" His voice grew louder.

Embarrassed, Anthony wanted to change the subject and picked up another frame on the shelf. It showed a stiff, serious couple in a black and white grainy photo, and the inscription read, "Bolt and Emma's wedding, Long Beach CA, January 20, 1929.

Bolt reached out, gently took the picture, stared at it and chuckled, "Those were happy, exciting times." He sighed deeply and pointed to his bride, "Emma was a real beauty, and as sweet as can be." He grinned at the memory and shook his head. "Yep, she sure had a way of melting a hard case like me to butter... just by a wink, a smile, and I would do anything for her."

Anthony watched his host set the photo back on the mantel very softly with both hands. "What happened to her?" He was surprised that he asked that question, but the words were out there, and he felt foolish.

"Emma died two years ago," Bolt gazed at the picture and sighed.

Anthony turned away and stared at the fire. Awkward silence filled the room, and the young vet's own sadness welled up inside, as he felt the guilt of causing the death of his wife, Amy again.

Finally, Bolt cleared his throat and looked down at the fireplace, "Emma and I settled in these mountains right after the war. Since then, our two daughters have grown and moved away. So, our lives revolved around each other. We were best friends, and she worked alongside me in my wood-crafting business until..." Bolt's voice cracked, and he said no more.

Anthony's knees buckled, and he slumped down on the couch from his own grief. Happy memories flashed, and he saw his wife's smile; then, just as quickly, he was haunted by guilt again. He felt hot sweat on his palms, and he wringed his hands. Slowly, he looked up to see his elder had been studying him intently. Anthony tried to turn away, but their eyes met again.

Bolt seemed to forget about his own grief and asked, "You've been through this, haven't you, son?"

Stunned by this question, Anthony's pent-up emotions boiled to the surface. "Well...I..." A lump in his throat choked off his words. He desperately needed to open up to someone, but it was too painful to speak.

Bolt moved slowly, sat down gently on a living room chair near the fireplace, and he lowered his head in silence. In that moment, Anthony's watery eyes observed the elder man in some kind of whispered prayer.

For the first time, in his life, the young man felt safe, while the fire crackled and flickered in the warm fireplace. No one had ever called him son before, and he wondered why this stranger referred to him in that fatherly-like-manner. Yet, there was a bond that connected them in a way that he could not understand.

Tears flowed down Anthony's cheeks, and his emotional wall melted away. Although he tried hard to maintain his manly dignity, great heaving sobs welled up from his chest, then burst through the blockage in his throat.

Shaky and embarrassed for not being able to keep his composure, he lowered his head. Before this, he had neatly locked away or numbed his emotions from others. Now, he felt like a blithering idiot.

Bolt knelt in front of the young man and squeezed his guest's shoulder. "That's all right, son. Looks like you've been carrying a huge burden. Now's the time to let it out."

Slowly, Anthony tried to regain control. "Amy was the sweetest…" His voice cracked, but he forced himself to go on. "It's all my fault." The grieving, bitter man's fist pounded his knees over and over. "If I hadn't been drunk, we would've never had that accident…she'd be alive today."

The elder man kept his hand on Anthony's shoulder in support, then said, "It's all right, son. Let it all out."

The young man looked up in agony. "I…didn't even get a chance to say goodbye…to say I love her." He sobbed uncontrollably, choked and tried to go on. "Amy was so lively one minute and…" His voice cracked again. Then, he blurted out, "Now she's gone! I killed her!"

"No need to beat yourself up over it, son." Bolt spoke firmly and sighed, "Let it go. Your worst enemy is right there." Bolt warmly touched the young man's forehead the same way as the mountain man had done in the midst of a raging blizzard.

"I don't understand. What do you mean by my worst enemy?"

"That's your own self-destructive thoughts. It sounds like this was an accident. You admitted that it was your fault, and you are paying a heavy price for your tragic mistake. You lost your dear wife, and now you're faced with grief, but you're punishing yourself with shame and guilt. These are the facts. Am I right?"

Anthony stared at his hands and shook his head, "But…I don't think I can go on."

"Son! Look at me!" Bolt commanded in a stern voice.

The young man raised his head and tried to focus with teary eyes.

"Now, you listen to me very carefully," Bolt noticed that Anthony started to lower his gaze again. "Look at me!"

When the heartbroken vet focused his eyes on him again, the elder continued, "Do you think your wife, Amy, wants you to go on like this?" Not waiting for an answer, he added, "Love is the most powerful force there is, son. Amy would want you to be happy and get on with your life. Do you believe that?"

"I guess so."

"Do you believe that God loves you?"

"How could he? I…"

"It's all right, son," Bolt interrupted with a softer, reassuring tone. "From now on, you'll be on a life-long journey. It won't be easy. You'll have many setbacks. It takes time to heal, to live fully and happily. Remember, son. You've been given a second chance at life. I know it's difficult. When my Emma died, I blamed myself because I was too caught up in my own success to be there when she needed me the most."

For a moment, Anthony put aside his own grief, and he felt empathy for the elder man. "What happened?"

Bolt leaned his elbows on the fireplace mantel and stared at the photos. "A storm barreled down from the north…much like this one, I reckon."

He stroked his wedding picture and exhaled, "When the storm approached, I had one thing on my mind. Leave for LA to receive an award and recognition for my works as a woodcarver. Emma wanted to stay and take care of a blind, elderly neighbor." Bolt lowered his gaze at the carpet, as though he was in deep thought and walked slowly around the living room.

"I didn't know that…" He began to wring his hands and speeded up his steps, "While I was gone, Emma rushed out of our home to get supplies. Unfortunately, it came in faster than anyone predicted, and she got caught in the blizzard. My dear Emma lost control of her car on an icy road…" His voice cracked, "She drove off a cliff in the dark."

The young vet observed Bolt's anguished expression, and it hurt to see his new friend in grief. He felt an overwhelming connection with this man, who invited him into his home, and accepted him unconditionally. "What did you do?" Anthony got up and gazed at him with a desire to provide comfort.

"When I got back home the next day, I couldn't find her anywhere. I called the police, and we all searched for her." Bolt stopped pacing back and forth, and he stared at the fireplace. His teary eyes and damp cheeks were bathed in an orange glow.

"Another two days went by, and the not-knowing, the worrying, the wondering where she was…it was so painful…" His voice cracked again, but he cleared his throat, "Finally, after the storm had past, her body was found near the wreckage by a hiker."

Anthony shook his head with concern, "Bolt, you don't have to…"

"I was shocked," Bolt interrupted and looked at him with reddened eyes. "When I held my award in my hands, all I could think about was my Emma. I was so angry with myself for not being here to protect her that I burned that meaningless plaque." Bolt sat down by the fire and sighed deeply again.

The young man sat across from him and, for a moment, neither said anything. Finally, Bolt spoke up, "I let my own worst enemy beat me up inside, and I blamed myself for a long time, son. It was so painful, I spent my share of days in a drunken stupor, so I wouldn't feel anything." He shook his head in disgust, "That was sure a waste of time, and I'm not proud of it."

Flames flickered and crackled, while the wind howled like a banshee trying to find a way inside. The men's shadows danced eerily on the walls by the fireplace, as they each tried to grapple with mutual emotions of grief.

Bolt gasped and puffed out air. "I thought I'd never be happy again, until, one night, I awoke from a restless sleep. I felt Emma beside me, like nothing happened. It was so real. She stroked my forehead with a warm hand, like she did every night. When I looked, she wasn't there. I knew she was telling me to get on with my life, and she wanted me to be happy."

The elder man leaned toward Anthony and said, "Same goes for you, son. Don't beat yourself up. No matter what happened, God is giving you another chance to make things right. Do you understand?"

Anthony looked into Bolt's eyes and nodded in silence. For the first time since his wife, Amy, died, he realized that he was not alone. Somehow, he felt a natural connection with the elder man, who shared deep sorrow and grief. As veterans, their bond was forged in that precious moment, and, in the safety of this mountain cabin, it became a refuge while the blizzard raged on.

"Okay," Bolt stood, glanced at a grandfather clock with its pendulum swaying back and forth on the hour of 11:00 p.m., "It's late and we're both tired. Come on, you can bunk in the spare room." He turned on a flashlight and headed down the hallway.

Anthony started to follow, but he heard a slight bumping noise in the kitchen, and he forgot about Bolt. Curious, he picked up a lit candle on the fireplace mantel and stepped into that room, as a shadow of the refrigerator creeped along the wall.

He squinted to make out a figure standing in the walk-in pantry. At first, he thought his mind was playing tricks on him, but then it moved.

Suddenly, the war-weary veteran's heart raced, and primitive survival instincts kicked in. He blew out the candle and backed away to make himself inconspicuous. Confused, he heard footsteps coming toward him.

5 Eagle Memories

A beam of light flashed in Anthony's face and lit up the kitchen. "Oh, there you are," Bolt walked in the doorway from behind him. "You alright, son?"

Startled, Anthony gasped and spun around, "Uh...yeah, sure." He turned and looked back at the walk-in pantry but nothing moved. "Must be exhausted. I thought I saw somebody in here."

Bolt shined the flashlight around the darkened room, "I don't see anything." He scratched his head and looked perplexed, "I thought you were coming with me to the spare bedroom. You ready now?"

Embarrassed, Anthony lowered his gaze, "Uh, sure." He started to leave the kitchen but spotted something on the tile floor. Curious, he picked it up.

"What's that?" Bolt shined the light on it.

"Looks like an eagle feather."

"I reckon it was blown in when I stepped out this morning," Bolt shrugged. "Come on, son, let's get some shut eye."

While they left the room, Anthony gently stuck the feather in his wool coat pocket.

In the hallway, Bolt stopped and pointed into a bedroom, "This is where you'll bunk for the night."

Anthony stepped in and looked around the room. "Wow," he whispered at the sight of an exquisitely carved headboard and wood-framed double bed. Slowly, he ran his fingers along a magnificent scene of tall snow-covered mountain peaks. In the center of this fine cedarwood was an intricately designed figure of a lone eagle, which flew wild and free over the landscape.

Awestruck, he remembered the woodcarver's sign outside. "Did you carve this?"

"Yep," The elder man nodded with a grin, "A long time ago."

Anthony respectfully rubbed his fingers on the wood and felt the texture of each carved-out groove in amazement. "Man...I've never seen anything like it." A deep longing stirred in him that he never experienced before. "I wish I could carve like that." Just as he spoke, awkwardness flushed over him. It was silly to be envious. Or, was it something else?

Bolt looked pleased, "Glad you like it, son."

Still in awe, the young man moved slowly around the room. A large cedar chest sat at the foot of the bed. "Wow!" On a carved lid, two eagles were perched on a tree limb in a scene that overlooked a pristine mountain lake. "I..." he stumbled for words while his fingers caressed the smooth surface of lacquered wood.

A tantalizing scent of cedar wafted into the air, as the young man lifted the lid of this intricately carved chest. He inhaled deeply through his nose and savored the fresh aroma. "You carved this, too?"

"Yep," Bolt chuckled with satisfaction.

"You must have a gift to..." The young man was so amazed, he had difficulty expressing himself. What was it about this old man that intrigued him so much? He felt clumsy as he tried to talk. "I mean...I guess it would take a lifetime for a guy like me to be so..." He turned away, feeling foolish.

The woodcarver studied him. "Son, it just takes a steady hand, eye for detail and..."

Anthony looked up with increased interest. "And, what?"

Bolt did not respond. Instead, the focus of his eyes seemed to slice deep into the young man's soul like a surgeon's knife. Feeling exposed, Anthony turned away again. He heard the wind howling outside, and the memory of being in that blizzard made him shiver. So, he sighed and rubbed his arms to warm himself.

"You've had a rough day, son." Bolt knelt and rummaged in the cedar chest, "Here, bunk down with these." He pulled out folded blankets and tossed them to Anthony. "Talk in the morning. Get some shut eye." He turned and abruptly left the room.

Exhausted, the young man quickly fell asleep. Sometime during the night, he awoke and was disoriented. Where was he? What was that scent?

"Ah…" he sighed in relief as the aroma of cedar filled his senses again, and he remembered that he was in his host's spare room. Unable to sleep, he turned on a flashlight beside the bed and examined the eagle feather he found earlier.

This stoked a childhood memory of a lonely, confused 12-year-old boy at a spring youth camp. While on a group hike, Anthony spotted an eagle perched high on a tree branch. It was the first time he had seen such an awe-inspiring-winged creature, so he stopped to admire its nobility. Unaware that the party had gone ahead, he watched, as the eagle took flight, and he followed it deeper into the forest.

Spellbound, the boy trekked further into a vast wilderness where he had a strange sense of becoming smaller. Yet, he was more invigorated than ever before, and he heard his own heart beat in the silence that peacefully engulfed him.

The raptor flew in a wide circle above him, then dove behind a hillside. Anthony ran over and was amazed at the verdurous splendor of a meadow bathed in golden wild flowers. Awestruck by this ephemeral, lush paradise, he felt like a speck of dust blown in on eternal cosmic winds.

Sparkling streams raced down several iridescent waterfalls, gurgled loudly in his ears, and flowed into a pristine lake. The boy hiked to a calm rocky area and sat on a boulder spotted with rust-red lichen. Snow-covered pinnacles were mirrored on the still water like monuments of inexplicable greatness. Above him, the eagle circled, and Anthony felt a presence he had never experienced before.

In this tranquil moment, he was truly at peace. He could see his reflection in the lake but noticed something else, to his left, several yards away. A large man appeared to be standing on a nearby boulder. The boy turned around but saw nothing there. When he glanced at the figure's reflection in the still water, it rippled and vanished. Though taken aback, he had no fear. Instead, he was giddy and laughed aloud. Anthony had an overwhelming sensation of being embraced by a loving force so powerful that joy swept over him.

"God…? Wow! You are real!" The boy giggled with an indescribable childlike wonder and delight. He leaned back on the rock, breathed in clean mountain air, and he watched the eagle soaring high above the treetops. As he observed this majestic bird, he wondered if it could be an angel sent by God.

Just when he thought of this amazing possibility, the eagle flew over some trees and vanished. Suddenly the boy felt abandoned and called out, "Don't go!"

Anthony scrambled up a steep, rocky slope to catch another glimpse but only saw more mountains. It was as though the eagle had never been there. Lost and alone, the boy trekked deeper into the wilderness. By late afternoon, he began to grow weary and could not go any further. Then, he heard the eagle call out. So, he continued on.

Finally, he came to a narrow mountain road and stood in the middle of a sharp curve. Where was he? Oblivious to impending danger, the boy looked around, and longed to see the eagle. Without warning, a loud roaring sound echoed through the canyon walls. Shocked, he froze, as a big rig barreled around that tight bend right at him. Paralyzed in fear, all the boy could do was stare at the monstrous truck, with its teeth-like grill and two glaring windows that hid any sign of a merciful driver. A split second, he would be dead.

Something rammed his shoulder with such tremendous force that he fell to the side of the road. Smoky, hot wind blasted his face and he landed hard in the dirt. A deafening roar shook the ground, and the metal monster disappeared around the bend. When Anthony stood up on shaky knees, he could not believe the horrendous sight before him.

There, on the road was the mangled body of his precious eagle. "No!" Anthony cried in panic and ran to the bird. Tears streamed down his cheeks while he picked it up and stroked the eagle's bloodstained feathers. Yet, the boy noticed something that surprised him. The eagle still had a pulse. It was alive. Anthony ripped off his shirt, gently wrapped its body and cradled it in his arms, and he realized this was the eagle that shoved him away from disaster. This angelic-like creature saved him. It was near death, and he did not know what to do.

Instinctively, the boy cried out, "God, please don't let him die!" He sobbed and held the bird up in the air. "It's all my fault! He risked his life for me!"

Anthony ran through a grove of giant sequoia trees with the eagle in his arms. Panicked, he stopped to catch his breath and peeked under his bloody shirt. The bird just gazed up at him, as though it could see into his soul. Never had he felt so loved, yet so helpless.

The boy held it gently, and he trekked along a deer path that meandered up a ridge. Hoping he could see the youth camp from higher up, he continued on. But all he saw was an endless forest and hope drained out of him. When he turned to go back down, he was startled by what he saw.

A large man stood a few feet away from him and blocked the trail. He looked wild in his crusty black bear coat, and he wore a coonskin hat with feathers sticking out from the sides. Long shoulder-length white hair blew in the wind, and his scruffy beard made him appear to be as fierce as a Viking about to attack. His penetrating blue eyes softened, and he smiled reassuringly. Then, Anthony recognized that he was the same man from the lake.

Unsure of what to make of this, the boy glanced at the badly injured bird in his hands and looked up at the stranger. The man grinned, nodded and held out a leathery hand.

Anthony was at peace and placed the eagle in the man's large palm. Gently, the mountain man raised up the eagle, and he sang a song in words that the boy could not comprehend. While a cool breeze swept along the ridge, Anthony took a deep breath, and he felt so alive and confident that all would be well.

Gradually, the song trailed off, and the only sound was a subtle breeze rustling through the trees. The boy tasted the fresh, clean air, and he inhaled deeply, then he relished the sensation of his lungs expanding.

For the first time in his life, the youth discovered the richness of his own breath. In awe, he watched, as the man gazed toward the heavens and said something in a strange language. Magically, the wind swooshed in; then, the stranger opened his mouth wide and took a breath.

Just as the mountain man held in fresh air, the wind subsided, and it felt as though time stood still. His lips touched the eagle's beak, and he breathed into the bird's lungs. Slowly the man raised the eagle high above his head, as though it was an offering to the heavens. A funnel of wind circled around his hands. The eagle's wings fluttered, and suddenly, it took flight with such majesty that it was like nothing ever happened. It flew higher and higher until it vanished in the sun's rays amidst parting clouds.

The boy shaded his eyes, scanned the horizon and asked, "Where did the eagle go?"

"You will see him again," the mountain man spoke in a soft, gentle tone, smiled peacefully, and added, "When you need him the most."

"But I don't understand...I have so many questions."

The man laughed, placed his hand on the boy's shoulder and smiled, "I can see why he chose you."

Young Anthony felt heat on his shoulder from the man's touch, and it flowed along both his arms, up his neck, head, then shot down throughout his extremities. His heart raced, and he had a strange sensation that he could fly like the eagle. The mountain man held up the boy's bloody shirt that had covered the bird, and he let it float away in a gust of wind. Anthony was so spellbound in this magical moment that he did not want to leave the mountain.

The man studied the boy intently, then knelt in front him, smiled reassuringly, and pressed his bloodstained large thumb on Anthony's bare chest, right over his heart. The boy felt a powerful jolt, and he blacked out. When he awoke, he was back in his bunk at the youth camp, while it was still twilight before the first sign of a morning glow.

Anthony sat up in his bunk, and he wondered if this was all a dream. While he pondered what had transpired, he felt a tingling sensation on his chest. He shined a flashlight on it, and he was startled to see a bright red spot the size of a man's thumb print. Thinking that no one would ever believe him, the boy decided to not say a word about it to anyone.

Years passed, as he grew to manhood, and gradually, the spot on his chest looked more like a birthmark. Meanwhile, the eagle visited him nightly in his dreams, and he believed that this majestic creature was sent by God to protect him.

This belief faded by the time Anthony was drafted into the Army and sent to Vietnam. During that tour, his senses were numbed by the blood on his hands that never seemed to wash off and the overpowering stench of death. As a medic, Corporal Anthony Lorenzo saved many of his brother's lives, but too many did not make it.

Feeling powerless to help in the midst of all this senseless violence, he grew increasingly resentful and angry. So, his repeated attempts at drowning his despair with alcohol quenched all dreams of the majestic eagle, and faith in God.

When the medic returned to the states, he just wanted to forget the war, but a couple of wild-eyed strangers spat in his face and called him a baby killer. This hurt as much as anything else he had gone through in the chaos of war.

Daily, he was haunted by the memory of the little Vietnamese girl he could not save.

While he remembered all this, he stood before a mirror in Bolt's cabin, and stared at his reflection, and it sickened him. Anthony went back to his bunk, and he thought of the two encounters with the mountain man and the eagle. Twice the stranger had left an odd thumbprint on his chest that gave him the strength to go on, and the young, weary vet longed to believe in that miracle again.

However, he still doubted that it actually happened. Perhaps, the eagle and the mountain man were just figments of a wild imagination grown out of despair.

While he rested on his bunk, Anthony whispered softly, "Oh please, God, if you are real, send me the eagle again. I promise that I will do whatever I can to change, with your help." Even as he said this, he still thought he was unworthy. He rolled over and pounded his fist on the pillow.

"Who am I kidding?" Anthony sat up, looked at the imaginary blood on his hands and remembered the last time he saw his wife's face. "I'm sorry, Amy! I never meant to hurt you! Please forgive me!"

For a moment, he stared at his reflection in the mirror and cried. "How can I be clean and live fully like a normal human being?"

Steven S. Foster

6 The Woodcarver

Anthony awoke to the tantalizing aroma of frying bacon and clanking sounds from the kitchen. Blurry-eyed, he tried to focus on the clock beside him, and it ticked at 5:00 a.m. Slowly, he remembered that he had stayed his first night in Bolt's cabin, so he dressed in the extra clothes that the elder man had given him. When he entered the kitchen, he found Bolt in front of the wood-burning stove with a skillet that sizzled and popped.

"Good morning, son. Grab a chair," Bolt gestured with a wave of the spatula toward the table, "Chow's almost ready."

"Thanks," Anthony heard the rumbling in his hungry stomach, as he glanced at the stove, "Need any help?"

"Nope," Bolt nodded again, "Go on, sit."

When the young vet scooted his chair in, Bolt piled a mound of yellow scrambled eggs on a large plate. Silently, he added half-dozen slices of bacon and brought over a separate dish stacked with blueberry pancakes. Anthony stared at all that food in disbelief, while his host set down a basket of fresh-baked biscuits and a bowl of sliced apples.

"You expect the two of us to eat all that?"

"Got a busy day ahead," Bolt sat and piled food on his plate. "You best keep your strength up, son."

Anthony laughed and thought there was no way he could take in such a huge meal, since he usually was not a big breakfast eater in the morning. "You're kidding, right?"

Judging by the way his host delved into his food without a word, Anthony knew this was no joke, so he shrugged and began to eat. He savored each juicy bite of steamy bacon and relished the taste of scrambled eggs in his mouth. After two large platefuls, that included the pancakes and biscuits, he realized how hungry he was, and every sip of hot coffee warmed him up.

"How about some apple pie that I saved from Jenny's kitchen?" Without expecting an answer, Bolt had already piled a slice on another plate for Anthony.

The young man glanced at Bolt's 5-foot, 10-inch muscular frame, with a thin waist, and asked, "If you eat like this all the time, how do you keep yourself fit?"

Bolt swung his leg over the back of his chair like a limber 20-year-old and sat down. "Breakfast is the most important meal of the day for me. Besides, I get lots of exercise and work hard the rest of the day." When he finished chewing a piece of the pie, he added, "You'll see what I mean and be glad you ate a good meal by the time we're done."

Anthony was even more intrigued. "What do you mean?"

Bolt leaned forward and looked directly at him. "Son, I've been thinking," he took a sip from his coffee mug, as though he wanted to weigh his words carefully, "First, we get your truck out from that snow yonder," he gestured with a wave of his hand.

The young man admired the rhythmic movements of Bolt's hands while he talked. It all appeared as though a master conductor was leading a grand orchestra. Yet, he had a simple, carefree quality about his gestures, as well. Anthony easily envisioned Bolt in a scene out of the old western frontier. In this backdrop, the rugged woodcarver clearly communicated in sign language with a great Sioux warrior.

"Second, we put you to work," Bolt interrupted his thoughts.

Anthony heard the words but was surprised by the blunt sound of it. "What?"

The elder man's expression looked sincere, like he deeply cared about Anthony. "Son, I reckon I know about what's ailing inside you." Bolt tapped his right first two fingers on the young man's chest and said, "I know the hurt in there. For a man, the best way to heal is to work and sweat it out through good physical labor that has a purpose. You got that?"

Without waiting for a response, Bolt added, "Let me put it another way…I could use an extra hand around here in my workshop. Since you appreciate my wood carving, I'd like you to work for me for as long as you like. Try it for a week or so, and, if you decide you want to stay on, you're welcome to continue."

Surprised by this offer, Anthony cleared his throat, "But you don't even know me."

Bolt shrugged, "I know enough."

"What do you need me to do?"

"Be my assistant. I need your help with my wood furniture business." Bolt looked into the young man's eyes and sighed, "I've had employees come and go, but I can tell there is something very special about you, son. The way you admired my woodcarving," he paused and tapped the young man's chest again, and added, "You have a passion for the work."

Anthony fidgeted in his chair. He wanted to say yes but felt so unworthy, and he could not understand why he was being offered such an amazing opportunity. After Amy's death, he had just walked away from a boring, tedious job as a machine operator on a conveyor belt that pushed meaningless products around. Now, he was offered a creative job that had purpose. How could he refuse? "Well, I…"

"I won't lie to you, son," Bolt interrupted. "You'll work until your back aches, but it's a good hurt when you know you've accomplished something worthwhile." The woodcarver studied him for a moment, then added, "Truth is, my previous assistants just didn't have the heart for it long-term."

"What makes you think I do?"

"Like I said, you have passion for the creative process, and it was obvious by the way you admired my wood carvings that you also have an eye for details." Bolt leaned back in his chair and observed the young man's expression. "It's okay, son. I can tell you have doubts about your worth and abilities. Instead of limiting yourself, you need to focus on what I see in you."

Anthony looked up and it seemed like Bolt could see right through to his soul. "What's that?"

Bolt smiled and boldly said, "Well, I see the spirit of an eagle in you, son. Trouble is you got a broken wing, and you think you can't fly. I know that you are a good soul, and you have a lot of potential for greatness. In fact, I think, if you stick with me, young fella, I'll prove to you that your spirit will soar like the eagle."

Anthony relaxed in his seat and sighed, "I'd like to believe that."

"Okay," Bolt smiled again, "If you want the job, I'll start you out at 100 bucks a week with room and board. Plus, you can eat all you want at Jenny's and put it on my tab. If you like the job and want to stay on after a month, I'd be proud to make you my apprentice. You'll learn an honest trade that you can feel good about, and it's the best way to heal, son. You in?"

"When do I start?" Anthony reached out a hand.

Bolt gripped him hard and grinned, "Right after we get your truck out of the snow."

Anthony winced in pain, pulled back his arm and chuckled, "That's if you don't kill me with another handshake."

While the weather briefly cleared, the men drove slowly on the mountain road and stopped to search along endless snowdrifts. After several hours, they discovered Anthony's truck buried deep in the snow, with only the antenna sticking up. Using shovels, they dug out a path to the asphalt, hooked up a hoist, and pulled the truck back to the main road. It took several attempts to get the vehicle started, and, finally, he was able to drive with Bolt following behind him.

At the cabin, they settled in front of the fireplace and it began to snow again. Hot coffee steamed from their mugs, and they were glad to be inside with the power back on. Anthony savored the aroma of peanut butter on warm toast, and it was all he needed to get by. With renewed energy, he asked, "So when can I see your workshop?"

Bolt smiled approvingly, stood up, put his coat on and strolled into the entryway. "Glad you asked, son. Let's go have a look see." Bolt opened the door and icy wind blew snowflakes around like a child's whirligig.

Eager to get started, Anthony followed and pulled up his jacket collar to protect his ears from the biting cold, to no avail. Struggling to keep his balance, he slipped in the ice three times before he met Bolt at the workshop. Together, they shoved the heavy steel door, which seemed frozen in the metal frame, and then it finally creaked open with some difficulty.

Once they entered, and the door slammed tight with a loud clunk, a scent of sawdust wafted into the young man's nostrils. He blinked and tried to focus but saw nothing in pervasive darkness. In that still moment, he felt strangely tranquil and relaxed. He heard a ruffling sound from the movement of Bolt's heavy jacket, and then a click. Instantly the shop lit up with bright overhanging lights that illuminated sturdy workbenches, saws, drills and other tools of the trade.

"Let's hope the power stays on," Bolt's bright blue eyes sparkled, and he grinned proudly.

Anthony's vision adjusted to his surroundings, and he was amazed at the sight. Silently, he began to stroll around the well-kept shop with tools hanging neatly on the walls. While he gazed upon exquisite works of art, he felt like he belonged there. Among the woodcarvings, he observed eagles in flight, deer leaping, and wolves on the hunt. It was so clear in the young man's mind that the woodcarver had a deep connection to nature, and he admired Bolt more than ever.

"Wow," Anthony whispered softly, as though he had just entered a sacred chamber. "Did you carve all these?"

"Yep, I reckon you could say they're my babies. A lot of labor went into each piece." Bolt's eyes shined like a proud father.

Slowly, Anthony approached several two-foot-tall figures on a shelf and he whispered, "amazing," in a low, hushed tone. Before him was a beautiful native American maiden, who sat with her suckling baby cradled at her partially exposed breast. Standing next to her was a tall, muscular warrior, who had a proud look as the protector of his family.

Anthony reached out his hand slowly within inches of the statues but held back, and he asked, "May I touch them?" His voice was reverent and almost breathless.

Bolt grinned and nodded approvingly, "I knew you would appreciate it."

The young man hesitated, glanced at the woodcarver, and he still felt insecure about somehow violating the sanctity of these masterpieces.

"Go ahead, run your fingers over the wood. Feel the texture. Sense the flow of the grains." The woodcarver waved a hand to assure him, "Go on, son."

Anthony noticed the signature at the base of the statue, and it read, "Bolt Mac Arthur." Softly, lovingly, the young man caressed the wood with his fingertips. A smile warmed his cheeks, and his eyes brightened. Deeply moved, he heard the eagle calling out to him within his spirit, and he knew that he must learn to skillfully carve wood in the same way.

The woodcarver laughed with delight at the young man's fondness of the craft and whispered, "I knew you were the one."

Anthony did not hear him while he was so engrossed in the fine details and curvatures of these graceful statuesque wonders. "It is so…I don't know how to describe it…it's magnificent… such splendor…and you capture the dignity of these people so well." He looked up and studied Bolt. "How could a guy like…"

The woodcarver smiled, "You mean a guy like me, who's hardened by the wind. A man, who looks as though he's been rounding up too many head of cattle, right?"

"Well…yeah," Anthony laughed awkwardly.

The woodcarver reached up at a top shelf, took a palm-sized carving and held it out. "Tell me what you see."

"A wooden horse."

Bolt put it back on the shelf. "It's more than that, son."

"What do you mean?"

Bolt waved a hand toward the shelf and smiled, "made that when I was five. It's a part of who I am."

Intrigued by this woodcarver even more, Anthony sat down on a stool and leaned his elbows on the counter. Never had he felt so enthralled by anyone before. Now, all he wanted was to sit in this workshop, smell the scent of sawdust, and listen to every word.

The elder war vet pulled out a small box made of cedar, then carefully unwrapped something in a red neckerchief. "My Pa gave me this knife and taught me to whittle."

Anthony leaned forward and was amazed to see a bone-handled knife with the detailed carving of an eagle in flight. "Awesome," he whispered with a sense of deep respect. He thought of nothing he could claim from his unknown ancestry as an orphan, and he admired the idea of anyone having such an heirloom to keep for himself.

The woodcarver held the knife in his opened palm, gazed at it and appeared to be in deep thought. "After a hard day's work on the ranch, we used to sit on the porch, and Pa told me stories about the old west. We carved while he talked, and I learned to appreciate what my hands could do."

"Sounds like you had some good times." The young man tried to remember his childhood, but it was all a blur of moving from one foster family to another.

"Yep. When the weather was nice, we camped in the Colorado mountains." He paused, as though he relived those days in his memories, and added, "I grew to respect the wilderness with all its wonders and unpredictability. I reckon I learned to listen, observe, and I got into a rhythm of all that was around me."

Nothing else was said, as the woodcarver picked up a partially completed piece, and he began to work in silence. In those moments, the young vet felt an unusual sense of belonging that he could not fully understand. Yet, this quiet solitude seemed right for him. If he had been anywhere else with any other person, it would have been unbearable without words being spoken between two people. Before this, he felt that he needed constant noise to muffle the ongoing traumatic memories of the war and the loss of his wife, Amy.

Now, with his mind at peace for the first time in over a year, he meandered around the workshop, and another carving caught his attention. It was a two-foot tall statue of a bald eagle with its wings spread out wide. The raptor's talons gripped a large fish that seemed to thrash wildly about. Anthony admired the realistic details, and he could almost hear the sound of splashing water.

Next to that piece, Anthony observed a carved eagle feeding several hungry chicks in a nest. Again, he heard the distinct call of the eagle deep within his spirit, and he longed to work with his hands in this sacred place. Strangely, he felt a tingling sensation on his chest, and he sensed the woodcarver's creative energy in the wood.

Time seemed to stand still, and he became aware of his breath: the slow intake of air, and his diaphragm expanded, then he observed the pleasing sensation of his own exhalation. In that sacred moment, he remembered his boyhood wilderness experience, when he felt being this alive, so clean and so vibrant in spirit.

Deeply transfixed, Anthony studied the way the carved-out mother eagle seemed to nurture and feed her young. Tiny featherless chicks appeared to be flapping their wings, with their beaks wide open, as their parent held a dangling piece of meat out for her little ones.

Anthony looked over at the woodcarver. "Uh, Bolt," he rubbed the thumbprint on his chest as the tingling intensified, "I know this may sound crazy, but I feel something about this carving. What inspired you to do this?"

The woodcarver strolled over and gazed upon his work in silence. Outside, the wind howled and vibrated against the walls. The young vet watched but said nothing. Finally, Bolt squatted and grabbed a handful of fresh sawdust that had been swept into a pile.

Quietly, he sprinkled it on the cold concrete floor, and, without making eye contact, the woodcarver whispered something. Anthony instinctively stepped closer, squatted beside the elder man and listened intently. Somehow, it felt right to do so.

"When my Emma died, I was so grief-stricken that I grabbed an ax and chopped wood for hours." Bolt continued to stare at that pile of dust until he said, "I got so tired, I fell face down in the dirt and sobbed until my gut ached. When my throat was dry, and the tears were gone, I sat up with the taste of earth in my mouth. All I could do was spit it out and yell, 'God help me!'"

The young vet had deep empathy for the woodcarver, since they shared their sorrows, but all Anthony could do was squat beside the elder vet in silence.

Bolt continued to stare at that pile of sawdust, and he finally said, "You know…a strange thing happened. I heard the call of an eagle, and I looked up as it circled overhead. Suddenly, I had a burst of energy that, to this day, I can't explain. I remember that I picked up a junk piece of wood, and I began to carve on it with my pocket knife."

Anthony watched in silence, as Bolt drew lines in the sawdust with his finger. The woodcarver wiped his eyes on his shirtsleeves and sniffed, "I whittled and used it as a model while I worked on a better piece of wood. Odd thing is the way it took shape without much effort on my part. I reckon the sense of freedom I saw in that eagle reminded me of Emma's spirit. So, I keep that statue as a reminder of her."

For a moment, they both said nothing, stood up and gazed upon the eagle statue. Anthony leaned in closer and studied the carved eaglets in a nest at the feet of the mother bird. He remembered that he saw photos on the fireplace mantle of what he thought might be the woodcarver's family. "You mentioned earlier that you have children?"

"Two daughters," Bolt went back to the workbench and carved again, "My oldest is Ann. She's 38. Haven't seen her in five years. She's in Germany with her husband, an Air Force Colonel. Linda's my youngest, but I don't know where she is. She left home at 19, and I'm not sure if she's still alive. Been over 15 years, and I tried to find her many times, but no luck."

Anthony began to feel awkward, like he had been intruding. So, he stood there and fidgeted.

"Yep," Bolt sighed, "Had two girls. No son." Woodchips dropped to the floor as he carved. "But...does no good to dwell on the past. I've had a good life."

The workshop grew silent, and Anthony instinctively picked up a push broom and swept the floor. Somehow, it felt right to put his hands to work, and the rhythmic swoosh, swoosh sounds helped to relax his restless mind. While he kept his pace near tall, well-organized shelves with stacks of cedar, pine, maple, oak and redwood; aromatic fragrances gave him peace.

Within those hollowed walls, no sacred music played, yet Anthony felt as though he was in a sanctuary. Here, the two men worked as a team. This made the hours go by quickly.

Often, the woodcarver asked, "Hold this piece for me, okay?"

Eagerly, the young novice gripped the wood, and he liked the feel of it in his hands.

"That's good, son. Hold it steady."

A saw buzzed, whirred, then it was silent again.

"Okay, now, we need to cut a groove here," Bolt held up the wood. "First, we'll double check to make sure this'll line up right." He glanced at a tool drawer, "Son, reach in there and get me the measuring tape."

"Got it," the novice slapped it into the woodcarver's hand.

Soon, they were connected by the same passion to create beauty out of pliable materials. After several hours of work, the woodcarver looked at the young man and smiled. "You've got a steady, hand, young fella."

The apprentice grinned, "Thanks."

"Can you see yourself doing this every day?"

"Maybe," Anthony hesitated and glanced at the sawdust on his hands. "I like the feel of it…but," he let out a deep sigh.

The woodcarver patted the young man's shoulder, "That's okay, son. I can see you still have doubts about your own abilities. Just take it a day at a time and see if this is what you want to do."

"Thanks."

7 The Intrusion

Working with the woodcarver went smoothly for three weeks until a blaring car horn intruded into his sanctity. Irritated by this invasion of his senses, Anthony glanced at a wall clock that ticked at 4:45 p.m. A fading winter sun had already dipped below the peaks to the west and radiated an orange glow in the clouds.

How many days had passed? He could not remember. Out the workshop window, he noticed a dingy-brown Ford pickup with two women sitting in the cab. What did they want?

A loud, irritating car horn blared again, and the young vet covered his ears to block out this intrusion of his tranquil work space. Bolt had already stepped outside to greet the women in a pick-up truck, and Anthony recognized one of them as Jenny, the café owner. Curious, and having a deep fondness for this elegant lady, he strolled over to the car while Bolt rushed to open her driver's side door.

"Jen, you alright?" Bolt looked worried as he grabbed the handle.

Of course," Jenny grinned, got out and stood next to him, "Just thought you might be hungry. I brought some fresh-baked chicken."

Bolt stood there with a dumbfounded expression, and he was oblivious to the other woman, who stood near the passenger side.

"Well?" Jenny interrupted his silence with a giggle and appealing smile. "Just don't stand there with your mouth gasping like a fish out of water. Help us out here." She reached across the seat and held a cardboard box filled with hot food wrapped in a thick towel.

Overtaken by the aroma of steamy chicken, Anthony felt hunger pangs and remembered that his last meal was an early breakfast, so he boldly stepped in front of Bolt. Without hesitation, he took the box from Jenny. "I'll help you."

Jenny grinned with gratitude and kissed him on the cheek. "Thanks, dear," she laughed and placed her hands on her petite hips, made a mock frown and glared at the woodcarver. "Now, Bolt Mac Arthur, what kind of greeting is this? Look at Anthony, and you'll see how it's done. Of all the times you men have been in my café the past several weeks, this young man has always been the perfect gentleman." She playfully wagged a finger in Bolt's face. "You could learn a thing or two about proper manners, you know."

The woodcarver blinked, raised his hand up, as though he was about to say something, but hesitated. Finally, he spoke, "Sorry, Jen, it's just that I was surprised to see you out here."

Jenny smirked with amusement, "Well, this is a very special occasion."

Meanwhile, Anthony watched the other woman, as she walked right past him, then stepped in between Bolt and Jenny. For a second, she stood toe to toe with Bolt, then grinned and giggled.

Anthony clumsily gripped the warm cardboard box, and he felt out of place. Strangely, he had a twinge of irritation, and he had no idea why. He wondered about this rude girl, who appeared to be about his age.

"Well," the young woman faced Bolt and smiled, "Don't you recognize me?"

Bolt's puzzled expression suddenly changed, and his eyes widened. "Sheri? Is that really you?"

Sheri hugged him and laughed, "It's so good to see you."

Bolt lifted her 5-foot, 3-inch, 130-pound frame off the ground and squeezed tightly. "Wow! You're all grown up!" He gently set her back down and grinned, "You must have been 18 and as skinny as a toothpick the last time I saw you."

"You remembered." Sheri kissed his cheek. "I knew you wouldn't forget."

"How could I? Ever since you were knee-high to a bunny rabbit, you had a way of getting yourself in trouble, young lady."

Sheri giggled and playfully slapped him on the chest. "I wasn't that bad."

"Oh yeah?" Bolt grinned and wagged his finger at her, "So, why was it that your Pa and I always had to rescue you? How about the time when you were eight, and you got lost near Bear Springs? It took us almost a day to find you."

Sheri looked up with a mischievous smirk, "I was only trying to find that little fawn to bring him home with me."

"You know, sometimes I thought you just wanted the attention," Bolt laughed and hugged her again. "It's so good to see you, kitten."

Jenny nudged him and teasingly said, "Okay, you've hogged enough of that attention from my daughter. Let's go inside and eat before the food gets cold."

Sheri held onto Bolt's right arm while Jenny took his left, and they headed to the front door. Anthony was so amused by this that he stood in the driveway while balancing the warm, flimsy box in his arms and watched them walk away. Then, he glanced at the goods, smelled the aroma of fresh-baked chicken, shrugged, and rushed to get inside with everyone else.

They gathered in the kitchen while Anthony helped Jenny to unload the box of fresh-cooked café delights. Soon the aroma wafted deliciously through the cabin while it was all being warmed up in the oven, and Anthony longed for the taste of Jenny's culinary wonders. While he set out plates and utensils, she quickly introduced him to Sheri, but all he managed was a shy nod, and he turned away.

"I'll help." Anthony took glasses out of the cupboard and his stomach growled. Embarrassed, he glanced at Sheri when she stood in the kitchen doorway with Bolt.

"I missed you so much," Sheri whispered to the woodcarver. "How are you?" She peeked over at Anthony and quickly diverted her eyes back to Bolt.

The young vet barely heard Bolt's response, but he did not make out all his words. Instead, he was uncomfortable with the odd feeling that Sheri was staring at him. So, he feigned disinterest by diverting his eyes to inanimate objects, like dishes, and he adjusted utensils on the table. Whenever Anthony thought she was not looking, he sneaked quick glimpses and listened intently to their conversation.

"Well, kitten, I reckon it's time you filled me in on what you've been up to these past three years."

Bolt strolled with Sheri into the living room and gestured for her to sit down. When she went to the couch, she paused and watched Bolt, as he stood and leaned against the fireplace. Anthony thought that it may have seemed odd to her, but this was the woodcarver's usual manner during their many conversations in the recent few weeks.

Sheri plopped on the sofa and let out a sigh. She removed a wool cap, and her long raven hair instantly flowed all the way to the curvy small of her back like a sudden waterfall. "I'm sure that Mom has told you about my half-hearted attempt at college life in New York, right?" Her tone turned sarcastic, and she looked toward the doorway where Jenny still worked in the kitchen.

Bolt stepped forward, reached down and gently squeezed her face in the palms of his hands, grinned and replied, "I want to hear it from you, young lady." He stepped back and leaned against the mantel again, then waited patiently for her response.

Sheri brushed a strand of hair away from her left eye and glanced at Anthony when he entered the living room with two glasses of iced tea. Feeling out of place, he quickly set the drinks down—one for Sheri and the other he left on the shelf for Bolt. Increasingly uneasy, the young veteran walked out of the room without a word.

"Okay..." She hesitated and seemed reluctant to say anymore but finally said, "I...dropped out of college after my second semester." She lowered her head as though she was ashamed. "Moved in with my starving-artist boyfriend. He was so broke and high on drugs, I worked as a waitress to support the both of us. It got so bad...I finally dumped him," tears streamed down her face and her voice cracked.

Anthony overheard this from the kitchen, and he noticed that the room was very quiet after Sheri dropped what sounded like an emotional bombshell. Immediately, he did not like this drama that was building up. She was disrupting his place of refuge where he calmed his own demons, and he resented her intrusion.

Bolt spoke up, "Uh, Kitten..."

"To top it off," Sheri interrupted in a loud, angry tone, "My no-good boyfriend showed up at my work, and he attacked me in front of customers! Then, the police came and arrested him! The next day, he was out and threatened to kill me! So, I ran away as far as I could go. Now, here I am crawling back to my mom as a total flop!" Sheri sniffed and wiped her damp cheeks with a sleeve. "But, of course, mom told you all that anyway."

Bolt's eyes widened, and he glanced at Jenny, who stood in the doorway while nervously wringing her hands on a towel. She wiped a tear from her cheek, saw that he was glaring at her with an obvious look of surprise, and she quickly vanished into the kitchen. Anthony watched her as she rushed to the sink and wildly scrubbed the dishes. Without saying a word, he went to her side and began the work of drying each plate that she slapped into his hand.

Meanwhile, Bolt tried to regain his composure, and he sat on the couch beside Sheri, who covered her face with her hands. "No..." he whispered softly, "Your mother didn't tell me, kitten. Did you think it would change the way I feel about you?"

Sheri hugged him tightly, "I missed you, Poppy." She cried and nestled her face on his shoulder. "Oh, why can't I find a decent man like you?"

Bolt noticed a tear running down her cheek and smiled tenderly, "Oh, come on now, what do we have here?" He caught the drop with his finger and pretended to place it in his pocket. "I reckon I'll just have to put this little tear with all the other magic drops I've collected from you, kitten. Now, make a wish. Then, it shall be granted."

Sheri laughed, sniffed and wiped her eyes on his shirt sleeve. "Oh, Poppy, I'm not a little girl anymore."

"Oh really," he teased. "Well, I'm still your godfather, and your Pa was my friend, so don't you forget that, young lady." He gently kissed her forehead.

During the next couple of hours, the four of them sat around a maple wood table, and they ate, laughed and told stories. After dinner, everybody pitched in to clean up, as they continued to enjoy each other's company. While Anthony put the dishes away, he sensed a deep closeness that these people shared, and he felt welcomed into this happy family atmosphere.

After the chores were done, Bolt held up a deck of cards. "Jen, remember when you and John used to come over for a game of poker, and we played for hours?"

Jenny laughed and sat down next to him. "We bet with piles of acorns, and that was hilarious. Emma won so much that her side of the table looked like a squirrel's booty of acorns."

"She was unbeatable," Bolt chuckled and held up the cards with a mischievous grin. "Well? Let's have some fun."

Bolt shuffled the deck, dealt the cards, and each person studied his or her individual hand. While they played, Anthony thought of the contrast between this gathering and poker games he had with his Army buddies. Usually, it was a tumultuous party, filled with heavy drinking and loud music.

This sparked his thirst for a cold beer, but he gradually forgot about it. The more they light-heartedly teased and laughed about gambling with acorns, the more he relaxed and enjoyed their company.

At one point, Jenny shuffled the deck and was about to deal the cards when she stopped and looked at Bolt. "I just remembered how John used to pull those crazy pranks."

Bolt burst out in laughter, "Yeah, we could never be sure who was going to be on the receiving end of his shenanigans."

Jenny glanced at Anthony and chuckled, "Oh, you just have to hear what Mr. Macho over here did."

Bolt rolled his eyes, slapped his cards face-down, laughed and replied, "Uh, oh."

Anthony looked at the obviously embarrassed woodcarver and chortled, "I got to hear this."

Bolt glanced over at Jenny, and she winked. Suddenly, he seemed to know what she was about to say. "No, not that story," he laughed and shook his head with light-hearted disapproval.

"Of course," Jenny giggled and looked at Anthony, "So, the four of us sat around talking late one night, when Mr. Macho here wasn't looking, and John tossed a bunch of caps into the fireplace. Then, he yelled, 'Incoming!' just as they exploded, 'pop, pop, pop!'" Jenny glanced at Bolt with a playful grin.

"What happened?" Anthony leaned forward with amusement.

Jenny laughed and hardly could contain herself. "Mr. Macho flopped on top of Emma in an effort to save her from disaster. It was so funny! Emma tried to push him off, while John rolled on the couch, laughing like a crazy hyena!"

Boisterous laughter filled the room, and Bolt mischievously grinned, "Well, what you so deliberately left out was about my part in the prank. The joke was that, when John set off the firecrackers, I was to roll on top of Emma in a mock attempt to save her."

Jenny giggled with delight and replied, "Yeah...well I like my version better." She winked and added, "Besides,

Emma was so mad that she didn't talk to you for the rest of the evening."

"Well, that's true, Bolt laughed and shook his head, "That was one of those pranks that didn't go as well as John and I expected."

Anthony laughed with everyone else, and he felt a freeing sensation when his lungs fully expanded. Hours drifted casually, and he could not remember having so much fun with a group of sober people. It was nothing like his drinking days with Army buddies at a sleazy bar in Da Nang, Vietnam, just a few months before. Here, it was good, clean socializing without the whores trying to steal his money and soul.

In that cabin, these two women fascinated the young veteran. He relished their delightful little gestures that mother and daughter made during their copious conversations. Both women tilted their heads slightly to the right, as they listened and nodded with sincere interest. They wore faded jeans like most country girls but were graceful and lady-like while they gestured with their hands to illustrate a point.

Both had high cheekbones, and waist-length raven hair that seemed to flow like streams down their backs. Jenny had a poise that comes with age, but a radiant playfulness that revealed a youthful vitality. She was soft-spoken one moment. The next, she would say something so profound, and direct to the point, that anyone in ear-shot always took notice. Anthony was in awe of her every delightful move. She had delicate white streaks in her hair, a couple of dark blemishes on her forehead, and, when she laughed, the lines on her face crinkled.

Sheri was a much younger image of her mother with smooth caramel flesh, and full supple lips that pouted one minute, then spread to a sweet smile the next. He also noticed the similarity she had with Bolt's statue of the nursing Native American woman. Since the piece was carved 20 years earlier, however, he wondered if Jenny may have been the original inspiration.

This idea made more sense, as he remembered that she mentioned her ancestry during a previous visit at the café. It was especially obvious while Jenny displayed her natural maternal ways around her daughter.

Yet, just as Sheri walked around the room, that is when Anthony noticed an annoying difference between mother and daughter. Jenny seemed to have all the noble qualities of a Cherokee woman, and each step was soft without any noticeable sound. Sheri, however, had an unrestrained clunky movement with each step.

"Anthony?" Bolt's voice awakened him from his thoughts, "It's your turn."

"What?" The young vet realized that everyone had been staring at him, "Oh, yeah, I'll take two cards."

Suddenly, they heard a loud thump from outside, and the lights flicked out. Bolt grabbed a flashlight and rushed to open the front door while they all followed.

"What happened?" Jenny peeked over his shoulder.

The woodcarver's light probed into the darkness and captured a beam of horizontal rain that blew against the cabin by buffeting winds. Slowly moving from left to right, the spotlight illuminated dancing bubbles in expanding ponds. Finally, it zeroed in on an oak tree branch that had fallen on Jenny's vehicle outside.

"My truck!"

"What?" Sheri rushed to her mother's side and peered out. "Oh no!"

Anthony felt cold, windswept droplets on his face and heard fierce ululation in his ears. His neck shivered from the icy wind, and he struggled to keep the front door from being forced all the way open by the storm's overwhelming power. Meanwhile, thick branches bitterly scratched the hood and windshield. "Man! There's no way you can go out tonight!"

"Come on, push!" Bolt yelled over the din, as they grappled and closed the door. Silent relief swept over the cabin when the door was finally latched tight. "Get some more wood on the fire," he calmly said to Anthony.

The woodcarver lit a kerosene lantern and checked the fuse box down the hall, then returned and frowned. "Sorry, Jen, I reckon you ladies will have to bunk here for the night."

"Maybe…" Jenny hesitated with a sigh, "I could just back up my truck, while you guys push the branch off, then I'll go around the tree and drive home."

"No!" Bolt's blunt outburst was so unlike him that everyone stared in surprise. As he looked at their bewildered expressions, he tried to soften his tone. "Please, Jenny...I won't let you go out there." His eyes narrowed slightly, "You know how dangerous it can be to drive in weather like this."

"But…"

Before Jenny could say another word, Bolt gently placed his finger to her lips, and shook his head, rested his hands on her shoulders, and whispered, "Did you forget what happened to Emma?"

Jenny hugged him tightly and kissed his right cheek. "I didn't forget, honey. I'm sorry. We'll stay."

Bolt's arms wrapped around her waist, and he glanced over at Anthony and Sheri with an awkward expression. Yet, he resigned to their observation of this affectionate scene and gently kissed Jenny on the forehead.

Sheri smiled at Anthony and they both shrugged, then strolled over to the fireplace in silence. Hot red, yellow flames reflected in their eyes and danced hypnotically before them. At the mantel, he lit a candle, then sat down on the couch, and he felt Sheri's arm brushing against his side when she plopped next to him.

No longer at ease, he slid over a few inches to prevent any further physical contact. She glanced at his reaction but said nothing. From there, Bolt and Jenny's voices faded to muffled whispers, as they held each other by the kitchen doorway.

Sheri crossed her arms and sighed, "Well, Bolt is stuck with us for the night."

Anthony observed that the elder couple continued to hold each other. "They seem to be more than just friends."

Sheri smiled with amusement, "Cute, aren't they?" She glanced at Anthony, while he grinned in the flickering candlelight and said, "My dad and Bolt were good friends for years. When dad and mom were divorced 10 years ago, and he moved away, Bolt promised to look after us. Being a man of his word, he stuck with us like glue."

Wood crackled in the fireplace, while they gazed upon the elder couple, who still embraced, and whispered softly. Sheri added, "I know one thing… Bolt Mac Arthur is the most trustworthy man I have ever known. You know what I mean?"

Anthony nodded, "Yeah, I noticed that."

"Bolt and his wife, Emma, kind of adopted me in a way," Sheri sighed. "Then, she died. That left Bolt and mom around. They grew on each other, I guess. Funny thing is…they're both crazy about each other but too stubborn to admit it out loud. Sometimes, they just hold on to each other for support, while they try to deal with their own loneliness." Sheri glanced at Anthony, "That's how it is with them."

Feeling his grief stir up, Anthony cleared his throat and all he could say was, "Yep."

Just as he said that, Jenny and Bolt strolled hand in hand and sat across from them. Sheri noticed that it was after midnight on the grandfather clock, looked over and asked, "What now, Mom?"

"We sleep here," Jenny glanced at Bolt, then back at Sheri. "It'll be easier for all of us, dear."

The woodcarver patted the couch, stood up and sighed, "Anthony, you bunk here. Ladies, I'll show you to your rooms."

Hours passed by slowly, while the thunderstorm raged and wind blew heavy rain sideways against the cabin walls outside. It seemed like the whole night sky had erupted and convulsed with explosive, nerve-shaking cracks, followed by rolling claps of thunder. Anthony tossed fitfully on the sofa, and he thought of his wife, Amy.

Nightmarish dreams agitated his convoluted mind, and he relived that fateful rainy night over and over. Worst of all, he could hear her screams and see the blood on his hands. If only he could make things right.

In one vivid dream, the eagle glided majestically, then it soared high above snowy ridges, circled, dove and swooped down, while Amy reached up from a mountain top. Her lovely face was so radiant, and she appeared to be at peace. Anguished in his sorrow, Anthony tried to run to her, but his feet were stuck in a wretched goo-like substance that had the malodor of decay. In a blink, she was gone. He wanted to cry out, but he felt as though he had lost his own voice.

Anthony awoke with his eyes wide open, and he stared into the darkness. For a moment, he listened to spattering rain on a metal roof, and eerie howls of wind against the shutters. Something brushed alongside the sofa, and he turned to see what it was but saw nothing in the dim light of a dying fire.

Unsure if he was still dreaming, he closed his eyes again in a futile attempt to sleep. As he tried to rest on his side, he noticed a cold draft of air that seemed to originate from the kitchen. He was startled by a slight thump and faint rustling in there, and he sat up.

Instinctually, his mind ducked into that survival mode of the jungle, and former Corporal Anthony Lorenzo threw off the blankets, then leapt to his feet. This was silly, he thought. He knew that he was in the woodcarver's refuge. So, why did he have this overwhelming sense of fight or flight? Slowly, he opened the swinging door to the kitchen and listened.

He shook his head at this foolishness and adjusted his eyes to the darkness. It had to be Bolt getting up early to make breakfast. Yet…there would be some kind of light from a lantern or something. Great, he thought. At least he should have picked up his flashlight by the sofa. How dumb was that?

Lorenzo heard a click, then a bump in there, so he rushed back to get his flashlight, armed himself with an iron poker from the fireplace, charged to the door again and stood at the ready for anything. "Bolt is that you?" he whispered softly. The only answer was the wind battering the shutters and pulsating rain on the rooftop. Okay, that's it, he thought. No more games.

Lorenzo kicked the door open and stabbed the darkness with his flashlight. The beam darted wildly and caused shadows to twist and bend in bizarre contortions.

Instantly, his mind flashed back to a rainy night in Vietnam. Soaked, stinking miserable, Corporal Lorenzo stood ankle-deep in mud and listened. Somewhere in the pitch-blackness of the jungle hid an unseen enemy but the only sound he heard was relentless pattering of rain drops.

Scared, he waited alongside his buddies. Seconds dragged on to what seemed like minutes of uncertainty until he felt a tap on a shoulder from his sergeant. With that signal, he sloshed in the muck and not-knowing if this would be his last moment alive. Then, another long agonizing minute passed, and he trekked on with that gut-wrenching fear.

Freezing, damp wind slapped him hard in the face, and his tormented mind awoke to the present moment. Realizing he was back in Bolt's cabin, he still was on high alert, and his heart raced anxiously in anticipation of any movement. Suddenly, the back door banged loudly against the outer wall.

Must be a bear, he thought, as he carefully stepped closer to the open door. At the threshold, he was acutely aware of the cold, wet soaking of his sock-covered feet on the wooden floor.

The flashlight beam jabbed into a stream of silvery rain drops outside, and he saw the lid of the firewood box was wide open. He heard an odd gasping sound and a loud bump, like something had fallen on the back steps. A shadowy figure appeared in the darkness, and Anthony wiped his wet, weary eyes.

"No! It can't be! Amy?" A gust of freezing wind swallowed his voice, and he lost his speech. Breathless, he could only stare in disbelief.

8 Awakening the Night

A loud scraping and grunting noise echoed from the wood bin out back. Startled, Anthony Lorenzo shined his flashlight on a hooded figure, and a gust of wind blew the hood back. "Amy?" He paused, "Oh, it's you! Sheri, are you out of your mind?"

She picked up an armful of firewood and smiled, "Oh, hi." Her boots loudly scuffed on wet wooden planks when she brushed past him and plopped several logs in front of the fireplace. Sheri sighed, turned around and looked at him, as though nothing was out of her ordinary routine, "Your light startled me, at first, but then I realized it was you."

Bewildered, Anthony followed her into the living room with his light glaring in her face. "What are you doing?" He blurted out in annoyance and disbelief.

Sheri ignored his question and reached over to the rack near the fireplace, "Where's the poker?"

Anthony frowned and handed her the iron poke, "Now what the heck is going on?"

Sheri stoked the fire while sparks flew like tiny red stars. "I'm putting more wood on the fire," she glanced at him with another smile.

"I know that, but why did you just go outside and get wood from the bin?" Sleepily, Anthony yawned and scratched his head in frustration. "It would've been easier to get some from the box inside, you know." He tried to see the clock but could not make it out with his tired eyes. "What time is it anyway?"

"I don't know." Sheri stood up, and, for the first time, she could see his obvious annoyance. "Oh, sorry, I didn't mean to wake you. I just couldn't sleep."

Anthony plopped down on the couch, rubbed his eyes and sighed, "Well…thanks for making that clear," He glared at her sarcastically, "That makes a lot of sense."

"Um…" Sheri pointed awkwardly toward the kitchen, "Okay, I won't bother you anymore. I'll just go make some tea."

Anthony closed his eyes and listened to that annoying clunky sound of her heavy boot steps into the kitchen. He tossed and turned for a few minutes and stared at the shadows dancing on the ceiling, as the fire sizzled. Restless, he leaped to his feet and burst into the kitchen, while Sheri was busy opening cupboards.

Sheri gasped and spun around, "You startled me!" The candle in her hand shook a little, and its flame quivered.

Anthony chuckled, "Now we're even." He opened a cupboard, got out a can of black tea bags, and handed it to her. "You freaked me out when you burst in from the porch like a half-crazed home invader!" He shined the flashlight on the wall clock and groaned, "Geez, it's 4:00 in the morning!"

Anthony shook his head in frustration, "Oh, well… I can't sleep either, so I might as well make some coffee."

"Sorry, I upset you." Sheri turned away sheepishly and sighed, "Um…since you're having coffee, I'd like some, too, please." She put aside the can of tea bags and sat with her hands folded on the table.

Anthony took a match and lit the lantern in front of Sheri, and she looked up with a smile. Quickly, he turned away, opened a can of coffee that released the rich aroma of fresh grounds into his senses, and he felt reinvigorated. He glimpsed over at Sheri, who flipped the pages of a newspaper in the dim light. Strands of straight raven hair dangled in her face, and she seemed to be focused on something.

Anthony scooped the grounds into a pot, and sneaked another quick peek, but he paused and studied her features, while she was engrossed in her reading. She wore a blue wool sweater with a hood that hung loose behind her. The sleeves were so long that even her knuckles were covered, and he admired the cute way her slender fingers gripped the paper.

Her nails were short and probably suited for work at the cafe. When Anthony put the pot on a gas stove, he glimpsed over again. For the first time, he noticed something he did not see before. Sheri had a small one-inch scar just above her right eye, which appeared to be a recent wound.

Immediately, he thought of her abusive boyfriend, and he winced at the thought of any man ever hitting a woman. How could a man proclaim his love for his lady, then hurt her at the same time? This made no sense to him.

Sadly, he thought of his wife, Amy, again, and how much he had deeply loved her. Anthony never wanted to hurt her, and he felt remorse over the tragic decision he made that fateful night. Nothing could change the outcome, and he knew that he would have to live with this guilt the rest of his life.

Sheri folded the newspaper, which made a rustling sound, and it reminded Anthony of how Amy used to read while she sipped her coffee after breakfast. Saturday mornings were always special, as they relaxed and discussed current events from the newspaper. Even in his darkest moments, she had a way of lighting a spark of hope in his embattled soul, and he tried to forget his horrific memories of war.

Finally, the coffee pot stopped percolating, so, Anthony poured the steaming, hot brew into a cup and placed it on the table. "Here you go, Amy."

"What?" Sheri looked up as she reached for a napkin.

Embarrassed, Anthony tried to correct himself, "Um, here you go Sheri."

"Thanks," Sheri examined the strong black liquid in her cup and added, "I like mine with cream. Do you have some?"

Anthony remembered that Amy enjoyed her coffee the same way, and he reached for a carton of milk and held it up for Sheri. "Will this do?"

"Yes, thank you." Sheri poured some milk in her cup and stirred it, while the spoon clanged softly. Then, she peeked through a few strands of her hair, which seemed to flow in front of her eyes. She brushed them away with her right hand and smiled, "Since you're going to be up, can we go sit by the fire? I'm freezing."

In the living room, Anthony stoked the flames, and cinders flared wildly in all directions. He added more wood, felt the warmth, and savored a scent of burning cedar in the air. When he turned around, he discovered that Sheri had sat on the end of the couch nearest the fire. She wore green baggy pajama pants that she probably borrowed from the woodcarver, and her legs were tucked to the side.

Anthony observed that she had taken her boots off, and she wore what appeared to be thin socks. Without a word, he grabbed a blanket from the hall closet and gently put it over her legs. "It's cold here, even with the fire."

"Yes, thank you," Sheri pulled it under her arms and sipped her coffee, while she cradled the cup with both hands, "You must have read my mind."

Remembering that Amy used to say the same thing, Anthony felt strangely awkward. He sat on the far side of the couch from Sheri, and they both sipped their coffee in silence. In those tranquil moments, he relaxed more and focused his gaze upon the hypnotic soft orange glow of the fireplace. Wind slowly moaned outside, as though it was dying, and wood crackled in the hearth, while shadows swayed on the walls around them.

Anthony glanced at Sheri but felt uncomfortable, because she gazed right back at him without saying anything. He fidgeted, lit another candle on the lampstand beside him, and she leaned forward like she was about to say something, yet she hesitated. Sheri sipped from her cup again with her eyes fixed on him. Anthony turned and watched a red-hot flaming log burn through its inner core, which made a slight hissing and popping sound.

Flashes of memory intruded his mind. In an instant, Lorenzo was back in a burning village, and a baby cried in his arms.

"Anthony?" A woman's voice softly spoke like she was calling him back to the present.

Army Medic, Anthony Lorenzo gasped for air, blinked, and his eyes felt damp. "What?"

"You okay?"

Anthony wiped his moist cheeks with a sleeve and cleared his throat. All he could do was nod, as he glimpsed Sheri's worried expression, and he turned away to prevent eye contact. In that moment of awakening, he wondered if he could ever have a normal life without those hellish memories.

"I'm sorry..." Sheri scooted a little closer, reached out and touched his hand, "I don't mean to pry, but, last night, when Bolt prepared the rooms for us, he mentioned that your wife died about a month ago."

He nodded quietly, took a sip from his cup and frowned, as it tasted cold and bitter.

"It must be very difficult for you," Sheri squeezed his hand.

Anthony felt uneasy, and he wanted to pull away, but could not move. Never had he been so torn between the desire for human touch and the impulse to pull away. How could he be worthy of such compassion? He lowered his gaze to the quivering dark liquid in his cup.

Sensing his apprehension, Sheri removed her hand and tried to change the subject. "Earlier you said you were from San Diego. Do you plan to go back soon?"

Anthony sighed with relief and looked up from his cup, "Well, for now, I think I'll stick around. Bolt asked me to help out in the workshop. Besides, there is something that I need to do here anyway."

"Oh? What's that?" Sheri smiled with interest.

Realizing his mistake of bringing up something that she could not possibly understand, he just sighed, "Nothing really." He scratched his head and tried to think of what to say. If he mentioned his desire to find the eagle with the mountain man out there in the wilderness, she would wonder about his sanity.

A small log cracked, fell into the fire and sizzled. Smoke billowed, and Anthony finally said, "I went to a spring camp near here when I was a kid, and I want to check out some sights that I remember." He noticed that she continued to study him in silence, so he lowered his gaze and did not like it. Why did she sit so close, anyway? He squirmed, and wanted to stand up, but could not move for some odd reason.

"How about your job in San Diego? Won't you be missed there?" She seemed to probe for anything to talk about.

Anthony thought for a moment and frowned, "At this point, I don't really care." His fists tensed up on his knees, and he felt like he was being squeezed into a narrow space by all these questions.

"Maybe…" Sheri paused, and Anthony looked up. Their eyes met, and he saw her compassionate demeanor that held him. Sheri continued, "Maybe you just need some time. You know…time to think and work things out here with Bolt."

Anthony nodded in agreement, and he gazed at the fire again. Another log sizzled, popped in the flames and smoke swirled upward; then, it suddenly took the shape of a tiny eagle in flight. He rubbed his eyes in disbelief, while it soared above the burning wood and vanished.

"Are you alright?"

"Why do you ask?" Anthony tried to look at her like nothing happened.

"You have this far-off look," Sheri reached out but pulled her hand back. "Now, don't get the wrong idea. I'm not trying to be forward or anything, but there's something about you that I understand. You know…like maybe I can help you."

Anthony suddenly stood up and leaned against the fireplace mantel. With his back to Sheri, he sighed, "Well, it'll be better for you if you don't get too involved. Once you see what a total mess I am, you would think I'm crazy." He glanced at her, then turned away again. "I don't think I could handle that right now."

Sheri came up behind him and put her hand on his upper arm. "Anthony…I didn't mean to upset you."

He felt the warmth and tenderness of her touch, and, without making eye contact, he whispered, "It's all right." He sensed her probing gaze as she stood near the fireplace.

"You must have loved your wife very much," Sheri sighed. "I'm sorry, please believe that I sincerely care, and I want to help you if I can."

Anthony did not respond, and he tried to not look at her. Somehow, it was wrong to get this close to another woman, especially this woman. Her sensitivity combined with obvious attractiveness was too much for him after losing his wife. To make matters worse, the guilt of accidentally causing Amy's death pained him even more whenever he looked into her eyes."

"Sorry, I…" Sheri hesitated, "I tend to jump into situations too fast." She turned to leave the room.

"No, wait, it's okay," Anthony gestured for her to come back, "Please don't go."

Sheri quietly sat down on a rocker opposite the fireplace and whispered, "All right," She lowered her gaze to the orange, red fall-like oak leaf designs on the carpeted floor, "I just thought it would help to talk about what you've been through."

"I know, but it's not easy," Anthony sighed and plopped on a nearby chair.

"Maybe I can relate to your hurt somehow, since I survived a lot of abuse by my insane boyfriend. When I ran away, it felt like all my dreams for a happy life had died, and I was broken inside. You know what I mean?"

Anthony nodded without making eye contact. "Yeah," his voice was a soft whisper, like a puff of smoke.

"We both lost…" Her voice quivered, and she tried to regain her composure. "I'm sorry, I guess I talk too much."

Forgetting his need to distance himself, Anthony reached out and touched her hand. "It's okay, Sheri."

With that simple gesture, they shared a brief moment in their grief. Yet, neither one looked at the other. Burning wood crackled in the fireplace and flames illuminated their faces in a warm, soft, red glow. He wanted to wipe away her tears, but memories vividly flashed in his mind, and he saw himself with Amy during happy times. Then, he felt uneasy, again, and he pulled back his hand.

Sheri quickly stood up and sighed. "Well…I guess I should go back to my room…uh, I mean your room and try to get some more rest. Thank you for letting me stay there." She hesitated near the fireplace as though she was not sure what to do next.

"That's a good idea," Anthony stared at his hands that rested in his lap.

"Good night," Sheri paused next to the mantel, and her face seemed hot in the candlelight. She gazed at him and pointed toward the hallway. "Okay…I'm leaving now."

Anthony nodded without a word. He unfolded the blankets that had been placed on a small corner table and spread them out on the couch again. Although he sensed her presence at the doorway, he kept busy. When he heard the slight ruffling of her clothing and clunky boot steps leaving the room, he threw a pillow down and sighed in relief. He blew out the candles, flopped on the cushions, and tried to clear his weary mind.

Flames had died down in the fireplace, while Anthony restlessly turned from side to side, and he agonized over what had occurred moments ago. Why did she linger like that? This was crazy, and he had no right to have any feelings stirring up so soon after Amy's death.

He pounded the couch with his fist and cursed himself for getting so close to another woman. Resentful, he plopped his face into the pillow and felt like smothering himself. After all, he was not worthy of any kind of life on this earth. Gasping for air, he rolled over, and stared at the ceiling.

Finally, Anthony was relieved when the power came back on, and the cabin thrived with activity as everyone gathered around the dining table for one of Bolt's hearty breakfasts. Warm conversations and laughter filled the morning air, and it felt good to be moving about, instead of languishing on that couch.

Later that morning, a bright sun glared through parting clouds and reflected off puddles in the driveway. Bolt and Anthony had cut away the oak tree branch from Jenny's dented vehicle. Soon, the women left, and Anthony was glad to be working outside. When he stayed focused on the chores in front of him, his mind temporarily cleared of toxic memories.

"Okay, son, hold that branch for me," Bolt ordered. Anthony gripped the limb that they both had lifted on two wooden horses. The woodcarver paused and said, "Ready?" Anthony nodded.

Bolt pulled on a string and his chain saw sputtered, whirred, chewed, then flung wood chips wildly in the air. Brown specks littered the still-wet earth at their feet. This went on for several hours, as they cut, hauled and stored the branches.

For the rest of the day, they built a dresser and cleaned the woodshop. Time seemed to go by fast, as they labored hard and lifted heavy materials. Meanwhile, they bent, twisted their backs, and Anthony loved every sweaty moment of working with his hands.

That night, hot water splashed on Anthony's shoulders and soothed his sore muscles, while he stood under a steaming shower. For a long time, he let it soak and run off his head and imagined that he was under a waterfall.

He scrubbed off the dirt and grime, then watched the soapsuds mixed with brown streams that swirled down the drain. It was a cleansing of his body, and he sensed a purifying of his spirit being renewed like he never felt before.

Back in his room, he rested in bed and stared at the ceiling. Light from a candle on a lampstand flickered and shadows danced above him. Although his body ached, he felt like he accomplished something by working with his hands.

"Yep," he whispered to himself. "It's been a good day." Throughout his busyness of cutting, hauling, building and cleaning, he did not think of all those sorrowful memories of his past.

He looked at his palms and smiled. "I like the feel of working with my hands." For a moment, he was content. Yet, he imagined the blood on his fingers again. Startled, Anthony got up, ran to the bathroom and scrubbed until his skin was sore. "How can I get clean?" he cried.

9 Back to Boot Camp

Anthony awoke one early morning with a jolt and sat up wide-eyed It had been one month since he started work with Bolt. Perhaps, the flashes were back, he thought. He heard loud scraping noises outside, stumbled out of bed and peeked through curtains, but it was still too dark. Something bumped against the side of the cabin, and he knew this was no dream.

Quickly, he tried to pull on his trousers and clumsily danced around on one foot at a time. Finally, he paused, sighed and focused on his balance; then, with better control, he got dressed and ran down the hall. He stopped at his mentor's room, noticed it was empty and yelled, "Hey, Bolt, where are you?"

Anthony grabbed the kitchen flashlight and rushed out on the back porch, as he heard more strange noises from behind the cabin. "Bolt?" Anthony yelled, but there was no answer. So, he stumbled around the corner, and he was surprised by the sight of a dark figure that seemed to move toward a hillside. "Bolt, is that you?" Still, only silence greeted him.

Anthony's boots slipped on a puddle of ice that froze overnight, but he gripped the wall and caught himself. "What the..." he muttered in disbelief, and he shined the flashlight further behind the cabin.

Confused, he rubbed his tired eyes and tried to adjust to the darkness and get a better perspective. Probing with the beam from his light, he finally spotted Bolt about 100 feet away. The woodcarver's headlamp guided him, as he trudged up an embankment, and he dragged something from behind. It appeared that Bolt had a harness around his waist, and he pulled a log approximately six feet in length. Strangely, he trekked in between several trees and disappeared from view.

Cold mist blew out of Anthony's nostrils, while he stared in astonishment and waited. Several minutes past, then Bolt came out from behind a thick conifer tree, unhitched the log, left it there, and started back down the hill.

"Good morning," Bolt shouted vigorously and waved with his right hand while the harness and chain dangled from his left.

"What are you doing?" Anthony studied his mentor, who had to be at least 60 but acted as though he was an extremely energetic 20-year-old.

"Exercise," the woodcarver pounded his chest and sniffed the crisp mountain air.

Anthony laughed, "Man, I can't believe this! You sure blow my mind from one minute to the next!"

Bolt smiled and waved a dismissive hand in the air, "I reckon that's supposed to mean something."
He chuckled with a mischievous grin, "Let's just say, I like to keep you on your toes, son."

"That's for sure. You're always trying to get me to do jumping jacks and sit ups with you." Anthony narrowed his eyes, "What's this all about? We didn't have chow yet."

"Forget breakfast, for now. It's part of your training, young fella."

"Uh, training?"

Bolt's expression became serious, as he stepped closer and put his hand on the young veteran's shoulder. "Talk to me, son. You still get night sweats?"

Anthony lowered his gaze and nodded.

"Look at me," Bolt spoke firmly.

Anthony raised his head and focused on his mentor's eyes. Like so many times he had done before, he knew it was important to pay close attention to his mentor. "Yes," he whispered in an almost inaudible tone.

"You still have horrific memory flashes, whether you're awake or asleep?"

"Yes, sir," Anthony's voice spoke louder and with more assurance that this old war veteran was there to help, as always.

"It's alright, son," Bolt spoke in his usual empathetic and understanding way. "Now, you know that I never ask you to do anything that I won't do myself." The woodcarver gazed into the young man's eyes, "When I got back from the war, in the Pacific, in 45, I thought I was going crazy. I had so many gory nightmares that I felt like I couldn't make it. You know what I mean?"

Anthony kept his focus on the woodcarver, "Yes, sir." After many talks, such as this, it became easier to look directly in the old veteran's eyes.

Bolt smiled, "Do you remember what I told you helped me the most?"

The young veteran nodded and answered, "Your friend, Cap. You both talked about your experiences and hiked the mountains together. You told me that, when one of you was down, the other one lifted him up."

"That's right, son. Now, it's your chance to heal with your buddy at your side. Part of that growing process is to work hard together: Not just in the workshop, but we also need to go on a strict daily exercise regimen for about a week. Then, we'll lay off for a while, and, when I think it's necessary, we'll do it again. This will be a cleansing process for both of us. There are things we will do together that I know will help us both. You in?"

Anthony nodded and grinned, "Whatever you say, Sergeant."

"Okay," the woodcarver patted Anthony on the back, "Follow my lead." Bolt put the harness back on and grabbed another one from a chain saw box on the porch. "This is how Cap and I did our week-long cleansings back in the old days," he grinned. "Here, put this on."

Anthony knew he could trust his mentor's lead and harnessed himself. Yet, with a playful tone, he teased, "I'm hitched up, partner. Now, where's my wagon?"

Bolt let out a vigorous laugh and slapped the young man on the back, "That's the spirit, son. Part of your training is to keep a good sense of humor." He waved a hand in a straight, horizontal slice, and pointed to a six-foot-long, 12-inch thick log. "There's your wagon!" The woodcarver's voice was like that of a game show host, as he laughed again.

"Got it!" Anthony nodded with a mischievous grin, "Who's riding and who's pulling?"

Bolt slapped him hard on the back again and laughed, "Just follow my lead." He wrapped the chain around the log and hitched the other end to a metal ring on the young vet's harness. "Now, take this," said Bolt, as he handed him a canteen of water and started up the hill. "I'll hook mine up yonder again. Meet me there."

The young vet started to pull and suddenly realized that he would have to work harder than he first thought. So, he leaned forward and took one step at a time. At the base of the hill, he stopped to catch his breath, looked up and saw the spry elder man about 100 feet ahead.

Vigorously, Bolt waved and yelled, "Come on, son, we're burning daylight." Without another word, he turned, dug in his boots and started pulling his log further up the hill.

Anthony took a few steps, slipped and caught himself with his hands in the damp soil. "He can't be that strong!" He groaned, started to climb, felt a jerk from the taut chain and glared at the heavy log. Frustrated at the dead weight, he sighed and thought of how out of shape he was from all that heavy drinking after his discharge.

Tempted to forget this crazy stunt, he looked to see the old man up the hill and said, "Okay, if you can do it, so can I!" Then, he skidded the log one scratch at a time.

His lungs ached, but he continued to go further, until he stopped near a chest-high boulder. Anthony gasped and tried to get enough air into his bursting lungs, and his heart raced. "Can't…uh…go on." He tried to breathe, but he felt faint.

"Sure, you can, young fella."

Startled, Anthony turned to the right, and he was stunned at the sight of his elder standing beside him. "Uh…how did you get here?"

"Just waiting for you, son," Bolt patted him lightly on the back and chuckled. "You were so busy pushing yourself, you blindly walked right by me. Good job. You made it."

"I did?" Anthony was surprised, but he just gasped for air.

"You sure did." The woodcarver nodded and pointed, "Take a look."

Anthony clumsily turned around and realized that he made it all the way to the top of that steep hill. "Cool!" He started to remove the harness and let out a deep weary sigh, "I'm glad that's over."

"Hold it, son," Bolt grabbed his arm and chuckled, "We're not done yet."

"You got to be kidding me!" Anthony's chest still heaved.

"Of course not," Bolt chortled and waved a hand toward the ridge. "The fun just started. We still need to go along the meadow over there and up that hill to the left." The woodcarver studied the young man and said, "It's okay, son. Take a breather. It takes time to get used to this 8,000-foot elevation."

Anthony relaxed and shielded his eyes through the glare of a bright morning sun that peeked over the eastern slope. "What's over there?"

The old woodcarver's blue eyes sparkled, and he smiled. "That's where the treasure is, young fella." Bolt gently tapped his own chest, just over the heart. "You can only understand it from in here, son. Once we get there, you'll see for yourself. It'll be worth the struggle ahead."

For several minutes, the men stood in silence. Anthony had grown accustomed to his mentor's ways over the past five weeks, and he sensed that he could savor these moments in peace. He was more relaxed, as he inhaled the cool, fresh mountain air, and his lungs no longer ached.

They looked out over the verdurous meadow and gazed into the vast clear blue sky. Their slow breathing synchronized like the many times they had worked together in the workshop, and it all felt right in the young veteran's heart and soul.

High above them, the great eagle circled, and Anthony spotted it. "You see that?"

"Yep," Bolt nodded with a smile, "That big guy has been watching us since we started." He let out a deep sigh, "Let's go. We're burning daylight."

Invigorated, Anthony felt cool, refreshing wind that blew off the ridge, and he inhaled deeply. Slowly, he exhaled and followed his mentor, while the heavy log dragged behind him. In this trek through the meadow, it was easier on his lungs.

Each step of his boots crunched on the well-worn gravelly trail, and it was obvious that Bolt had hiked it many times before. Tiny rocks and small frozen puddles made it slick, and he had to be mindful of the unstable surface. He felt his boots slip so often that this added to his heightened awareness.

The young man was so focused that he lost track of where Bolt had gone. Gradually, his heels dug into the steep hillside, and his back ached. Fatigued, Anthony tried to catch his breath, and his heart pounded while the log grew heavier. Fortunately, he found brief moments of relief when he turned into one of the many switchbacks on the trail. There, it leveled off, and he caught his breath, somewhat, then, he was back on a steep footing again.

Finally, at a curve in the trail, Anthony stopped and leaned against a car-sized boulder. He felt a cool breeze cutting deep into his jacket-covered sweaty flesh, and he shivered. In that moment, he noticed how sore his leg muscles were, and he looked up the hill but saw no sign of the woodcarver.

Nearby, he heard a fluttering movement, like that of someone shaking out laundry on a bright sunny day. So, Anthony turned toward the sound and spotted the eagle, as it glided low along the ridge, and he watched in awe of its massive wings. That is when he saw Bolt waving high on a ridge above him.

Surprised, Anthony groaned, "That guy must be superhuman!" Embarrassed by his inability to keep up with a man old enough to be his grandfather, he groaned and yanked hard on the chain. "I'll show him!"

Just as the heavy log slid forward a few inches, a sharp pain shot through the young man's shoulders. So, he adjusted the harness to balance the burden of a log dragged against nature's force of gravity. It constantly wanted to go down, but he begged to drive it upwards, and his legs quivered with each agonizing step. "Come on!"

Morning sunrays blinked through tree leaves, and he shaded his eyes with his right hand. Temporarily blinded, he longed for the sunglasses that he left in his bedroom. Determined, Anthony dug in his heels and trekked on while he sucked in every precious breath of air.

Several times, his knees buckled, then he fell and scraped the palms of his hands in slippery rocks. He forced himself to get up, however, and he followed his mentor with fierce determination. Constantly, he tried to see where Bolt was up the hill, but tall pines blocked his view, and he grunted with every step.

Minutes pulsed by endlessly while his body ran out of energy, and he could go no further. Anthony's sore feet came to a halt on that lonely mountainside, and he lost his will to go on. This was crazy, he thought. Doubt crept in, and he began to question the whole purpose of this bizarre exercise.

June 1969: Quang Tin Province, Vietnam.

Suddenly, a nightmarish war-torn memory invaded his weary mind. There, he saw himself struggling up a steep hill in a vain attempt to rescue an unknown wounded soldier. Under heavy fire, he was pinned down. He could neither go up or down. Trained as a medic, he knew he had to save his embattled brother. He wanted to help, but every time he lifted his head, bullets ricocheted everywhere.

A voice called out from above him, and he agonized deep in his heart to not leave a man behind. But how? All he managed was to taste dirt on that lonely ridge in Vietnam. Yet, he heard a groan, so he stood up and ran into a barrage.

Just then, roaring jets flew in low, and they struck with a deafening explosion, followed by a fire ball on the ridge above him. Searing heat swooped down in a wave, and he dove under a small outcrop.

Desperately, he dug into dirt. Eerie silence creeped in, followed by a strange ringing in his ears. Shocked by the blast and heat, he could not move. Out of nowhere, someone grabbed his arm, and he felt himself being dragged down that parched hillside.

Anthony awoke in the present moment, gagged, choked, spat out the dirt in his mouth and realized that he was no longer in Vietnam. Instead, he had belly-crawled on a trail in the Sierra Nevada mountains. Shaken, but relieved, he stood up and brushed himself off. Feeling light-headed, the young, weary vet remembered that he had not eaten anything since last night, and he heard a low growl in his woozy stomach. Still haunted, he thought about the man he could not save.

Yet, he had to focus on his immediate needs and tasted the dust on his tongue and remembered the canteen that his mentor gave him. So, he searched and found it among the rocks a few feet away. He sipped and sloshed the soothing water in his parched mouth, spat it out and took several swallows. More determined, he started up the trail and skidded the log behind him, as he wondered what happened to Bolt.

No matter what, Anthony knew that his mentor would not want him to quit, so he trekked further up the trail.

Along an eastern ridge, the eagle circled above a bright yellow globe of the rising sun, and he figured it was about eight or so.

With the eagle in sight, the young man felt renewed energy, and he finally made it to the top of another hill. Just as he adjusted the harness, he heard footsteps, and he was relieved to see the woodcarver.

"Good job, son," Bolt grinned, "I knew you could do it."

Anthony noticed that the woodcarver's harness and log was gone. "Where were you?"

Bolt waved a hand toward a quaint two-story chalet in a clearing about several hundred feet away. "Over there. I just dropped off my log, and now it's your turn." He turned and headed toward the cabin. "Let's go."

Anthony followed and dragged his log to a pile of wood behind the structure. "I don't get it. Why are we doing this?"

"Drop it here," Bolt pointed and grinned with satisfaction. "These logs will be cut and used for firewood later. We could have hauled them up here the easy way, in my truck, but the purpose of this exercise is to build up endurance. It also purifies the mind."

Anthony released his load but was confused. "Why and how did you leave me in the dust back there?"

His mentor studied him for a moment, then said, "Well...as to the how...I've been doing this on and off for years, son. I'm in better shape, as a result. That's okay. We'll take a day off tomorrow. Then, we'll go at it again the next day."

"But...why did you go on without me back there?" Anthony felt embarrassed and humbled.

"The why is simple, son." His mentor put a hand on the young man's shoulder and looked directly into his eyes. "You had to face your demons on your own. Later, we'll talk about it. You have to sweat it out, son. You understand?"

Anthony's stomach had a low rumble, and he rubbed his belly. "Right now, all I care about is getting some chow. Man...I am so hungry; I could chew on the bark from these logs."

"Let's do something about that," Bolt laughed and slapped the young man's back. "Come on, I want you to meet someone very special. You're in for a real treat."

Anthony rubbed his sore neck and followed his mentor to the front of the cabin. Suddenly, a large male chocolate lab with floppy ears ran, skittered and leaped down the porch steps. His tail wagged and signaled a friendly greeting, while he ran toward them. Boundless with energy, he had the eternal grin of a happy dog. A wet tongue dangled and dribbled, when he plopped his massive paws on Bolt's chest.

"Hello, Cocoa," Bolt staggered backward, dug in his heels and scratched behind the lab's ears, "How are you doing, boy?"

Satisfied with that greeting, Cocoa jumped up and placed his paws on Anthony's chest, and licked his face. "You sure are friendly," the young man chuckled, glanced at Bolt, then teased, "So, this must be my treat, right?"

Cocoa plopped his rear in the driveway and looked up with pleading eyes, while his tail flagged in a rhythm all its own. Bolt laughed and pointed to the dog, "You just said the magic word."

The woodcarver reached into his pocket and took out beef jerky, "Here boy." Cocoa snapped it into his mouth, chewed, swallowed and looked up for more. Bolt smiled and glanced at Anthony, "Around here, you've got to be prepared."

Cocoa's tail thumped back and forth on the ground, but he stood up, turned his head and sniffed the air. An unmistakable scent of cooked bacon wafted toward them. Ignoring the men, the dog rushed back to the cabin.

"Come on, son," Bolt waved, "Now you'll see why we're here."

10 Art Treasures

Anthony and Bolt eagerly tramped up redwood steps of a two-story chalet. Just as the woodcarver was about to knock, a figure appeared in an oval stained-glass window and the door swung open. Immediately, they were greeted by a petite elderly woman with a sweet, radiant smile.

"Good morning, Bolt," her eyes did not blink, and she looked straight ahead. "Breakfast is ready," she leaned closer and blindly kissed his cheek.

"Thanks, I'm starving. I brought more firewood for you, Lucille. Oh, I want you to meet a friend of mine," he nudged the young man to step forward. "Lucille, this is Anthony."

Lucille reached out, and Anthony felt the warmth and softness of her hand. She smiled pleasantly, then stroked the natural lines of his palm with her delicate fingers. "It's so nice to meet you, young man. You have good, rough hands like a working man. I like that." Her voice was melodious and pleasing to his ears.

"I'm glad to meet you, too," Anthony immediately liked this delightful lady.

Lucille paused in the doorway with her hand still in his, and she smiled pleasantly. At her side, Cocoa sniffed and excitedly wagged his tail. She wore a green knit sweater over a blue dress that had red carnations in the design, long wool socks, and moccasins with sheepskin lining. While she lingered, the young man began to feel a little shy and uncertain about what to do next.

Finally, she asked, "Anthony, may I see you better?" She held her palms up to his face.

Puzzled by this, Anthony glanced at Bolt, who nodded and smiled to reassure him. After a brief hesitation, the young vet shrugged, "Okay."

Lucille placed her hands on his face and felt with soft, smooth fingers. "You have a nice, friendly face, I can tell." She giggled almost childlike, "I can see you don't like to shave. What color is your hair, dear?"

"Uh...it's brown." He lowered his head slightly, "I'm not much to look at."

"Oh, where are my manners? Come in boys," Lucille turned and walked through an arched entryway. "Come," she waved them in and disappeared into the kitchen.

Immediately, Anthony was amazed at the sight of numerous paintings scattered everywhere he looked. Many were in stacks of five or six against the walls and furniture. Mingled with the aroma of cooked bacon was the rich scent of what smelled like mahogany and cedar. Oil colors depicting mountains, deserts, beaches, and an assortment of adobe churches hung on walls.

From his rough, amateurish point of view, they seemed to be exquisitely detailed. Anthony's pulse lowered, and he browsed from one painting to the other, like he was in some magnificent art museum. Each step he took was reverent and thoughtful.

"Wow," he whispered and gazed upon a painting that both surprised and intrigued him at the same time. There, before him, was a scene of a boy, about 12 or so, who stood on a rocky mountaintop with arms outstretched. An eagle soared gracefully in a turquoise sky, and it appeared to stare at him with omniscience.

"Makes you wonder, doesn't it?"

Startled, Anthony spun around to see the woodcarver intently studying the painting. "Um...yeah, I..." He was so captivated that he forgot that anyone else had been in the room.

"Come sit at the table, boys," Lucille called out from the kitchen.

Bolt pulled back a sturdy maple wood chair and sniffed the air, "Smells mighty good, Lucille." When the men sat, he added, "I meant to get here sooner, but we were busy in the shop. How are you holding up?"

"Just fine, dear. Sheri and Jenny stop by and help a lot," Lucille smiled elegantly as she brought a large bowl of scrambled eggs to the table. "Cocoa and I kept warm by the fire, during the past cold nights."

Anthony watched in amazement, while Lucille served the meal. Her blindness was obvious by the way she felt for utensils, but she moved gracefully, and this fascinated him even more. Her voice was gentle and humble in tone while she also seemed confident for such an elderly, blind woman living alone.

"Hmmm, this is delicious, Lucille," Bolt's eyes widened, and he took another bite.

"Yeah, thanks," Anthony spoke up with a mouthful and kept shoveling ravenously.

"You are both welcome, boys. Oh, would you like more coffee?"

The woodcarver stood up quickly and gently placed a hand on her shoulder, "I'll get it, Lucille. Here, please have a seat." He scooted out a chair. "You can sit here."

Lucille elegantly tucked the hem of her dress to the side and sat next to Anthony. "Thank you, dear."

Bolt set a cup of coffee in front of her and smiled, "I'll get you some eggs and bacon."

Lucille giggled and waved a hand in the air, "Oh, no thank you, honey." She shook her head playfully, "You know that I don't eat much." She laughed a little louder,

"Besides, I always have my meals while standing next to the sink. After all, I get messy." She had a look of mischief and appeared to enjoy her own delightful sense of humor. "Now, stop fussing over me and sit down."

While Anthony ate, he looked around the room and observed that oil paintings seemed to be everywhere. Into a hallway, he noticed several stacks of artwork were leaned against the walls. This, he estimated, must have added up to a least 20 pieces, there, alone. From a partial view of the living room, he saw even more. In awe, he had a sense of being in a shrine of artistic greatness that he never saw before.

Finally, Anthony could not hold back his curiosity any longer. "Lucille, you have so many beautiful paintings here. I'd really like to know more about them."

Lucille's soft, rosy cheeks brightened, as she smiled, "Oh, yes," she held out her hands wide, "All these masterpieces are the work of my late husband, Julian. He was a wonderful artist and such a strong outdoorsman. Wasn't he, Bolt?"

"Yes, he was," Bolt agreed and nodded to his young apprentice. "You see, Julian and I were good friends, and we explored much of this wilderness together."

The woodcarver put his fork down and stared ahead, as though he remembered something profound. "Julian had a way of capturing such beauty wherever he went. He was my mentor, my teacher of the arts. Not only that…he also was a role model of integrity. He showed me how to savor and live in each moment of life with such passion, and he had a wild sense of humor."

Bolt patted Lucille's hand and said, "I owe much of my artistic achievements to Julian, you know."

He looked directly at the young vet and added, "Fact is, he made me promise to pass on everything I learned to someone else when the right person came along."

Lucille smiled and giggled like an awestruck schoolgirl, "Oh, he was such a wonderful man. He was so strong and handsome and, oh, what a dancer." She sighed and added, "Julian had a way of sweeping me right off my feet." She hugged herself and swayed in her chair. "Anthony, would you like to see a photograph of my husband?"

"Yes, I would."

Lucille wiped her hands on a rose-patterned apron, got up, held her dog's leash and patted his head. "Come on, Cocoa, help me find my picture box."

When she walked down the hall with Cocoa, Anthony leaned forward and whispered to Bolt, "When did Julian die?"

"Almost six years ago," Bolt spoke softly with his arms resting thoughtfully on his chest. "They had been married about 55 years."

Anthony's eyes widened at the realization and sighed, "Wow, she must be close to 90."

"Lucille doesn't discuss her age, son. That is not proper, you know. But the closest I can figure, she must be at least 87 or 88, I reckon." Bolt scratched the white streaks of his beard, as though he was in deep thought again. "She lost much of her eyesight about five years ago." Bolt smiled and said, "Naturally, that didn't slow her down. She's as feisty and independent as ever."

"She is amazing," Anthony whispered reverently. "How does she get around so well, being blind, I mean?"

"Lucille memorized every inch of this place, and she can still make out shapes of people as we move about. Plus, she's a retired teacher with a keen mind, and her hearing is so acute, she can sense the amount of coffee being poured into a cup."

Bolt spotted a cobweb in a corner, "Of course, she needs help to take care of some details." He aimed his right finger and mimicked a pistol at a target. "Okay, spider…I'll take care of you later. I am not going to let you bite the lady of this house."

Anthony studied the way his mentor stared at that cobweb like a sharpshooter. There was no way that spider would survive the morning. He was about to tease when Lucille returned with a small, lacquered wooden container the size of a shoebox. The young man was delighted to see Bolt's handiwork of a carved eagle on the lid, and it had his favorite scent of cedar.

"Here you go, dear," she placed it on the table and smiled, "Can you find Julian's picture for me?"

Bolt thumbed through a pile of photos along with what appeared to be important papers. "Here it is, Lucille," he respectfully placed it in her hands.

Lucille let out a sigh and nestled the well-worn photo close to her heart. For a moment, she just smiled, and her eyes dampened. Tiny tear drops were embellished in between the lids of her eyes like sparkling diamonds. Then, she handed it to Anthony and spoke softly, "I still remember taking that picture myself when we were both very young."

Although the faded brown photograph was tattered, Anthony observed a tall, slender-built man with a pipe in his mouth, who stood near a mountain lake. Julian wore a Stetson, and he had a paintbrush in his hand with an easel in front of him. In the background, there was something on a tree branch, and the young man realized that is was an eagle perched like an alert sentinel ready for action.

In that moment, Anthony had a strange connection to the man in the photo. Why did he feel so moved, so sad, and so lost in the image that stared back at him? Oddly, it reminded him of when the mountain man had saved him from freezing to death in the blizzard. He was told that it takes time to heal his badly wounded soul. The eagle would lead him to others for long-term healing, he remembered.

"You alright, son?" Bolt's voice suddenly jolted his mind back to the present.

"What?" Anthony looked up from the photograph and said, "Uh...yeah...sure. Just tired, I guess."

Bolt scooted his chair back and stood up. "I'll get you another cup of coffee."

Anthony watched, as the woodcarver poured that steaming brew. Then, he glimpsed Lucille, who smiled peacefully, yet so blindly ahead. She had such a sweet, almost angelic expression, and he admired her like she was a long-lost saintly grandmother. Could Lucille, Bolt, Sheri and Jenny be the others the mountain man talked about? What was the bond he felt for the image of Julian in the photograph?

Anthony examined it again. Perhaps the connection he had was that Lucille's late husband, Julian, lived, breathed and loved this woman. Julian had given her so much happiness and created such beautiful masterpieces that thrived in her memory.

Although the artist had passed away, there was a continuity of his love and passion. His legacy will reverberate in the hearts and minds of admirers for generations to come, and people will need to see the works of art, he thought. But, for now, she clings to all of these treasures, and it would be difficult for Lucille to release her treasures for any public displays in galleries.

The young man looked at his new friends, and he knew that he was in the right place. Since they all shared similar sorrows, he no longer felt alone. "Very nice, Lucille," Anthony placed the photograph back into her hands. "Thanks for showing it to me." Overcome with grief over the loss of his wife, Amy, he could say no more, while guilt and shame stirred up inside him again.

She smiled and cradled it close to her heart, "We had such good times together."

"Well…" Bolt got up from his chair, and abruptly changed the subject, "I enjoyed the breakfast, Lucille. Now, you relax, and we'll do the dishes for you, okay?"

"Oh, thank you, dear." Lucille carefully returned the photo to the box and closed the lid.

Bolt washed the dishes, and Anthony dried them, while he admired Lucille's contented expression, and she patted Cocoa. She looked so adorable when she talked affectionately in a babyish voice to her dog, like he was a little person.

"You are such a good boy," she thoroughly rubbed behind his ears.

In happy response, Cocoa tilted his head back and panted while his slobbery tongue dangled in sheer pleasure. "Okay, sit."

Cocoa plopped his rear, sniffed and looked up expectantly. Lucille chortled with delight, reached into her apron pocket and pulled out a treat. Ravenously, Cocoa chomped, crunched, swallowed and looked up for more. "That's all, dear. One's enough for now. I don't want you to get fat."

Bolt laughed, patted Cocoa's plump belly and teased, "I think it's too late for that. You spoiled him rotten a long time ago."

"Well, he's my dog. So, I'll spoil him if I want to," Lucille giggled playfully and immediately gave him another treat. "See?"

"You are hopeless," Bolt shook his head and laughed.

Anthony put the last plate in the cupboard and admired the way these two long-time friends bantered with each other. So, he decided to contribute with his own little tease and said, "Maybe I better stay with you, Lucille. I have to work too hard for my food at Bolt's house."

"Oh, yeah?" Bolt grinned mischievously, grabbed a broom and looked like he was about to swat Anthony. Suddenly, he spun around, knocked down the spider in the corner, stomped his boot and yelled, "Ah, ha! Got you!"

"Oh, dear," said Lucille with a light-hearted giggle, "You boys had better settle down. Don't break anything."

"Okay, Lucille, we'll be good." Bolt put the broom away, sat next to her, and gently patted her hand.

"You better be good," she laughed.

Bolt smiled and affectionately kissed her cheek. "It's a good thing you're here to keep us in line."

"Well, somebody has to."

Anthony leaned against the sink and enjoyed their banter. "Yeah," he added with his own teasing, "Bolt's a real handful alright."

"You stay out of this," Bolt glanced at the young man with a playful grin. He laughed, "I tell ya, Lucille, these young-ins are downright talkative."

"Well, it wouldn't hurt to listen to what the youth have to say once in a while," Lucille giggled again. "You might learn something."

Anthony grinned, "Yeah boss."

"Well, I can see that I'm being bushwhacked by you two," Bolt laughed and pecked her cheek. "I reckon it's time I leave before you hurt my feelings."

"That'll be the day," Lucille laughed.

Bolt lightly patted her hand and smiled. "Well, my dear lady, is there anything you need before we head back down the hill?"

11 Blind Faith

I need just one thing before you boys leave," Lucille smiled. "Do you know what that is, dear?"

"Yes, Lucille," Bolt patted her hand affectionately, "I'll get the book." He scooted his chair back and strolled into the living room.

Anthony watched, as Bolt returned with a large, black Bible in his hand, and the woodcarver sat at the table. While Bolt opened a thick leather cover, the morning sun beamed a smoky orange ray of light through the kitchen window and onto the page. Surprised by this unexpected religious gesture, the young man backed up against the counter. For the first time, he began to feel uncomfortable.

Yet, Anthony was intrigued by Lucille, who sat quietly. She clasped her delicate hands together and waited serenely for the woodcarver while he turned the pages. Although her skin was well-worn with age, her face had a creamy, softness that shined in the morning sun and made her seem younger.

Curly white hair hung a few inches above her shoulders and some strands had a reddish tint in the sunlight. Her slow, deep breathing easily allowed her thin diaphragm to rise and lower with a tranquil meditative appearance. This was beyond the young man's comprehension, and just being in her presence calmed his restless soul.

"Where would you like me to read, Lucille?" Bolt looked up from the open Bible.

She smiled pleasantly and placed her hand on the Bible, "Start where you left off the last time you were here. Remember? You were about to read Isaiah 40:28."

Bolt laughed, "You have a wonderful memory, Lucille. That's exactly the page I turned to read." He cleared his throat and began with the words, "Hast thou not known? Hast thou not heard, that the everlasting God, the Lord, the Creator of the ends of the earth, faint not, neither is weary?"

Anthony furrowed his brow at the sound of this religious tone, and he backed away toward the door. Suddenly, he felt so unclean around these pious people, and he looked at the imaginary blood on his palms and wiped them on his shirt in disgust. Slowly, he reached for the backdoor knob, and he wanted to run back out into that wretched private hell where he knew he belonged.

The door creaked open slightly, and he felt the bleakness creeping in. Just as he was about to run, he noticed a strange popping sensation in his ears when Bolt read a verse that caught his attention. So, he gently closed the door and listened.

"Even the youths shall faint and be weary, and the young men shall utterly fail." Bolt paused and said, "That's verse 30."

Anthony's eyes widened, as those words pierced his heart and spoke directly to him. Sure, he was weary. Yes, he failed so miserably as a human being that it sickened him.

Bolt continued, "Verse 31 says…But they that wait upon the Lord…" Lucille boldly interrupted and continued, "shall renew their strength; they shall mount up with wings as eagles. They shall run, and not be weary; and they shall walk, and not faint." She leaned back in her chair and smiled contentedly.

Anthony removed his grip on the doorknob and he stepped closer. He leaned over Bolt's shoulder, and he looked at the passage where the woodcarver had his finger. His mentor grinned and nodded at him, and the young man realized that she had quoted it exactly as it was written.

These powerful words seemed to echo over and over in Anthony's mind, "they shall mount up with wings as eagles…" He scratched his head, then remembered his dream of Amy, as she flew off on a giant eagle, and he desperately wanted to ask what it all meant. Instead, he quietly sat down next to Lucille, and he was inexplicably drawn into this impromptu devotional.

Lucille folded her hands on her lap, and she smiled happily, "I just love that part, don't you boys?"

"Yes, Lucille," Bolt grinned, "Especially when you recite it so well."

Anthony started to ask about the eagle, but Lucille gently squeezed each man's hand and said, "Let's pray. Dear God, we thank you for…"

The young man did not hear her words. He sat there and was drawn to her loving presence. Never had he known anyone with such simple faith and conviction. While this soft-spoken, humble lady spoke, memories of his childhood flashed in his mind like old faded photographs.

There he was, a four-old boy, crying with his face to the rear window, as his parents drove away from his grandmother to move from Boston to southern California. That was the last he had seen her. Later, he found out that she passed away.

Now, here was Lucille, the perfect grandmother type, and he wished she had been with him during those difficult days as a boy, especially when his father was drunk and could not hold a job for very long. Another painful memory snapped him to the age of nine. His father, who had been drinking all night, stumbled into their apartment, fell to the floor and died.

During the funeral, rain splattered on the coffin, and no one showed up to pay respects, except Anthony and his mother. He stood under an umbrella, stared at puddles near his feet, and he blocked out all emotions, while an unknown cleric mumbled a prayer. The boy's father had always demanded that he must be tough, because men don't cry. So, he stoically followed orders and counted droplets on the walkway. Then, one day, his mother left the house, and she never returned.

Anthony rubbed his eyes to forget, and he wished he could have a stiff drink to numb the pain again. Slowly, he became aware of the present moment, and he observed Bolt while Lucille prayed. This elder man seemed so strong, yet serene and compassionate about the needs of people. The young vet thought of the faded image of an intoxicated, bitter parent, who told him to be tough but obviously had a weak, undisciplined soul.

Instead, Bolt was nothing like the father, who had died so long ago and left a wound that still festered in his heart. Anthony saw the woodcarver as a man of oak-like hardness on the outside, but honest and forthright enough to shed real tears over the loss of his wife, Emma.

In those moments, he gave himself permission to be present in Lucille's kitchen while she prayed. Though broken in spirit, the young man wondered if, perhaps, these people were drawn into his miserable existence for a purpose.

Anthony's thoughts drifted back to when he was dying in the snow. That is when the mountain man had touched his heart and saved him, then kept him warm enough to survive in the blizzard. He was told to follow the eagle to other people, and he would find healing for his wounded soul.

Now, Anthony questioned, who was this mountain man, and what role did the eagle have in his life? Were they angels? Was this all part of God's plan? But why? All these queries rapidly fired in his mind, and he wanted to believe there was some grand purpose to all this, but he was in a bitter quandary about his self-worth.

While he pondered this, he became aware of Lucille's voice, as she said, "We also thank, you, God, for sending Anthony to us. This young man is truly a blessing. Amen."

Blessing? Astonished, Anthony held his breath in disbelief. How could he possibly be a blessing? He had nothing to offer these decent, caring people but they had so much that appealed to him.

"That was right nice, Lucille," Bolt affectionately squeezed her hand. "Now, if you don't mind, I'd like to do a few chores before we leave. Anthony can help me."

"Thank you, dear," Lucille smiled peacefully, "You are such a thoughtful gentleman. I don't know what I would do without you."

"You are welcome, Lucille. You have been a blessing to so many people over the years, I am honored to be of assistance." Bolt grabbed a toolbox under the kitchen sink, "I want to fix a small leak on the faucet. Anthony, take that broom over there and knock down any pesky spider webs you find in the corners of the house."

Later, when Bolt was satisfied that they had done enough chores for the day, he said, "Well, Lucille, it's time for us to leave. We need to get back to the workshop."

Lucille kissed his cheek, "Thank you for everything, dear. You have been so kind as always."

Then, she held out her hand to Anthony and smiled, "Thank you, young man. God is with you. I can sense it."

Deeply transfixed by her words, Anthony did not know how to respond. For the first time, he noticed her eyes were like the sky on a bright sunny day. With this awareness, he had an epiphany--although Lucille was blind, she could see with a heart of unconditional love and understanding. At this precise moment, he knew that he wanted to be in her presence. From then on, he eagerly aspired to follow her lead and live in peace with himself.

Yet, all he could say was, "Thanks, I enjoyed meeting you." What? He thought to himself. Is that all you can say to such a beautifully insightful lady?

"Are you going to be all right, Lucille?" asked Bolt, as he interrupted the young man's self-deprecating thoughts. The woodcarver studied dark clouds overhead with a worried expression. "I don't like the looks of this weather."

"Oh, yes, don't worry about me, dear. Since Sheri came back home last month, she stops by to check on me daily. You know how I am anyway. Every night before I go to bed, I ask God to give me one more day and he does. I learned a long time ago to take one day at a time and just be grateful for everything. Besides, I need to care for Julian's paintings, so that keeps me going."

Bolt looked concerned and sighed, "You really shouldn't have all of Julian's artwork stored in one location, Lucille. What if there's a fire? Why don't you let my agent, Daniel, come out and see what he can do to sell some of them for you?"

Lucille just smiled confidently and stared blindly ahead. "Oh, my dear, wonderful friend, we have this same discussion every time you come up here. Don't be such a worrywart, dear."

The woodcarver nodded his head reluctantly and sighed, "All right, Lucille."

She kissed his cheek, again, "Someday, I'll call your agent, but, right now, I like having a part of Julian around a little longer."

Bolt shrugged, "Just don't wait too long." He knelt and patted Cocoa, taking the time to give this wildly affectionate dog a caring rub. "Okay, boy, you take good care of the lady of the house while I'm gone." He paused and held the frisky canine's head, then looked directly into the lab's playful eyes, "And, don't go chasing after rabbits anymore."

Bolt stood up and looked at menacing black clouds that sailed along the late, afternoon horizon. He gave Lucille one last peck on her cheek, "I'll be back the day after tomorrow. I reckon we'll see rain soon." As he took two steps forward, he paused, looked back and smiled, "Remember that I love you." He glanced at the overcast sky again and took to the trail without looking back.

Lucille blindly waved and smiled contentedly, "I know, dear. I love you, too. Now, get going."

Anthony looked on in amazement. This was the first time his mentor spoke those three words of affection, since he started working for the woodcarver. Bolt talked about his love for his late wife, Emma, and he demonstrated a sincere warmth and caring for Jenny and her daughter, Sheri. Yet, the young man was still surprised by the sound of it.

This planted a seed in his own aching heart about the true meaning of compassion for another human being. He did not remember any one time that he actually heard his parents say, "I love you." Yet, it seemed like a natural thing to do for someone you cared about, he thought.

Several heavy drops pelted the young man's face, and he knew it was time to head back before it got worse. "Good bye, Lucille," Anthony followed Bolt, who already went on ahead at his usual rapid stride.

A pale sun filtered through thickening clouds, and cold wind whistled between swaying tree branches, while they trekked in silence toward Bolt's cabin. Each man exhaled moist air and dwelled on personal thoughts during their brisk hike down the mountain. Anthony was relieved that it was easier and faster heading on the decline of the path without a log dragging behind as dead weight.

Soon, they were back inside the cabin, and the late afternoon sky grew menacingly dark. Dense rain uproariously battered the rooftop, as if Thor himself brutally tried to break in. Loud claps of thunder shook and rattled any sane man's nerves. The men ignored it all, and they relaxed by the fireplace with steaming cups of hot cocoa.

Crumbs from hot raison muffins dribbled on their plates, while they both sat quietly and listened to nature's havoc outside. Anthony had a lot on his mind; and, he finally spoke up, "I got a question that's bugging me."

"Shoot."

The young man scratched his beard, "I still don't understand why we just didn't take our load of firewood to Lucille in the pickup truck? That would have been so easy, man."

"Easy isn't always best, son."

"What do you mean?" Anthony sipped the hot cocoa and wiped his whiskers above the upper lip with a napkin.

"Think about it, son," Bolt looked up from his mug. "What have you gained by doing it the hard way?"

Anthony rubbed his throbbing right shoulder and grumbled, "Sore muscles."

His mentor let out his usual hearty laugh, "When you're in better shape, that won't be a problem." Bolt looked serious again and paused, "Come on now, think."

The young apprentice warily felt like a student in the midst of a lecture. He had to come up with a suitable answer to please his instructor. So, he shrugged and replied, "Well, I guess it's good exercise."

Bolt grinned with approval and slapped his shoulder, "Right! Our bodies were made for work, not to just sit around on our royal rumps. If we don't challenge ourselves, we're going to shrivel up and die of inactivity way before our time." His mentor suddenly stood up, walked over to the fireplace and stared into the flames.

Anthony enjoyed the familiar way Bolt got worked up about a subject. His nostrils flared, while he paced back and forth, and his voice seemed more forceful. This happened often in the workshop, and it was fun for the apprentice to interact with him. How could he pass up another intellectually stimulating opportunity for both of them to blow off steam?

So, the young vet chose to challenge him, knowing that the old war veteran loved a heated debate. "Well, I understand that part, but we still could've been up that hill in no time with the truck."

"True." Suddenly, his mentor spun around and glared with those piercing blue eyes. He seemed intimidating with that hawkish nose, and he had grit in his voice like the grinding of sandstone. "Now, let me ask you something. Back in the city, when you're in a mall or a tall building, do you take the elevator or climb the stairs?"

Oh, this is going to be good, the young apprentice chuckled to himself, "Well, I…"

"That's the problem!" Bolt interrupted, "People take the easy way for everything. They drive to a store and park as close as they can to the front door. They sit for hours and watch their favorite game on TV, and they're killing themselves while their muscles atrophy!"

Anthony laughed and took a mock defensive position with his fists like a fighter trying to block a punch to the jaw, "Whoa, man!"

Bolt's expression softened, and he smiled, "I reckon I came on too strong." He turned and stared at the fireplace, again, as though he was in deep thought. After a moment of silence, he sighed, "You know, son, there's more to it than just the exercise."

"What do you mean?" Anthony looked at his mentor with fascination, and he deeply admired Bolt's conviction and sincerity.

"Truth is…I am a proud, stubborn man. But, the work to get up that hill clears my mind. I reckon it humbles me, and I'm better prepared to meet Lucille." Bolt smiled, "That wonderful lady may be blind, but she has more faith, warmth and compassion than anyone I ever met."

Anthony nodded in agreement, and he was impressed with his friend's integrity.

Several months flew by, rapidly, as the two men worked together in the woodshop and it was early spring and warmer. Gradually, their log-pulling routine up the hill to Lucille's place had tapered off to twice a month, and it usually came on Saturdays.

Each time they visited, Anthony felt stronger, and he looked forward to their breakfasts, chores around the house, and their light-hearted discussions. For the young man, it was more like a second home with Lucille, and he cherished these moments.

It was especially meaningful, during occasional evening visits, when Jenny and Sheri joined them for dinner at Lucille's place. Sheri came in one day with a small bouquet of carnations and handed them to her informally adopted grandmother, Lucille, and smiled, "Here, Grammy, these are for you."

Lucille snuggled her face into the blossoms and sniffed contentedly, "Oh, thank you, dear. You always bring me such nice, fresh flowers, and I love to breath in these aromas."

Sheri kissed her cheek, "You are so welcome, Grammy. I enjoy the chance to bring these to you. I'll put them in a vase. Now, please sit down with Bolt and Anthony. Mom and I brought baked chicken and fresh salad from the café. Dinner is about to be served."

Anthony admired how caring and supportive Sheri and Jenny were of Lucille. More and more, it felt like the family atmosphere that he missed as a child growing up in numerous foster homes.

To the young man, he had it all—Bolt was like a father, Jenny, the motherly type, Lucille, like a grandmother; and Sheri was more like a…long-lost sister, or something else. The latter…he was not sure what to think.

The following month passed by quickly, and they all continued to meet at least once a week. His demons were still there, however, just under the surface of his happiness.

Overwhelming pernicious doubts came in waves, and his own lack of self-worth reared its angry head. He had a punishing sense that he did not deserve this new, emotionally secure life-style, and, that any moment, it would all go up in flames.

That made him melancholic and moody sometimes, and he tried to not get overly happy. Even with his mentor's support, he still knew it was only a matter of time when he would be tested. So, Anthony braced himself for the inevitable downfall ahead.

12 Hell's Fury

Hot, dry Santa Ana winds blasted Anthony's face when he opened his truck door and stood in the driveway near Bolt's cabin. On that miserable September day, a dust devil swirled and hissed about 20 feet in front of him, like a serpent ready to strike. He sniffed the air and smelled burned timbers. Uneasy, he looked toward the northeast, and saw thick, black smoke that billowed over the ridge.

Suddenly, a terrifying wall of flames rose up, as though demonic forces had erupted from the mountain. This sparked memories of numerous conflicts in Vietnam. Medic, Anthony Lorenzo's war-weary instincts curdled, and he had to act fast before hell took over the land. Immediately, he reached into the truck's cab and leaned heavily on the horn. Bolt rushed out of the shop and saw the fiery invasion, steamrolling directly at them.

A dirt splotched vehicle raced over to the site and congealed Lorenzo's twisted reality. He was back in the heat of battle, and the only way to survive was to fight his way out.

A resolute driver slammed on the brakes and yelled, "I just heard on the radio! There's a forest fire heading this way!" White knuckles gripped the steering wheel, and she looked horrified. "What are we going to do, Poppy?"

Sheri's voice and lovely face awakened Lorenzo back to the present moment. Stunned by this abrupt change of perception, he blinked and remembered that he was in the Sierra Nevada mountains of California. Instantly, he was thrust far away from the brutality of war in Asia.

Still, his mind was on high alert, and he knew there was no time to lose. "It's coming in fast!" he heard his voice call out and it somehow got muffled in a fierce wind.

Bolt pointed up the flaming ridge and yelled, "Looks like it'll hit Lucille's place first!" He slapped Lorenzo on the back and ordered, "You go with Sheri! Get Lucille and Cocoa out! Grab Julian's paintings! Get as many as you can! Take everything to Jenny's place! Move!" Bolt spun around and ran to the workshop.

"What are you going to do?" Lorenzo yelled out and coughed, while thick smoke swirled around his face.

"I'll make a stand here!" Bolt slammed the door behind him.

Lorenzo tapped the hood of Sheri's pickup truck and ordered, "Go on!" I'll drive mine and meet you there!"

When they reached Lucille's place, brakes screeched, and a dusty vortex temporarily swallowed up their trucks. Sheri stormed into the front door without knocking and yelled, "Grammy!"

"I'm coming!" Lucille appeared in the hallway with a small suitcase and said, "Bolt just called me, and I knew you were on your way! I have my emergency pack ready!" Cocoa nervously pulled on a short leash and whimpered at her side.

"Wow!" said Lorenzo, as he rushed in from behind. "You are prepared!"

Lucille confidently handed him the case and smiled, "My late husband, Julian, taught me to be ready for anything," she proudly shared.

"Okay! Let's get you in the truck!" Lorenzo carefully held her right arm, while Sheri grabbed Cocoa's leash. Once they had their dear Grammy, and her dog secured in Sheri's truck, he handed Lucille her suitcase. "Stay here!" he commanded firmly. "Sheri and I will get Julian's paintings!"

Lucille gripped the bag tight on her lap and had a stoic expression. "Thank you, dear."

Frantically, they grabbed as many paintings as they could carry and piled them in both truck beds. Sheri cradled several more in her arms and unloaded a stack in the back of her truck. Just as she did so, demonic flames rose up and fiercely licked nearby trees.

"Tony! The fire! It's here!" Sheri watched, in horror, as the monstrous firestorm roared, crackled and devoured trees without mercy.

Lorenzo dashed out while he carried more paintings and stacked them in his truck. "Now get out of here! I'll go for another run!"

Sheri grabbed his arm and shouted, "No! It's too risky!"

Lorenzo kissed her on the cheek and assured, "I'll be right behind you! Now get!" He ran back in and rummaged for anything that seemed valuable to Lucille.

Sheri drove off, just as strong hot winds blew embers onto the roof and front porch. With his arms full, Lorenzo ran for the door but skidded to a halt. Flames blocked his escape. So, he darted through the kitchen and clumsily turned the backdoor knob, but almost dropped his precious cargo, as he juggled to keep everything in his grip.

Lorenzo cursed his own stupidity and quickly had to set the paintings on the kitchen counter first. Better focused, he easily opened the door, grabbed Lucille's priceless treasures and ran. In his mad race, he stumbled down the back steps and fell to his knees. Yet, he protectively held on to the paintings like a father would cradle his own baby. Carefully, he stood up with everything still in his arms. Suddenly, he heard a loud explosion, and he felt burning heat on his neck.

Briefly stunned, Lorenzo's memory flashed back to Vietnam again. He heard multiple tat-a-tat-a-tat shots.

Bullets pock-marked wildly at his feet and a mortar exploded nearby. Instinctively, the medic only had one mission—to save the severely wounded soldier, who was carried on his back amidst heavy fire.

"Hang on! I got you!" Finally, he made it to safety and placed the blood-soaked body down. "I'll get you out of here!" Lorenzo held the 19-year-old boy's hand tight.

The terrified soldier gasped, "Doc, how bad is it?"

"You'll be okay!" The medic began first aid, and he looked into the wounded soldier's eyes. "You'll be back home before you know it."

More shots rang out and bullets pockmarked the ground. Lorenzo covered his brother with his body. Nearby, someone gasped, "I'm hit!"

"Tat-a-tat! Tat-a-tat!"

"Doc!" Someone called out a few feet away. "Help me!"

"Hey, doc!" Another man yelled. "Get the hell over here!"

The medic looked up and saw more soldiers down. For a moment, he froze. How could he get to them all? It was too much to take!

Exhausted and numb, Lorenzo awoke to the present, and he looked down at the artwork he just saved. Brutal, unforgiving winds blew fiery sparks all around him.

Desperate, he pulled a tarp from the back of his truck over his precious cargo; then, he firmly tied it down. Several wind-driven embers burned the back of his neck, and he felt searing pain on his flesh.

So, he ran, climbed into the truck, and he had to get out fast. Just as he turned the key and started the engine, he took one quick look at Grammy Lucille's home being eaten alive, and he could do nothing. It will be gone soon, he thought.

Lorenzo bitterly floored the accelerator, and the truck lurched forward. He swerved around the next curve, while three fire trucks passed him, and they headed right to Lucille's place. Just as they went by, he waved at Jake, the driver, a friend he met during numerous visits at Jenny's Cafe.

Although he knew it was too late to save the structure, he admired the dedication of these volunteer firemen, as they raced toward the danger. Saddened by Lucille's devastating loss, he wiped tears from his eyes, gripped the steering wheel and focused on the road ahead.

When Lorenzo passed Bolt's cabin, he stopped briefly on the hill to check on the property. Down below, he observed more fire trucks and men ensconced around the compound. He coughed, cleared his throat and remembered that Bolt had mentioned this was to be set up for an emergency base of operations in case of a forest fire.

As a precaution, all foliage had been cut away from the buildings long ago. A nearby stream provided water for tankers as needed. Well-built structures, made of masonry and metal roofs, easily withstood a natural disaster. For the fire fighters, it was an ideal command post. Encouraged by this sight, he felt more hopeful that the woodcarver's compound was safe. So, he proceeded to Jenny's place as ordered.

When Anthony Lorenzo drove to the café, he barely had a chance to open his door, as Sheri rushed over and hugged him. "You made it!" She giggled and planted a kiss on his lips.

Still numb from his battle, Anthony tried to keep his balance while she continued to cling to him. In a clumsy attempt to maintain his composure, he looked over her shoulder and asked, "Uh…where's Lucille?"

Sheri giggled with relief again and smiled, "Grammy's fine." She took a deep breath and hugged him tight, "I am so glad you're here! I was so scared!"

"Me too!" Anthony awkwardly released himself from her grip, untied the ropes on his pickup and quickly pulled back the heavy tarp. "Let's get these unloaded!"

"I'll get some help!" Sheri rushed into the crowded café of evacuees from cabins up the ridge. "Okay, guys! We got another batch!"

Without hesitation, five burly men came out and unloaded the valuable cargo. "You want these to go in the same place as the others?" asked a local truck driver with a toothpick dangling from his mouth.

Sheri grinned with satisfaction and nodded, "Yep! Take them all back in the storeroom." She stood by with her hands on her hips and watched the men quickly and efficiently haul out Lucille's priceless treasure.

Pleased with the help, Sheri held Anthony's hand and enthusiastically directed him to the front door. "Come on! You have to see this!"

Anthony felt the warmth of her hand, as they followed the workers to a storeroom. Each man carefully stacked the paintings against a wall with the others that Sheri brought over, and one big fella grabbed clean table cloths from a cabinet. Together, they reverently spread out the material and covered all the paintings around the concrete basement, as though everything was sacred.

"Thank you, men!" Sheri gratefully patted their shoulders as they left the storeroom.

One of them smiled, "Glad to help. Just let us know whatever Lucille needs, and we'll take care of it."

Sheri grinned happily, held Anthony's hand and led him into the dining room. "Let's go see Grammy."

At the doorway, they watched a dozen men and women, while everyone hovered around Lucille, who sat at a booth. "Is there anything that we can get you, Mrs. Hart?" asked a young lady, who handed her a glass of water.

Another woman patted Cocoa while his tail slowly ticked back and forth. Then, the lady affectionately leaned closer to Lucille Hart, "Whatever you need, we're here for you, dear."

Sheri put her arms around Anthony and rested her head on his shoulder. "I don't think we need to worry about Grammy," she smiled contently. "Most of these people have known her as Mrs. Hart since they were kids. Grammy was their school teacher, and she had a positive influence in their lives."

For a moment, Anthony forgot his awkwardness about Sheri's affections, and he grinned to see so many caring people around this dear lady. Even several customers became servers and kitchen help for their fellow patrons.

"Looks like she's in good hands," he said with a chuckle. It seemed natural, at that point, to keep his arm around her waist.

Jenny came over with a tray in her hands and smiled, "Why don't you two relax for a while."

Anthony's eyes felt tired, while he slid into a booth with Sheri. "I'm beat."

"You look terrible!"

Jenny set down two glasses of water and confirmed it. "She's right, you know!"

Sheri grabbed a napkin, dipped it in a glass and wiped his soot-covered face. Anthony felt the cool dampness of it, and he noticed for the first time how Sheri's eyes had more of a hazel color. Her mother's eyes were darker, but they both had features of part Cherokee ancestry.

With his gaze on her, Anthony thought about her father's Irish heritage, which added a rich mixture in her skin tone. Meanwhile, she looked at him with such compassion, and he liked the softness of her touch. Gently and lovingly, she rubbed his forehead, paused to see if she did enough, then wiped some more.

"How's that?" Sheri studied his face, then touched up his beard and gently plucked out some ashen debris with her slender fingers.

"Much better," he gratefully smiled. "Thanks. You would make a great nurse. Did you take courses in college?"

Sheri glanced at her mother, who walked by with another tray, "No, Mom has always been my role model. I learned a lot from her." Sheri glimpsed Anthony's shirt and sighed, "Do you realize that you have burn holes all over your clothes?"

Anthony looked at his frayed sleeves, "Ah…that's nothing new to me." He shrugged, while another memory of the war flashed in his mind.

Sheri thoughtfully patted his arm, "Come on, you can clean up, and I'll get you a fresh shirt." She grinned with a slight tease and added, "You don't mind wearing something that says Jenny's Café on it, do you?"

"Thanks, but I have to get back," Anthony worried, "Bolt needs my help."

"No, not yet," Sheri squeezed his hand, "You need to get cleaned up first."

"Well, I…" Anthony hesitated, and he saw by her determined expression that she sincerely cared about him. He sighed and nodded, "Okay, but I have to hurry."

In the employee's restroom, Anthony gladly removed his shirt and tossed it in the trash can. Quickly, he thoroughly scrubbed his face and upper torso with a thick lather of soap. He rinsed off and was about to dry but heard a knock at the door, so he opened it.

Sheri peeked in and handed him a towel. "Here, use this," she stared and added, "It's better than paper towels."

Anthony grabbed the towel and covered his wet torso with slight embarrassment and quickly slammed the door. He dried himself furiously and looked at his reflection in the mirror. "What's wrong with you, man?" He lectured himself with a frown, "Lighten up, okay!" He glared at the mirror but heard another knock at the door. So, he held the towel in front of him and opened it again.

"Here, you'll need this," Sheri handed him a shirt with a label, 'Jenny's Café,' on the front. She paused and stared at him with an odd grin. This really annoyed him, but he tried to ignore her peculiar behavior.

"Thanks!" Anthony grabbed it and slammed the door. He quickly put on the shirt, opened the door, and he was surprised to see Sheri standing there like an inspector.

"Let me see," she examined him closely and wiped his forehead with a damp cloth and smiled, "Okay." She gazed into his eyes with a sincere expression of compassion, "You feel better?"

Anthony fidgeted like a school boy in the nurse's office, "Yeah, thanks." He sighed and quickly turned away, "I have to go!"

Sheri held his arm and smiled, "You don't have to rush. I heard that Bolt and the guys are safe. The fire is heading west now."

"Thanks, I'll see you later."

"I'm coming with you!"

Anthony placed a hand on her shoulder and shook his head, "No! You stay here!" Just as the words came out of his mouth, he knew that it was futile.

Sheri stubbornly glared and insisted, "I want to see Poppy. Besides, I can cook for the men. I'm sure they're hungry."

"Okay," he let out a deep sigh, "Hurry! It's getting dark now!"

They rushed out to the truck, and Anthony had an uneasy feeling about taking her with him. As he started the engine, he glanced up the mountain, and he did not like the look of it.

13 Aftermath

When Anthony drove into Bolt's driveway, headlight beams bounced off the walls of the cabin and woodshop. "Where is everybody?" He glanced at Sheri with increased uneasiness, and they slowly stepped out. Hot winds blew swirls of dust at their feet, and it all seemed so eerie. It was as though the entire crew vanished in a puff of smoke. "I don't get it! All the fire trucks are gone!"

Sheri gripped his arm, while they cautiously walked around the deserted compound. "This is weird," she nudged closer, "Shouldn't somebody still be here?"

Their flashlights illuminated deep tire tracks in the mud, and boot prints scattered in all directions. Ghostly shadows danced on drenched buildings and water dribbled to the ground from the eaves. Surprised, Anthony wiped a wet wall with his palm and sighed, "Looks like they soaked everything down before they pulled out."

Anthony yelled, "Bolt!" He stepped up on the porch and opened the damp front door of the cabin while his light searched the living room. The couches were still arranged in horseshoe fashion, but the fireplace—the heart of this refuge—was dead. Nothing moved. Empty and forlorn, the house appeared as though it had been evacuated in a hurry.

Sheri peeked in, squeezed his arm and whispered, "I never saw it so..."

"Spooky," Anthony warily backed away, "Okay, let's go check the workshop."

Flashlight beams bounced along the compound and stopped. "Bolt's Jeep is gone," Anthony turned and scanned the horizon. "Well, at least the wind has shifted away from us." To the west, he saw a bright glow in the sky. "Maybe that's why nobody's here. They all must've followed the flames over the next ridge. It's dark at Lucille's place."

Sheri anxiously held his arm with both hands, "Let's go up there and look around."

When they drove to Lucille's property, it was difficult to see how much damage was done with only the headlights. The burned-out structure appeared to be a ghostly ruin in the shadows of night. An overwhelming smoky stench of charred wood lingered, and they also smelled heavy dampness from firehoses that soaked the entire area. Broken glass and debris crunched under their feet, while they scouted the terrain.

Anthony picked up a wet piece of wood and looked around the site, "Nothing seems to be burning here now." He tossed it over his shoulder. "It's strange that they all left. Someone should've stayed to watch for flare ups."

"That's my job," said a gruff voice in the darkness.

Startled, Anthony spun around and shined the light on a figure, who sat on a nearby boulder. The young vet squinted to see who was there, and then he recognized the man. "Bolt?" Is that you?"

"Who else would it be?" Bolt shot back, with a tone of sarcasm.

Relieved, Anthony laughed, ran over to his mentor. "You old buzzard!" Bolt stood up, and they slapped each other on their backs like long lost brothers.

"Poppy!" Sheri kissed Bolt on the cheek, "What happened?"

The woodcarver sat back down on the boulder, let out a weary sigh and held up his right palm. "Hold on a second," Bolt's voice sounded gravelly, as he reached to his side and gulped down water from his canteen, "Ah…much better. My throat's a little parched."

"You okay?" Anthony shined the light in his mentor's face.

Bolt covered his eyes and groaned, "Hey! Point that somewhere else!"

"Sorry," Anthony turned the beam away, but he still tried to get a good look at Bolt.

Sheri repeated, "You okay? We were worried about you."

"Yeah, what happened?" Anthony insisted.

"Alright," Bolt waved a hand in front of them, "Stop nagging!" The woodcarver leaned forward with his palms resting on his knees and sighed, "You remember Tom?"

Anthony stood there and looked intently at his mentor, "Yeah, yeah, I know Tom, our volunteer fire captain. He's a good man. Go on."

"Well…" Bolt reached for his canteen again and took several gulps, then let out another loud sigh and cleared his throat. "Tom and I saw how the wind shifted to the west…away from us. So, we drove here to check on our men. They were able to control this site, while the wind kept blowing the flames toward Dollar Lake."

Bolt coughed and spat several times, "We agreed that the rocky terrain up there could slow it down, and they needed to go in the direction of the wind. So, I decided to watch for any hot spots here."

Anthony scanned faint silhouettes of the tree line in amazement, "I don't see any sparks or lit up areas anywhere. I don't get it."

"Remember how we talked about the eagle?" Bolt coughed again.

"What eagle?" responded Sheri and nudged the woodcarver's arm.

"How can I forget?"

"Okay…what are you are talking about?" Sheri sighed and glanced at both of them.

Bolt reached out and held Sheri's hand. "Well, Kitten…you are not going to believe this, but I'll tell you anyway. Monster flames came at us on all three sides of us and heat was so intense, and we were trapped…" He hesitated.

"What happened, Poppy?" Sheri insisted.

"Let me guess," Anthony interrupted. "The eagle flew in, right?"

"Yep," Bolt waved a hand across his chest, "The eagle came out of nowhere. He flew in low, just between us and the fire. It happened so fast, there's no way that it makes any sense. All I know is that we heard this ear-piercing swooshing sound and the fire went out like a giant had snuffed out a thousand candles."

"Okay, Poppy, now you're freaking me out," Sheri laughed. "If anybody else told me that, I would think they were on LSD or something." She hugged him affectionately. "But it came from you, Poppy, so, I believe you."

"It's true, Sheri," Anthony placed his hand on her shoulder, "Bolt and I have similar experiences that just can't be explained scientifically."

"Yep," Bolt grinned, "Tom saw it with his own eyes, and we gladly accepted our good fortune. So, with an all clear, Tom ordered the men to head toward the lake, and I agreed to stay behind with my walky-talky, in case anything changed."

Fatigued, but relieved, Anthony plopped next to Bolt and stared silently at flickering stars in the sky. Clouds drifted amid these ancient celestial gems like great sailing ships. He felt numb, as though the air had been knocked out of him, and he tried to inhale. He coughed from the lingering odor of burned-out ruins that once was the home of the grand lady he had grown to love as a grandmother.

Sheri snuggled up to Bolt on the other side of him. "What do we do now, Poppy?"

"Take it one day at a time, Kitten." Bolt shined his flashlight toward the ruins. "For now, I see a tall chimney standing amidst the rubble of my dear friend's home. Do you realize that Julian built that place 45 years ago? That's a lot of memories in there."

Sheri smiled, "I know, Grammy used to tell me how happy they were back then."

"Yep," Bolt paused, as though he was in deep thought and laughed, "They used to joke that Julian constantly chased Lucille around the house in those days. Of course, she would say she never could out run him. Then, she'd wink at me and say, 'Not that I really wanted to.'"

"Oh, come on, you two!" Anthony exploded in a rage. "Don't you see what's happened here?" He picked up a rock and threw it into the ashes. "All those great times just went up in smoke!" He furiously tossed another rock with a loud grunt. "Look at that, man! It's the end of an era for that wonderful lady! It's over!"

"Maybe, maybe not," Bolt stood up, threw a stick and sighed, "That's up to Lucille. How is she anyway?"

Sheri walked over and leaned on Bolt with her arm in his, "She's fine. A lot of people are looking after her right now. We all know how feisty she is anyway." Sheri tossed a rock and it bounced off a beam that had fallen against the chimney. Oddly twisted, it appeared as a ghostly apparition in Bolt's flashlight beam. "Hey! That's kind of fun." Sheri laughed and wildly launched another missile like a mischievous little girl.

"Go ahead. Have your kicks. Lucille is over 85 years-old!" Anthony ran over and kicked a charred piece of wood. "Look at it! You can't expect her to come back to this mess, do you?"

"Well, like I said, that's up to her," Bolt firmly raised his voice but was more controlled in his tone.

"That's crazy!" Anthony yelled in a bitter rage.

"What's crazy?" Sheri spoke up loudly and placed her hands on her hips with increased annoyance at his pessimistic attitude.

Frustrated that he could not get through to them, Anthony groaned and rubbed his forehead like a man in agony. "Don't you people get it? This is all one big cosmic joke played on a sweet, old lady. That was her shrine in there. She cherished her husband and the beautiful paintings he left for her. Now look at it!"

Bolt kicked a burned piece of wood, "What's your point, son?"

Anthony sighed deeply, knelt and grabbed a handful of ashes, then let it sprinkle to the ground. "This is what life's all about—dust to dust, ashes to ashes. We are born, and, in a twinkling of an eye, we're gone. What's it all for? Nobody really cares."

"God cares," Sheri knelt and touched his shoulder. "And, I care too."

"Yeah, well…" Anthony stood up and tossed another rock into the pile, "God has a strange way of showing it, don't you think?"

"You're forgetting something, young fella," Bolt waved a hand in the air, "Remember those times, like this afternoon, when the eagle was sent to save us?"

Anthony smirked, "Well, today his timing was off! Don't you think that it would have been better to stop the fire before Lucille's house was burned down?"

"Son, I'm not smart enough to answer that. Nor, do I want to speculate on things that are beyond my control and understanding." Bolt put his arm on Anthony's shoulder, "No one said life is fair, young fella. Things happen. That's just the way it is. So, you do the best with what you have and leave it all in God's hands. It's how I made it through many difficult times over my years on this planet."

Anthony sniffed and wiped tears from his eyes; then, he dropped to his knees in the dirt. "I know Bolt. It's just that I've seen so much suffering, and it hurts." Bitter and confused, his voice cracked, and he tried to control himself.

His mentor fondly patted the young apprentice on the back, "I understand exactly how you feel. When Emma died, I desperately wanted to cling to the way it was before the accident. But I had to let go of what I desired and accepted the truth that she was gone. Gradually, I realized that I had to live in the present moment without resentment. You understand?"

Anthony searched the heavens and focused on the north star. "I know you are right, but it is so difficult to accept what has happened to Lucille."

War-weary, his voice cracked with pent up sorrow. "Oh, please, God," he cried out, and he raised his hands to the cosmos as a way of letting go. "I just don't understand but help me to believe that you are in control. Give me peace."

Like a mud slide, his memories gushed out—the dying baby in his arms while a Vietnamese village burns; the wounded men he saved in combat, and those who died. Then, the ultimate tragedy and shame--the burden of responsibility for the accidental death of his lovely wife, Amy. Now he witnessed the destruction of Lucille's home. This was like another knot in a long string of tragic events that choked his emotions, and he could not untie.

Sheri knelt beside Anthony and quietly nestled with her arm on his shoulders. Embarrassed, he tried to keep from having this emotional breakdown in front of Sheri, and he gasped for air but could not stop himself. All he managed to do was just let out all that toxic anguish, shame and despair.

He felt his mentor on his opposite side, then he listened to their words, and he knew they were praying for him. Their warmth of human kindness and compassion circulated peacefully in his soul, and he felt his body relax in their empathic embrace. Never had he experienced such love and understanding. Gradually, his pulse slowed and the sorrowful tears dried up.

In the silence of their embrace, he remembered that his father insisted men don't cry. Above all, his dad had drilled into him, "You never, ever show emotions around a woman or anyone else because they will only think of you as weak." You had to be tough. So, the young man always pushed his emotions deep inside.

Back in the present, Anthony Lorenzo felt the warmth of Bolt and Sheri beside him. Time had passed quickly since he met the woodcarver, and these two war veterans talked honestly about their thoughts and emotions. As a result, he experienced gradual healing and a little more clarity of mind.

Now, he found himself in the presence of a sensitive and caring woman. While Sheri listened and held him tight, she did not act like he was less of a man. Instead, she supported him, not just in words but with unconditional love and acceptance.

During those quiet moments, with all three of them on their knees, in the dirt, Anthony discovered that it was okay to shed tears. They're comfort, support and acceptance were all he needed to help him heal.

Cleansed and strangely renewed, he rose up and brushed off the ashen dirt from his knees. Relieved of his anguish, he reached out, and they all embraced each other. Humbly, Anthony said, "Thank you."

"How are we going to help Grammy?" asked Sheri, as they strolled toward their vehicles.

Bolt opened the passenger side door of Anthony's pickup, "Lucille can stay at my place tonight."

Sheri slid in on the seat and asked, "Then what, Poppy?"

"It's up to her," Bolt responded. "We'll ask her in the morning."

Anthony sat next to Sheri and looked at Bolt. "What are you going to do now?"

"I'll keep an eye on things here for a little while longer." His mentor leaned in and kissed Sheri's forehead, then he closed the door. "Bring Lucille to our cabin. I'll be right along by the time you get her there." He patted the hood twice, "Now go on."

14 Getting Together

Santa Ana winds slowed to a dry breeze outside the woodcarver's cabin the next morning. Inside, the place thrived with activity, as Jenny and Sheri just stepped through the front door with their arms full of groceries. Bags ruffled on the kitchen counter, and the women chattered while Anthony poured coffee for Lucille. With everyone together, it felt like home to him, and he did not want it to end.

"Here you go, Grammy," said the young man, with satisfaction. "I stirred in the cream, just the way you like it."

"Thank you, dear," Lucille smiled warmly, "You are always so thoughtful." Cocoa rested his head on her lap, and she gently rubbed behind his ears.

Bolt stood by the stove and studied the items that were removed from the bags. "Let's see how you did, ladies. Okay, we got peppers, celery, tomatoes, mushrooms, ground beef and a little bit of this and a little of that." Then, he held up a jar, with a mischievous grin, and he was pleased with the inventory. "And, the sauce!" He nodded to Jenny and her daughter, "Great job, you two."

Bolt eagerly opened a wax paper wrapper and plopped the beef into a large skillet. "Okay, operation omelet will now commence," he playfully announced and held out his hand to Sheri, "Pepper?"

Sheri giggled and slapped it into his palm like a nurse, "Pepper!"

Bolt sprinkled it wildly over the sizzling beef. "Ah, yes!" he teased with "Tis the season to be merry." He held out a hand again, "Salt?"

"Salt!" Sheri laughed and slapped it into his palm.

Delighted with their little performance, Bolt reached out, "Spatula?"

"Spatula!" Sheri grinned and plopped it into his hand, "You are a true culinary master."

"Of course." Bolt parried to the left and right with the utensil, "On guard!" With grand flair, he stabbed into the frying meat and scrambled it thoroughly. "Ah, hah!"

Jenny laughed along with Bolt's clownish humor and grabbed a cutting board, "Sheri, hand me the peppers and knife."

Bolt nodded with a witty, "Chop! Chop!"

"Here, Mom," Sheri giggled, "While you're doing that, I'll get the eggs ready."

Anthony laughed with delight at seeing everyone so cheerful. "I'll set the table."

As if to add to the jovial atmosphere, Lucille gleefully added, "Well, whatever you do, don't break anything."

"Who? Me?" Just as Anthony tried to play along with the antics, he dropped a glass and it shattered on the floor. "Oops!"

Finally, Bolt held up the skillet, "Feast your eyes on this culinary masterpiece! We have bright red and green peppers, tomatoes and sliced mushrooms all piled on top of ground beef with melted cheese and eggs." Pleased with this huge omelet, he served it on individual plates and proclaimed, "Breakfast is served."

When everyone prepared to eat, they naturally joined hands like they had done many times during the past several months. Lucille chuckled and bowed her head, "Thank you, dear Lord, for this meal and the crazy company we keep. Amen."

They all laughed together and ate in silence for a few moments, while Anthony began fidgeting. He wondered how they would bring up the sensitive subject of Lucille's future, and he thought that no one wanted to stifle the jovial air of the room. Gradually, they each looked at each other, as if to see who would speak first.

Bolt glanced around the room, leaned close to Lucille and placed his hand in hers, "We are all sorry about the loss of your home."

She sipped her coffee slowly, and, with a calm, gracious smile, she set her cup on the table, "Nothing stays the same, dear, except change, of course. That is the one constant in life. We can all agree that everything changes."

Relieved by her response, the woodcarver sighed, "You seem to be accepting this very well."

Lucille giggled with her usual easy-going sense of humor, and, with light, playful sarcasm, she smiled, "Well, I could start kicking and screaming." She reassuringly squeezed his hand, "But, I really don't think that would accomplish much, do you?"

Bolt burst out that familiar vigorous laughter Anthony grew to love, "Yeah, I remember the time I…"

Jenny whispered to Anthony, "Get ready for another tall tale."

Bolt glared with a mischievous grin and chuckled, "Don't interrupt me."

Jenny laughed and shrugged, "Who's stopping you?"

"I remember when I was about 13, I reckon, and I was angry over my kid brother's teasing when I stepped on mushy cow pie. So, I punched my fist into the barn door, which added to my misery. My Pa came over and wagged his finger, 'Son, you just got yourself knee-deep in cow dung! Did that make you feel any better?' Before I could answer, Pa threw a bucket of cold water in my face and yelled, 'Cool off!'"

Bolt looked serious at everyone and said, "Pa sneered at me like one angry bull and spoke real frank, 'You got until sundown to patch up that hole in the barn door!'"

Jenny whispered to Anthony, "Here it comes."

"So, that day I learned, number one, don't punch your fist in a barn door. It's downright painful. Number two, I got splashed in the face with cold water because of number one. Number three, I had to clean up my own mess, because I didn't accept that things didn't go my way in the first place."

"Your point is?" asked Jenny with a teasing smirk.

"The point is, don't go kicking and screaming when you're stuck knee-deep in cow dung. Wear thick boots and accept it while you trudge your way out of the muck."

Everyone cheered, and Lucille laughed with a light-hearted smile. "Amen to that!"

"Hey, that reminds me," Anthony spoke boldly and turned to Lucille, "Why don't you live with us until we rebuild your house? Okay, Grammy?"

No one said anything, and everybody looked at each other with relief that the question was finally in the open. Lucille chuckled, "Well, I wouldn't mind living here, but last night you boys snored louder than two grizzly bears in hibernation."

Everyone nervously laughed, until Bolt jokingly replied, "How about we wear muzzles? Will that be enough to convince you?"

Sheri interrupted, "You can stay with us, Grammy. Right, mom?"

"Of course," Jenny nodded and smiled, "That would be perfect."

Lucille let out a sigh, "You know how much I dearly love each one of you. When I called my daughter last night, however, she invited me to come live with her in

Portland, Oregon. Susan and her husband, Ron, will be here next week to pick me up."

Bolt placed his palm on her hand and smiled, "That's great. I haven't seen Susan and Ron for several years. How are they doing?"

"They seem to be happy together, after 40 years of marriage," shared Lucille, with a proud smile. "Susan is still teaching third graders, and Ron's accounting firm is prospering well. Of course, their son, Tom, and their daughter, Debbie, have families of their own and moved to different states back east." Lucille patted his arm, "You know how that is."

"I sure do." Bolt looked concerned and asked, "Do you think you will be happy so far away from the home you've lived in for 45 years?"

Lucille patted his arm confidently again, "Well, I carry my home inside me, so I'm certain that I'll be happy wherever I go. That's the beauty of free will. I choose to be joyful." Lucille paused, as though she was in deep thought. Then, she added, "That doesn't mean I like what's happened, but I accept the things I cannot change. If I can make things better, I will. Okay, dear?"

"Of course," Bolt patted her hand. "It's not always easy or fun, but you've got the best survival skills I've ever known. That's one of the many reasons why I am going to miss you so much, Lucille."

Anthony listened to these two wise elders, as they talked softly and humbly about life, like there was no one else in the room. While he greatly admired them, he kept silent and was content to just be in their presence. This was natural for him whenever they all got together as a family on many occasions.

Gradually, he became aware that Jenny and Sheri had been washing dishes at the kitchen sink, and he glanced over his shoulder, "I'll help." He grabbed a towel and gladly dried each plate while he affectionately observed Bolt and Lucille.

Lucille turned toward Sheri and smiled, "I'll be glad to stay with you two tonight. Thank you, dear."

Sheri and Jenny looked at each other, and their eyes widened as though they just won a prize. "Great!" they both exclaimed with delighted grins in unison.

"Hey, I know!" Sheri beamed with excitement, "Let's have a slumber party in our pajamas tonight!"

Lucille giggled with delight, "Oh, I haven't been at a slumber party since I was a little girl." She paused for a second and smiled, "Uh, can I borrow pajamas from one of you girls?" She giggled like it was no big deal. "I have nothing to wear."

Sheri glanced at Jenny and knelt beside Lucille, "Oh, that's right. You need new clothes after you lost everything in the fire. I know what would be fun, Grammy. We'll go down the mountain and shop in the city today."

"That's an excellent idea." Jenny put the last dish away and warmly smiled, "We'll have lunch and make it a girl's day out! Okay, Grammy?"

Lucille happily rubbed her hands together and laughed, "Oh, that would be so much fun! I haven't done that in ages!"

Sheri rushed over to Lucille and hugged her. "Come on, Grammy! It's party time."

Anthony and Bolt watched the ladies, as they drove off, and they glanced at each other. "Looks like we're on our own," the woodcarver smiled.

The young apprentice soaked up the silence and sighed deeply, "Yep, it's a good day to work in the shop."

Cocoa stood up from under the table, walked sullenly to the men and whimpered. Anthony knelt and stroked the lab's thick fur. "It's okay, boy, we didn't forget about you."

Bolt patted Cocoa, "Let's go outside and we'll play fetch with a stick for a while."

Cocoa barked, looked up at Bolt and happily wagged its tail while charging wildly toward the door. Massive paws skidded down the hallway, and the lab stopped with its tongue flapping and dripping saliva on the wooden floor.

"Wow!" Anthony laughed, "Slow down, boy." Just as they opened the door, Cocoa darted off and ran up the driveway. "Hey!" Anthony took out after him and yelled, "Cocoa! Get back here!"

Bolt frowned, "Forget it! There's no way you'll catch up with that crazy dog!"

Anthony stopped in the driveway and sighed, "Yeah, you're right." "Well, at least we know where he's going."

"Yeah," Bolt lifted his hat and stroked his hair back. "Looks like Cocoa is heading back up to Lucille's place." He ran to his parked Jeep near the workshop and yelled, "Come on, let's go fetch him before he gets in trouble."

Anthony rushed over, grabbed the passenger side door handle. "Yep. If he goes and chases after a deer, no telling what'll happen."

15 Deep in Dung

The men quickly hopped in Bolt's Jeep, as Cocoa ran and disappeared into the forest. "Cocoa must be taking a short cut. I reckon he'll get there first." The woodcarver released a brake, floored the gas pedal, and the wheels spun ahead.

When they reached the ruins of Lucille's home, there was no sign of Cocoa anywhere. So, Anthony and Bolt leaped out and scanned the area. "Cocoa!" Bolt called out, "Here, boy, got a treat for you!"

Suddenly, a jackrabbit jumped from behind the same boulder they sat on the night before. Right behind it was the lab in full pursuit. "No Cocoa!" Bolt yelled and turned to Anthony, frowned and sighed, "That didn't go very well."

Anthony started to run after the dog, then he stopped in his tracks and glanced back at his mentor. "Well, come on!"

Bolt shook his head and waved to the young man. "No, we can't chase after him in that burned-out forest, son."

"Why?" Anthony demanded, "We have to get Cocoa!"

"Hold it," Bolt held up his palm, "Take a deep breath and think. You know as well as I do why we can't go running in there without food, water and flashlights at the bare minimum, son. We could be stuck up there at night if we go off half-cocked."

"But we…" Anthony stopped himself.

"I know, son, we need to do something, but we could get disoriented along that charred ridge up there. A lot of twisted branches are probably on the ground and that could make it dangerous." He let out a sigh and shook his head. "Although I know the area very well, everything has changed."

"So, what do we do now?"

"You know the answer to that, young fella. Stop reacting and think. What did your combat experience teach you?"

"Okay, okay," groaned Anthony, with increased frustration. "We wait, see and devise a plan to get in, accomplish our mission and get back out safely."

His mentor smiled, "You know, you remind me of the days of my youth. One of the most difficult things we had to do was hurry up and wait." Bolt let out his healthy laugh, "That was not one of my best qualities."

Anthony plopped his rear on the boulder. "Alright, we wait and hope that Cocoa will get tired, and maybe he'll find his own way back."

"You keep watch," Bolt started the Jeep's engine. "I'll get some gear just in case Cocoa doesn't come back in the next hour."

While the young man waited, he was aware of how the weather had cooled, and the mountains became a remarkable study in contrasts between devastation and renewal. The hillside where Lucille had lived was desolate with blackened trees.

Some land still had partially burned trunks with leaves. A nearby shed was completely unscathed, and small plots of ground had tiny yellow flowers that gently swayed in the breeze. Even the deep scars of tire tracks had beaten-down patches of wild grass with a few verdant blades that already began to rise up in defiance.

This inspired the young man to have hope. "Cocoa!" he called out and looked toward the direction where the lab had disappeared into the charred forest. "Cocoa! Come, boy!" Anthony strolled closer to the tree line, watched and waited. At first, only a slight breeze stirred; then, he heard what sounded like barking somewhere in the distant hills.

"Cocoa?" he muttered to himself and intently listened. There it was again. The young man barely picked up a far-off, very faint sound of barking, and he cupped his hands around his mouth, then yelled, "Cocoa! Cocoa!" He paused and waited again, but he heard only a slight rustling of the wind in his ears.

Another, more pronounced sound piqued his interest, and he recognized the familiar roar of Bolt's Jeep heading back up the hill. Relieved, Anthony turned to see the woodcarver drive up with a loud screech of the brakes and a plume of dust and ashes.

When Bolt got out, Anthony ran to him, "I heard barking that came from the ridge up there!"

"Great!" Bolt grabbed a backpack and threw it to Anthony. "Here, take this."

Anthony caught the heavy pack with both hands and immediately slipped it on his shoulders. "Cocoa sounded like he was way up there. I could barely hear him."

Bolt picked up another backpack and put it on, pulled out some rope, and he scanned the ridge for a moment. "Okay, we're going to take this one step at a time."

"Got it!" Anthony nodded in agreement.

"We have no idea how long this will take." Bolt slung the rope over his shoulder. "Cocoa may head back soon. Then again, he may not."

Anthony turned and started to leave. "Let's go!"

"Not yet."

The young man spun around and sighed, "Okay, I'm too much in a hurry, right?"

"I know, son, I feel the same way." Bolt gave Anthony a hard hat with a lamp attached to it and pulled out another one for himself. "This may take a while, so we have to be prepared for the long haul."

Anthony slipped off his backpack, set it on the hood and unzipped the flap. "You're right, I should know better," the young Army veteran remembered his training and opened up the pack. "Okay, let's go over our supplies."

"It's all there, son," Bolt handed him a canteen. "We've got food, water, flashlights, jackets and…" His mentor handed the young man a sleeved hatchet and a hunting knife. "Here, put these on your belt."

"You think of everything."

"Okay." Bolt pulled out a rifle and slung it over his shoulder, then noticed the young vet's eyes widen in what appeared to be surprise. "What's wrong?"

"Uh, nothing," Anthony laughed "For a second there, I thought I was back in Nam." He pointed to Bolt's backpack and teased, "Got any grenades in there?"

Bolt grinned and waved, "Head em up! Move out!" Then, he marched on.

Anthony grabbed his gear, "Stop saying that."

Bolt hummed while they headed up the trail. "Okay, how about, off to work we go?"

"Or, we can sing, 'We're off to see the wizard!'" Anthony laughed and got in step with his friend, as they trekked on.

After hiking for several minutes, Bolt halted in his tracks. "Okay, let's take stock of the situation." He took out a roll of bright, red ribbon from his backpack, cut off a strip and gave it to Anthony, "Wrap one of these around that branch over there."

Anthony secured the ribbon and scanned the terrain. "You're right. We've hiked up here so many times, but it sure looks like an alien landscape now."

"Always adapt to the constant changes, son."

Bolt knelt and examined the trail, "I see Cocoa's prints going up that a way."

The men followed ashen tracks in silence, and they studied the area while going deeper. Bright sun beamed through barren tree tops and made it easier to see the debris-cluttered path ahead. Yet, they had to stop often to carefully climb over fallen branches and a few charred remains of animals everywhere they trekked. About a hundred feet or so, they tied more ribbons along the way.

"Cocoa!" They called out often, "Cocoa! Cocoa!" Only the wind in the trees greeted them, but they kept going.

"Hold it," Bolt held up a hand, knelt and studied the ground. "I don't see any tracks." He stood up and scanned the terrain with binoculars. "Cocoa!"

The men listened, then Bolt lifted his canteen and took several swigs. Anthony did the same, and they glanced at each other. Just at that moment, they spotted the eagle, as it flew low and landed on a fallen tree trunk about 200 feet up the hill.

"What do you think of that?" Bolt nodded toward the eagle.

Anthony shrugged, "I think he's showing us the way."

Without a word, they carefully climbed over twisted branches and marched toward the eagle. When they came within a dozen paces, it flew another couple hundred feet or so, then perched on a branch again. The men followed, and it took off and landed further up ahead. So, they kept this pace until it seemed to vanish into the fading light before the sun set over the next ridge.

"It's getting dark," Bolt clicked on his headlamp. "We have to be very careful now." He handed Anthony one end of a rope, "Secure it real tight around your waist and let's stay close. We could easily trip or fall into something."

Anthony turned on his lamp and tied the rope. "Listen! I heard something!"

"Yep, it sounds like barking somewhere up there," Bolt waved a hand toward the west.

Anthony eagerly rushed ahead. "I hear it! Let's go!"

"Watch your step, son!"

Suddenly, Anthony felt his boots slipping from under him, and he slid right off a steep ravine. This caused an immediate chain reaction, as the rope jerked hard on Bolt's waist. So, he dug in with his heels, but gravity took over, and he plopped hard in the dirt on his rear and kept sliding toward edge. Frantically, Bolt gripped the rope with his right hand, while his left arm flailed out to grab anything to hold onto, like riding a raging bull.

Bolt gripped a branch, but it snapped, and he kept sliding. He caught another one and that broke. Finally, the heels of his boots dug into a tree root, and his body jerked to an abrupt halt, just inches from the edge. "Anthony! You alright?"

"Yeah, I think so," the young man responded with a shaky voice. "My right foot is barely wedged on a rock." Instinctively, he tried to look down, and he felt his toes slipping. Then, he lost his footing and dangled wildly at the end of his rope.

Bolt felt the downward pull, and he dug in his heels to keep from sliding further. Frantically, he turned to his left, then his right, and he looked for anything to grab and spotted a partially burned tree trunk. It appeared to be about six inches wide in the dim light. "Stay calm, son!" He grunted, twisted and stretched, then gripped it tight with his right hand.

Anthony felt the dead weight of his backpack, and he knew that he had to act fast and release it, or they both could fall into the abyss. So, he tried to yank off the strap from his left shoulder but his body dangled wildly while he struggled to get a foothold. The rope jerked him down a few inches. Bolt let go of the branch, gripped tighter and dug in with his heels again. Yet, he kept slipping further to the edge.

In that instant, the tragic memory of Amy's death, flashed in his mind, and he thought, I'm not worthy to live! Take the knife and cut the rope! End it, now!

Former Army Medic, Anthony Lorenzo knew it was his own worst enemy--his destructive self. "No!" he whispered in resistance to this temptation. Desperately, he struggled to break free from the pack, while his body scraped against the cliff. Yet, the more he fought, the more of a burden he was on his mentor. No way was he going to risk the life of his friend any longer. He had to act now! So, he tried again, but, for some strange reason, the backpack was stuck.

"God! Help me!" Lorenzo yelled so loud; he could hear his own echo off surrounding peaks.

In the darkness, their lifeline yanked tighter around Bolt's waist, and he dug in with his heels. He reached and grabbed the tree with one hand again, and the rope with the other. "It's okay, son! I got you!"

"No! I can't let you do this!" Suddenly, Lorenzo remembered the knife. He gripped the handle, pulled it out of the sheath and cut the left shoulder strap. The pack slipped, and he wiggled the whole dead weight off. Finally, his heavy burden dropped into the abyss, and he felt instant relief.

Immediately, Bolt felt it, too. "You okay?"

"Yeah!" Lorenzo sighed, and his adrenaline pumped with renewed energy. More determined, he inhaled, reached and dug his left-hand fingers into a tiny outcrop, and he slowly exhaled. With his right foot, he sensed a slight foothold, and this gave him better control. "Okay, Bolt, try pulling while I work it from here."

Encouraged by a lighter drag on his hands, Bolt yelled, "On the count of three, I'll pull while you look for anything to hold on to. Copy that?"

"Copy!"

"One, two, three!" Bolt yanked with both hands on the rope, while he dug his heels in the dirt.

In turn, Lorenzo reached for one tiny crevice at a time and lifted himself further up. Yet, his foot slipped, and he dropped down a few inches but gained a grip on some other crack in the rocky ledge.

Bolt felt the jerk downward again and held tight. "You alright?"

"Yeah!" Lorenzo groaned, "Let's do this!"

Bolt took a deep breath, slowly exhaled and pulled forward one hand at a time. As it became easier, he asked, "How are you doing?"

"Almost there," Lorenzo grabbed a small ledge, dug, kicked the toes of his boots in and pulled with all his energy. Slowly, he could feel his body lifting, but he still worried. "Please, God!" He grunted painfully as he slid higher with his torso rubbing and scraping into the rocky cliff side. "Come on!" he groaned fiercely.

Laboriously, Bolt pulled on the rope. "Sounds like you're close."

"Yeah," Lorenzo tried to see in the darkness, "It feels like my fingers are on the ledge now. Where are you?"

"Right above you! Hang on!" Bolt grunted, then yanked hand over hand.

Finally, Anthony made it to the top and pulled harder until he was flat on his belly, and suddenly, he laughed crazily with relief. Then, Bolt reached out to the young man, and they both held on, laughing, gasping for air, and neither one wanted to let go of the other.

Bolt breathed heavily, then blew out a loud, "Phew! Do me a favor!"

"What's that?" Anthony gasped for air and chuckled.

"Don't you ever do that again!"

"Copy that!" Anthony laughed again and savored his own breath with such a rich passion for life that he looked to the heavens and whispered, "Thank you, God!"

"You got that right!" Bolt hugged him again. In doing so, he accidentally bumped the headlamp switch off, and they could not see each other in the darkness. "Oops!" So, he reached and turned it back on. "Okay, let's have a look see."

"Hey! You're blinding me, man!" Anthony covered his eyes and laughed with the fullness of his renewed life.

Bolt grinned, "Now we're even! Hey! Where's your hardhat?"

"Down there!" Anthony kept giggling like a drunkard, but he was never soberer and higher on life than at that precious moment.

"I see your pack is gone," Bolt sighed with relief. "That extra weight could've killed us both!"

"Yep," Lorenzo stomped his feet and rubbed his pants, then laughed.

"What's wrong with you?" Bolt grinned, "You got something in your britches?"

Anthony looked at his mentor with embarrassment, "My pants are a little wet."

Bolt slapped Anthony on the back with more chuckling, "Fear has a way of draining that all out! I remember back in 42, when…"

Anthony interrupted, "If this is going to be another long tale, let's start back and you can tell me all about it on the way, okay?"

Bolt laughed again, "That's a great idea. You can dry off on the way down." He reached into his backpack and gave Anthony the extra flashlight. "Here, you focus on our path, and I'll watch for the markers. Steady as she goes."

"Aye, Aye, captain," Anthony saluted playfully. He shined the beam from left to right to get oriented and sighed, "Where's the edge of the cliff? I can't see it!"

"It's two paces behind you, son."

Anthony glanced at his feet, observed twisted branches, and he knew they had to be extremely careful with each precarious step. "Okay," he sighed, "I can see this is not going to be easy." Aware of this dangerous terrain, they both paused, and it was like a switch that turned off all humorous banter.

Now solemn, Bolt asked, "Ready?"

"Yep," Anthony anxiously kept one hand on the rope around his waist, "Looks like we'll have to take one step at a time and stay close to each other."

Bolt tightened the knot on his torso, then wrapped the extra length of rope around his shoulder. "Let's bring in the slack. Keep your light focused on the ground ahead, and I'll be right behind you."

"Affirmative," said the young vet in a sober voice. He cautiously lifted his foot over one fallen branch after another, and he felt the tightness of the rope behind him.

Neither said a word. The beam from the woodcarver's headlamp scanned ahead for any sign of a ribbon that marked their trail. A cool breeze nipped the backs of their necks, and both men knew the temperature would plummet in the night. Finally, after slogging for what seemed like an hour, they trudged to an abrupt halt.

"I heard something!" Anthony cocked his head and listened.

"Sounds like barking way up on the southern ridge," Bolt grabbed Anthony's shoulder. "Wait! I hear more than one!" He let out a deep sigh and turned toward the sound, as the beam of his headlamp revealed dancing shadows from twisted branches. "I've heard this before, son."

"What is it?" Anthony cocked his head and listened to what seemed like a whole pack of wild dogs on a brutal chase of their prey.

Suddenly, they heard a blood-curdling scream very similar to that of a human baby in excruciating agony. Vicious growling, yelping and barking echoed through the mountains. Anthony imagined a half-dozen wild dogs attacking and ripping apart the flesh of some hapless animal.

A queasy feeling stirred in his gut, as though he was back on patrol in the jungle. "Okay, man, I've heard a lot of scary things at night, but do you mind telling what's going on up there?"

"A pack of coyotes just caught a nice, fat jackrabbit, I reckon. Usually they're solitary hunters, but sometimes they prowl as a group." Bolt paused and listened to increasingly louder growls like their prey was being torn apart. "I actually witnessed an attack many years ago, son. What you heard was the very second that rabbit was ripped into by the pack, and it cries out much like a baby screaming."

"What about Cocoa?"

Bolt patted the young man on his shoulder and tried to reassure him. "I reckon Cocoa found his way back home by now."

"But he could still be out there," Anthony looked toward the barking noises.

"Nothing we can do now," Bolt sighed and started walking, "Let's go."

Both men tramped on in silence. Soon, they spotted a red ribbon on a tree. Encouraged, they persevered down the mountain and followed their markers back to Lucille's place. Muscle-weary, they called out to the lab, but there was no response. So, without another word, the men tossed in what was left of their gear in the back of Bolt's Jeep. They both let out a groan in unison, as they climbed into the front seat.

Bolt puffed out air, paused and started the engine. "Let's go home, son."

Anthony sat quietly on the way back, and he liked the warm words of 'home' and 'son.' Yes, he thought to himself, he was truly at home with this man that he grew to love like a father, and he knew he could never return to his old life.

It was before dawn the next morning when they heard scratching at the front door. There, on the porch was a bedraggled, stinky, almost unidentifiable Cocoa with grimy matted fur and a forlorn, downward look of shame over a wild night out.

"Oh, man!" Anthony covered his nose, "What is that smell?" Cocoa rubbed against his legs and smeared malodorous brown stains on his pants. "Ah, that's gross!"

Bolt gagged, "Whoa! Son, you just got yourself knee-deep in dung!" The woodcarver backed away and laughed, "Cocoa must've rolled in something strong enough to knock out a horse! Quick! Let's give him a bath before the ladies get here!"

Cocoa looked up, snorted, leaped off the porch and ran to the back of the cabin.

"Hey! Come back here!" Bolt yelled.

Anthony laughed, as they both stood there, "Well, I don't think he liked to hear you say bath."

"Nope," the woodcarver let out a weary sigh. For a moment, he paused, then his eyes widened. "Hey! What are we standing here for? Come on!"

They both chased Cocoa in circles. Every time they were close enough to grab the dog, he darted and got away. When he ran to the front yard again, "Bolt shouted, "You go around the back, and we'll head him off!"

Anthony finally caught up, grabbed Cocoa by the collar, and yelled, "I got you now!" Suddenly, he slipped and splashed face-down into a mud puddle.

Bolt rushed over, and he fell in. Quickly, he staggered to his feet, and they both wrestled a wet, stinky dog back into the house.

"Hurry!" Anthony pulled, and Bolt pushed Cocoa from the rear down the hall and into the bathroom.

Bolt slammed the door, and with the three of them locked inside, he nodded to the bathtub, "Turn on the water!"

While they wrestled and scrubbed Cocoa, Anthony glanced at the wall clock, "We don't have much time! Lucille will be back soon!"

16 Fond Farewells

It was a bright, sunny morning when everyone gathered at Jenny's Cafe for Lucille's farewell party, and the place was packed with friends and family. The guest of honor sat graciously at the end of five tables all joined together. Jenny presented her with a large, double-layered chocolate cake and placed it reverently before her like a trophy.

"This is for you, Grammy. It's your favorite chocolate cake." Written in white frosting were the words, "To your new, happy life, Lucille! Love, from Your Bear Mountain Family!"

"You may now kiss the cake," added Bolt with his usual mischievous grin.

Lucille smiled happily, "Thank you everyone." She laughed and teased with, "Now, where's my ice cream!"

Everyone clapped, cheered and shouted, "Speech!" Lucille giggled like a school girl and held up her hands, "Thank you, all, but you know I never give speeches, for fear that my dentures may fall out!"

Everyone laughed with admiration for this grand lady, then paused and waited to hear more from her.

Lucille turned to a woman in her early 60's and said, "Oh, for those who have not met my daughter, I'd like to introduce my dear, sweet, Susan. She has invited me to come and live with her. May I not be a burden to her in any way."

Susan had a kind, gentle smile that Anthony admired right away, and she said, "Thank you, mom. I'm glad to be here, and, no, you will never be a burden. In fact, I need you to teach me how to crochet," she leaned into her mother. "I want to make up for being too stubborn to learn from you when I was a crazy teenager."

Lucille giggled with her usual playfulness, "I would love to do that, dear. Uh, what's crochet?"

Everyone laughed, and one man of about 40ish stood up, then said, "Remember me, Mrs. Hart? It's Tommy Jameson. I was in your fourth-grade class."

Without a beat, Lucille responded, "Yes, I remember. You were the boy who kept pulling that girl's hair. Um…what was her name? Oh yes, I think it was Becky."

"That was me, Mrs. Hart." A stocky woman with a radiant smile stood up and said, I married him."

Lucille playfully grinned and giggled, "Oh, dear, I hope you waited until after the end of my class."

Everyone clapped and lovingly cheered again. Someone yelled, "Good one, Mrs. Hart!"

Anthony admired the way so many people loved and respected her. That was her greatest legacy. Before the loss of sight Lucille was a teacher, active in the community, and she inspired everyone with a positive, not-judgmental acceptance of all those in need. She did not preach faith. She lived it. As a result, people were drawn to her as a role model of unconditional love.

"Oh, where are my manners?" Lucille stood up and turned to a short, chubby man with graying hair and a bald patch on the back of his head. "Please, everyone, I would like to introduce my son-in-law, Ron. He has always been so supportive and a true gentleman in my family."

Ron sat with a shy grin, and he looked embarrassed through his thick glasses, as though he was not used to the attention. Anthony observed his somewhat awkward mannerisms. He was about to make up his mind that he did not like this geeky-looking fellow, when Bolt nudged him and said, "He's a great guy. You'll like him."

Later, when the party wound down, and people had left, it was only Anthony there with Bolt, Jenny, Sheri, Lucille, Susan and Ron. Everyone sat close together, talked softly, and it seemed like no one wanted to leave, especially the young man. There was an odd sense about the atmosphere in that room. To Anthony, it was difficult to put into words. How could he explain that warm, cozy feeling one gets when he deeply cares about someone so inspirational in his life?

Is this what it feels like to be part of loving family, he wondered? All he knew for sure was that he enjoyed how Susan rested her head on Ron's shoulder while Lucille did the same with Bolt, then Jenny leaned affectionately on his opposite side. And Sheri? Where was Sheri, he asked himself?

Just as he pondered that question, someone brushed up to him. He turned to see Sheri with her arm under his, and she let out a sweet, refreshing sigh, "Isn't it nice here? I've never felt so close to a group of people like this before."

"Yeah, I feel the same way," Anthony gazed into her eyes, and he was glad to see her.

He did not hear the soft-spoken conversations around him, until Lucille said, "I think we should all have a family meeting about something very important."

All eyes turned to Grammy, and she smiled, "It's time that we decide what is the best way to preserve Julian's paintings. Bolt has said many times that I should put my husband's masterpieces in a safe place. Well, I confess that I have been very stubborn and unwilling to part with them. As a result, I almost lost all of them in the fire." Lucille's voice cracked with emotion, "Bolt, will you please tell them?"

Bolt cleared his throat, stood up and made eye contact with everyone in the room. "Lucille has asked me to be Executor of her property here, so I talked with Susan and Ron to get their opinion. They have agreed to have me proceed in the interests of not only Lucille, but what she wants for the family. Ron has also stated that his lawyer will help with any legal documents in the coming days ahead."

"Um…" Lucille started to speak, then wiped her eyes with a napkin.

"Yes, Lucille, please go ahead," Bolt sat down and waited for her to continue.

"As you all know, I love each one of you dearly. To me, it doesn't matter that we're not all of the same blood-line. We are what society now calls the extended family," she laughed and added, "Whatever that means." She sniffed and wiped her eyes again.

"Anyway, the point is, you are my family. So, before Bolt takes any paintings out of that back storeroom, I invite each of you to go one at a time and pick out a piece that seems to speak to you. You will choose prayerfully from your heart. If you hear an inner voice that says, please take me home, then I want you to bring it here and describe to me what you see."

Anthony immediately felt out of place, and he squirmed in his seat. As if to sense this, Sheri whispered in his ear, "That means you, too."

Unwilling to accept Grammy's loving gesture, Anthony said, "But I don't think I…"

Lucille interrupted with a firm tone, "Don't give me that I am not worthy talk again, young man." She sighed and softened her voice, "If you hadn't been here, I would have lost most of Julian's artwork. Sheri was wonderful, but she couldn't have done it by herself, and Bolt was not able to be in two places at once. Also, you have helped me many times around the house during the past year. You are like a grandson to me. So, I am truly grateful for your love and support. Okay, dear?"

Anthony glanced around and saw reassuring nods, then he felt more at ease. "Yes, thank you, Grammy."

Lucille let out a sigh again and smiled, "Okay, let's start with Susan and Ron as a couple. Please go and prayerfully look for the paintings that await you. When you enter that room, I want you to hold each other's hands as a sign of your love and commitment to each other. After you choose the one that appeals to you, please bring it here and tell me what you see."

Anthony observed how the café had a quiet, sacred air of reverence when the couple stood up and left the room. Sheri sat close to him, and he was aware of his own, steady breathing. Everyone waited patiently in anticipation of their return. The only movement was from Jenny, as she left for a moment and came back with a pitcher of water; then, she filled everyone's glasses and snuggled next to Bolt.

When Susan and Ron strolled back into the room, they each carried a framed oil painting. "Okay, mom, we're ready," said Susan, while she stood close to Lucille.

"Tell me what you see, dear," her mother waited with a tranquil smile.

Susan leaned the two-foot length artwork on a table. "This has always been my favorite. It's the one that shows Dad, holding me in his arms, when I was three years old, and you're standing close to us. We're at a lookout with Mt. Whitney in the background."

"Yes, I like that, too," Lucille nodded in agreement. "Your Dad loved to get a self-portrait worked in with us as a family. How about you, Ron?"

"Well," he gazed at his chosen piece, "I found this one that shows Susan and me posing in front of Cliff House Inn." Ron smiled over the pleasant thought of the past. "Julian tried to get us to stand still, so he could do a quick sketch, but we were hungry and just wanted to get inside. I never saw anybody draw so fast. He must've painted that from memory later."

Lucille laughed, "Yes, Julian tried to get me in there, too, but I insisted that he just concentrate on you two together. When he painted the scene, and we saw how cute you both looked, we were glad that he did."

After each person made a choice of paintings to keep, Anthony picked out a piece that caught his attention. "I like this one, Lucille." held up a three-foot-long framed oil painting, and he studied it with curiosity and wonder. "It shows a boy, about 12 years-old, in the mountains with an eagle overhead. You know, Grammy, I really don't understand how Julian came up with this scene. It looks like my memory of an experience that I had at that age."

"Yes," Lucille smiled happily, "I remember when Julian worked on that scene, and he mentioned that it came to him in a dream. He couldn't sleep after that, so he stayed up all night to work on it."

Anthony shook his head in amazement, "It's like he was actually there." The young apprentice noticed something else, and his eyes widened with increased interest. "Bolt, check this out."

His mentor studied the oil painting and nodded, "Yeah, I see a man standing on that peak in the background, and he appears to gaze right back at us."

"Do you notice how he's dressed?" Anthony pointed to the man in the picture, "He's wearing a coon-skin cap, and he looks a lot like the mountain man I saw."

"You're right." Bolt leaned closer. "I remember that Julian talked about an encounter with a mountain man and the eagle when he was a boy."

Lucille grinned, "Oh, yes, Julian told me when his father took him hunting, they were caught in a freak snow storm. In their race to build a lean-to shelter, his father accidentally cut his leg with a hatchet. Julian patched him as best he could and stopped the bleeding but worried when his dad developed a fever and was delirious."

"Uh, huh…" Bolt looked at the painting again. "Yeah, I remember he told me the storm passed, but they had to stay put. After several days, they were starving, so Julian prayed for food and help. Moments later, an eagle landed and dropped a freshly caught rabbit at their feet. Julian gutted, skinned and cooked the meat over a fire, then ate it, but he could not get his father to respond. So, he prayed and held his father's hand."

"Yes, when he opened his eyes, the mountain man appeared," said Lucille. "The stranger cleaned the wound, then applied a poultice, and he pressed a thumb on the father's chest. After that, he touched Julian the same way. This was like a jolt of heat and energy to both of them.

When the stranger turned and started to leave, Julian begged him to stay, but the man said he already did more than he was allowed. There would be strangers who will be inspired to provide more help, as needed. Julian asked his name, and he just smiled. 'Call me, Watchman.' Then, he walked away and vanished."

"Yeah," Bolt agreed, "The Watchman told Julian to follow the eagle and they would be safe in their journey home. So, with his father's renewed strength, Julian dismantled the lean-to and used the wood to build a make-shift sled. He pulled his father through the snow, and he was surprised that he had the strength to keep going. They followed the eagle until they were rescued by two men in a wagon."

Anthony studied his painting again, "You know, as I look at this and hear Julian's story, it makes me wonder how many of his paintings did he include the eagle and the Watchman."

Bolt grinned at this idea, turned to the group and said, "This could be fun. Let's all take a look at those paintings again."

Everyone followed the woodcarver and his apprentice, while Jenny took Lucille's hand. "You want to come with us, Grammy?"

"I wouldn't miss this for anything, dear," Lucille giggled, "I like puzzles." She held Jenny's hand and was led into the storeroom.

When they all stood together, Bolt nodded, "Ron, you and Susan examine this stack here. Sheri, you take this. Jen, you look at these. Anthony, you help me over here."

Each person began sorting out the paintings and Sheri held up one with a look of amusement. "Okay, Poppy, I don't see a haystack and there's no needle," she playfully teased. "So, what exactly are we looking for?"

Bolt laughed along with her sense of humor. "Well, kitten, just look for any sign of a man or an eagle somewhere in any of these scenes and call out when you do." Bolt held up one, put it down and looked at another. Then, he stopped and pointed, "Like this," he placed his finger on a tranquil view of a lake that reflected majestic peaks in the background.

"Where?" Jenny leaned over his shoulder, "I don't see anything."

Bolt set it down on a counter, under better light and tapped on a far corner of the painting. "There, you see that?"

"You're right," Jenny's eyes seemed to sparkle over this mystery.

Susan looked closer, "He sure looks a mountain man all right."

"Here's another one," Ron held up a painting of a meadow. "See?" he used a pen from his pocket as a pointer. "And, look over on the branch of this tree. It's an eagle."

"I count six more over here." Anthony held up his stack, and he sorted through each one. "They all show a mountain man and an eagle somewhere in each scene."

"I don't get it, Pop," Sheri leaned closer, "Who is this mountain man?"

"That's a good question, kitten." Bolt glanced at Anthony and shrugged, "We have been trying to figure that out ourselves."

Anthony rubbed his whiskered chin as he contemplated. "Yeah, all we know is that his name is Watchman. That gives us a clue."

"So, he's a Watchman of what?" asked Susan.

"Well," Lucille smiled, "Julian had talked about this, and we came to the conclusion that he was sent by God to watch over people wandering in the wilderness."

"Like an angel?" asked Jenny.

"Perhaps," Grammy shrugged slightly, "Whatever he is, I am sure God will use any animal or anything to help people in need."

Sheri said, "I had my own guardian angel when I was 12 years-old. Sometimes I explored a nearby trail after school, and out of nowhere, a stray, friendly collie dog showed up. He followed me around like he knew me. I called him Buddy, because he stayed close to me. Then, one day, Buddy ran over to some bushes and growled. I saw a strange man lurking like he was ready to attack me, and I was so scared, I ran back to our house. I never saw the stranger or the dog again."

Anthony nodded with understanding, "The eagle has been like that to me."

Lucille said, "Well, I read that God satisfies our years with good things, so that our youth is renewed like the eagle. I think the eagle represents a renewal, a new beginning for all those in need. What do you think, Bolt?"

"That sounds about right." He glanced at his young apprentice, "I reckon the eagle is a symbol of second chances for those who need to start a new life after a tragic loss."

"Speaking of starting a new life," Susan glanced at her watch, "Mom, are you ready to leave for our trip to Portland?"

"Oh, yes," Lucille patted her daughter's arm and smiled happily, "I didn't have a lot to pack, so I'm ready to go, dear."

"Ron said, "If you need anything, Mom, we'll get it along the way."

"This will be fun," Susan held Lucille's hand. "Like I mentioned on the phone, Ron has a week off from work, and it will be our vacation trip together." She kissed her mother's cheek, "Remember how you liked to walk barefoot in the sand at the beach?"

"Oh, yes," Lucille laughed and smiled, "I'm looking forward to it again."

"First, we'll stay in Morro Bay, and we can stroll together and feel the sand between our toes. Then, we'll drive up to the Pine Ridge Inn where you and Dad took me when I was a little girl. Won't that be great, Mom?"

Lucille gushed with excitement, "Oh my goodness, is that place still there?"

"Yes, Mom, we checked it out on the way over here. And then, we will go…"

"Oh, wait!" Lucille interrupted, "What about Cocoa?" She hesitated. "I know you said he can come with us, but that's a long way, dear."

"Don't worry about that, Mom," assured Susan. "We have plenty of room for him. Ron and I have everything all worked out along the way. When we get home, Cocoa will have his own fenced backyard to run around, and he can come in whenever you want him to, okay?"

"Let's go, then." Lucille giggled with delight, turned around and asked, "Where is he anyway?"

"Cocoa is right here, Mom," Ron brought in her frisky lab.

Lucille knelt and patted Cocoa while his tail wagged and tapped, tapped against a table leg. She sniffed his fur and sighed, "Oh, you smell so good. I can tell that the boys took real good care of you."

Bolt and Anthony glanced at each other with relief. "Cocoa was no problem at all, Grammy," Anthony said with an awkward grin, as he looked back at Bolt and shrugged.

Lucille hugged each man graciously. "Thank you, boys." Then, she smiled happily, "Okay, I'm ready to go."

Moments later, after all their affectionate goodbyes, Ron drove off with Susan, Lucille and Cocoa. While everyone waved, Anthony had mixed emotions of sadness and joy, as the car pulled out of the parking lot for the last time. He was sad that Lucille was leaving but glad to see that she would be happy living with her daughter and son-in-law. Although he would miss her, the young man was certain that this big change was in the best interests of his dear Grammy and that comforted him.

Deep down, he also felt a raw emptiness in his heart, knowing that he no longer could enjoy his visits with her. This caused uncertainty about his own future, and he had a sense of walking on a razor's edge of instability.

So, as he strolled back to his pickup truck, Sheri came alongside and put her arm in his. "I'm going to miss Grammy."

Anthony felt the warmth of her hand, as she squeezed his, and he nodded, "Yeah, me too."

"I don't think I'll ever get used to not having Grammy around." Sheri stopped and gazed into his eyes. "It's so difficult to see her leave us. What do you think, Tony?"

For a moment, Anthony paused, then he remembered something that his mentor had said recently. "Well, sometimes we just have to accept the direction someone takes and love them enough to let them go their own way."

17 Letting Go

Bolt and Anthony loaded up some of Julian's oil paintings into the back of a sky-blue delivery van on a Tuesday morning. It had bright red letters on the side that advertised Jenny's Café. When Jenny stepped out of the service door, her soft raven-hair glistened with a slight bluish tint from the sun's reflection off the vehicle.

She hugged each man and smiled, "Have a safe trip."

"Thanks for the use of your van, Jenny." Bolt kissed her cheek and held her close, "This really helps while I get the brakes fixed on my truck."

Sheri came out of the back door with a thermos and smiled affectionately, "Here, Poppy." She glanced at Anthony and nodded, "You both need hot, fresh coffee on your way to San Diego."

"Thanks," Bolt took the thermos and handed it to Anthony. "We'll be back in several days. A friend of mine plans to exhibit these pieces on Saturday, and she's confident that Julian's work will be a success."

"What about the other paintings?"

"We catalogued everything," Bolt assured her. "The rest of them will be stored in my shop. When we get back, Anthony and I will figure out the next step."

He lovingly stroked Sheri's face with his right hand and smiled, "I reckon it'll all work out just fine."

"Bye, Poppy," Sheri hugged Bolt, then kissed him on the cheek.

Anthony was about to open the driver's side door when Sheri turned and wrapped her arms tight around his waist. Then, she smacked her lips hard on his mouth and lingered in a long passionate kiss. Embarrassed by her sudden assertiveness, the young man was aware that they were being watched by Bolt and Jenny.

He tried to push her away, but she held him tighter, until she finally released him with a loud smack of their lips. The young man gasped for air and firmly demanded, "What was that for?" He breathed heavily and glanced wide-eyed over at his mentor and Sheri's mother, as they looked on with surprised expressions.

Sheri smiled forthrightly and patted him on the chest, "Oh, just a little something for you to think about during that long, boring drive." She turned and sauntered back in the café without another word.

Bolt glared at Jenny and whispered, "What just happened?"

"Don't look at me," Jenny giggled with a smirk. "She's your goddaughter."

"Very funny," Bolt frowned and observed the young man's dazed appearance. "Look at him! Now he's a mess!"

Anthony clumsily lifted his foot to get into the van but slipped twice; then, he slid into the seat and white-knuckled the steering wheel. Unable to speak, he just stared ahead, as though he was in some kind of trance.

Bolt sighed and shook his head with increased annoyance, "You see what she did!" With a low grumbling, he gritted his teeth, stepped up on the driver's side floorboard, and he gruffly ordered, "Move over!"

Anthony turned his head and still looked disoriented. "I thought I was supposed to drive."

Bolt growled, "Move! I'm driving!" He gestured toward the young man, with a flip of his hand, "Go!"

Anthony sighed and groaned, "Okay!" He rolled his eyes and reluctantly slid to the passenger side.

His mentor plopped into the driver's seat and reached for the keys but paused and exhaled loudly. "Alright," he huffed, "Give me the keys."

"What keys?" The young man still looked puzzled, until his eyes widened, and he remembered they were in his pocket. "Oh, yeah!" He pulled them out and sheepishly handed them to his elder.

Bolt snatched the keys from his hand and started the engine. He let out a deep sigh of irritation and frowned at Jenny, who stood by the driver's side door.

Jenny held a hand over her mouth with amusement and snickered, "I think she broke him."

At first, Bolt tried to look fiercely angry but could not hold back from seeing the humor in the whole silly affair, and he chuckled, "We'll be back in a few days." He smiled and whispered softly, "I love you, Jen."

Jenny waved and smiled affectionately, "Bye, I love you, too."

When they arrived in San Diego, Anthony felt apprehension about his return to the city he once adored. Before the tragic loss of his wife, Amy, they enjoyed many bright sunny days, and their strolls along sandy beaches. This time, the unique, lively charm of places like Old Town and Balboa Park all seemed clouded over with the memory of the most horrific mistake he ever made in his life.

Even during the delivery of Julian's masterpieces, the young man was in a somber mood. Once they had set out the paintings in the Pacific Beach gallery, Anthony went back outside and sat on a bench. Seagulls noisily squawked and swooped around a fisherman, who gutted a fish, and its blood streamed down a drain in a nearby sink. A cool, brisk breeze wafted the odor of fresh catch in a bucket.

Meanwhile, his mentor focused on business discussions with the owner inside. Although the woodcarver tried to encourage his apprentice to be present for this productive exchange of thoughts and ideas about art displays, Anthony had to get away.

So, the young veteran of a far-off war sat on that lonely bench with a stream of bitter memories, while a fisherman's radio played, "Sittin on the dock of the bay." At first, the darkness of his own thoughts prevailed in his mind. Yet, there was something else that stirred deep in his wounded soul, and it resonated from the ebb and flow of ocean waves. It was as though nature's rhythm began to soothe him, and he gave himself permission to just listen without judgement.

In that moment of awareness, Anthony observed a V-shaped squadron of pelicans gliding in formation over rolling swells, and he sensed the harmonious flow of life. Even as he listened to a cacophony of squawking seagulls, he noticed the humorous behavior of these pesky winged rodents of the shore. He could not help to have a slight grin on his face when these comical thieves tried to steal anything in their sight.

These masterful robbers were determined to snatch someone's unattended hotdog or zero in on a fisherman's fresh catch right off a line. All was fair game. Passersby had to stay alert and watch for aerial bird bombings. One crafty woman attempted to outsmart them with her umbrella that had splatters of white seagull droppings, as she strolled on the pier. Observing all this made it difficult for the young vet to stay melancholic for very long.

To his pleasant surprise, he felt a natural lift in his bedraggled, downcast spirit, so he stood up and took a deep breath of ocean air. Each step felt lighter during his stroll along the salty, wooden pier, and it was good to be alone in this refreshing time and place, he thought. Renewed, Anthony stopped at the edge of a pier and looked over a wooden rail to observe the fish, as they darted, just below the surface. This calmed his restless mind, and he smiled with delight in that present moment.

A couple strolled by, while they affectionately held hands, and it stirred up mixed emotions. At first, he missed his wife and guilt swept over him, but something more soothing flowed over him. It was a hopeful thought that maybe he could start his life anew. A vision flashed in his mind, and he saw the eagle soaring high above him, He thought, perhaps, he could be forgiven and actually live again.

"There you are," said a familiar voice behind him.

Anthony turned and made eye contact with his easy-going mentor, and this confirmed his hope for a better life. Bolt smiled pleasantly, "I thought I might find you here." He came alongside of the apprentice and looked around, then added, "Yep, this is the perfect place to clear your mind, son."

"Thanks, I needed this time out here." For a moment, he gazed at drifting clouds overhead, and he looked at Bolt. "Could you do me a favor?"

"Sure."

"Would you mind if we drive over to Amy's gravesite?"

"I'd be glad to," assured his mentor. "I'll take you now, if you want."

Anthony nodded, "I'm ready."

Later, when Bolt drove through the manicured grounds of a cemetery with white statues of angels and brightly-colored flowers everywhere, Anthony felt at ease. He knew it was time for closure, and he was glad they parked near the gravesite. When he got out of the van with a bouquet in his hand, it was so quiet and peaceful that he could almost hear his own heartbeat.

"I'll wait here." Bolt kept his hands on the steering wheel.

Anthony paused and felt he needed support. "Come with me, okay?"

Bolt stepped out and placed his hand on the young vet's shoulder, "I'd be honored, son."

Anthony knelt before Amy's headstone, placed a pot of mums and bowed his head, "I am so sorry, Amy." His voice cracked, and tears flowed down his cheeks. "It was my fault. Please forgive me." While he cried remorsefully, he realized that she was not really there. Just the body. So, he looked up and said, "She's with you now, God."

A gentle breeze fluttered bright yellow petals, and the emotionally broken young man felt a sensation on his skin. It was like Amy had caressed his cheek with her hand. For a moment, it seemed so real that he turned to look but she was not there. Somehow, he knew that she forgave him and it was time to start living again.

His mentor quietly stepped closer and stood silently beside him. This assured Anthony of his dignity and respect, and that was all he needed in his moment of closure.

18 Becoming Stronger

Anthony and his mentor busily worked on the final touches of an oak wood dresser when the telephone rang that Wednesday afternoon. "I'll get it," said the apprentice. Sawdust stuck to his palm, so he delicately picked up the woodshop phone with his thumb and forefinger. "Hello? Who? Oh, hi, Grammy. How are you?" He signaled with a wave of his hand for Bolt to come over.

"Is that Lucille?" Bolt leaned close to listen in on the conversation.

"Yes, Grammy, we're both here." Anthony held out the phone with their ears on each side of the piece. "Go ahead, Grammy. We're listening."

"I just called to let you know that I am so happy here with Susan and Ron."

"We're glad for you, Grammy," said Anthony.

The woodcarver leaned closer and cocked his head to hear better, "Tell us more, Lucille. What do you like about it there?"

"Well, I have my own cozy room that's perfect for me. Susan and I walk in the neighborhood almost daily, and everyone is so friendly here. Cocoa loves to run around in the backyard. There are plenty of birds and squirrels he can chase after, and it's funny because he never hurts them. He just likes to chase anything that moves. So, I think he's enjoying every minute of it."

"Knowing you and Cocoa are happy there means a lot to us," said Bolt.

"Oh, thank you for that recent check on the sale of some of Julian's paintings."

"You're welcome, Lucille. Everyone is fascinated with Julian's work, and I'm sure that more will sell very soon."

"I'm glad to know that people are inspired by my husband's paintings. Julian would be pleased."

Bolt had difficulty, as he tried to make out her words, and he held the phone closer. "Is that Cocoa I hear barking?"

"Yes, Cocoa is at the back door, and he knows to bark twice as if to say open up. So, I need to let him in before he forgets his manners and keeps barking. Tell Jenny and Sheri that I said hello. I'll call in a few days. I love you both. Goodbye."

Relieved to hear that Lucille had settled in to her new home, the men said their farewells and decided to have a break. Bolt grabbed two bananas from a wooden bowl he kept on top of the workshop refrigerator and tossed one to his apprentice.

"Let's take a look at that piece you've been working on," The woodcarver peeled back the sides of his banana and took a bite.

His apprentice put his snack to the side and held up a six-inch by two-inch pine with lines etched into it. "It's not much to rave about." When Anthony placed it on the work bench, he felt childish embarrassment.

"Don't worry about it, son." His mentor examined the piece and smiled reassuringly, "I see an eagle in the wood here. You've got the shape of its upright torso, and the wings are folded in like its perched on something. Getting the form of its head, beak and eyes can be a challenge, but it's there, just waiting to come out."

"I don't know, man." The apprentice shook his head and grumbled, "It's so hard to do this. I keep making too many mistakes."

"That's all part of the learning process, son." The woodcarver looked him in the eyes and smiled, "To succeed, you have to fail many times before you get it right."

Still doubting his own abilities, Anthony lowered his gaze to the bench. "You've said that before, and I want to do this, but every time I take that carving knife in my hand, I'm afraid I'll cut too much off."

"That's okay." His mentor patted the young man's shoulder, "It's good that you're aware of that fear. Now, you go beyond that negative idea here." Bolt tapped his apprentice on the forehead, then patted his chest and added, "Look deep inside and ask yourself, what is it that I want to do with this wood?"

"Well, I want to make an eagle, of course," sighed Anthony, with slight frustration, as he stared at what seemed like an amateurish attempt to make art.

"Okay," his mentor tossed a sketch pad and pencil on the workbench, "Show me what you see in that wood." Bolt opened the refrigerator and turned to him, "Looks like Sheri left us some orange juice. Do you want some?"

Anthony nodded, bit into his banana, chewed, then he began to draw with increased tension in his jaw and fingers. Observing this, Bolt poured the juice into a glass filled with ice and placed it beside the apprentice. Without a word, Anthony gripped the pencil tightly and made a harsh scratch, scratch of the lead point and abrupt swish, swish of the eraser. Then, he angrily crumpled up the paper, tossed it in the trash, and he tried again, but he seemed increasingly annoyed with himself.

"What's going on inside you, son?"

"I don't know, man," groaned the apprentice. With increased irritation in his voice, he blurted out, "I'm trying to draw."

"Okay, look at me," his mentor said softly.

Anthony focused on the woodcarver, knowing that he was about to receive another wise teaching moment, and he had better concentrate. After more than a year of his apprenticeship, he respectfully responded with his usual, "Yes sir."

"Put your pencil down and listen. You've done very well before, and you have progressed a lot. I am so proud of you. But, suddenly, you are digressing, and now you are trying too hard. You can't force it. So, what's going on inside you, son?" His mentor spoke with a sincere, steady command of the situation.

Anthony dropped the pencil on the table and felt tension in his neck. "I'll never be as good as you."

"Oh, so that's what this is about?" His mentor sighed, "This is not a competition, son. Just be yourself. Go with your own gut. You've got real talent."

The woodcarver looked intently into the young apprentice's eyes, "Now relax, take a deep breath and slowly let it out." Bolt glanced at the sketch, "Okay, now write the letter, 'T', for tense, at the top of that paper and set it to the side. Then, turn to another page and breath in and out again before you do anything else."

The apprentice obediently did as he was told, looked up and felt more at ease.

"Now, close your eyes and just enjoy the sensation of your breathing through your nostrils. Okay… exhale slowly. You're doing fine, but I need you to sit up straight," said his mentor, as he gently pressed his palm on the apprentice's mid-chest area. "Do you feel that, son?"

The apprentice kept his eyes closed and nodded with complete trust in his mentor. This compassionate, calm teaching helped him to relax and be more focused.

"Okay, that's your sternum. Keep your back straight and take another deep breath until you feel your abdomen expand." Bolt watched with approval while his pupil followed through as instructed. "That's good. Now, with your eyes closed, see that eagle coming out of your piece of wood. Take your time. Keep that slow, steady breathing." The woodcarver took his hand away and observed his student. He whispered, "This is not about me. It's what you want for yourself."

With each in and out breath, the apprentice began to feel more confident. Gradually, with his eyes still closed, an image appeared in his mind. That is such a beautiful eagle, he thought. Anthony smiled peacefully, and he felt a slight smile on his face, while tension melted away.

"Good, now, open your eyes and tell me how you feel."

"Relaxed," The apprentice opened his eyes. "What did you do? Hypnotize me?"

His mentor laughed, "No, son, all I did was guide you to that positive side of yourself. You need to ignore the enemy within that negative, self-destructive side that's been attacking you for way too long. It's time for you to see who you truly are as a human being and a great artisan in your own right."

"That's awesome, man," the apprentice shook his head in amazement. "Where did you learn that, anyway?"

"Well, I had my own doubts when I was a young artist." Bolt patted Anthony's shoulder and smiled, "Fortunately, Lucille's husband, Julian, took me under his wing, and he became my friend and mentor. He observed the same tension in me, so he taught me to be focused, and I never forgot his caring, patient support of my work as a woodcarver."

Bolt looked him in the eyes, "Now, I want you to promise me something."

"What's that?"

"Make this practice a part of your lifestyle. "Live it. Breathe it. And remember, you already have talent, and you just need to be mindful with each creative step of your artwork. Be aware that these doubts may hit you again no matter how long you perfect your skills." His mentor smiled and added, "When the time is right, I want you to pass it on to someone else. Can you do that for me?"

"I would be honored to do so, Bolt," the apprentice grinned with more confidence.

"Okay, now pick up that pencil and draw what you see in your mind and heart."

Anthony's was more relaxed, and his pencil flowed freely. Without any mental blockage, he drew easily, and the eagle appeared majestically on the paper, just the way he envisioned it. "How's that?"

"Perfect!" Bolt patted him on the back, "Now, pin those papers on the wall over there as a reminder." The woodcarver turned and studied the unfinished pinewood again, "Next, I want you to get out your carving knife and hold it gently in your hand. Don't do anything yet. Just close your eyes for a moment and breath in and out slowly and visualize that eagle wanting to show itself to you."

With his inner vision, the apprentice smiled, "I can picture it in my mind."

"Now, open your eyes and think of your carving knife as a surgeon's instrument that will bring new life to your patient. At the very top of that stub of pine, use your knife to carve out the lines of an eagle's head, eyes and beak. Focus and don't think of anything else. Go ahead and set him free, son."

The young apprentice sensed his own freedom of expression, while he relaxed and let the knife carve where it needed to go. Slowly, the bird's eyes began to form, and the rounding of the head took shape, and the student was pleased. Then, the curvature of the beak appeared, with each meticulous caress of his blade, and he was satisfied.

"Very nice," whispered his mentor, "Now, gently, respectfully set your knife on the workbench and breath in and out with gratitude for the privilege of working with your hands."

Thrilled with learning from his wise teacher, Anthony plopped his carving knife down with a clunk and grinned, "I did it, man! Look at that!"

"You sure did, son." The woodcarver laughed and paused, "There's just one thing you forgot."

"What?"

"Your carving was excellent as usual. Still, I want you to think about how you placed the knife down. Tell me, son."

The apprentice remembered, "I didn't set my knife down the way you instructed."

"That's right. Now, always remember what I'm about to tell you. Pick up the carving knife, feel it in your hand and examine the curvature of the blade with respect for this tool of the trade. Do this every single time you begin your work. Alright?"

Anthony eagerly nodded and grinned, "Okay!" He started to pick up the knife but felt his mentor's hand on his wrist. So, he looked up.

"Son, I can't stress this enough…" The woodcarver focused directly in his eyes. "You must do this every single time you begin your work. If you do exactly as I instructed, when you feel the doubts come in waves, you will be able to rise above the swells and triumph."

Bolt patted the young man's shoulder, "Okay...when you're ready, I want you to pick up your knife gently and have a grateful attitude for your ability to use your hands."

The apprentice inhaled calmly and picked up the master tool of his craft. For the first time, he examined the sharpness and curvature of the blade. Mindfully, he felt the smooth handle in his fingers, and he gently placed it in front of him with respect.

"Perfect. You're making great progress, and I'm very proud of you, son. Just remember to think positively of yourself and always maintain the utmost respect and dignity for your woodworking skills."

The apprentice grinned, "I appreciate all that you've done for me, Bolt. I promise I won't let you down."

His mentor smiled and placed his hand on the young man's shoulder. "My only concern is that you might give up and let yourself down. But, if you stick with it, son, you'll become a master woodcarver and furniture maker. You'll always have a good, honest way to make a living, and, if you love what you're doing, it won't feel like work."

Anthony nodded and eagerly stood up, "Well, our lesson is over. Shouldn't we get back to finishing that dresser?"

Bolt glanced at the clock on the wall and smiled proudly, "It's 3:00 in the afternoon already. Let's quit for the day. After your breakthrough, you deserve to do whatever you want, so go out and have some fun."

"Thanks," Anthony rushed to his locker and grabbed a bar of soap on the shelf, and he enthusiastically placed it on a counter near the deep sink. "What are you going to do?" he asked while he removed his shirt to wash himself off.

The woodcarver shrugged, "I need to make some calls to a few friends on behalf of Julian's artwork. I'll see if I can rustle up more exhibits to bring in some sales and help with Lucille's finances."

"That's good." The young man eagerly scrubbed his face, head and torso with a heavy lather of soap. Satisfied with his progress, he wanted to go celebrate.

"Oh, by the way," said the woodcarver, "I have something for you." He pulled out a small envelope from a drawer.

"What is it?" Anthony rinsed off and dried himself with a shop towel.

"Jenny gave me some photos she finally developed from last summer when we all camped and swam at Silver Lake." Bolt handed it to him.

Anthony thumbed through the pictures and laughed, "Oh, man! Look at us!" He shook his head and smiled, "We sure had a good time that weekend!"

"Yeah, I like the one with you and Sheri tossing around the ball." Bolt laughed and pointed at the photo, "See how you've changed? Take a look in the mirror on your locker door."

Anthony chuckled, as he glimpsed an image of his chubby, out-of-shape self from almost a year ago. Then, he studied his more muscular build that reflected back to him. "You're right! Thanks to you, man, I've gotten a whole lot stronger, and I feel much better now."

His mentor nodded in agreement, smiled, turned and started toward the door, "Okay, son," he gestured with his hand across his chest and sliced it in the air, "Go on. Get out of here. Enjoy yourself."

It was 4:00 that afternoon when Anthony drove up to Jenny's Café. The young man was so excited about going out and having fun that he rushed right over to Sheri while she waited on a group of eight, who were about to order. "Hey Sheri!" He ignored the crowd of people, stepped right up and greeted her impetuously, "I'm free for the night! Let's go out somewhere!"

Startled and embarrassed by Anthony's sudden intrusion in a packed restaurant, Sheri frowned and gritted her teeth, "I'm busy! Can't you see that?"

"Come on, Sheri!" Anthony forgot all manner of décor, and he rudely demanded, "Tell your Mom that you need to take some time off!"

"Stop bothering me!" Sheri brushed her hand in front of his face, "Go!" She angrily turned away and tried to focus on her customers.

"You heard the young lady!"

Anthony turned to see a large, burly man towering over him. Although he felt it would be suicidal, he wanted so much to slug this guy, but his common sense prevailed. He looked around and saw a crowd of angry people glaring at him, and he realized he had been acting like a jerk. How could he be so stupid?

Humiliated, the young man huffed and shook his head at his own undignified behavior, then stormed out of that café in a rage. Next thing he knew, he drove like a madman down the mountain without even thinking about what he was doing. By then, it was dark; and, later, he sped aimlessly through city streets.

Strangely, he became aware of how idiotic he behaved, but it was like his old ego-self had taken control, and he got lost in his own destructive melodrama. A few hours ago, he had been praised by his mentor, and he actually believed he was a much stronger person. Instead, he drove around like a depressed teenager on over-active hormones.

When Anthony turned a corner, he noticed a five-foot tall cross on top of an old dilapidated building, with a sign that read Hope Mission. A haggard group of men stood in line to get inside, and that depressed him even more.

Ahead, he spotted the blinking neon lights of a bar, and he said to himself, "What's the use? Who am I kidding? I'll never change!" So, he parked in front, opened the barroom's door and was blasted by loud rock music that was so intense he covered his ears.

Stunned, he backed away and headed toward his pickup truck. He had been so used to the peace and solitude of his refuge; it was too much to take all at once.

Just as he opened the driver's side door, he heard a sensuous female voice, "You look lost," said a woman, who stepped out of the darkness. "How can I be of service to you, honey?" She wore a skin-tight red mini skirt that revealed much of her legs and little to the imagination. On full display was her bosom that bulged out of a low neckline and advertised like a cheap airbrushed magazine cover.

This marketing ploy was nothing new for the young Vietnam veteran. As he glimpsed this ostentatious package, he remembered the streets of Saigon. There was always a heavy price for such demeaning merchandise, as this, and many of his buddies had suffered the sickening consequences. You pay to play and lose your humanity.

"Sorry, not interested, I'm heading back home."

Her seductive voice whispered, "You don't know what you're missing, honey."

Aware of the trap, Anthony ignored her siren's song and drove up the mountain. Cool, refreshing air blew in his open window, and he thought of the foibles of mankind. Raw, barebones sadness settled over him, as the faces of people flashed in his mind.

Clearly, he saw the hungry look of the temptress, and he had an epiphany. This woman was a human being, who desperately needed a way out of her own personal hell.

Where did this awakening come from? It had to be Grammy's influence. She planted a seed of unconditional love and acceptance. Now, her virtuous compassion had grown in him to where he looked at people differently for the first time in his life.

Anthony parked his truck next to the workshop almost an hour later. The living room light was on at the cabin, and he just could not bring himself to go back inside. Still irritated about his own foolishness and unsure of what to do with himself, he sneaked over to the shop. He glanced at the home, saw no movement and hoped that Bolt did not notice.

Sullen, Anthony turned on the light, then he quietly strolled over to his workbench. There, he felt completely at ease, and all he wanted was to practice his carving skills in solitude. With a knife handle in his hands, the apprentice guided the blade along the grain of the same pinewood piece he was working on earlier that day. His mentor's previous instructions guided him to trust his own instincts, and he shaped the eagle's head on that malleable material. These soothing moments were so satisfying that he was not aware of anything else.

To his right, the metal shop door clunked loudly and startled him out of his concentration. This caused a knee-jerk reaction, and he dropped his knife.

"You alright, son?" asked Bolt. "Sheri called twice already. She sounded worried."

"Uh, yeah," Anthony looked up from his carving and sighed, "I wanted to practice on this wood more. What do you think?"

His mentor examined it with keen interest. "Let's see…the lines are very well defined on the eagle's breast, and I like how you revealed the natural curvature of its beak. I'm pleased with it, son."

"Thanks," the apprentice gazed at his piece and was about to say something when the annoying ring of the telephone intruded on his concentration.

Bolt picked it up and answered, "Hello. Oh, hi Sheri. Yep, he's here."

"Tell her I'll call back," Anthony picked up his knife and tried to appear that he was engrossed in his work.

The woodcarver frowned and spoke in the phone again, "Sorry, Sheri, he can't come to the phone yet. He'll call back soon."

Bolt put the receiver down and shook his head with displeasure, "Okay, son, what's going on?"

Anthony sighed and carefully set his knife on the bench, "I messed up, man. I acted like a jerk when I asked Sheri to go out with me while she was busy working. What's worse is that everybody watched me make a complete fool of myself." He slapped his forehead, "How could I be so stupid?"

Bolt chuckled, "Oh, I thought you robbed the place," he said with a light-hearted teasing grin.

"Come on, man!" Anthony stood up and paced the floor, "It's not funny."

"Alright, let's be serious then," Bolt stood and leaned against the workbench with his arms crossed. "You made a fool of yourself and now you're too embarrassed, so you'll hide in here like a whiny puppy, feeling sorry for yourself. Is that it?" His mentor pretended to play an imaginary violin and stuck out his lower lip.

Anthony glanced at his clownish expression and tried not to laugh. "Come on, Bolt," he shook his head and let out a controlled chuckle.

"Did you ever stop to think how Sheri feels?" Bolt glared sternly, "Truth is, that poor girl already told me, but I was waiting to hear it from you, son. You were so out of character that she could no longer concentrate on her work, and she worried about you."

"Sorry, man".

"Don't tell me, son," Bolt spoke with increased firmness, then picked up the phone and gestured to the young man.

Anthony took it, dialed the number and blew out a deep sigh, "Hello, Sheri, it's me, your village idiot. What? Yeah, I'm fine. I'm sorry for my rude behavior. Will you forgive me? Oh, thanks, Sheri. Uh, you get off at 4:30 tomorrow afternoon? Uh, hu…um…yeah, sure, that'd be nice. See you then. Bye."

Anthony hung up the phone and looked at Bolt, "Can you believe that? She forgave me, and she still wants to go out. She was more worried than upset."

"That girl has a lot of spunk!" Bolt laughed, "She sure knows what she wants; and she's downright crazy about you!"

"Ah man don't even think it! I'm so messed up that, if I got involved, I would only hurt Sheri." Anthony groaned and rubbed his forehead, "I never want to do her any harm! I'd rather die first!"

"Well, that's a bit melodramatic. Besides, you're not as bad as you think you are, young fella. What you need to understand is that Sheri is sharp, and she cares deeply about the needs of others."

"I know, and that's what I admire about her."

"Sheri's also stubborn. I was there the day that girl was born, and she burst out kicking and screaming in the backseat of her parent's car. She shot into this world so fast that we couldn't get her to the hospital in time. I watched her grow up, and I know that when she makes up her mind, there's nothing you can do about it." He laughed, "Unless you run off like a skittish mule."

"Well, I'm not scared of her, if that's what you mean," Anthony sighed and carved with his knife again. Finally, he looked at his mentor and frowned, "I'm more worried that I'll do something really stupid. Like I said, I don't want to do anything to hurt Sheri."

Anthony looked at the carving, "I actually like her feistiness." He gently scraped the wood with sandpaper and blew the dust away. "In fact, I like her a lot."

"Have you told her?"

"Nah," Anthony shrugged and carved another line on the eagle's wing, "Why should I?"

His mentor came alongside and examined his work. "Looks good, son. Now, if you put as much effort in your love life as your work, you might have a chance to be truly happy."

"You're right, as usual," Anthony set his piece down. "It's time that I make things right."

19 Get it Right

A watch on Anthony's wrist had the time of 5:00 p.m. when he arrived at Jenny's Café. He was determined to not louse up his first official date with Sheri. Expecting to see angry customers glaring at him, after his rude behavior the night before, he felt relief when nobody seemed to notice when he walked in.

Jenny greeted him with her usual smile and a hug. "Hi, Anthony, have a seat. Sheri just got off work, and she's getting ready in our cabin out back. Coffee?"

"Yep, thanks," Anthony sat at the counter and looked around the busy café. A cacophony of clanging dishes and boisterous voices invaded his ears.

"Here you go, honey," she placed a steaming cup in front of him.

"Uh, Jenny," Anthony looked up sheepishly, "Sorry about last night."

Jenny waved a hand in the air and smiled, "Don't worry about it, honey." She chuckled, "You just livened up the place, that's all."

Anthony nervously waited and kept looking at his watch, as he drank one cup of coffee, then another. Minutes passed slowly, and he constantly glanced at the time—it ticked 5:30, 5:40 and 5:50. What's taking her so long, he wondered.

Finally, it dawned on him that this was exactly what happened whenever he took out his late wife, Amy. Of course, that was the cardinal rule for a man to wait and wait for his date. He chuckled at the poetic humor of his own restless thoughts and stared at his watch again.

By 6:00, Anthony was rewarded for his patience by a stunning young lady that sauntered graciously into the room. Surprised by her unusual elegance, his eyes widened, and he gazed upon Sheri, while her long raven hair flowed like a veil down her lower back. Sparkling silver earrings dangled and swayed in a graceful tick, tock movement, as she strolled toward him. She wore a lovely turquoise stone that nestled pleasingly in a V-shaped neckline of her blue dress.

It was obvious to Anthony that Sheri put a lot of thought in what she wore for their night out, and he was pleased. She seemed to know precisely how to dress, in a manner, that revealed her smooth, youthful flesh without being ostentatious. Her shoulders were slightly covered by two inches of ruffles, and she left just enough to the imagination.

"Wow! Sheri, you are gorgeous!" Anthony stood up and stared with such approbation, that he felt breathless with awe.

"Thank you," Sheri humbly smiled. "Sorry to keep you waiting so long. I guess I'm not used to dressing up, being a country girl and all."

"Sheri, you are the most beautiful country girl I have ever seen," Anthony was so euphoric that he almost felt light-headed with delight.

Jenny came over and hugged her daughter, "Oh, you look lovely," she smiled, "I can't remember the last time you wore a pretty dress. Okay, have fun tonight." She kissed Anthony on his cheek. "I trust you to bring her home safely, dear."

"I'll take good care of Sheri," Anthony smiled. "I promise."

Sheri kissed his cheek. "I know you wanted to surprise me with a drive down the mountain to the city but where are you taking me?"

"Well, first we have reservations at the Viva Senorita's Restaurant on main street. I remembered you told me that you liked Mexican food. It has a nice ambience there."

"Oh," Sheri giggled and smiled, "Now, you're trying to impress me with a fancy word like ambience." Her voice was breathy, as she pronounced each syllable.

Anthony held up his palm and grinned, "I confess that I had no idea what it meant until I called Lucille for advice on how to talk like I had some kind of education. You like it?"

Sheri nodded with a giggle, "I like it."

"Oh, after dinner, we'll stroll along the river walk and enjoy those fancy lights that reflect on the water." Anthony glanced at his watch, "It's getting late. We better go."

Anthony held her hand, and they both strolled outside. To the young man, it all had to be a perfect night out, even at the risk of being chivalrously corny. So, he led Sheri to the passenger side, opened the door, and he bowed with a wave of his arm, "My lady."

"Well, this is different," she said with a lovely smile. "I'm used to us getting in and out like two buddies at a work site," Sheri laughed and gracefully turned her legs to slip into the seat, while revealing just enough of her smooth flesh above her knees.

She watched Anthony, as he rushed to the driver's side and got in. "Oh, this is nice. I've never seen your pickup truck look so shiny. And, you are being such a gentleman." She kissed his cheek, "Thank you for making it a special evening together."

"You are welcome, my lady," he grinned.

Sheri laughed and leaned closer, "You keep calling me lady. Okay, what did you do with the caveman Tony that I know?"

Anthony smiled, turned the key and started the engine, "He's off for the evening."

Later, Anthony drove as close to the entrance of the Viva Senorita Restaurant as he could, then got out and opened Sheri's door. With a bow, he said, "My lady, may I have the honor of escorting you to dinner?"

She held out her hand and playfully acted like royalty, "You may."

They strolled arm in arm into an extravagant atrium with a myriad of exotic flowers in waist-tall decorative ceramic pots. Sheri sniffed and smiled happily, "Oh it smells wonderful in here." Several fountains gave it a cool airy feel and the flow of water was soothing to both of them. She leaned in and whispered in his ear, "This is so nice."

Anthony nodded and smiled with satisfaction. It was just as he hoped it would be since he drove here earlier to set up all the details in advance. At the elaborately designed archway, the restaurant opened wide to numerous private booths and circular tables. Well-dressed Mariachi strolled, played and sang throughout the establishment, and the young man glimpsed the delighted expression of his date.

At a podium, the Maître d greeted them with a handsome smile, nodded and said, "Welcome, Senor Lorenzo. We have been expecting you and your lovely lady." While still focused on the couple, he snapped his fingers and a gentleman waiter escorted them to a private booth.

Sheri slid into one side and Anthony sat across from her in order to be face to face. This was ideal since he could admire her every gesture as they dined together. For a moment, they just gazed at each other until he realized that the waiter said something. He looked up to see the server leaning toward him. "Yes?" asked Anthony.

"Si, Senor Lorenzo. As I was saying, I am Miquel. It is my honor to serve you and the senorita this evening." Miquel waved and someone brought glasses of water, but Anthony did not notice, for his eyes only saw Sheri's beautiful face. Menus were placed before them, and he heard what sounded like the waiter said he would return.

Somewhere in the background, music played, people talked, laughed, and yet all the transfixed young man focused on was his lady across the table. He had dated many girls in high school and fell in love with his late wife, but now this was different. It seemed like he could not move. Perhaps he put too much into this, and it had to be wild infatuation.

"It's so amazing," Sheri spoke breathlessly. "Everything is so perfect. Even the maître d recognized you immediately." Sheri leaned closer and grinned playfully, "Oh, I get it. You live a secret life and you've been here many times with other women. Is that it?"

"How did you know?" Anthony teased. He had no intention of admitting that he had been here earlier, and he even slipped a $50-dollar-bill to the host as a way of guaranteeing flawless service. Nor did he want Sheri to know that his crazy gesture cost him a half-week's pay. If anything did go wrong, it be would his own doing, and he worried about the possibility while all went smoothly so far.

After two hours of dining and enjoying the evening with his date, Anthony was pleased with himself, as he drove Sheri to the river walk. Before they arrived, he noticed a large fountain with red, blue and green lights that shined on the water at a downtown park. "Cool," he turned over and parked, "Let's go see that first."

It was the perfect place to stroll with his date on this romantic night out. Numerous couples and families, with their children, stood around and admired the magnificent aquatic display. So, Anthony and Sheri sat on a bench and observed the dancing colorful waterfalls.

To his surprise, what entertained them the most was the chaotic running, laughing and playing of children. Never before had he experienced so much fun watching little kids as they bounced off each other. He was even more pleased to see Sheri's delighted expression, and she giggled happily. Nothing could go wrong now, he thought.

Then, it happened. Brakes screeched in the middle of a busy street. Startled, Anthony looked, just when a car swerved around a fallen man. The enraged driver swore obscenities and drove off. A woman screamed next to the victim, dropped to her knees and cried out, "Help me!" She desperately hugged him, "Oh, please, Johnny! Don't die! Please God!"

Without thinking, Anthony Lorenzo's medic training kicked in, and he leaped to his feet. "Wait here!" He glanced at Sheri.

Lorenzo sprinted through busy traffic to help and almost got side-swiped. Drivers slammed on their brakes; cars swerved in all directions. A large man stopped and signaled about the danger ahead. Cars halted. Another guy leapt out of his car and tried to lift up the fallen pedestrian. He kept struggling, but the victim slid out of his arms.

"I'm a medic," Lorenzo tapped the good Samaritan's shoulder. "I'll take it from here. Thanks."

The man smiled and nodded. "I'm glad you're here. I got a bad back."

"That's okay. You did what you could."

"I'll help direct the traffic." He turned and waved at cars to go around.

Lorenzo knelt beside the fallen pedestrian. "Are you hurt?"

"Nah, I just slipped. Where's my cane?" Tipsy, he tried to stand, but spun around in confusion, then fell into the young veteran's arms.

The woman cried. "Come on, Johnny. Get up!"

Another man rushed to his side. "How can I help?"

"Take her hand." Lorenzo glanced at the distraught lady. "Come on, let's get them off the road." The medic lifted the victim on his shoulders, just as he had done many times in combat, then he darted between cars to the sidewalk.

Once they made it to a patch of grass, a woman driver yelled, "Let's go, honey. We don't want to miss our flight."

"Okay," the volunteer helper waved, rushed back to his car, and they drove away.

Vehicles started moving again while Lorenzo examined the victim's eyelids. Abruptly, the man sat up, pushed his hand away and yelled, "I'm okay! Leave me alone!"

"Johnny!" The woman knelt and hugged her him. "Don't do that! He just saved your life!"

Lorenzo noticed that the man wore a tattered Army fatigue shirt with corporal's stripes, and he wore a dog tag with a name, Hobbs, on it. "Calm down, I'm here to help."

The man groaned, "Don't bother! I'm not worth it!"

The medic compassionately tapped him on the shoulder and tried to assure him, "You're Johnny Hobbs, aren't you? My name is Anthony Lorenzo. Are you hurt?"

"How'd you know my name?" asked Hobbs.

Lorenzo smiled reassuringly and pointed to the tags dangling from his chest, "That's your name, isn't it?"

Hobbs coughed and tried to stand up but plopped on his rear again. "So, what!"

Lorenzo glanced at the corporal stripes and asked, "Where'd you serve, Johnny?

"I fought in Nam! Who cares? Most of my buddies are dead! And what did that get me? A purple heart! That's it, man! I can't get a job! I can't take care of my woman! I can't even take care of myself!"

Lorenzo looked at the woman and smiled, "You must be Johnny's lady."

Sheri rushed over to her and asked, "What's your name, honey?"

The woman looked up with a surprised expression and grinned, "Nobody ever called me lady before. I'm Rosie," she said with a nervous giggle. "Johnny's my husband. I'm his wife," she nervously giggled and proudly announced their bond as a married couple.

"My name is Sheri. We're here to help you."

Lorenzo examined Johnny's swollen red face, filthy hands and noticed that he had no shoes for his dirty feet. "Were you hit by that car?"

"Nah, I'm okay."

"Can you stand up?"

"Yeah, but I need my cane to get around. I got a bum knee."

"Let's get you over to the park bench." The medic helped Johnny up and sat him down. "Okay, take it easy."

He looked back to see how the women were doing. "We'll get your lady over in a minute."

"Come on, Rosie." Sheri took her hand, and, just as they stood up, Rosie slipped on wet grass, stumbled backward, then reached for anything to catch herself. This caused a chain of mishaps, as the woman grabbed Sheri's arm, and they both tumbled to the sidewalk. Sheri struggled to get Rosie and herself off the grimy surface but she scraped her knees, and her blue dress was badly soiled by dirt and grime until they managed to right themselves.

Yet, Sheri remained calm, and she put her arm around the woman's waist to keep their balance. "You okay, hon?"

"Yes," Rosie's eyes widened, "Oh, I'm sorry I messed up your pretty dress!"

Johnny sat on the bench, while Rosie plopped down and snuggled with her man. They both reeked from an obvious lack of hygiene. Anthony and Sheri faced them, stood side by side together, took stock of this bizarre situation and wondered what to do next. Sadly, the young vet noticed Sheri's tarnished dress, and he thought that was it. He just ruined his first official date with this lovely lady, and she will never want to date him again.

To Anthony's surprise, she smiled and squeezed his hand, "Well, what do we do now, Tony?"

The young man looked deeply into her reassuring eyes and brushed back her raven hair. "Sorry, sweetie, I really wanted our date to be special."

Sheri wrapped her arm around his waist while he stroked her face. "We're in this together, no matter what. They both examined the pathetic, lost souls in front of them and Sheri said, "Well, we can't just leave them like this."

The medic sighed and nodded, "You're right." In that moment of observing Johnny Hobbs, the young vet saw himself sitting there, and he vividly remembered his own experience of despair and self-destructiveness. Tears welled up in his eyes, and he was struck with empathy and compassion for this fellow Vietnam War Veteran—a brother in desperate need of his help.

People walked by, stared and gossiped, but they were in their own little worlds, and this was his reality. It was up to Anthony to do something. In that brief moment, he felt Sheri's arm in his, and he knew that this caring lady would stand by him.

So, with his aching heart wide open to Johnny Hobbs, the medic leaned in and asked, "Where do you live?"

An angry voice from behind him yelled, "Don't mess with that baby killer! He's nothing but trash, man!"

The medic ignored it and calmly held out a hand to his brother. "Come, Johnny, let's get you and Rosie home."

Former Army corporal Hobbs just lowered his head in shame, but his woman looked up and smiled like everything was okay, "Me and Johnny sleep on cardboard behind the museum over there." She pointed to a building across the street.

For the first time, Anthony and Sheri had a good look at Rosie's grimy face. The poor woman's short hair was all matted and she constantly scratched her head. She wore a ragged green sweater over a baggy ankle-length dress that appeared to be too big for her. Her left foot had a beat-up red tennis shoe. On the right, her toes protruded through an under-sized indescribable brown shoe.

Anthony and Sheri gazed into each other's eyes, and they had a mutual awareness that meshed into one overriding thought. Through all that ugliness, they numinously awakened to Rosie's ethereal beauty inside.

Something miraculous had taken place in their hearts, and it was beyond any mortal comprehension. They both noticed how the homeless woman leaned closer to her man. It was as though this malnourished couple was magnetically attached to each other.

By looking ever deeper, Anthony saw that they were like anyone else. As husband and wife, they were loving human beings with a desire to be happy and thrive in life. They were not like the trashy cardboard they had to sleep on in a back alley.

Sure, they were ugly in the sight of the more fortunate. But, Lorenzo sensed that Johnny and Rosie had a story to tell, and they were people that fell on hard times. Under similar circumstances, Anthony and Sheri could get kicked into the dirt and have a hell of a time to get back up.

The war vet knew what it was like to fall flat on his face. He also experienced the unconditional love of others, who helped him to get back up and live fully with dignity.

As he pondered his next move, he had a clear inner vision of the Eagle in his mind. It circled with such majesty and splendor overhead, and it called out to him. He saw the Watchman, who reached out and touched him with an energy to keep going and not give up. Anthony felt he had been given a second chance to make things right in his life. As a result, he felt spiritually stronger than ever before.

Naturally it felt right to reach out and give this couple an opportunity to rise above their despair. With the medic's heart wide open, he looked at his date for the evening, and this stirred his compassion even more.

Sheri tried to keep herself together, but tears streamed down her face in empathy for these human beings. "Oh, Tony," she sniffed and gazed at him with pleading, moist eyes, "We have to help them."

Anthony wiped the tears from her cheeks with his thumb, "I know, sweetie." He drew her closer and put aside his desire for a perfect night out. "Are you ready?"

"Yes," Sheri smiled, as a park lamp revealed streaks of dirt on her face, "I'm ready."

Anthony looked at the couple and humbly asked, "How can we help you two?"

20 Wild Night Out

Rosie looked up from that dirty park bench and smiled. "Thank you for asking how you can help," she snuggled closer to her weary husband, "I've been praying for a miracle but Johnny doesn't believe in it. So, I just don't know what to do."

"When was the last time you two had anything to eat," asked Sheri.

"Oh, last night we found some fries and half a burger in the dumpster," Rosie placed her arm on her husband's shoulder. "Ain't that right, Johnny."

Sheri reached out to Rosie and asked, "Would you like to have dinner with us someplace nearby?"

Rosie smiled, eagerly took Sheri's hand and said, "Oh, we'd sure like that."

She nudged against her husband's shoulder and chuckled, "Right, Johnny?"

Hobbs looked up with a lost, pathetic expression of hopelessness, "We'd like to eat, but we got no money, man."

"It's on us," the medic helped Johnny to his feet. "Let's get some chow." He glanced at a place across the street, "Come on, I'll help you walk over to Mack's Take Out." To provide a sense of dignity, he added, "Maybe you can buy us lunch another day."

Sheri guided Rosie and all four managed to struggle over to the street corner. While Lorenzo observed the red light, he said, "This time we'll go through the cross walk." When it changed to green, they worked their way to the other side.

For a moment, he stopped, watched the uncaring drivers, sighed and said, "Johnny, do me a favor. Next time, don't go running out in the middle of traffic."

At the take-out stand, Rosie and Johnny plopped down on outside chairs while looking haggard and hungry. Moments later, Anthony and Sheri brought a bag of burgers with fries, and they carried two sodas. They placed everything on a round metal table in front of the emaciated couple.

Immediately, Rosie took out the food, served one for Johnny, then another for herself. She stopped and looked up, "Oh dear, where's your food?"

Impressed by Rosie's thoughtful concern, Anthony pulled out a chair for Sheri, sat down beside her and nodded, "We already ate. Go ahead, help yourselves."

Rosie smiled, "Thank you for being so kind to us." She opened the wrapper and gave it to her man, "Come on, Johnny, you need to eat, honey." She patiently waited to make sure he started first.

Anthony and Sheri observed Rosie's sincere maternal affections for her man but Johnny seemed so down-trodden. Finally, he looked up sheepishly at his woman, took a bite of his hamburger and slowly chewed. It was only after he began to eat that Rosie nodded with satisfaction. She slowly ate with an admirable sense of grace and dignity for a homeless person on the street.

"How long have you been together?" asked Anthony.

Rosie sipped from a soda straw and looked up with a smile, "Oh, me and Johnny met in Chicago about three years ago." She bit into the burger and chewed slowly.

Sheri leaned in with interest, "How did you meet?"

For the first time, Johnny perked up and grinned with a little spark of joy, "We bumped into each other inside a grocery store. When our carts banged together, our eyes met, and it was love at first sight, man."

Rosie giggled and rubbed his scruffy beard, "Yeah, I couldn't resist his puppy dog eyes."

"How did you wind up here?" Realizing there was a story unfolding, Anthony leaned forward with increased curiosity.

Johnny looked at Rosie and seemed to have a twinkle in his eyes, "We both had good jobs after we graduated from high school. I worked as a welder for a construction company and made good wages."

Rosie kept her gaze on him, "I always liked helping people, and I enjoyed my job as a waitress at a nice restaurant downtown. At night, I took nursing classes, and I hoped to serve in a hospital someday. When Johnny asked me to marry him, I was so excited to be his wife, but my parents wanted us to wait another year. So, we eloped. We were very happy in our little one-bedroom apartment. It was really nice."

Johnny frowned with a look of increased sobriety, or perhaps it was unadulterated rage. "It all went to hell when I got drafted, man," he huffed and his eyes glared wildly like a bull with no place to charge.

Anthony nodded, "I hear you, man. It happened to me too."

Johnny's expression softened, and he focused steadily at Anthony, "I wanted to do my duty but, like so many guys, I was confused. I really wanted to believe that our country could do no wrong, so I did what I was told. You know what I mean?"

The medic nodded with understanding again, "Yeah, I sure do, man."

Rosie squeezed Johnny's hand, "When he came back with a purple heart and a shattered leg, he couldn't get a job." Rosie choked up and tears dribbled down her cheeks.

"It's okay, hon," Sheri leaned closer and rubbed Rosie's arm, "Go on."

"Well…it's hard to talk about," Rosie glanced at Johnny's tense features and patted his tight-fisted right hand. "You see…my boss demanded that I stay late and help him with closing one night."

Her sad eyes glistened like rocks below a waterfall, and she patted her moist cheek with a napkin. Determined to talk more, she cleared her throat and it finally gushed out. "He…he tried to force himself on me and tore my dress, then I ran away! I was so scared that I never went back!" Rosie began to cry.

Johnny tried to comfort his wife and held her close. "I wanted to beat him up bad! But he wasn't worth me going to jail! I had to take care of Rosie! With both of us out of work, we couldn't afford our rent, and we were evicted. Her mom and dad were struggling financially, and my parents were bitterly divorced. We tried to sleep in our car, but it snowed. So, we drove out here and hoped to make a fresh start. Our car broke down, and the city towed it away with all our stuff inside. We had to hock everything, just to survive, but we still wound up living on the street."

Anthony noticed that both of them wore twine around their ring fingers and nodded, "Is that why you're wearing those?" He pointed to their tightly-held hands.

Suddenly, their expressions changed, and they looked into each other's eyes with an obvious deep affection that only true lovers will ever comprehend. Johnny kept his complete focus on Rosie, "No matter what happens, we are husband and wife."

Rosie did not even blink, "I am his. He is mine."

Anthony glanced at Sheri, as she tried to hold back tears. In that moment, he knew that he had to be the one to speak about the practical side of this love story. "Well, you can't live in squalor forever, man. There's got to be a way out."

Johnny looked at him with surprise, "Don't you get it? We hit bottom, and we're neck-deep in the gutter! What do you expect us to do, man?"

"Hey! I got it!" Anthony stood up with increasing irritation at their plight, "You both hit bottom. So, is this where you want to be?"

"No…" Johnny's voice lowered, and he turned away with a hopeless look of shame, "But…"

Anthony shook his head and let out a deep sigh, "I understand what you are going through," he interrupted. I also know that you are better than this, man!" He held out an open hand to Rosie, "Look at your wife! She deserves to be treated with dignity, and so do you, Johnny! You hit bottom, right? So, you can stay there or work your way back up! You are good people!"

Sheri gripped Anthony's arm, "I think what Tony is trying to say is that you still have a choice." She looked seriously at the couple, "We don't mean to sound judgmental. Toni and I both know that under similar circumstances, we could wind up the same way. But, it's time to ask yourselves, do we want to live like this? Yes or no?"

Johnny and Rosie looked at each other and they both said, "No, of course not."

Anthony sighed again, "Okay, I believe you. It's not going to be easy. But, if you are willing to work at it, we'll help in whatever way we can."

Rosie smiled and patted her husband's chest. "Johnny needs a job, and he'll be okay."

"You need to survive first." Anthony glanced down the street, "There's a mission a few blocks away. Let's see if we can get you cleaned up and in temporary shelter for the night. We'll figure out the rest tomorrow."

"Why are you trying to help us, man?" asked Johnny.

Anthony smiled, "I hit bottom once, and a friend helped me out of that pit. I wanted to repay him in some way, but he just said that I should pass on a good turn to the next person in need. So, that's exactly what I intend to do."

Johnny shook his head with concern, "We appreciate your help, but I don't think we can get in the mission this late at night."

Rosie nudged him, "Come on, Johnny, have faith, honey."

Sheri chuckled and placed her hand in Rosie's palm, "Yes, we all need it."

Anthony reached out, "Well, I'm not much for praying out loud, but how about we join hands and stick with Rosie's faith? She's got enough to go around for all of us."

It seemed natural that everyone huddled quietly. So, Anthony paused, then spoke simply and from the heart, "We ask that Johnny and Rosie get shelter tonight. Also, please help them to find work and a decent home to live in. Thank you, God."

When the couples walked up to the mission's door, Johnny limped over with the medic's help and was apprehensive. "I don't think they'll let us in now. They've turned us down because there was no room before."

Rosie optimistically smiled, "They will, Johnny." She kissed her husband's cheek and assured him, "You just need to trust in God, honey."

Although Anthony had his doubts, he knocked and waited, not knowing what to expect. He knocked again and prayed in his heart, please God, open up to this desperate couple in need. He knocked and waited for the third time.

Finally, the big wooden door opened wide, and a tall man appeared with a welcoming smile. "Hello," he greeted them warmly, "My name is Pastor Gabe. May I help you?"

The young vet reached out his hand with relief. "My name is Anthony Lorenzo, a former Army medic. May we come in? My friends need help."

Pastor Gabe smiled kindly and shook his hand. "Yes, please join me. I think you could be the answer to my prayers." There was something about his eyes that seemed familiar to Anthony, but he did not know why.

They stepped into a dimly lit entryway, and the pastor said, "Let's go into my office, and we can get acquainted."

While they all entered in silence, Anthony noticed the room was well-lit, orderly and the walls had oil paintings of mountain peaks. Pastor Gabe stepped behind a simple wooden desk and sat in a swivel chair. He leaned forward with his big arms outstretched in front of him. His palms relaxed in what appeared to be a gesture of open-heartedness, and he had a calm, assuring smile.

Without a word, he waited until the two couples entered and stood near the doorway. He spoke softly, "I'm happy to see you all here this evening. Before we continue, Anthony, would you please close my office door, so we don't wake anyone? Thank you, Brother."

Anthony did so, and he was about to speak when Pastor Gabe said, "Have a seat." He pointed to some folding chairs stacked alongside a metal file cabinet. "Go ahead and get those out. Now, let's all sit together and talk as friends."

When they were seated, Pastor Gabe smiled, "You must be the ones I prayed for tonight."

Surprised by this announcement, Anthony said, "Well, we also did some praying." He turned and introduced Sheri and added, "We came to get help for our friends, Johnny and Rosie here."

"Perfect," Pastor Gabe smiled warmly again, "You prayed. I prayed. You need help. I need help. So, let's work on a plan together."

Rosie hugged her husband, "See, Johnny, everything will be fine."

"Ah, yes," Pastor Gabe chuckled, "You are Rosie, alright." His eyes seemed to twinkle with delight. "You are the rose, the blooming of optimistic wonder. God sent the very person I requested for our mission."

"Well, I have no idea what you're talking about, sir," Johnny glared pessimistically, "We just need to have shelter for the night."

"Of course, you shall, brother John, the blessed one," said the minister. "Let me explain. Recently, our husband and wife team were transferred to another assignment, and I'm in urgent need of replacements."

Anthony laughed with relief and surprise, "Wow! This is nothing like what we expected."

Pastor Gabe grinned, "Now, there's stalwart brother Anthony. You remind me of Anthony, the Great, the wise monk, who went into the wilderness on his quest for truth."

Rosie smiled and leaned forward in her chair, "We would be happy to help in any way we can, Pastor Gabe." She turned to her husband, "Right, Johnny?"

"Alright, honey," Johnny frowned suspiciously, "Don't get too excited. Let's find out what this is all about first."

"It's simple," said Pastor Gabe. "John, I need you to manage the men's section down the hall. Rose, I need you to care for the women's area. You both will make sure that all our guests have fresh towels, soap, toiletries and a change of clothes. Together you will run the kitchen operations during the service of our meals. For now, it's late. Let's get you both cleaned up and we'll provide you with a change of clothes and your own private staff bedroom to sleep in."

Rosie gushed with excitement and hugged her husband, "You hear that, Johnny? We can sleep in our own room tonight!"

Pastor Gabe chuckled and shrugged with humility. "Well, it's not much, but it will be comfortable. If you want the job, you'll receive a salary, three meals a day and a simple place to live. So, think about it and let me know in the morning."

"We don't to have wait!" Johnny leaped to his feet with renewed enthusiasm, "We accept!"

"Good, let's get started." Pastor Gabe stood up, opened a storeroom door and pointed, "As you can see, we have donated clothes in here. You two pick out something to wear. Anthony, you hold John's clean apparel; Sheri, you're in charge of Rosie's items. While you get what is needed, I'll round up soap and towels. When you're ready, just follow me to the men's and women's showers."

Moments later, Pastor Gabe led them first to the door of a lady's section. He smiled warmly at Rosie, and he handed her a bar of soap and wash cloth. "Here, Sister Rose, you take this for your shower." He turned and smiled at Sheri and said, "Hold this towel for her. When you two are done, please return to my office. Thank you, ladies."

Further down the hall, Pastor Gabe explained the same protocol to the men, and he left. Everyone had a sense of excitement and anticipation, as Johnny and Rosie had their first shower in more than a month. Anthony and Sheri expressed relief and satisfaction to know that their new friends would have a chance to be clean and secure again. Eagerly, they all hurried back to the office to learn more about the possibilities ahead.

Upon entering the room, Anthony was surprised to see that Pastor Gabe busily folded small pieces of paper on his desk. Remembering a brief tour in Japan, before Vietnam, the young vet recognized it as the art of origami. He was delighted to observe four figures in the shapes of eagles.

While everyone took their seats, Anthony grinned and glanced at the desktop, "I see you're familiar with origami."

Pastor Gabe precisely folded the last piece and smiled with a mild sense of accomplishment, "Yes, it's a hobby of mine." He handed each person a three-inch-tall paper eagle, "Here, please accept these humble gifts as a blessing for all of you to have good health. May your hearts be filled with peace.

"Thank you." Deeply moved by this simple, honorable presentation, Anthony asked, "What inspired you to do this?"

"Well…" Pastor Gabe looked up and seemed to be in deep thought, "Many years ago, I was called to the bedside of a dying 12-year-old girl in Hiroshima. Before she passed away, I had a chance to witness her strength of character, and she taught me to fold paper into origami. She was such a precious child, and I make these in honor of her memory whenever I can. For me, it is my humble demonstration of prayerfully asking God to give each of you a peaceful heart and long life."

Johnny Hobbs frowned and angrily blurted out, "How can I ever have a peaceful heart knowing that I was the only one to survive an ambush that wiped out my platoon? I should have died with them!"

Pastor Gabe's expression changed, and his eyes reddened with a look of empathy. He stood up and faced the broken Vietnam Veteran, "I am deeply saddened for you, my friend." The pastor placed a hand over the man's heart, "You have been wounded badly here in your soul." He pressed his thumb on Johnny's chest. "This will help to soothe you, Brother John."

Immediately, Johnny inhaled air, as though he was breathing for the first time since his tragedy. His body jerked backwards like he had been shocked by a powerful jolt of electricity. His eyelids blinked and opened wide with a look of awakening in his spirit.

"What just happened?" Johnny's countenance seemed brighter, and he chuckled joyously.

"You have been given a second chance, brother John." Pastor Gabe embraced him compassionately, "Of course, this feeling you have will gradually wear off, but it'll be up to you to revitalize yourself through daily prayer and hard work."

Just then, Anthony's eyes widened with awareness and he laughed, "Hey! I know you! Now I understand. You are the Watchman! It all makes sense now!"

Pastor Gabe shrugged, "We are all watchers and stewards of our fellow men. No one can stand alone, for we are all interconnected in this fragile world. We each must listen to the call of the eagle and do whatever we can to support the other."

"That's right, Anthony!" exclaimed Rosie. "You saw our need for shelter, and you helped us when no one even bothered to look at us!"

"Well, I think we've done enough for one night," Pastor Gabe waved a hand in the air. "Brother John, why don't you and Rosie get some rest? You'll have a busy day tomorrow."

Johnny chuckled and his eyes sparkled, "Thank you, Pastor Gabe, I think we will. Come on, honey."

Rosie hugged Sheri, and she reached out to Anthony. "Thank you for everything. Will we see you again?"

Anthony hugged her, then he did the same with John. "Yes, of course, we'd like that very much."

Pastor Gabe laughed and opened his arms wide, "Ah, yes, now for a five-person huddle." Magnetically, everyone joined in a group hug. At that moment, Anthony realized that the Watchman was a giant of a man, and his massive arms embraced them so affectionately that all were content to linger under his protection.

"Here's the game plan," he grinned playfully. "John, you grab the ball, and Rose, you go after him and make a pass in your room. Anthony, you lead off with Sheri and get on home. Now, break!" He beamed with satisfaction about his own silly performance. "I always wanted to say that."

It was after 2:00 a.m. when Anthony brought Sheri home, and they stood outside the front door. For a moment, they gazed into each other's eyes, then Sheri said, "Well, that was a wild night out."

Anthony looked at Sheri's badly soiled dress and sighed, "I am so sorry for the mess I made." He tried to wipe a dirty streak from her cheek with his thumb. "I wanted our first date to be perfect. Now, I wouldn't be surprised if you refused to go out with me again."

Sheri giggled and patted him on the chest, "Oh, you are not going to get rid of me that easily. I'll admit it wasn't the kind of date I expected but it was definitely an adventure I'll never forget."

"You mean…" he chuckled, "You actually want to date after all I put you through?"

"Of course," Sheri gave him a quick kiss and gazed into his eyes again, "Besides, we see each other at the café and around Bolt's place anyway. We've done a lot together this past year, and I'd like us to go beyond this buddy, buddy thing and see what happens."

"I'd like that," Anthony smiled, "But I tend to make a mess of things, and I don't want to hurt you."

Suddenly, the door flung open and Jenny glared at them. "Where have you two been? I know you are adults, but you had me worried! Oh my! Sheri, you've got dirt all over your dress!" Jenny pulled her daughter inside, then slammed the door.

Worried that it was over between them, Anthony went to his truck and drove away. Little did he know about the wild ride ahead.

Steven S. Foster

21 Wild Ride

Morning sunlight flickered through tall, verdurous pine trees that swayed in a gentle breeze. Anthony shaded his eyes and strolled on a nearby trail behind Bolt's cabin. He did not sleep well during the night, for he worried about any repercussions from his wild, late hours out with Sheri.

Yet, he sensed that it was best to wait for Jenny to calm down. He hoped that Sheri could convince her mother about what happened during their crazy date together. With this on his mind, the apprentice did not rush to work.

Above him, the eagle perched on a high branch and called out as if to say, 'I am here.' That was enough to remind him that he needed to focus on his job as a woodcarver's apprentice. He picked up his pace and rushed back to the workshop.

"Good morning, son." Bolt glanced over with his usual easy-going disposition, while he set out some tools for the work ahead. "Welcome back," he grinned, Sheri called a few minutes ago, but I couldn't find you."

"Thanks, I went for a walk to clear my head. I'll call her now."

Worried about how Sheri's mother felt, he hesitated but forced himself to pick up the phone and dialed. "Hello, Sheri. Uh…sorry about last night. I didn't mean to upset your mom. Is she okay? Oh, good. I'm glad to hear that."

He glanced at Bolt, who seemed to be focused on his work. "Yeah, I agree, we should go back and check on them this afternoon. I'll see what I can do. Right, I'll call you soon."

The apprentice hung up the phone, put on his gloves and quietly concentrated on his apprenticeship with the woodcarver. After so much time of working side by side, it was natural to get into an easy flow, and he moved in rhythm with his mentor. Together, they attached a panel to an oak wood dresser. Once in place, Anthony gently tapped, tapped on a chisel with his mallet.

"Perfect, son," his mentor observed and nodded with satisfaction. "That's it. Just go slowly with the grain," he whispered softly. "I can see a bear beginning to take shape with your carving knife."

Hours passed quickly and during a break, the young vet had a chance to talk about his wild night out with Sheri. Bolt listened intently, while Anthony described their encounter with Johnny, Rosie, and he especially zeroed in on the details of Pastor Gabe.

"So, you think he is the Watchman?" Bolt leaned against a workbench and folded his arms, as he pondered the possibility. "Well, that's interesting," he scratched his beard and had a twinkle of curiosity in his eyes. "We've had personal encounters with this Watchman in the wilderness. Now, he shows up as a pastor in an urban rescue mission."

"Yep," Anthony placed a paper origami-shaped eagle on the table. "That's not all. Pastor Gabe gave this to me as a blessing, and he also said he was called to the bedside of a dying girl in Hiroshima, Japan, years ago."

The woodcarver picked it up and admired this simple gift, "Ah, yes," he nodded and smiled, "I'm familiar with the custom. It expresses hope and a peaceful long life for the person who receives it. This Watchman fella sure gets around."

"Yeah, one thing is for sure, Pastor Gabe appeared at the right time for our new friends, Johnny and Rosie. If it wasn't for him, I don't think they could have survived in those streets for very long."

"Don't forget your involvement, son." His mentor placed a sturdy hand on the apprentice's shoulder and smiled, "Pastor Gabe did say we are all watchmen, and we must help our fellow man, didn't he?"

Anthony studied the origami eagle and smiled, "Yep."

Bolt was silent, as though he was in deep thought. For a moment, he stared out the window and observed a dozen birds while they fed on seed that he spread out on the ground earlier that morning. "You know, I reckon our idea that the Watchman helps those in the wilderness may still apply here."

"How's that?"

"Well, it seems the Japanese girl was lost and dying in her own wilderness of despair. And, the Watchman had been called to help ease her suffering. Then, he showed up in a rescue mission downtown." Bolt paused to think about this and said, "As a result, he helped to save Johnny and Rosie from their own urban desert."

"I agree," Anthony nodded, "It's beginning to make sense now, and I think there's probably more to it, but I can't figure it out yet."

Just as Bolt was about to say something, the phone rang, and Anthony picked it up. "Hello? Oh, hi, Sheri. What? Sorry, I got busy and lost track of time," he noticed the clock on the wall was 2:30 p.m. "You're right. Okay, hold on."

The apprentice turned to his mentor and asked, "Do you mind if I take off early? Sheri and I have to go back down the mountain." Bolt smiled and nodded affirmatively. Anthony talked in the phone again, "I'll be there in half-an-hour."

Anthony put the phone down and stared at the receiver on the wall, "Well, that's interesting. After that wild night out, Sheri still wants to get together and take some pies to the mission for their late afternoon meal. She called Rosie, and I just got volunteered to help serve and clean up for the evening."

Bolt had his familiar mischievous grin and jokingly asked, "Okay, for the record, is this your second date? If so, maybe you better take extra clothes to change into."

Anthony chuckled and shrugged, "Nah, all we're doing is helping out our new friends. That's it. So, don't make a big deal about anything."

"Well, like I said before…" Bolt laughed with a wave of his hand, "Sheri's feisty, stubborn and she'll stand by you no matter what happens. So, you better watch out." He grinned and teased, "You should know that she's already made up her mind about what she wants in a relationship."

"I watched Sheri in action, and I don't like to admit it, but you're right."

"Of course, I am, son. Come to think of it, Sheri's a lot like her mother. Together, they're double trouble, and they'll melt your heart like butter."

When Anthony walked into the Café, Jenny greeted him near the counter with a hug and warm smile. "Sheri will be out in a minute."

"I thought you would be mad at me."

"It's alright. My daughter explained the whole thing." Jenny poured a cup of coffee, "If your second date is anything like the first, you had better drink this. You may need it," she grinned with a teasing look.

"Second date?" Anthony was perplexed.

"That's right, Tony," said Sheri from behind him, as she leaned in and kissed his cheek.

Anthony spun around and noticed that she wore blue jeans, running shoes and a green button-down shirt with rolled-up sleeves above her elbows. She had a small backpack slung over her shoulder like she was well-prepared for anything.

"I have extra clothes, and I'm ready to go out for our date."

Anthony scratched his beard in confusion, "I thought we were just volunteering at the mission."

Sheri tilted her head slightly and asked, "Are we going out tonight or not?"

"Of course." Anthony admired the way her long raven pony tail swayed gently from side to side as she leaned forward with hands on her hips. Yet, he tried to be firm, "Now, let's get something straight here. We're supposed to volunteer at the mission, and I plan to get you right home afterwards," he insisted. Then, he stood up and faced her in a mock attempt at defiance. "So, it's technically not a date."

"Okay," Sheri said with a playful nod, "Once we go out that door together, that will be our second date no matter what we do." She wagged a finger in his face and smirked, "You got that, Tony?"

Anthony turned to Jenny hoping for her support, but she shrugged and chuckled, "Don't look at me. Once she makes up her mind and…"

"Yeah, yeah, I've heard that before!" Anthony grabbed Sheri's hand and pulled her out the door. "Phew! You are driving me crazy, woman! Come on! It's not a date!"

Jenny watched them arguing like two kids on a playground and laughed.

"It's a date!"

"No, it's not a date!"

Anthony drove down the mountain in silence. Sheri sat with her arms folded in front of her. In those annoying moments, they just ignored each other while they sat in the same vehicle. Irritated by this absurdity, he glanced at her pouty face and wanted to say something, but he did not know how to thaw out her chilly mood.

Maybe he could tell a joke. No, he thought, that would never work. He took a quick glimpse again, and she looked so lovely, even without her makeup. Then, it dawned on him. There were only two words he needed to say.

Finally, he spoke up, "I'm sorry."

Sheri placed a hand on his knee and said, "It's alright, Tony. I guess I'm being silly. I just thought that with all the things we've done together, that it would be nice to think of whatever we do as a date."

"Yeah, you're right, sweetie." Anthony drove in silence for a moment and sighed, "You know, for me, I think of a date when I can take you out some place real special."

"Hey, I know," Sheri giggled and patted his knee, "Whenever we do that, we can call it our hot date! How's that?"

Anthony chuckled, reached out, and they shook hands, "Agreed! Hot date it is!" He drove in silence a little further down the road, then he began to get confused again. "Um, so what we're doing now is not a date, right?"

"We're together, so it's a date." Sheri had a smug and determined look with her arms crossed. "It's just not a hot date, like, you know, with all that dressy, romantic stuff going on."

Anthony gripped the steering wheel tighter and let out a sigh, "Woman, you are…"

"I know, I'm driving you crazy," Sheri giggled and still looked straight ahead. "You'll get used to it."

About five miles before the mountain road led to congested city streets, Sheri saw the eagle had landed on a tree branch along the side. "Look at that, Tony," She pointed, as the great raptor flapped its wings.

Anthony heard the call of the eagle in his mind. "Did you hear that?"

"Hear what?"

Anthony glanced in the rearview mirror and saw a car racing around a sharp curve and down the mountain toward them. "Uh, oh!" He gripped the steering wheel tight, and he shouted, "There's a maniac behind us, and he's coming fast! Hold on!"

In his mirror, Anthony stared in shock at the cold, unemotional face of a driver, who came at them without any attempt to slow down. Instinctively, the young vet swerved onto the shoulder just as the lunatic turned sharply to the left with a horrific roar of his engine. Yet, he clipped Anthony's side mirror and ripped it off with a loud clunk and an ear-piercing screech of tires.

While the speeding car passed, it slid wildly back and forth along the road until the driver regained control. Madly, he raced down the mountain at a pace of what appeared to be more than a hundred miles an hour.

Anthony took his foot off the accelerator and steadily held the steering wheel. Gently, he pressed on the brake to prevent skidding on slippery gravel until the pickup truck came to a complete stop. First, he heard sirens echoing from the mountain road above them. Then, it increased to a deafening scream, as two police cars raced passed them toward the valley below. To his right, he saw the edge of a cliff that dropped a thousand feet.

Instantly, he realized that if he had panicked and slammed on the brakes, he would have lost control and gone right over the cliff. Relieved, he looked at Sheri's terrified expression, "You okay, babe?" He gently put his hand on cheek and sighed. "Phew, that was close!"

Sheri attempted to maintain her tough, country-girl image and nervously laughed at the realization of how they could have been killed. She tried to find humor in this crazy situation and chuckled, "Yep," this is definitely a date." She gave him a quick peck on his cheek and sighed, "What's next, big guy? Sky diving?"

Her light-hearted reaction to a near tragedy relieved the tension, and he smiled, "I think we'll just go right to the mission, do our volunteer service, and then I promise to get you home in one piece. How's that?"

"What?" Sheri teased, "No roller coaster ride?"

Anthony shook his head and laughed, "You are a real handful, you know that?"

Sheri poked him in the ribs, "Oh, yeah?"

"Yeah!" Tony leaned in and tickled her.

Sheri playfully screamed, giggled, and she tried to push him away, then they wrestled and rolled around in the front seat until she yelled, "I give up!"

Anthony brushed his hair back and caught his breath. "Okay, what are we doing today?"

Sheri breathed heavily, "Um, skiing?"

"Oh yeah!" Anthony tickled her again, "You going to be a good girl now?"

Sheri giggled, "Okay!" She gasped and smiled, "I'll be a good girl!"

"Alright!" Anthony glared with a humorous mock of superiority. "I'm in charge!" He sat up straight and started to pull out, but he suddenly heard sirens. So, he stepped on the brake, just as another police car raced down the mountain.

Anthony glanced at Sheri and turned on the radio. At first, it crackled and whirred until he finally caught the tail-end of a news report. "Police are still in pursuit of a murder suspect on highway...buzz, whirl..." Quickly, he turned the knob back and forth to no avail.

The young vet looked at the steep ridge to his left and groaned, "I never did get very good reception in this area." He listened to the swoosh of the wind in nearby trees, stared at the rearview mirror, and with a shrug, he added, "Looks clear..." He felt Sheri's arm in his, and he paused, "Um...maybe I'll just wait a little longer, just to be sure." Worried for her safety, he sighed, "Can't take any chances, babe."

In his hesitation, he saw the shattered remains of his side mirror on the pavement, just in front of the truck. Then, as if to reassure him, the eagle flew by and headed down the mountain. So, Anthony slowly pulled onto the road, and he kept a sharp eye on any possible traffic that might come around the bend at a high rate of speed.

Two miles further down the road, the radio crackled again. The announcer's voice faded in and out and finally said, "The suspect's vehicle rammed into the side of a building on 30th street and exploded into a ball of flames. Police on the scene confirmed the suspect is dead. Firefighters are now trying to control the blaze. The public is advised to stay clear of the area near the intersection of Alameda and Durango street."

Anthony stopped at a red light and sighed with relief, "That's several miles away from the mission. We should be okay. What do you think, babe?"

"Let's keep going," Sheri pointed up ahead. "You can take the next left. We'll get there quicker that way, she sighed and seemed to finally relax, "Besides, it'll be nice to see Johnny and Rosie again."

Anthony drove in silence for a few minutes and turned left on 9th street, about a mile away from the mission. At first, it all seemed calm and traffic was light. The sun glared off passing vehicles, and only a few pedestrians walked on hot sidewalks. The pickup truck's air conditioning provided no relief, so he turned it off and rolled the windows down. Soon, his shirt stuck to sweaty flesh as a dry, stifling heat baked the cab's interior.

A report on the radio said, "This is Friday, August 2nd, 4:00 p.m., and the temperature is 98 degrees. It's scorching outside. The air is thick with smog. So, it is best to stay indoors until the sun goes down. There will be a full moon tonight with hazy skies."

While Anthony drove on, he spotted a half-dozen men in a brawl outside a local tavern. Fists and feet beat and kicked a man down. Men yelled and cursed. Women screamed, yet they incited further violence, and the brutality continued unabated.

The young vet barely heard Sheri's voice mention something about how horrible it was to see people act this way. Yet, to this former Army medic, he had seen it all. So, he turned away and kept driving. All he thought about was to get her to safety, away from all this mayhem.

Determined, Anthony Lorenzo focused on the road. A car suddenly raced through a red light, and barely missed them as they entered the intersection. Frightened, Sheri gripped the dash board. Yet, the Vietnam Veteran felt numb.

Memories of mutilated bodies and the stench of death flashed in his mind. He was in his element. Was it real? He did not know. Nor, did he care. All he knew was that he had to get this girl to a safe place—the rescue mission with its five-foot white cross perched on the roof like a beacon pointing to the heavens.

To his left, someone cursed and yelled obscenities. Anthony glanced to see a man, who shoved another, much smaller man to the pavement of a parking lot. At the center of it all, was an obvious woman of the night. She flailed her purse wildly in what appeared to be in defense of the shorter individual, who fell to the ground and held up his arms to protect his face. Still, the young vet turned away and kept his eyes on the obstacle course ahead.

Drivers swerved madly in and out of traffic. At the wheel, was the medic. In his mind, shots fired, bombs exploded, bodies flew all around him. His perception of reality was distorted. All he could see was the bad of people's behavior. He forgot to look for the good qualities of love, compassion and human dignity. Focused, he drove on with a clear objective—to save a life.

In his war-torn mind, he kept hearing something. What was it? Lorenzo cocked his head and drove strategically in and out of an endless battle. Deep inside of him the eagle called out. This awakened him to the present moment, and he slammed on the brakes. Relieved to see stateside city streets, he looked at his lovely passenger, and realized that she stared at him with a worried look.

"You okay, Tony?" She pointed to the red light where he stopped half-way in a cross walk. "You came up so close, I wasn't sure if you were headed right through that light."

"Yeah, I'm alright," he sighed as the signal blinked to green and he drove on. "Must be a lot of crazy people out tonight." Lorenzo white-knuckled the steering wheel and looked ahead, "It's stirring up too many ugly memories that are hard to shake."

"I've never seen it like this before." Sheri watched several shirtless men as they darted in and out of traffic, and she pointed to her right, "What's going on over at the market?"

Anthony glanced over, and there, on the sidewalk was something he could not ignore. "What the hell!"

Sweat dribbled down his heated face. He slammed hard on his brakes with a loud screech of tires. Enraged by what he saw on a nearby sidewalk, the war vet had to act before it was too late.

Sheri gasped, held onto the dashboard and yelled, "Oh, no! This can't be happening!"

Anthony gripped the door handle and yelled, "Stay here!"

A woman screamed, "Help me!"

The medic's heart raced. He was at war again!

22 Instincts of a Medic

Sheri yelled, "Tony! Look!"

There, in front of a market, a desperate, frightened mother screamed and held her baby tightly to her breast. A big, brutal man slapped her face. She fell to the ground. Her child flew out of her arms and landed on the grass. The attacker grabbed her purse and ran.

Lorenzo leaped out of his truck. The thief slammed right into the passenger side of the truck, flew over the hood to the other side and crashed head first on the asphalt. Stunned, he moaned at Lorenzo's feet.

Without hesitation, Lorenzo reached under his seat and pulled out a roll of duct tape, grabbed the man by the collar and hog-tied him. Around and around, Lorenzo swirled the tape on the enemy's legs, arms, face and head so tight, so fast, that it was all he could to keep from killing him.

Adrenaline pumping, heart racing, Lorenzo was still at war. He ignored the bloody face of the enemy at his feet, who was left harmless in a fetal position and unable to hurt anyone else. The medic rushed to the side of the fallen victim.

To his amazement, Sheri was already there with a little baby girl crying in her arms. "Sheesh," she whispered soothingly, "It's alright. You're safe now."

Relieved to see that Sheri had this under control, he tapped her shoulder, "Thanks, babe!"

For a split second, he remembered his failed attempt to save a baby girl in Vietnam, but he focused on the present emergency. "You're doing great, sweetie! I'll check the mother!" He knelt beside the unconscious victim and monitored her pulse. "She's still alive!"

Suddenly, she gagged and the medic opened her mouth and realized that she choked on her own tongue. Worried, he tilted her head back, lifted her chin and cleared her throat with his finger, so she could breath. Then, she gasped, choked and her eyes opened wide in shock. "Where's my baby?"

"She's okay, hon," said Sheri in a soothing voice. "She's right here."

"I want my baby!" The mother held out her arms, "Give her to me!"

Lorenzo adjusted the victim, so she could lean back on his chest, and he admired the way Sheri tearfully handed the baby to her mother. Just when the little girl stopped crying, Sheri leaned in and examined the woman's bruised face.

"It's alright now," assured Sheri, "You're safe with us. What's your name?"

The mother hummed softly and rocked her baby. Without taking her eyes off her child, she said, "My name's Kathy." She giggled nervously with relief, "This is my little girl, Danielle. My husband's name is Daniel, so we thought it would be fun to give her this name. He likes to call her his Danny-girl."

Sirens blared in the distance, and it grew louder, as emergency vehicles were on their way. The medic asked, "Where is your husband now?"

Kathy kissed Danielle's forehead and sighed, "Dan is a Marine and he's stationed somewhere in Vietnam. We write each other every single day."

Anthony became aware that a crowd of onlookers had gathered around. Tires screeched and sirens were silenced. Police rushed to the scene.

"Okay, everyone, move back!" ordered a policeman.

"I saw the whole thing, officer!" exclaimed a bystander. He pointed to the hog-tied attacker and yelled, "That dirt-bag beat up this lady here and stole her purse!"

"Yeah, I saw it, too!" yelled someone else. He turned to Lorenzo and pointed, "This guy's a hero, man! I never saw anyone take control so fast in my life!"

Several other officers came in to restore order, and the first policeman calmly said, "Okay, one at time. Anybody, who is a witness, please gather to the side. We'll take your statements now."

Just then, two medics came and knelt beside the victim. Relieved to see them take over, Anthony stood up and took Sheri's hand. "Let's go, babe."

"Whoa, not yet," said the officer. "Looks like you got everything under control here, but I need a statement from you."

Anthony took a deep breath, sighed and waved a hand toward the bystanders. "Well, like they said, that scum over there beat up this lady and grabbed her purse." The vet glanced at the vanquished attacker, still bound in duct tape, while two policemen placed him in a squad car. "All I did was to make sure he didn't get away."

Several other officers looked up from their notepads while interviewing witnesses and chuckled, "You sure did," someone said.

"Yep," said another. "Who would've thought of using duct tape?" He added, "That sure made our job easier."

The policeman laughed, shook his head, grinned and asked, "So what's your name?"

"Anthony Lorenzo."

The officer looked up from his notepad, "That sounds familiar." He studied the young vet's face. "I know you from somewhere, but I can't place it."

For the next several minutes, all the vital information was written down. A squad car whisked the suspect away, while the young mother and her baby were taken to the hospital for observation. Finally, Anthony and Sheri left the scene and headed to the mission in silence.

By the time they arrived, meals were being served to bedraggled men and women, who lined up with trays at a counter. Several volunteers helped to hand out food, while Johnny and Rosie busily rushed in and out from the kitchen. With quick nods and greetings, Anthony and Sheri put on aprons and took places at the serving line.

It was all happening fast, as more and more hungry people came in, but Anthony felt at ease in this environment. For the young veteran, it seemed so right to be there, and he liked to make eye contact with each person that he served. Beside him, Sheri smiled at everyone, and he enjoyed her friendly manner. Every individual had been treated with sincere lovingkindness and respect.

This became a refuge from the chaos outside, and it had an orderly feel, while everyone quietly and gratefully accepted the food that was served to them. Anthony especially noticed one elderly couple in particular. Although frail in appearance at first, the man's hazel eyes sparkled through the lens of his glasses. Slender built at about 5-feet, 8-inches tall, he was slightly stooped. He wore a tan-colored beret tilted to the left, and it gave him a look of youthful jauntiness.

Anthony served him a hot bowl of stew and made eye contact, "Good evening, sir."

"Well, greetings to you, too," said the distinguished elder man with a warm smile. "Thank you."

He took the steaming bowl in his frail hands and placed it carefully on the woman's tray next to him. "Here you go, honey."

"Thank you, dear," said a petite lady of about 5-feet in height. She wore a simple yellow dress with red carnation designs and a narrow-brimmed hat with colorful artificial flowers on top.

Anthony smiled, glanced at their wedding rings, and he admired the thoughtful way the man treated his wife. This warmed his heart, while he placed another bowl of stew on the counter. "Here you go, sir."

"Thank you, young fella." The gentleman had an air of sophistication with his white goatee that Anthony liked.

Although the medic felt drawn to them, he had to keep the line moving. So, he glanced over between servings, and he noticed the way they strolled across the dining hall to a table. It was obvious that they were in love, as they sat closely and quietly together, and he thought of how nice it would be to live a long life with someone special. Before they started to eat, this lovely couple held hands, bowed their heads and said a simple prayer.

Rose glanced at Anthony, while he watched them. She leaned in, then whispered, "Pastor Gabe said to look for an elderly couple." She nodded with a smile, "I think they're the ones he talked about. That must be Benjamin and Margret Schuller. They're retired teachers and they live in a studio apartment around the corner. Both are on a tight fixed income, and they come here for dinner every day."

"That reminds me," Anthony looked around, "Where is Pastor Gabe?"

"Oh, he left this morning," Rose smiled warmly, while she set out more plates. "He mentioned something about another assignment, and he'll be back, but he wasn't sure when."

"That figures," Anthony laughed and kept handing out bowls of stew. He had a feeling that Pastor Gabe or the Watchman was out saving a lost soul in the wilderness somewhere.

Anthony smiled and served a slender man, who shyly took a bowl in both hands. "Here you go, sir. Enjoy your meal."

The man seemed to be disoriented and ignored Anthony, as he walked away with his stew. Yet, the medic was grateful for the privilege of helping all these people without judgement. The room had a rich diversity of hungry human beings—blacks, whites, Hispanics, Asians all mingling peacefully together. Some were drug addicts, alcoholics, or mentally ill, but others may have been like the Schuller couple, and they just needed a little help to survive. All were welcome.

At first, it all went so smoothly, but Anthony noticed a slight tingling sensation above his heart, and he scratched it. In an instant, it was like being in a calm pool of water, and he felt that something was about to stir it up. Intuitively, he heard a faint call of the eagle amidst the cacophony of dishes clanging. He paused and saw that Johnny Hobbs had been scratching his chest with a look of puzzlement.

Something did not feel right, and both men scanned the room, as though they sensed that something was about to happen. Everything seemed outwardly alright, but Anthony heard the eagle in his mind again, and that sensation on his chest intensified. On high alert, the hardened war vet stepped away from the serving counter. He slowly moved along rows of tables while keeping a sharp eye on the crowd.

Meanwhile, Hobbs had set up position behind the counter, near a freezer and warily focused on the front entrance. Both men glanced at each other, nodded and waited. Still, nothing happened. The medic began to think he was getting jumpy after his rough day outside. So, he looked over at Hobbs, who shrugged, went back to his station and started to serve again.

Convinced that his imagination had gone wacky, Anthony headed over to the counter. He was about to pick up a spoon when he noticed a huge bear of man with a fierce, angry expression in the front doorway. The beast's eyes were cold and dark like that of a shark, and he glared menacingly at everyone. Suddenly, without saying a word, he deliberately forced his way toward the serving line.

Both war vets glanced at each other and nodded in anticipation. The medic knew that it was not going to go well, so he silently prayed. Then, he remembered something he had witnessed overseas, and he strolled over to Hobbs.

"Did you ever see a mongoose and a cobra fight in a cage?" asked Anthony.

Johnny nodded with a chuckle, "Yeah, all my buddies lost a lot of money betting on the cobra. Instead, that mongoose out-maneuvered, danced, then pounced."

Anthony slapped him on the shoulder, "That's right. The mongoose bit the head off the cobra within seconds. I think we may have to do a little mongoose dance ourselves."

Johnny glanced at the big man and nodded, "You lead, I'll follow."

"Got any duct tape?"

"Funny, you should mention it," Johnny pulled out a roll from the drawer and handed it to him, "Pastor Gabe gave this to me earlier and said we might need it."

"Why am I not surprised?"

Just as he turned, Anthony saw the big man in line. Suddenly, the intruder grabbed a tray from a much shorter man in front of him and demanded with a booming voice, "Get out of my way!"

"Hey! You can't do that!" yelled the smaller fella.

"Move!" the giant shoved him across the room like he was a bag of trash.

Another man grabbed his arm and yelled, "Leave him alone!"

The beast pushed this guy aside and growled, "Who's next?" He glared and snorted, "Come on! I'll take you all on!" He shook his fist wildly in a bizarre challenge. "Well, what are you waiting for?" Gruffly, he pulled back his long coat and gritted his teeth.

"He's got a knife!" People screamed and ran for the door. Volunteers behind the counter froze.

Wary, the medic quickly adapted to the increased danger, changed his tactics, and he set the roll of tape down, then calmly stepped around the counter. "It's okay, man."

"Who are you?" growled the beast.

"Anthony Lorenzo. What's yours?" He spoke softly, and he knew that his only chance of preventing further violence was to try and talk him down.

"Stay back!" the beast pulled out a long blade from his belt. "You come any closer, and I'll gut you like I've killed all the rest of them gooks!"

Lorenzo recognized the knife as the type used in hand-to-hand combat, and he knew that any physical confrontation would be fatal. So, he smiled calmly, stood completely still and tried to empathize in some way. "It's okay, man, you must've had a rough day. What's your beef? Maybe I can help."

"Stop staring at me!" The beast blinked and rubbed his forehead, "My head hurts."

Lorenzo relaxed and lowered his gaze, "I know, man. Sometimes, I get em, too." The medic stepped closer. "It's alright."

"I told you to stay back!"

The medic smiled reassuringly, "You must be hungry. Can I get you some chow?"

"I haven't eaten in two days." The beast gripped his head, as though he was in pain and groaned wearily. "I can't find a job! No one wants to hire me! I was trained to kill! That's all I know, man! What am I supposed to do? Beg?"

Lorenzo easily stepped closer to the counter and smiled, "You don't have to beg, my friend. I'll be glad to get you something to eat."

Abruptly, the beast pointed the knife at him. "Get back! I don't trust you!" He rubbed his head again and groaned, "I can't trust anybody after what the Sergeant did."

Lorenzo calmly stepped back, "Okay, take it easy. I'm only trying to help." He silently prayed and sensed that this badly wounded soul did not really want to harm him. "Talk to me, man. What did the Sergeant do?"

The beast gripped his head in pain and groaned. "Sergeant Raines ordered me to get the girl out!" Tears ran down his cheeks and he choked up. "I did what I was told...you know what I mean? I followed orders, man."

"I hear you," the medic whispered. "Go on, I'm listening."

The beast gasped for air, as though he was holding his breath in a long painful struggle, and blurted out, "She had to be no more than 14, you know, about the age of my little sister." Streams of tears ran down his cheeks and nostrils, "I...I did what I was ordered."

"It's alright," the medic looked at the poor brute with compassion, "I understand."

"He wanted to find out where the VC were hiding. He kept beating her to get intel! I thought...no way! This is Sergeant Raines! He wouldn't do that! I trusted him, and he took good care of me! So, when he ordered me to go in and kill the gooks, I'd do it just for him! You know what I mean? I saw what he did to that girl, and I thought this can't be happening!"

"I know, man."

Lorenzo glanced around and saw the faces of so many people, who were too terrified to move. Sheri stared from across the counter with a horrified expression, and she turned away with tears in her eyes. In his peripheral vision, he noticed that Johnny Hobbs had stealthily ducked into a back room to call for help. It was just a matter of time, and he sensed that the only way to free this guy of his demons was to let him talk.

The beast stared blankly ahead and sighed, "After he was through torturing her, Sergeant Raines gave an order to kill her. I said, no way man! She's just a kid!" The big man's eyes widened in shock.

"Then, he swore at me like it was all my fault, and he slit her throat! She died at my feet! I watched and did nothing!"

Traumatized by this tragic memory, he dropped his knife. His gaze softened. "I'm sick of killing, man! I don't want to hurt anybody."

The medic looked into the man's eyes, and he saw that hate, rage and bitterness drained right out of him. "I know you don't. You just need help. I'm here for you."

The now beaten warrior rubbed his head in agony again. He fell to his knees, raised his arms in surrender and cried, "Oh God, please help me!" Broken-hearted, he sobbed uncontrollably.

The medic kicked the blade away, knelt and placed a hand on the man's shoulder like a brother. "It's alright, let it all out." Anthony glanced at Hobbs, who just came out of the back room, and they both nodded with understanding that help was on the way.

Sirens blared for the third time in one day. Yet, in the chaos of police rushing in to take over, the medic continued to comfort a broken man he did not know.

23 Howling at the Moon

Sirens screamed louder, as a half-dozen emergency vehicles approached, and the police swarmed into the rescue mission. Amidst all this chaos, the medic calmly stood up and sadly watched the broken man being hand-cuffed and taken away.

Just when Anthony turned around, Sheri ran over, hugged him tightly and gushed, "Oh, Tony!"

Relieved and emotionally drained, the medic kissed her forehead and her flesh was clammy. Worried, he gazed into her glassy eyes, and she seemed pale. "You okay, babe?"

"Tony, I…" Sheri began to faint, and he immediately picked her up, then carried her to a chair.

Gently, the medic set her upright on the seat and held her shoulders, "Look at me, sweetie."

Sheri tried to focus, but she had difficulty sitting straight. So, Anthony brushed back her hair with his fingers, "You'll be okay." He held her face in his palms and examined her moist eyes, "You've been through a lot today, so it's alright to feel a little dizzy. Now, lean forward with your head down."

She did as he instructed, then Rosie rushed to them with a wet cloth, and he wiped Sheri's forehead and face. Gradually, Sheri began to feel better but looked like she was about to cry. Anthony held her in his arms, "Go ahead, let it out." She snuggled into his shoulder and wept from all the sorrow that she had witnessed in one day.

For the next few moments, nothing else mattered to Anthony. Everyone around him seemed to disappear and all he wanted was to comfort Sheri, as she cried.

Slowly, Sheri regained her composure, sniffed and looked up with teary eyes. "I'm sorry, Tony, I thought I was tough, and I could handle anything."

Anthony wiped her face with the damp cloth and smiled reassuringly, "It's alright, sweetie. It's been a crazy day." Just as he comforted her, he heard footsteps.

"We meet again!" said the same police officer, who interviewed them earlier.

Anthony stood up and laughed, "Yeah, we have to stop meeting like this," he teased. "People will talk, you know."

The officer shook his head with a look of admiration and chuckled, "Witnesses are all saying the same thing. You stayed so calm and were able to talk that guy down."

The medic shrugged, "He's a lost soul, man. He just needed someone to guide him back to a caring world. That's all."

"Well, you were the perfect guy to do it," the officer paused and seemed to be in deep thought. "Oh, yeah," he clapped his palms together, as though he had an epiphany. "Now, I remember who you are. You're Corporal Anthony Lorenzo, the medic." He reached out and they shook hands. "I'm Tom Hatfield. We never officially met, since we were in different platoons, but..."

The officer paused and glanced at Sheri while she stood up. "I remember you, too. Hello, Sheri, it's been, what? An hour or so since we last spoke, and here we are again."

Sheri weakly tried to smile, but she still felt dizzy and sat down. Still concerned, Anthony knelt and wiped her face with the damp cloth again, then looked up at the officer. "I think she'll be alright in a minute."

"She your lady?" Hatfield nodded and smiled compassionately.

"Yep, she's my lady." Anthony stood up and glanced at Sheri with a smile.

Sheri raised her head in surprise, gazed with moist eyes and kissed Anthony's hand. She immediately got to her feet with renewed energy and wrapped her arm around his waist. "You mean that, Tony?"

He kissed her forehead, "Of course."

Hatfield grinned, "You two are a perfect match." He patted the medic's shoulder and said, "I saw you at Quang Tin."

"Oh, yeah," Anthony studied him, "Sorry, I don't remember meeting you."

"Well, that's because I was on a ridge with the 101st. The Major and I watched you through our binoculars," Hatfield grinned and looked at Sheri. "This guy should've gotten a medal."

"Forget it!" The medic frowned, "I don't need it!"

"Come on, man!" Hatfield looked at him with admiration and respect. "I watched you carry a wounded soldier to safety in a hail of bullets. Then, instead of hunkering down like most of us guys, you went right back up that hill to get the second man under heavy fire, but they were hitting us hard. So, we called in an airstrike."

Anthony nodded and laughed, "Yeah, you guys cut it a bit too close. Wow…talk about friendly fire. I thought I'd get fried up there. I don't know how I made it."

"That's what I'd like to know," Hatfield lifted his cap up and scratched his head. "Say, who was that guy running with you anyway?"

"What guy?"

"You know," Hatfield tapped him on the shoulder again, "That big guy. You were dodging bullets and heading right into a barrage. I couldn't believe it, man! All of a sudden, out of nowhere was this guy running in front of you. Then, when our napalm blew up the ridge, he jumped right on top of you. We thought you were both dead. When it all cleared, you stumbled back down the hill. That guy just vanished in all those flames."

"All I can say is, I'm grateful to be alive," Anthony put his arm around Sheri.

Hatfield smiled and nodded, "Yeah, I'm glad you're here, too. You made my job a lot easier. It seems like every time there's a full moon on a hot Friday night like this, everybody goes crazy, and we're always short-handed."

"You got that right," Anthony shook the officer's hand. "Maybe we'll meet under better circumstances next time."

"Hey, that's a great idea," Hatfield wrote his name and precinct number on a piece of paper. "Here, take this, call me and leave a message. They'll reach me in the field. I'm sure my wife, Cindy, would like to meet you folks. We could all go out for dinner or something." He slapped Anthony on the shoulder like they were best buddies, "What do you say?"

Anthony smiled, took the note, and they shook hands, "I'd like that."

Hatfield waved and rushed toward the door, "It's going to be a long night!"

Anthony took Sheri's hand, "Come on, babe, let's get you home."

"I want to say good night to Rose and Johnny first." Sheri looked to see the smiling couple as they headed over.

"Hey!" Johnny laughed with relief and he gave Anthony a bear hug. "I'm so glad you didn't have to do the mongoose dance!"

"Yeah, when I saw that knife, I knew that it was a bad idea! What's really strange is that when I looked him in the eyes, I realized that it could've been me holding the blade! We all got our demons, man!"

"Mongoose dance?" Rosie giggled and twirled around. "That sounds like fun. How do you groove to that?"

"Yeah, Tony." Sheri side-bumped him with her hip. "Show us."

Anthony laughed and rubbed his beard thoughtfully. "I have no idea. I figured I'd kind of wing it."

Sheri slapped him on the chest and giggled. "Come on, buster. You're not getting off that easily."

Anthony made a fake maneuver like he was about to fall back. "Hey, don't get so rough, woman," he playfully groaned, "Can't you see how fragile I am?"

"Oh, you poor baby," Sheri laughed and poked him in the ribs. "We're not leaving until you show us the mongoose dance."

"Okay," Anthony let out a sigh, "Um…let's see now," he scratched his whiskers, "I think it goes something like this." Suddenly, he grabbed Sheri's hand and spun her around, then let her fall into his arms and wildly planted a kiss.

Sheri giggled and pretended to swoon, "Now, I think I'm dizzy again."

"I have the perfect remedy, my dear." Without another word, Anthony grabbed Sheri and lifted her over his shoulders. "Okay, just keep your head down, and you'll be fine."

"Tony!" With her head and arms dangling, she playfully beat him on the back with her fists, "Let me down, you brute!"

"Not until you promise to be a good girl!" Anthony slapped her on the rear, and he marched to the front entrance with Sheri still pretending to put up a fight, but she giggled the whole time.

Later, Anthony drove up the mountain and noticed a bright lunar ball, as it seemed to float high above a moonlit peak. "Wow, it's beautiful, honey."

"Let's pull over and look at it for a while," Sheri sighed.

"You sure, babe?" Anthony worried about getting her home safely.

"Yes, Tony, just for a little while. It'll be alright."

Anthony glanced at the man in the moon, as he seemed to smile down upon them. "Okay, sweetie, we'll make it quick, and then I need to get you home."

"Oh, look, Tony," Sheri pointed, "There's a lookout."

"Yeah, it's a perfect spot." Anthony drove into a wide parking area, and there were no other cars.

When they got out, Sheri sighed, "This is nice. We've got the whole place to ourselves."

Anthony took her hand and smiled, "Yeah, after all the craziness we went through today, it's about time." He put his arm around her waist and drew her closer. In that quiet stillness, they stood by the truck and observed a white globe that lit up the peaks all around them.

Sheri inhaled deeply and giggled, "Oh, the air is much cooler up here." She leaned in, hugged him tight and rested her head on his shoulder.

"Yeah," Anthony sniffed, "And, a whole lot cleaner," he let out a deep sigh. "I love these mountains." He quickly got out a stored jacket that he kept behind the seat, placed it on her shoulder and rubbed her back. "This'll keep you warm, sweetie."

"Sheri snuggled in his arms. "Yep, it's a date," she giggled.

Anthony squeezed her closer and chuckled, "Yep, it's a hot date, babe."

"You know something?" Sheri rested her head on Anthony's shoulder.

"What?" He felt a slight breeze, and her hair tickled his cheek.

"Let's make this our scenic view whenever we drive up the mountain." Sheri gazed into his eyes, "Okay?"

"I'd like that," Anthony smiled and brushed back strands of air from her face.

Moments passed, and they felt so alive and free. Several clouds drifted over and temporarily blocked out the lunar brightness. Then, it cleared again, and as if they were on que, both of them smiled and spontaneously howled at the moon. Together, they laughed at their own silliness, kissed and lingered together. Nothing else mattered.

Another cool breeze caused Sheri to shiver. Anthony held her closer and rubbed her back, as she snuggled into his chest. "Okay, babe, I better get you home."

24 Death Warmed Over

A nthony knew that something was wrong when he knocked on the bedroom door that Tuesday morning. He listened but had no answer. "Bolt," he tapped with his knuckle again. "You awake? It's after 6:00."

"Come in," said a raspy voice.

Anthony opened the door slowly, and he could not believe the sight of his tough-as-steel mentor all tucked under heavy blankets. Bolt laid there in a fetal position, coughed, choked, sniffled and shivered.

"Bolt!" Anthony rushed to his side. "You look terrible!"

"I reckon I got the flu," groaned the wheezy woodcarver.

"Man, I've never seen you so sick before!"

Bolt pulled back the covers and sat up, "I'll be alright," he coughed, sniffed and nodded to his neatly-hung clothes nearby, "Grab my pants over there."

The apprentice glanced at a finely-carved maple valet chair beside the bed. Bolt had his usual well-organized layout of clothes that hung neatly on the rack every night before going to bed. "You aren't fit to go anywhere." Anthony grabbed his mentor's shoulders and nudged him but felt resistance. "Come on now, don't fight me on this."

Bolt weakly plopped back on the sheets and coughed, "We have to get that shipment out." His voice sounded like sandpaper rubbing on wood, and he sniffled, then grabbed a tissue from a box on the lampstand.

For the first time, Anthony noticed a trash can full of snotty tissues, with some that Bolt must have missed and were scattered on the floor. He felt Bolt's hot, sweaty forehead with the palm of his hand. "Man, you look like death warmed over! You obviously have a high fever!"

Bolt tried to focus with his red eyes and groaned like a bear that had been hit with a tranquilizer dart. He wheezed and gasped, "What about the..."

"Don't worry," Anthony interrupted, "When the truck gets here, I'll make sure all the wood furniture we built gets loaded up for delivery in San Diego."

"We got too much riding on this, son," the woodcarver's gravelly voice was barely audible and sweat dribbled down his face. "Hey, where are you going?" He tried to lift up his head, while Anthony started to leave the room.

"Be right back." Anthony quickly rushed to an adjacent bathroom. He returned with a wet washcloth and wiped his mentor's face, "That feel better?"

Bolt grabbed the cloth from him and growled, "Give me that! I can do it myself!"

"Whoa!" Anthony held up his hands as if to surrender. "Now, I finally get to see the stubborn, cantankerous side of macho Bolt." Anthony sat down on the nearby chair next to a reading lamp and sighed, "You, old coot! Can't you see that I'm trying to help you?"

"I don't need your help!" Suddenly, he let out an uproarious sneeze and blew his nose, and he clumsily wiped the mucous from his gray beard. "We're burning daylight!"

The woodcarver growled angrily, yanked off the blankets again and demanded, "Get my pants! Got work to do!" He sniffed, rubbed his red nostrils and swore something that sounded like obscenities from his Celtic ancestry.

"Alright," sighed Anthony calmly. He reached over and picked up the pants, then turned to see Bolt had drifted off with a loud snore. "You, old buzzard," he whispered softly, "That's better. Now get some sleep."

In the kitchen, Anthony rummaged through cupboards, and he was pleased to see five cans of chicken noodle soup and another four of beef broth left over from last winter's stash. "Let's see," he talked to himself, "Got some tea, plenty of coffee, and, oh, I see a lemon here. Perfect, that'll help."

For the next couple hours, Anthony paced anxiously around the house and every few minutes, he peeked in the open door to check on his patient. Bolt had always been so strong. Now, he seemed frail.

Worried, the medic entered the room often, sat by the bed and prayed. Yet, he got restless again, and he glanced at the grandfather clock on the fireplace mantel. "It's after ten. Why is that delivery truck so late? That shipment should have gone out over an hour ago."

He tried to keep busy, and he remembered origami. So, he tore several pages from a colorful magazine and cut the paper into pieces. Gradually, he began to make an eagle. Soon, he formed a half-dozen shapes of the raptor, and this relaxed his mind.

Feeling stiff, he remembered some basic Tai Chi moves that he had learned from a South Vietnamese Army Sergeant during a lull in fighting. A friendship developed between them, as they practiced the benefits of balance and martial arts. That inspired him to take up position in the backyard of Bolt's cabin. There, it all flowed easily in his memory, and he slowly glided his body with ease.

In the present, he thought of the meaning of each powerful slow-motion gesture of hands and feet. Grounded between earth and heaven, he was connected deeply to all that was around him. Visually, he became aware of the eagle perched on a branch nearby. He listened to every sound of the rustling of leaves in a light breeze. Nothing went unnoticed.

Abruptly, he heard a truck's engine roaring, and its tires rumbled on the gravelly driveway in front of the cabin. "Beep! Beep!" An intrusive horn blared out the arrival of the expected pickup. Finally, it was time for the scheduled shipment to go out.

Anthony glanced at his wristwatch and frowned. "They're two-hours late!" he groaned and shook his head with displeasure. He knew that the woodcarver always insisted on promptness. "Phew! He's not going to like this."

Before Anthony went to the front, he stepped inside and peeked in on Bolt and was relieved to see his patient still asleep. Satisfied, he rushed to greet the two-man crew, who stood by the van. "Hi, I'm glad you made it. Name's Anthony. What's yours?" He smiled and reached out a hand.

Instead of a mutual, friendly greeting, the men just stood there with frowns on their faces. "We're in a hurry!" growled the driver, a big man, who must have weighed over 300 pounds, with a massive belly that protruded over his belt buckle. He glared menacingly, and he made no attempt to reciprocate with a handshake. The other, more slender man stood by the passenger side door. He appeared nervous and unsure of his stance.

Anthony Lorenzo kept calm, with his focus on the big man. "I can see why you're in a hurry, considering that you showed up two-hours late." He shrugged and smiled, "I understand. Things happen."

The big man ignored him, glared at his anxious partner and yelled, "Lower the lift and open the door! Let's load up!"

With that bark of orders, the slender man's eyes widened in what looked like fear, and he ran to the back. In his hurry, he stumbled twice, got up, pressed a button, and the elevator whirred and lowered to the ground with a clunk. He peeked timidly around the side, paused, then waited for the next command.

"Well!" growled the big man. "Just don't stand there, you idiot! Get the dolly out!"

Lorenzo watched and listened, while the timid fella jerkily rushed and clanged around in the back. "You might want to slow down," he said to the big man. "I have valuable cargo here."

"Don't tell me what to do!" The brute stepped forward aggressively, then stopped about two-feet away and glared with clenched fists.

Lorenzo stayed calm, but he noticed a lingering odor of alcohol on the man's breath. Slowly, he strolled around the truck. "Okay, I just want to be sure that the shipment is in good hands." He kicked the tires, glanced in the open door of the cab and spotted something that he did not like. "What's this?" Lorenzo grabbed a whiskey bottle wrapped in a brown paper bag on the front seat.

"Hey! That's none of your business!"

Lorenzo threw it hard against the truck and shattered the glass. "It is now!"

"I'll get you for this!" The big man lunged with his fist.

Lorenzo side-stepped and allowed a muscular arm to go off center. He used the leverage of the attacker's own weight, grabbed an oncoming wrist and pulled with minor physical effort. Lorenzo kicked his groin, and the beast slammed head first into the truck. His body went limp and flopped against the hood. Blood dribbled down from the forehead, and he groaned in pain.

Lorenzo spun around and faced the timid guy. "Don't move!"

Frightened and shaky, the slender man said, "I didn't do anything, man!"

"That's the problem!" Lorenzo glared at him. "You did nothing to stop him in the first place!"

"I'm sorry!" he lowered his gaze to the ground. "I need this job and I got a family to support!"

Lorenzo shook his head in disgust. "You make me sick! As long as there're cowards like you, we'll always have trouble makers like him around!"

"What am I supposed to do?" The timid man nodded toward the attacker, "He threatened to break my arm if I said or did anything!"

"Stop whining! Bring the dolly over here!" Lorenzo noticed the big man's body started to slide off the hood, so he gripped the guy's belt to keep him from falling.

Just when the timid man rushed the hand truck to the front, Anthony commanded, "Set it up behind him! Now brace yourself, and I'll lean this refrigerator on it!"

The limp body plopped backward, and the slender fella strained to keep his balance, while trying to hold the dolly with a struggle and groaned, "He's heavy!"

Lorenzo rushed to his side and helped, "Come on, push it to the back! Move!"

The dolly's wheels slid and wobbled behind the truck, and they loaded it up. Lorenzo tapped the switch, and the elevator door rose to the storage bed. "Okay! Lower Mr. Beer Belly here! Now, take your shirt off!"

"What?"

"You heard me!"

The timid man reluctantly removed his shirt. "Now what?"

"Wrap it around his forehead to stop the bleeding!"
Lorenzo looked on with mounting indignation. "Now, tie
it tight with the sleeves of your shirt!" While this was
being done, Lorenzo grabbed a roll of packing tape from
a tool box nearby, then wound it around the opponent's
hands and feet.

After the cowardly man tied his shirt, he asked, "Now
what?"

Lorenzo pointed to a pile of blankets used to cover
furniture. "Lay those down! We're going to make a
bedding for your charming buddy here!"

Quickly, the timid man spread out the blankets, and
Anthony ordered, "Okay, on the count of three, we're
going to roll him over. One, two, three!"

Finally, they turned the big man on his back, and he
looked up in a daze. "What happened?"

The medic lifted the man's eyelids and examined him.
"You'll be fine. Comfy now?"

"I feel sick to my stomach!" The big man suddenly
lifted his head and vomited right into the timid guy's face.

"Oh! Yuck!" Stunned, the slender fellow stood up with
a sickened, mortified expression.

"Take this!" Lorenzo tossed another blanket. "Wipe
yourself! Now let's lock it up! Get that hog off our
property!"

The poor fellow stumbled out and the lift plopped to
the ground. Gagging, he rushed to the driver's side, while
wiping his face and climbed in. Seeing the keys still in the
ignition, he turned on the engine.

"Now, drive to the Sheriff's station in Crest Ridge!
You've got 15 minutes to turn yourself in! I'll call them!
So, you better get there!"

The timid man whimpered, "But, I'll lose my job!"

Lorenzo looked at him with pity and sighed, "I'll call your boss and say you helped me to restrain the driver. Maybe that'll be enough. I'll also make it clear that the company's contract is terminated!" He slammed the driver's door hard and yelled, "Now get out of here!"

Just as the truck left, Anthony dashed to the cabin and checked on Bolt. Relieved to see that his mentor still rested peacefully, he called the Sheriff and reported the incident.

With that done, he dialed the number for the moving company and canceled their agreement to pick up any shipments. Calmly, he explained that their driver was drunk, and the other worker helped to detain the fool. Any further communication will have to be with the Sheriff.

After Anthony cancelled that disappointing business arrangement, he still needed a way to deliver the shipment on time. He contacted three other companies and discovered that it would take a couple of days before any pick up could be made. This worried Anthony, and he knew it would cause further delay. So, he contacted Levinson's Furniture.

"Hello, Mr. Levinson, this is Anthony Lorenzo. I work for Bolt MacArthur."

"Yes, how may I help you?"

"Bolt is sick, and he can't come to the phone. I had to fire the delivery company, and I just want to give you a heads up. So far, I'm having difficulty finding someone else to deliver your order on time."

"No! That's not acceptable! Get Bolt on the line!" demanded Levinson. "Bolt MacArthur is never late!"

Anthony remained calm, "I apologize, sir. Like I said, Bolt is sick and can't come to the phone. I am responsible for his shipment." The apprentice examined the paper work. "According to the order, we have until 8:30 a.m. tomorrow. Correct?"

"That's right." Levinson paused, then said, "Bolt always gave me his word. That's like gold to me. Do you understand?"

"Yes, sir. Let me put it this way, Mr. Levinson. I have worked for Bolt MacArthur for more than a year-and-half now. He is like a father to me. You have my word that I will get the furniture to you on time, just as he promised you."

Levinson sighed and said, "Okay, I can tell by the sound of your voice that you are sincere, and since you work for Bolt, I believe I can trust you. My advertising has already gone out, and my customers are expecting to see Bolt MacArthur's finely crafted wood furniture here when I open the doors at 9:00 in the morning. I accept your word, young man."

"Consider it done, Mr. Levinson."

When Anthony hung up, he looked in on Bolt, who was still sound asleep. Disappointed to see that he could not ask his mentor for advice, he wondered how the master woodcarver would handle this crisis. As he pondered the dilemma, he quietly set an origami eagle on the lampstand and prayed in silence.

"God, please help me," he whispered, "I have no idea how to get this shipment out on time. Show me the way for everyone's sake. Thanks."

Desperate for an answer, Anthony strolled out to the workshop and stood by the old flat bed truck that was used to haul wood. He examined the dirty, exposed surface and sighed, "Nah, this'll never do." He scanned the western sky and worried about the dark clouds. "Bolt's furniture is too valuable."

A low rumble from distant thunder signaled an ominous warning to keep his mentor's property safe for the long-haul south. Anthony scratched his beard, "I need an enclosed delivery truck."

He rushed back into the shop and rummaged through a storage bin. "There's got to be a big enough tarp here somewhere." He pulled out one and examined it. "Nah! That'll never work! It has too many worn spots!"

Increasingly worried, the apprentice searched around and finally, he found a tarp that looked better. "Okay, now I got something."

Quickly, he carried it outside. Just as he spread out the material to measure it, a gust of wind blew it wildly in his hands. Thunder roared again. It was closer.

Anthony looked up and saw thick, black clouds. Trees swayed and lightening flashed. "Now what?"

25 Mr. Grumpy

Anthony had to act fast, so he went to the kitchen and called the café. "Hello, Jenny, I don't mean to worry you, but Bolt is sick with the flu. I need help."

"Well, I'm not surprised. A lot of my customers have been sick for several days now. Half my crew are out, too. We're about to close down for a few days until this epidemic is over."

"I'm sorry to hear that, Jenny. But, I'm sure it's the best thing to do." Anthony sighed, "Anyway, I need to get two things done. First, can I get Sheri to stay with Bolt for the next 48 hours or so?"

"Of course, hon, I'll help, too. What's the second thing?"

"I need somebody with a truck to get our shipment out right away," Anthony worriedly glanced at the wall clock. It was after 1:00 p.m.

"Hold on a minute. Tom, our regular customer just pulled up in his rig outside. I'll get him."

"Thanks, Jenny, I'll wait." Anthony fidgeted, and he knew every minute counted down to the deadline.

Finally, after what seemed like long, agonizing minutes, he heard Tom, the truck driver. "Hey, Anthony, Jenny says you and Bolt need help."

"That's right, Tom. I know it's a lot to ask, but we have to get our furniture to San Diego by tomorrow morning. Can you give us a hand?"

"Well, Bolt MacArthur has always been there for me and my family." Tom paused, then said, "I think it might work. You see, I've got to pick up a load at the harbor there by noon tomorrow. I have plenty of space to take what you need."

"Great!" Anthony sighed with relief. "I knew I could count on you, Tom. So, when can you get here?"

"Well, I just came in for coffee, then I need to drive up to see my wife and kids. Let's see…shower, get some chow. Um, I can get there about 5:00 this evening. Will that work?"

"Perfect! I need to see this through, and I gave my word on it. So, I'll go with you and even help with your load afterwards. In fact, I'll guarantee you'll be well-paid for this, my friend."

"Are you kidding me?" Tom chuckled on the phone. "Bolt MacArthur helped me so many times, it'll be an honor to do a good turn for you guys!"

"Thanks, Tom. Say hi to Linda and the kids. I'll see you soon."

Anthony hung up and checked on his patient, who was already getting out of bed. "Hey, Bolt, glad to see you're awake."

"Got to go pee," Bolt coughed and dizzily stumbled toward the bathroom.

"Let me help you." Anthony grabbed his arm, "You look shaky."

Bolt pulled away and growled irritably, "I don't need your help!"

Anthony released him and stepped back. "Okay, boss."

Bolt grumbled, wheezed, shuffled to the bathroom, then slammed the door.

This was all new to the apprentice, as he plopped on the chair next to the bed. Not only was he trying to care for his mentor for the first time, but he also had to get along with a downright grumpy sick patient. On top of that, he felt protective of the woodcarver's property and reputation, and it sure did not look like he could count on

Bolt for support. It was all up to him to keep the operation running smoothly.

So, when Bolt came out and went back to bed, Anthony said nothing about what happened with the shipment or his plans to make the deadline on his own. Instead, he paused in the doorway. "I'll get you some hot soup."

"No, I'll do it myself when I'm ready." Bolt coughed, sniffled and sighed, "I don't want you waiting on me!" He waved a hand weakly and growled, "Get out of here!"

Anthony quickly closed the door in silence. This was a waste of time to try and reason with him, he thought. Meanwhile, he kept busy around the house and listened out for his mentor. He cleaned windows, counters and anything else close by, in case he was needed.

Finally, Sheri and Jenny showed up, just as he was about to go stir-crazy.

"I'm glad to see you," he sighed with relief. "Bolt won't let me do anything for him, and he's sick as a starving papa bear in the heat of summer!"

Jenny laughed, "That's because you're a man."

Sheri hugged Anthony and patted his chest, "You just let us women folk handle this." She giggled and glanced down the hall. "I guess he's still held up in his man cave?"

"Yeah, but I wouldn't go in there, if I were you. He's ornery enough to bite your heads off."

"Don't worry," Jenny held up a thermos. "We know how to handle him." She glanced at Sheri and nodded, "Come on."

Anthony followed them into the kitchen, and Jenny took out a bowl from a cupboard, then poured hot chicken soup from the thermos. Surprised, he said, "I already got some canned soup in the cupboard."

"Well, we have the magic potion right in here," Jenny tapped the steaming container.

"Sheri, go out to the car and get the other two thermoses. This could be a long night, and Mr. Grumpy is going to need it."

Anthony watched Sheri, as she left and shook his head with puzzlement, "Say, what are you ladies up to, anyway?"

Jenny glanced at the bowl of hot, steaming soup and grinned knowingly. "This is made from a secret recipe. A year before Emma died, she shared the ingredients with me. Once he takes a whiff of this, I'll have him eating out of my hands."

"Now, this I got to see," Anthony followed Jenny, and Sheri came in behind him.

When they entered, Bolt was on his side and he coughed miserably. "Go away!" he growled. "How many times do I have to tell you to leave me alone!"

"It's me, honey," Jenny whispered softly and sweetly. "I got something for you."

Bolt rolled over with a look of surprise and sighed, "Oh, sorry, Jen. I didn't know you here."

"I'm here, too, Poppy." Sheri leaned over and felt his forehead. "I'll get you a washcloth." She went into the bathroom, just as Anthony did earlier. Then, she returned and wiped his face. "That feel better, Poppy?"

Bolt relaxed and smiled weakly, "Yeah, kitten. I reckon that feels right nice."

Anthony watched in amazement, but he said nothing when Jenny sat on the bed with the tempting magic potion. Steam rose from the enticing soup, and she brought it closer to the woodcarver's nostrils; then, he sniffed, and his eyes widened.

"Oh," he sighed and inhaled the aroma, "That smells good."

"Of course, it does, honey." Jenny held the hot bowl and let him take it all in. "This is from Emma's secret recipe, and she gave it to me so that I could give it to you whenever you need it. This was her way of saying how much she loved you."

"My dear, Emma," Bolt sniffled in a way that was difficult to tell whether it entailed a twinge of sentimentality or a bad case of the flu. "I'd sure like to have some now. I'm hungry as a mountain lion in winter."

Sheri fluffed up an extra pillow and smiled, "Okay, Poppy, sit up and I'll get you nice and comfy, so you can have Emma's soup."

Bolt eagerly lifted himself, while Sheri tucked it behind his back, and the sick patient strangely seemed a little more energetic. Surprised, Anthony looked on but said nothing.

Jenny sat beside the bed and stirred the soup softly, then took the spoon to her lips and gently blew off the steam.

"Here you go, honey," Jenny held the spoon to Bolt's awaiting lips.

Bolt slurped in the savory chicken soup and sighed contently, "Ah, that's so good."

Jenny glanced at Anthony with a smug expression, then turned to Bolt and held out the spoon again. For the next few minutes, Bolt was back to his well-mannered self and all seemed normal, as long as Anthony did not offer to help in any way. Yet, the apprentice did not mind the extra support since he knew that his mentor was in good hands.

When Tom drove up in the big rig, Anthony greeted him with a handshake and smile, "You're right on time. Thanks, my friend."

"Glad to help." Tom opened the back of his trailer, "Let's load up."

Soon, they had all of Bolt's wooden furniture secured, and Anthony was relieved to see the eagle circling overhead. With the shipment deadline looming, Anthony eagerly climbed in the truck, then he placed an origami on the dash board and said, "Ready whenever you are."

Tom glanced at the carefully folded paper-shaped eagle, "What's that for?"

"Think of it as a blessing," Anthony tapped on the dash. "It's something I learned from a good friend."

Tom chuckled, "Roger that." He started the engine. "Let's rock and roll." He turned on the radio and Bob Dylan sang, "You better start swimming, or you'll sink like a stone, for the times they are a-changin."

As the truck headed down the mountain, the mission was clear--safely deliver the valuable cargo ahead of schedule, if possible, but at least on time.

Later, when they drove into the city, Tom glanced at the setting sun and frowned, "We got a long night ahead."

"Yep."

"Traffic's heavy up ahead."

Anthony observed the long line of cars stopped at a red light, as they slowed down. "Got a couple hundred miles to go. What time do you think we'll make it to San Diego?"

Tom braked to a stop behind the cars, "Don't know for sure…it all depends on what we encounter on the way there."

"Like what?"

Tom nodded to the traffic in front of them, "Like this…or just about anything else. "After 10 years of driving these long hauls, I've learned to be prepared for blown tires, brakes going out, accidents, sudden storms and a dozen other crazy things."

"So, why do you keep doing this, anyway?"

"Got to support my family, man." Tom observed the light, as it blinked to green and cars started to move forward. "It's all I know."

"Uh, oh!" Anthony glanced out his side window and frowned.

"What's wrong?"

"I don't like the look of them clouds to the northwest."

Tom turned his head to look. "Yep. A storm's brewing and heading in our direction. "I heard a forecast on the radio earlier that a massive pineapple express will blow in by tonight."

"Ah, man," Anthony groaned, "Why didn't you tell me?"

"Does it matter?" Tom glanced at him and chuckled. "You have to get your furniture to San Diego, and I need to pick up my load at the dock no matter what.

"Yeah, you're right. We have no choice." Anthony shook his head and watched the menacing black clouds roll in along the coast. He peeked at his watch and sighed, "Sure hope we make the delivery on time."

Steven S. Foster

26 Skunk Works!

Red tail lights flashed ahead for miles, and Anthony Lorenzo knew this was trouble. Tom down-shifted and the big rig slowed to a dead stop. Cars were backed up on the southbound lanes for miles. Windshield wipers hypnotically sloshed away rain drops in a vain attempt to clear the view in the dark.

"Must be an accident," Tom nodded to Anthony, "Check the front tire. I think I might've run over something."

"Roger," Anthony put on a raincoat, slipped on his leather gloves and grabbed a flashlight. He was about to open the passenger door when Tom tapped his shoulder.

"While you look, I'll give a holler on the radio." Tom glimpsed a passing northbound 18-wheeler, then picked up his CB mike. "Breaker one-niner, how 'bout you, north-bound?"

The radio crackled when Lorenzo stepped out, and he felt eerily exposed to the unknown. A memory flashed to an ambush in Vietnam, just as his boot sloshed in a puddle. "Pop! Pop!" In an instant, an invisible sniper fired, and his buddy was dead beside him. "Okay, man, get your head on straight," he muttered and focused on the present moment.

Rain drops splattered all around, so, he covered his head with the water-proof hood of his coat. His flashlight beam searched the pavement, and he saw nothing, except glittering pools. When he started to get back inside, something dark under the wheel-well caught his eye, and he examined it closer. It appeared to be a crumpled piece of tire that must have been on the road.

Worried, Lorenzo opened the door and looked at Tom. "There's a clump of old rubber stuck in the wheel-well."

"That figures," Tom pointed behind the seat. "Grab the tire iron. We truckers call that road trash under there an alligator. That thing will chew up the underbelly when we head down the road. So, try and pry it out of there, pronto."

"Copy!" Lorenzo took the tool in hand, and he carefully probed at it first, while he made sure to not damage the truck's front tire. Then, with a good, strong grip, he pulled the piece toward him, and it jammed in again. So, he pried and struggled for several long agonizing minutes in the unrelenting downpour. Finally, he yanked the rubber all the way out, and he tossed it into a ditch alongside the road.

Back in the cab, Anthony pulled his rain coat and gloves off. "Got it! What'd you find out on the radio?"

"I heard there's a 4-wheeler pile up about three miles south of us." Tom glanced over, "Traffic's been backed up for several hours now, and a buddy said it's starting to move."

Just as he said that, a car in front of them jerked forward and stopped. "Okay, baby," Tom kissed the origami eagle and grinned, "Let's do it." He shifted into gear, and the truck edged forward.

"Rock and roll!" Anthony tapped a drumbeat with his fingers on the dash, "Tap a tap."

Inch by inch, the truck's peevish pace reminded the young vet of a sloth he had observed in a zoo. The humor of that mental image helped him to accept each moment without judgment. No use fighting what you cannot control, he remembered his mentor's advice. Allow it to just happen. So, he decided to focus on his goal of delivering the furniture on time and not worry about the results.

Tom nodded to a turnoff about a 100-feet ahead. "That's the old frontage road. We'll go that route and save time."

Several cars made the same maneuver, and Tom drove to the right easily. Soon, they made clear headway of 45 miles an hour. "Looking good!" Encouraged, he tapped the dash board and began singing along with Diana Ross on the radio. "Ain't no mountain high enough to keep me from you babe."

"Sing it baby!" Anthony tapped his knees to the beat. Then, he glanced at his buddy and joked, "Not you! Her!"

Meanwhile, rain pelted metal, glass, earth. Nothing was spared. Windshield wipers endlessly swished and swashed in a futile attempt to keep up. Both men blindly tried to perceive up, down, sideways, but it was difficult to make out land versus sky.

So, Tom downshifted and slowed to a crawl of 20, then 10 miles an hour. Anthony wiped the window with a rag as best as he could, while Tom turned on the defroster. Gradually, the rain dissipated. Yet, the fickle air changed like an angry woman scorned. Within seconds, another deluge furiously battered the truck, as it edged forward.

Soon, the rain let up again. Then, the cars ahead disappeared in a thick fog bank, and they were alone in a void. Anthony shined a flash light to the side and it bounced off an eerie gray opacity.

"Whoa, this is creepy, man." Tom white-knuckled the steering wheel and slowed the truck to 5 miles an hour. "I've never seen it this bad before."

Anthony wiped the side window again and warily nodded in agreement, but he tried to provide some humor, "Yep, we live in a world of constant changes. Do you remember who said that?"

Tom chuckled, "I haven't the foggiest idea."

"I just said it!"

"Okay, wise guy," Tom laughed nervously and wiped his side window with a sleeve, then leaned forward with a worried look. "So, how about changing the weather for us while you're making jokes?"

"Hold it!" Anthony Lorenzo grabbed Tom's arm. "I see something."

They slowed to a halt. "What is it?" Tom squinted his eyes, "I can't see a thing."

"I don't like the looks of this." Lorenzo put his rain coat on and cautiously stepped out. "I'll check."

Tom watched and, for a moment, it seemed like Lorenzo had vanished into nothingness. Deathly silence swept over the truck. Nothing moved. Tom anxiously glanced from side to side but only saw the headlights that bounced off a wall of fog. Even the chatter of his CB radio had whisked away. Music died, and he waited.

"Thump! Thump!" Startled by sudden pounding on his door, Tom rolled the window down and looked out.

"Boo!" Anthony shined a flashlight under his chin and made a spooky Halloween-like face. "It's me! Is that you?"

"Oh man!" Tom groaned with relief, "You scared the crap out of me!"

"So, that's what I smell." Anthony teased, "I thought it was your dirty sox behind the seat."

"Very funny."

"Seriously…" Anthony leaned against the window, "There's a tree trunk that's fallen on the road ahead. But I think we can get around it. Go slowly to the left, and I'll guide you." He stepped down and patted the side door.

Tom nodded with worried look. "Just don't get too close. I'm as blind as a deer in headlights." Carefully, he drove forward and kept his eyes on Anthony as best as he could in thick fog that darkened his mood.

Anthony took several steps in front of the truck and to Tom's left, then disappeared again. Yet, the driver made out a bouncing flashlight beam that waved him to move forward. Ever so tediously slow, he steered the rig around a dark object on the road. Finally, he pulled it safely away from the obstacle and his guide signaled to halt. The brakes screeched slightly, and Tom sighed with relief.

Anthony climbed aboard and grinned, "Okay, I think it's clear now."

Tom slowly accelerated, and the truck moved forward. Within minutes, headlight beams shined on ghostly tree branches that swayed in a strange gust of wind. "Looks like the fog is clearing. It'll be okay now."

"Bam!"

"What was that?" Tom looked up at a bizarre dent in the ceiling.

"Something must've hit the roof. I'll check." Anthony tried to open his door, but it was jammed. "Won't budge!" A memory of an ambush flashed in his mind again but he ignored it. "Okay, we have to get out on your side."

"Geez, this is creeping me out, man." Tom groaned and stepped out to examine the damage. "Ah, man!" He peeked through the open door and sighed, "You are not going to believe this!" Have a look see!"

Not liking the sound of it, the wary war vet slid out of the driver's side, and they both walked around. There, they shined flashlight beams on a two-foot-wide tree branch that had fallen on the roof. Part of it jammed against a top edge of the passenger side door.

Stunned, they listened to scratching like the sound of finger nails on a chalk board. In that split second, they could not stop the branches from slipping further.

Tom groaned and watched helplessly. "No! No! No!" Yet, the whole mass followed the force of gravity and began to slide off a damp, slippery metal roof. Abruptly, it slammed hard onto the hood with a sickening clunk, while entangled cable wires grabbed the antenna and ripped it off.

"Well that does it!" Tom cursed and tossed his cap to the wet pavement. "We just lost our communications!" He picked up his hat, sighed and grumbled, "Come on, help me to push all this crap off the hood, so we can get out of here!"

Anthony studied the tangled mess of branches with twisted cables, and he had an idea. "Let's use some leverage here." He picked up a smaller branch that was about five-feet long. "Okay, back up your rig, and I'll hold things in place. That heavy piece should slide right off."

Tom grumbled, climbed into the cab and slowly reversed, while Anthony steadied himself with the branch. Wood scraped against metal until the twisted branches clumped to the ground, then Tom leapt down to check. "Great, that freed us up!" He pulled on cables entwined in branches and sighed, "There's no way to repair this!"

"Maybe we can save the antenna, at least." Anthony pulled out his pocket knife, cut it free and examined it, "This might still be good. Let's take it."

Tom climbed back into the cab and yelled, "Alright! This place gives me the creeps!"

Anthony got in and dropped the pieces behind the seat. "Let's get out of here!"

After a late-night long haul, they made it to a dimly-lit rest stop off the highway, and Tom pulled in the parking lot. "Let's make a quick pit stop."

"Great," Anthony hopped out, "I'll race you!" He took off toward the restroom, as Tom ran behind him, and they both chuckled like a couple of kids on a playground.

Just when they rushed by a metal trash can, a raccoon leaped out with a candy wrapper dangling from its mouth. Startled, the men jumped back, as the frightened animal made a wild dash across their path.

"Ah, man!" Tom swore, gripped his crotch and ran inside. "Got to go!"

"Geez!" Anthony chuckled and sighed, "That was crazy!"

After the men relieved themselves, they eagerly ran back to the truck but stopped suddenly. "What the…" Tom looked in shock at what he saw.

"Is that what I think it is?" Anthony leaned forward and squinted his eyes at the rear wheel-well of the rig. He turned on his flashlight and shined it.

"Yep, that's a skunk sitting right on your tire like he owns it!"

Tom looked warily at the animal, "You got any ideas on how to get that little devil out of there?"

Anthony shook his head, "Not without getting sprayed." He found a discarded can and picked it up. "Maybe this'll scare him out." He tossed and skidded it under the trailer, but the skunk did not budge.

"Now what?" Tom frowned with disappointment.

"Start the engine. That'll do it."

"I don't know, man," Tom groaned, cautiously walked to the cab and climbed aboard. "I don't like it!" He glared out the open side window, "What if he sprays anyway?"

"That's the risk we have to take! Okay, wait before you start it up…" Anthony backed away about 50 feet and yelled, "Now, go ahead. I'll watch from here!"

Tom shook his head, frowned, cursed, and glared at Anthony, "Well, I sure hope you're comfy now."

"I'm ready."

Tom gripped the steering wheel tight and sighed, as he looked at Anthony, "I don't like this one bit!"

Anthony shrugged, "No sweat, man! It's like ripping off a band aid! So, let her rip!"

Tom sighed, "Okay, here we go!" He started the engine, blew his horn, and he glanced out the side mirror. Suddenly, that skunk leaped off the tire, and, in a panic, left a trail of sulfuric, malodorous spray right in the wheel-well.

Seeing this, Anthony held his nose and darted back to the truck, then gasped for air when he climbed aboard. "Let's get out of here!"

Tom sniffed and frowned, "That skunk left his mark, didn't he?"

"Well, I wouldn't stick my head back there if I were you," Anthony puffed out, "Phew!"

27 City Skunks!

Finally, after traffic jams and the calls of nature, they reached San Diego. It was about 1:00 a.m. when Tom drove his rig into the parking lot of a run-down motel. "I'm beat! We'll bunk here!"

"You know this place?" Anthony looked out the window and a red neon sign blinked, "Seaside Inn." Below that, it had the words, "Vacancy."

"Yep, it doesn't look like much, but it's close to Levinson's Furniture. Besides, I don't want to stay at the truck stop out on the highway. That place is crawling with lot lizards this time of night."

"Lot lizards?" Anthony laughed with a puzzled expression.

"Yeah, you know, prostitutes, man. Between them and drug dealers, they're slithering around from one truck to another. If you turn your lights on, they'll scatter back into the dark and hide."

"Forget that, man!" Anthony studied the motel parking lot and began to worry. "We better park within eyesight. I can't afford to have anything go wrong now."

Settled inside a sparse room with two twin beds, the men took turns in a tiny stand-up shower and bathroom. When Tom came out, he noticed that his friend stared out a gap in the faded window curtain. "You worried?"

On high alert, the war vet sighed and kept a close watch on the truck that was parked sideways near the road. With a clear view of the cab and part of the trailer's rear, he said, "Can't take any chances," he looked straight ahead and did not blink, "They're out there…I feel it."

"Ah, come on, there's nobody out there." Tom plopped on the bed and sleepily gazed at a 13-inch, black and white TV on the dresser. "Let's get some shut eye," he yawned and snuggled into his pillow. The screen flickered, as brief news reports flashed images of ongoing anti-war demonstrations. With the volume down low, the weary men were numb to the chaos that reverberated through the country.

Anthony Lorenzo glanced at Tom, who had drifted off peacefully. Yet, he stood ready to face an unseen enemy, and he was unable to sleep. So, he stared out the window and the minutes ticked by slowly. Gradually, he yawned more and rubbed his weary eyes, then gave himself permission to plop on the bed for a few minutes. It will be okay. No need to get paranoid, he thought.

Soon, the young vet dreamed of the eagle that flew gracefully in a clear, blue sky. Ever watchful, the great raptor glided majestically over mountains, lakes and streams. It was such a beautiful dream, and Anthony did not want it to end. In his ethereal bliss, he began to see through the eyes of the eagle, and he became one with this heavenly symbol of spiritual freedom.

Deeper in his dream, Lucille spoke soothingly to his weary soul, "They that wait upon the Lord shall renew their strength; they shall mount up with wings like eagles."

Suddenly, he awoke, sat up and listened. What was that? Something stirred outside, and he leaped to his feet. Cautiously, he peeked through the curtain but saw nothing. On edge, he stared at the truck parked across the lot for a long time.

Lorenzo was about to close his tired eyes again, when four shadowy figures appeared behind the trailer. He slid the motel window open a crack, listened and watched them tamper with the padlock. They appeared to be in their early teens and skittish like young bulls trying to prove themselves. Yet, he knew that it was foolish to even consider a confrontation, since they recklessly brandished handguns.

So, he turned to the lampstand and reached for the phone to call police. Just as he was about to dial, he noticed that two of them looked under the stinky rear wheel-well. This piqued his interest, and he wondered if they thought an extra key was hidden there. Lorenzo held his breath and waited with anticipation.

"That's it, you punks," he whispered to himself. "Take a good whiff."

"What's that smell?" One kid bumped his head, and he jerked away from the stench.

Lorenzo chuckled when they backed away with hands on their mouths. One tall figure gagged and suddenly vomited. Another yelled, "Ah, gross, man! You're making me sick!" He up-chucked and heaved uncontrollably while the others gagged.

At this hilarious sight, Lorenzo could not ignore the temptation. So, he gave in and shouted, "Freeze!" That's all he had to do, and they scattered like frightened flies.

Startled, Tom jerked awake, and he stumbled out of bed so fast, that he tripped on the blankets and laid there on the carpeted floor. "What was that?" Slowly, he stood up, unhurt but embarrassed, and he rubbed his tired eyes. He looked over at Lorenzo, who still laughed at this joyous confusion.

"You wouldn't believe me it, if I told you," he grinned. "It's okay, go back to sleep."

Tom scratched his scalp and grumbled something that sounded like he'd rather be home with his wife and kids. What was he doing here in the first place? Then, the worn-out trucker plopped back into bed, and he snored almost instantly.

At about 5:00 a.m., Tom and Anthony walked to a nearby 24-hour coffee shop for breakfast. When they looked over the menu inside, Tom sighed, "Man, I am so hungry, I could eat an elephant."

"How about skunk meat and eggs," Anthony teased.

"I'll pass," Tom shook his head. "Say, that reminds me," he looked up from the menu, "We need to clean out that wheel-well before we deliver your furniture."

After breakfast, they purchased a heavy-duty cleaning solution, rags and a bucket at a hardware store. Then, they scrubbed the wheel-well and used a hose at the motel. Anthony sniffed and nodded, "That's better. What do you think?"

Tom shrugged, "It'll have to do but it kind of sticks in my sinuses like glue, no matter what."

"Well, I don't know about you, but I'm going to shower." Anthony quickly wound up the hose and put it to the side of the building.

Tom nodded, "You go first. I'll put this stuff away."

By 7:30 a.m., Tom drove the big rig to Levinson's Furniture, shut off the engine and glanced at the back-loading dock. "What time did Mr. Levinson say he would be here?"

"Between 7:45 to 8:00," Anthony stepped out and kept the passenger side door open. "He should be here soon."

Moments later, a car pulled up and parked by the back door. A tall, slender man in his 50's got out and walked towards them. He had a well-dressed, distinguished appearance, with his blue tie, black blazer and grey side burns along his light brown hair.

"You must be Anthony Lorenzo," he smiled and shook his hand warmly.

Anthony was immediately impressed and smiled back, "That's right, sir."

"Call me, David," Levinson grinned with a look of satisfaction. "You're early. That's good."

"Yes sir," Anthony nodded to the truck driver. "This is my friend, Tom. I couldn't have done it without him."

David shook the trucker's hand enthusiastically. "Of course, that's what makes life worthwhile. People helping each other." He grinned and nodded at the truck, "Okay, let's see what you have for me."

Mr. Levinson stood by and watched, as the men unloaded all the finely-crafted wood furniture on the dock. He slowly strolled around and examined each piece. "Very nice." With a look of admiration, he ran his fingers along the wood. "Yes," he whispered reverently, "Bolt MacArthur out-did himself. I am very pleased."

"Thank you, sir," Anthony nodded, "Bolt will be happy to hear that."

Mr. Levinson leaned closer to an eagle carving on a dresser. "Ah, yes," he slowly felt along the wings and looked up. "So, Anthony, how much of this is your work?"

"Well, Bolt and I work as a team, sir." Anthony humbly lowered his gaze and added, "I'm just an apprentice and I still have a lot to learn."

Mr. Levinson put his hand on the apprentice's shoulder and said, "Don't say, 'just'. You work for Bolt MacArthur, so that means you do high quality craftsmanship. Am I right?"

"I do my best," Anthony grinned and liked the way this man talked, and it was obvious that he cared about people. Mr. Levinson had an admirable trenchant gentlemanly quality that the young veteran had not seen before.

"Okay, let's get everything in the showroom and meet in my office afterwards."

Later, at his desk, Mr. Levinson signed off on the paper work and handed Anthony a check. "You did a great job. Next time we do business, I'll know that I can count on you to follow through, young man."

"Thank you, sir," Anthony shook his hand, "It's been a pleasure to serve you."

Several hours later, Tom and Anthony picked up a load at the harbor and drove downtown on their way out of the city. Ahead, they spotted hundreds of people, who marched toward them with anti-war signs. The street was completely blocked, as the mob raged closer and streamed around the truck on both sides.

In Anthony's side-mirror, he saw police in riot gear, and they rushed up from behind the truck. Unable to go anywhere, he sighed, "Uh, oh! We've got trouble!"

Suddenly, both opposing sides converged, and the truck was surrounded by angry protestors and aggressive policemen. Stuck in the midst of this angry crowd, the two men kept their windows rolled up and looked on in shock. People pushed, shouted and waved their signs while the police shoved with shields and wielded batons. The out-of-control mob squeezed in so tight, that the truck shook wildly.

What started out as a peaceful anti-war demonstration turned into a pitched battle when a lone protestor climbed on the truck's hood and waved a sign with bold, red letters, "Stop the War!" Then, an officer armed with a baton jumped on the running board and whacked the intruder's shins. This escalated into a brawl, as the man fell to the pavement and protestors retaliated with fists, rocks and sticks.

Anthony Lorenzo felt like he was in Vietnam, as someone's bloody face was smeared across his side window. Sickened, he watched while people kicked, screamed and slugged it out. Troops of well-protected riot police turned back the tide in a hail of tear gas canisters, and they pushed back demonstrators further up the street and away from the truck with shields and batons.

Amidst all this mayhem, Lorenzo focused on two teenagers in the retreating crowd. One, a boy of 16 or 17, tried to help a girl, who was about 14. Her forehead was bleeding, and she fell near a storefront doorway. In a panic, the young male ran away, while more police rushed by without noticing the girl.

Lorenzo heard the faint call of the eagle in his mind again, and he saw that the mob had dispersed. His medic instinct kicked in, and he leaped out of the truck, then rushed to her aid. It all happened so fast, and, before he had time to think, he knelt at her side. The girl was conscious, and she tried to stand up.

"Take it easy. You have a head wound. My name is Anthony. I'm a trained medic, and I'm here to help you."

"Where's Larry?" The girl appeared to be dazed and confused.

"It's alright," the medic had her lean back on his knee, "Is Larry your boyfriend?"

"Yes," she began to cry and seemed frightened.

"What's your name?"

"Brandi."

Tom ran over with a first aid kit and knelt with them. "Is she okay?"

"Yeah, she'll be fine," Lorenzo nodded toward the truck, "get my jacket."

Tom brought the coat out and handed it to him. "What's she doing out here, anyway?" He leaned closer and appeared to be worried. "She must be about the same age as my daughter."

The medic ignored his concern and focused on the girl. "Okay, Brandi, I need you to lay back for a little while, so I can be sure you'll be okay." He gently slid the jacket behind her head as she relaxed.

Lorenzo applied pressure to the 4-inch gash on her forehead and checked her eyes. "I have to stop the bleeding, so you need to be very still. Okay, Brandi, just relax and tell me about yourself. What's your last name?"

"Watson," she winced and tears streamed down her cheeks.

The medic monitored her pulse and examined her eyes again, "You're doing fine, Brandi." He continued to apply pressure on her wound and smiled, "Do you know where you are right now?"

"San Diego." Brandi seemed to relax more and she gazed at him with clearer eyes.

"Do you live nearby?

"No, I'm from up north."

The medic observed that the bleeding had stopped, so he cleaned and bandaged the wound. It did not appear to be serious, but he took no chances. To keep the girl still, he talked with a soothing tone. "So, how did you wind up here, Brandi?"

"My boyfriend said we had to go and fight against the war," Brandi looked bewildered. "I thought we were just going to demonstrate peacefully, you know." She groaned, shook her head in confusion and tried to get up.

"Okay," he gently held her shoulders and said, "Slow down, relax. Take your time and talk slowly."

Brandi laid back, rested her head on his jacket again and sighed, "A lot of us kept our cool, until my boyfriend and a few other guys started throwing rocks at that cop. Everybody pushed and shoved, then I fell on the sidewalk."

Lorenzo wiped several minor scratches on her face. "Well, I'm sure most of the them were peaceful, Brandi. Unfortunately, people get overheated and use violence to fight for peace," he shook his head at the irony. "Kind of crazy, don't you think?"

Tom leaned closer, "Do your parents know you're here, Brandi?"

"No." She lowered her head and let out a deep sigh.

"You look about the same age as my daughter. How old are you anyway?" Tom seemed to be so worried that he had difficulty keeping calm.

"I'm 18," she said smugly.

Tom shook his head like a father, who just caught his daughter in a lie. "Come on, young lady. How old are you really?"

"Alright," she sighed, "I'm 14. My Mom and Dad would kill me if they knew I was here."

"Brandi, my guess is that your parents are so worried that they will hug you as soon as they see you. You need to get home right now."

"I can't."

"Why not?"

"I ran away with my boyfriend," Brandi's eyes teared up. "I'm from Santa Barbara."

"A true boyfriend wouldn't leave you on the sidewalk like this, young lady." Tom smiled and patted her hand, "You need to be with your parents, who love you."

Tom sighed, stood up and saw an ambulance driving by, so he ran out and flagged it down. For a moment, he talked with the emergency personnel, then he rushed back, as they followed with a gurney.

"Okay, young lady, these gentlemen will help you," Tom smiled reassuringly and said, "When you get home, tell your parents that you love them."

While Tom drove the truck away, he glanced in the rearview mirror. "I sure hope she gets home alright."

"Brandi will be okay, Tom." Anthony looked in the side mirror and watched, as the medics wheeled her gurney to the ambulance. "We all get lost in our own personal wilderness sometimes. I know because I've been there. You helped that girl when she needed it the most." Anthony reached out and they shook hands. "You did the right thing, my friend."

"Now all I want to do is get home. I miss my wife and kids."

Anthony stared out the side window in silence. Telephone poles, trees and landscape passed by in a blur, and he longed to get back to his refuge in the mountains. Ahead, he spotted a gas station and pointed to a phone booth, "Let's stop, and you can call your family, okay?"

"Good idea." Tom pulled up and got out of the truck. He picked up the receiver while the glass door was still opened and glanced at Anthony, "I'll make it quick, then you can call Bolt."

"Okay, I'll wait," Anthony leaned back in the seat and closed his weary eyes. It had been two days since he had a good night's sleep. He looked forward to a shower and rest in the place he called home with his mentor.

In these quiet, restful moments, Anthony visualized his work with the woodcarver. He felt the pliable wood in his hands and saw the knife slowly carving out the shape of a beautiful eagle in flight. While the young apprentice focused on each detail in his mind, he heard the soothing voice of his mentor, "That's good, son. I'm proud of you."

Anthony felt a smile on his face, and he kept his eyes closed. Then, it dawned on him that he had no horrific flashes of that far-off war in Vietnam. Instead, his mind was completely at peace.

A few minutes later, Tom stepped out of the booth and frowned, "I couldn't get through, so I called the operator. All the lines are down in the mountains, due to a lightning strike."

"Well…I'll see if I can call Bolt. Maybe his phone is still working." Anthony dialed, listened and hung up. "It's dead there, too."

28 Eagle Mates

All the lights were off when Tom drove his rig into Bolt's compound, and Anthony glanced at his watch. "It's after midnight," he stepped out of the truck. "They're probably sound asleep."

"I'll wait here while you check on the place," Tom gripped the steering wheel with a worried look.

"No, you get on home to your family." Anthony closed the door and walked up the steps. "I'll be alright. That lightning must've knocked out the power along with the phone lines."

"Okay," Tom smiled, "I'll see you later." He shifted his gears and drove off.

When Anthony stepped on the porch, he paused and focused his weary eyes in the darkness. Just as he entered the cabin, a flashlight beam greeted him from down the hallway. "Oh, Tony! I missed you so much!" Sheri hugged him and asked, "Did you make the delivery on time?"

"Yep," Anthony gave her a quick kiss and looked down the hallway. "How's Mr. Grumpy? Is he still like a growly bear?"

"Oh, he's fine," Sheri giggled, "Mr. Grumpy is now more like a teddy bear." She rubbed his cheek with her palm, "You look beat."

Anthony sighed and plopped on the couch next to the dying coals of the fireplace. "Yep," He looked up, as Sheri stood beside him and stroked her fingers through his hair. Then he said, "It's good to be home, babe."

Sheri kissed his forehead and gazed into his eyes, "Well, you just take it easy, and I'll get you something to drink. I have some orange juice or iced tea."

"Thanks, I'll just have a glass of water instead." He leaned back and rested his head, while she went into the kitchen. Weary, he started to doze off but felt Sheri, as she sat next to him with a glass of water in her hands. "What?"

Sheri smiled, "You went out like a light...here's your water."

"Thanks," He sipped from his glass, "So, what's going on with Bolt?"

Sheri patted his chest, "Like I said, he's fine. He is so finicky, though."

"What do you mean?"

"Oh, you know," Sheri got up and stirred the simmering embers of the fireplace with a clank, clank of an iron poke, "Pop wants his soup hot, but not too hot." She jabbed at the flickering wood and paused, while the flames grew brighter, "He was so sick with a 106-degree fever the other day that we tried to get him in the hospital, but you know how stubborn he gets."

Anthony leaned forward and laughed, "I can imagine how that went down."

Sheri giggled and shook her head, "Yeah, Pop really freaked out. He insisted that hospitals are where you go to die. No way was he going there! I never saw Pop so pig-headed before!"

"What did you do about it?"

"Well, Poppy said he would only talk to Dr. Benjamin, so I called him instead."

Anthony slapped his knee and laughed, "Our village veterinarian!"

Sheri placed her hands on her curvy hips and grinned, "That's right! I think Pop knew that Doc would back him up. After all, they've been friends for years." She cocked her head and mimicked the doctor, "'Oh, you'll be fine. Just rest in bed. No need to go to the hospital,'" Sheri giggled, as she explained it, "'You'll be fit as a horse in no time.'"

"I wish I could have seen that!" Anthony sighed, leaned back and closed his eyes. "I'm glad you were here, babe."

Sheri knelt at his feet, "You look so tired. Why don't you get some sleep? I can stay another night."

Anthony groaned, as he got up from the couch. "I just need a hot shower, then I'll get to bed."

Later, Anthony awoke from a dream about two eagles and the watchman. It was 2:55 a.m. Unable to comprehend its meaning, he got up and checked on his mentor, who rested peacefully. So, he went into the kitchen and made some tea. He added wood to the fireplace and sat in the living room with a sketch pad and doodled. He sipped from a steamy mug and until he heard slip, slip of slippers in the hallway.

Sheri appeared in the glow of a fireplace while she put on her robe. "I heard you get up," she yawned, let out a deep sigh and stretched her arms. For a split second, he noticed the supple curves of her breasts under a white night gown; then, she closed her robe. "You okay?" She tied the belt with an air of sensuousness that he had not seen before.

"Yeah," Anthony paused and noticed the way Sheri stood next to the fireplace and rubbed her hands together for warmth. For some strange reason, he could not divert from observing her subtle moves. She brushed back strands of raven hair, while she knelt by the fire, and her cheeks had an orange radiance that softly caressed her face. In that moment, the young man was awakened to her beauty more than ever. "I'm just feeling restless," he yawned.

Sheri looked up and asked, "What do you feel restless about?" She leaned closer to the fireplace, rubbed her hands to warm up near the flames and waited to hear his answer.

Anthony vaguely heard her voice but took a sip of his tea and admired how the Navaho Mesa robe flowed gracefully along her feminine curves. Never had he seen such simple elegance from a woman, who wore a robe before. Why did he find this so attractive? He remembered the bar girls of Saigon, and he thought of how scantily clad they were in such ostentatious, seductive display.

Now, here was Sheri wearing nothing fancy--just a robe. All these thoughts flashed in split seconds, and he was not clearly aware of Sheri's question.

"Why are you staring at me like that?" Sheri interrupted his thoughts, "You okay?"

"What?" Anthony blinked his eyes, "Oh, nothing. I was just thinking of…um…how nice it was for you to look after Bolt." Feeling embarrassed, he could not think of anything else to say.

"Thanks, Tony," Sheri sat down and snuggled up to him. "Pop has always helped me in so many ways. It's the least I can do."

Anthony tried to ignore her warm body, as she rubbed against him, but it was becoming increasingly difficult to do so. "Yeah, I know, Bolt has done a lot for me, too." Sheri naturally rested her head on his shoulder, and he became keenly aware of her sweet aroma. Strands of hair brushed up and tickled his cheek. She smelled so fresh that he had to say something. "I like your perfume."

Sheri giggled, "Oh, I just washed my hair before going to bed." She sat up and shivered, "It's freezing tonight. Maybe I should get more clothes on. I'll be right back."

Just as Sheri started to leave, Anthony gently took her hand and smiled. "That's okay, sweetie, I'll put more wood on the fire." He added two small logs, then stoked the flames with a poker, "How's that?"

"Perfect," Sheri nodded, "While you do that, I'll make us some hot chocolate." She went into the kitchen, and he eagerly puffed a bellows on the fire.

When Sheri returned with hot mugs, she noticed that he had spread out blankets and extra cushions on the carpet next to the fireplace. "That's a great idea," she handed him a mug and sat on the floor beside him. "I am so cold right now."

"Me, too," Anthony took a sip, "I can't sleep anyway." He was about to lay a blanket over her but remembered his tragedy with his wife, Amy, and he felt it was best to cool it. Instead, he placed it at her feet, leaned back and sighed, "This will give us a chance to talk."

Sheri took the blanket, pulled it under her arms and slowly sipped from her mug and sighed, "This is much better. So, what do you want to talk about, honey?"

Anthony reached over and picked up his sketch pad and pencil from a lampstand. "Since you've taken some art classes, I'd like to get your opinion of a drawing I started when I woke up from a dream."

Sheri studied the pencil sketch of a wilderness scene. "Oh, I see you drew two eagles flying together. I like the intricate details of their wings," she paused. "This is very good, Tony."

Anthony observed her expression and asked, "Can you give me any suggestions on how to improve this? I struggle with things like clouds and the eagle's talons."

Sheri cocked her head and said, "Well, let's see…" she examined it carefully, "The curvature of your lines may need some practice. Show me how you hold your pencil."

Anthony picked it up and began to draw. It was obvious to her that he held the pencil too tight while his lines were stiff and jerky.

"You need to relax," Sheri spoke softly. "Hold it lightly in your fingers. Can I show you?"

"Please do. I feel so clumsy sometimes," Anthony handed it to her and watched.

"Okay, see how I hold it very gently in my hand." She gracefully, freely swirled the simplicity of clouds without hesitancy. "Now, you try it."

Anthony admired her slender fingers and the way she glided her hand. So, he reached out, took the pencil and drew more easily. "Yeah, I see what you mean now," he paused. "Bolt keeps working with me on this, but you add a nice touch, babe."

"That's better," she placed her hand on his in an attempt to guide him along. "Hang loose, honey."

Anthony tried to not think of the warmth of her soft touch. So, he relaxed as she conducted every move of his fingers. "Oh, this makes more sense. It's kind of like holding the carving knife." He sighed, "I think I'm too much of a perfectionist." More at ease, he loosely sketched in the swirls of clouds.

Sheri let go and watched, as he drew freely. "There, that's very nice." She leaned back on a cushion and smiled, "I can see you've learned a lot from the great Bolt MacArthur. In fact, he's told me how proud he is of you."

Anthony set the pad and pencil down, then moved closer to Sheri. "I really enjoy drawing and carving into wood. Sometimes, I can see a clear image in that pliable material, and I want to set it free. Does that sound crazy?"

Sheri rolled to his side and put her warm hand on his face, "Of course not. It just shows that you've caught Bolt's vision for his craft," she whispered.

"Well, that's not surprising," Anthony chuckled, "You know, the more I immerse myself in woodwork with Bolt, the fewer nightmares I have about Nam. For that, I am truly grateful. It's nice to work on something meaningful."

Sheri kissed his cheek, "I'm glad."

Anthony rolled on his back, and, for a moment, he stared at the dancing shadows on the ceiling from the fireplace. "You know, it's amazing. In the middle of the night, I had a peaceful dream about two eagles and the watchman, so it felt natural to just get up, and I sketched it from memory."

"I'd love to have the same passion for art as you," Sheri snuggled and rested her head on his chest. "Maybe if I listen to the beat of your heart, I'll get inspired."

"You hear anything?"

Sheri lifted her head slightly and rubbed her ear. "Yeah, and you're burning me!"

"Oh," Anthony felt above his heart and laughed, "That's where the Watchman placed his thumb and revived me when I almost died in the blizzard. Sometimes, I get a tingling, heated sensation just before something is about to happen."

"Oh, how interesting," Sheri teased and giggled. "What do you think is going to happen?" She leaned in and listened. "I'm hearing a thump, thump, like a woodpecker tapping on a tree." She rubbed her ear again, "You are hot."

"Okay, stop it now," Anthony laughed and forgot his self-control.

"Let me see it." Sheri unbuttoned his shirt and looked, "You have a red thumb print close to your heart." She sighed and rubbed the spot with her finger. "You weren't kidding!" She kept her hand there and felt his heated heartbeat.

"Now, you did it," Anthony laughed and slipped his hand under her robe. He touched just above her heart. "Let me check you out."

Sheri giggled and feigned resistance. "That tinkles!"

"Okay, hold still, and I'll give you a nice love brand on your heart." Anthony and Sheri wrestled, then he gently pressed his thumb into her flesh. "There!" He laughed, "Got you now!" Suddenly, they both felt a jolt of static electricity, as they kept their hands on each other's chest.

"What was that?" Sheri gasped and rubbed above her left breast. "It feels hot!"

"Let me see!" Stunned by the energy that surged between them, he opened her robe, just enough to see a bright red circular mark in the shape of a thumb print.

"Wow! I don't believe it!" He gazed into her eyes. "Sorry, sweetie, I was just playing around. You okay?"

Sheri appeared to be dazed and had watery eyes. "I feel kind of funny." She tried to sit up, but Anthony gently nudged her to lay back.

"Rest a minute." He stood up, rushed to the kitchen and returned with a glass of water, "Here, drink this." Anthony helped her to sit up.

After several sips, she sighed, "I'm okay." She blinked and wiped her eyes with her fingers. "It's strange. Everything seems brighter somehow." She easily got up and looked around. "I feel lighter. It's weird…but in a good way, I think."

Curious, Anthony leaned closer, "Let me try something." Gently, he touched above her heart again, and the sensuousness of her flesh ignited a desire for her that was stronger than ever. Yet, he tried to keep his composure as best as he could. "Now, you place your hand on my chest at the same time."

Just as they touched each other, a mysterious energy flowed through their bodies without restraint. Surprised, they gazed into each other's eyes. Instead of shock, they were empowered in a pulsating sensation that bonded their souls into one. This made them feel giddy, and they smiled in amazement, while they were fused into a tranquil, cosmic force that magnetically drew them even closer.

During those peaceful moments, they continued to hold each other until Anthony heard the call of more than one eagle in his mind, and then, he leaned back. "Did you hear that?"

"Yes," Sheri turned her head and listened, "It sounds like two eagles. What does it mean, Tony?"

"I'm not sure," Anthony closed his eyes. "In my mind, I can see what appears to be eagle mates, just as clearly as in my dream. Okay, I'd like to try something, sweetie," he lovingly placed his palm over her eyes. "Do you see them?"

"Yes, Tony. It's like having some kind of inner vision. Do you think God is sending a message to us, somehow?"

Anthony released his hand, and they both gazed into each other's eyes in wonder. "Sheri, all I know is…"

"Yes, Tony?"

Anthony smiled, "Sheri, I don't think I've ever felt happier and more alive than at this moment."

"Oh, Tony, I feel the same way," Sheri leaned closer and they embraced.

Anthony awoke the next morning with Sheri beside him, and he wondered what happened during the night. He scratched his head and worried that they may have gotten carried away during their passionate moments together. While she slept, he noticed how lovely she looked even in her peaceful slumber. Perhaps it was all part of his dream, he wondered.

Just then, Anthony heard footsteps from down the hall. He sat up and looked at his mentor standing in the living room. Surprised, the young man sleepily rubbed his eyes and tried to focus, but he only yawned.

"Good morning," said Bolt, as he stretched his arms out and yawned as though it was contagious. "Glad to see you, son. How are you?"

Embarrassed, Anthony glanced at the lump under the blanket beside him and tried to change the subject. "You look better. How are you feeling?"

"Great! What's for breakfast? I'm hungry!"

Suddenly, the blanket stirred and out popped Sheri with her hair all mussed up in her face. "What?" Sheri brushed the strands away and looked startled to see Bolt.

Her godfather chuckled, grinned and nodded, "Well, I see you two had a pleasant night together."

"Poppy!" Sheri quickly stood up with her robe still on and gasped, "It's not what you think!"

Bolt shrugged, "All I'm thinking about is breakfast." He waved to the couple, "Come on, let's eat."

After they ate together, Anthony and Sheri strolled hand in hand through a grove of nearby pine trees. Subtle and pure was the breeze and sunlit needles swayed, as though all the world danced to a rhythm that only nature could provide. Nothing else mattered, while they gazed at each other and smiled. It seemed as though music reverberated in their veins, and they felt light on their feet.

"The sky is so bright this morning." Anthony scanned the landscape with binoculars. "Maybe we'll see the eagle today."

"Oh, there he is!" Sheri pointed directly above them.

Anthony turned his gaze upwards and spotted the raptor, as it circled. Then, suddenly, it flew over to a tree branch. "Wow! He just landed beside another eagle! Here, check it out!"

Sheri took the binoculars. "Yeah, it's rare to see a pair this close to our area."

"The one on the left is kind of preening the bigger eagle." Anthony pointed to the branch, "Must be his mate."

"Oh, look, they flew off together!" Sheri followed their direction through the binoculars. "Now, they are zipping around and doing some wild aerobatics!"

"Yeah, they're swooping, chasing and spinning in cartwheels!" Anthony nodded and grinned in amazement.

"It's a courtship dance," Sheri handed him the binoculars. "See how they fly up real high, then dive together."

"Yeah," Anthony focused through the lens, "How do you know it's a courtship?"

When I was 13, my dad and I hiked on Eagle Ridge, and we saw a similar display." Sheri shaded her eyes with a hand, and she looked skyward. "I thought the two eagles were fighting, but he explained that it was a mating ritual."

"Look at that!" Anthony watched in awe. "The eagles have locked talons, and one is upside down. They're tumbling to the earth! That's crazy!"

"It's okay, Tony," Sheri assured him, "You'll see."

Suddenly, the eagles released themselves, just a few feet from a jagged outcrop. From this death-defying maneuver, they flew high up and continued their wild aerobatics with such precision that only stunt pilots could ever dream of accomplishing.

After several more twists and turns, they nose-dived, leveled off and landed on a branch together. There, the eagles preened each other in silence.

"Wow!" Anthony yelled, leaped and cheered like he was at a football game. He had seen the eagle perform so many amazing stunts, but nothing that topped this grand finale.

Sheri giggled with delight and hugged him. "Aren't they beautiful!"

"Yeah!" Anthony kissed her cheek. "Just think, we saw this together! It's got to be a once-in-a-lifetime experience!" He let out a sigh and chuckled with satisfaction.

Back in the cabin, Bolt sat by the fireplace with a cup of coffee, and he looked up from his newspaper, as Anthony and Sheri came in. "I feel a lot better now, but I reckon I'll take it easy for another day. How was it outside?"

"Oh, Poppy!" Sheri breathlessly rushed over and knelt beside him. "We saw two eagles in a courtship flight!"

"Yeah!" Anthony grinned, still wide-eyed with wonder. "They locked talons and tumbled almost to the ground!"

"Really?" Bolt set his newspaper down and smiled in surprise. "You both saw it together?"

"It was awesome, Poppy!" Sheri still tried to catch her breath and sighed, "They flew up and down and made so many twists and turns that I got dizzy watching it all!"

Bolt slapped his knee and stood up. "Do you realize what this means?" He wrapped his arms around both them and grinned, "There is a legendary belief that says when a young single couple witnesses the eagle's courtship ritual together, they will be blessed as mates for life!"

Anthony and Sheri gazed at each other knowingly and smiled.

"You don't look surprised," Bolt chuckled.

Anthony glanced at Sheri, then said, "Something else happened last night."

Bolt turned away and laughed, "I don't want to know about it, son." He shook his head and held a hand up. "Whatever happened between you two in private is none of my business."

Sheri grabbed his hand in her palms and looked seriously into his eyes, "It's not what you think, Poppy!"

Bolt softened his gaze, "Okay, kitten, what are you trying to tell me?"

"Remember how you and Tony talked about the mark of the Watchman?" Sheri waited for his answer in an effort to emphasize her point.

Bolt nodded, "Yes, kitten, go on."

Sheri started to speak but looked at Anthony and sighed, "You explain it, Tony."

Anthony felt awkward and embarrassed. Finally, he scratched his beard and said, "Well, Sheri and I were just clowning around when she put her hand on my chest mark, and I...um, jokingly touched above her heart at the same time." Anthony rolled his eyes and sighed, "Oh, man, this sounds crazy."

"What Tony is trying to say, Poppy, is that there was some kind of heated energy surge between us, and now I got a mark just like his!" Sheri giggled and put a hand over her heart, "See?" She partially opened the top of her shirt, just enough to reveal the red thumbprint.

Bolt's eyes widened, then he slapped his knee again and laughed, "The Watchman sure has a sense of humor!"

"What does it mean, Poppy?"

Bolt laughed, hugged her, then stepped back and grinned with a look of satisfaction. "Okay, Kitten, let me put it this way. Do you love this guy?"

"Uh, huh," Sheri nodded breathlessly, "Yes, I do."

Bolt looked at Anthony and asked, "Son, do you love my goddaughter?"

"Yes." Anthony gazed into Sheri's eyes.

"Well, there you have it," Bolt chuckled, kissed Sheri's cheek and shook Anthony's hand. "I think the Watchman is sending you a clear message that you are meant to be soul mates for life. Love moves in mysterious ways. Now, it's up to you to decide for yourselves."

Moments later, Anthony and Sheri stood by her pickup truck, and she smiled, then lovingly held his hand. "Well, what do you think?"

"About what?"

Sheri chuckled slightly, "You know…what Pop said about being soul mates for life."

Anthony felt the warmth of Sheri's hand and saw the tender, loving way she looked up to him. A slight breeze caressed her face and he gently stroked her hair away from her eyes. "Sheri, I…" He hesitated. Why was it so difficult to say those three words that were in his heart?

Sheri smiled and kept her affectionate gaze on him. "Yes, Tony?"

Anthony lowered his head and noticed a tiny beetle as it crawled in the dirt at his feet. His thoughts were on the tragic accident that caused the death of his wife, Amy. How could he be worthy of sharing his life with Sheri after he made such a fatal mistake? "Sheri, I…care about you a lot."

"What's bothering you, honey?" Sheri warmly placed her hand on his cheek. "I've seen that lost look before."

Anthony focused on her lovely face again, and he thought of how nice it would be to wake up every morning and see her smile. "I need you to help me. I just feel that I'm not good enough." He groaned at how stupid that sounded. "I'm sorry, babe, I don't want to ever hurt you."

Sheri embraced him, "I know, Tony." She snuggled and rested her head on his chest. "It's okay, I understand, you've suffered a lot."

"I just need some more time to work things out." Anthony held her close, and he felt her unconditional love.

Sheri sighed and looked with moist eyes, "That's okay, I am here for you, Tony. No matter what happens, I will always love you."

"Sheri, I…"

Wings fluttered just above his head, and Anthony turned to see an eagle, as it flew and landed on the roof. He gazed into Sheri's eyes, "I…"

Another eagle passed in front of them and perched itself next to what appeared to be its mate. Sheri chuckled and nodded, "I think they're waiting to hear what you have to say to me, Tony."

"I love you, Sheri," Anthony smiled and brushed back her hair, as a gentle breeze caressed her face again. "Thank you for being patient and giving me enough time to get my head screwed on straight."

Sheri rested her head on his chest again. "I love you, too. We have our whole lives together, so there's no need to rush."

"Okay," Anthony opened her driver's side door, "Do you want to go see a movie down in the city this Saturday?"

Sheri kissed his cheek and slid into the seat, "I can't," She turned on the engine and smiled, "Have to work." She closed the door and looked at him with an odd expression that confused him.

"Oh, yeah, I forgot. Um…how about Friday night?" Anthony rested his arm on the open window.

Sheri patted his hand and smiled, "Let's wait a while, so you can have more time to think about what you want to do in life." She pressed down on the accelerator and drove off in a cloud of dust in his face.

Anthony coughed and waved a hand to clear the air, as he watched her drive away. The two eagles flew off and disappeared in the forest. A cool gust of wind blew in, and he felt a chill in the air.

Dark clouds drifted over a ridge to the west and several leaves skittered across his feet. For a moment, he just stood there in front of Bolt's cabin, shivered and wondered what just happened.

29 Cause and Effect

Bright, flashing red lights glared through the kitchen window. Surprised by this sudden intrusion, Anthony glanced at the clock. It was 5:15 a.m., and he just made the morning coffee while Bolt turned over blueberry pancakes in a skillet.

"It's the Sheriff!" Anthony ran and opened the front door to see Deputy Hughes, as he came up the porch steps. "What's wrong?"

"We just got a report of a missing 4-year-old boy from a campsite at Logan Spring."

Bolt appeared in the doorway, "How can we help?"

"We need your tracking skills and all the volunteers we can get." Deputy Hughes frowned and looked worried, "According to his parents, the boy was sleeping in their tent with them, but, somehow, he disappeared in the night."

Bolt shined a flashlight at the outside temperature gauge on the porch wall. "How long?"

"Possibly an hour or two."

"It's 40 degrees out!" Bolt grabbed a jacket and cap from the hook by the inside door and tossed them to Anthony. Then, he put on his coat and Stetson hat. "We'll follow you!"

At the camp, a dozen men and women had already gathered around emergency vehicles and more came in. Headlights shined on Sheriff Hamlin's map, as he leaned it on the hood of Bolt's Jeep. "Okay," he pointed and said, "The stream is here and about a quarter of a mile to the east is the lookout with a sheer cliff that drops down 1,500 feet."

Bolt looked to the east and saw an orange glow of the sunrise about to peek over a ridge. "We'll be able to see better soon." He glanced around, "Where are the search dogs?"

"Clancy is bringing his up now," Sheriff Hamlin nodded over to a pickup truck that just drove up.

"What's the boy's name?" Anthony Lorenzo felt a tingling sensation and scratched the heated mark above his heart. He glanced at Bolt, who still gazed toward the east with increased interest.

"Tommy Reed," Sheriff Hamlin looked over to a young couple in their mid-20's. "His parents are right there being interviewed by one of our deputies now."

Bolt noticed that Clancy went to them and took what appeared to be the boy's jacket. The two dogs sniffed it wildly, then barked, pulled on Clancy's leashes and headed west. "What was Tommy wearing?"

"Just his pajamas and socks. Nothing else."

Lorenzo heard the call of the eagle in his mind again and glanced at Bolt, who nodded as though he picked up the sound, too. "I think we should go east."

"Agreed," Bolt waved a hand to the young vet, "Let's go."

"But the dogs went west," Sheriff Hamlin frowned.

"It's best to fan out," Bolt glanced at the sun that rose over Carson's Peak, and he jogged ahead with Lorenzo.

When they reached the lookout, both men yelled, "Tommy! Tommy!"

Bolt knelt and examined the trail, "Too many prints here to make out anything." He stood up and scanned the terrain, "Tommy!"

"Tommy!" Lorenzo urgently searched off the trail. "He's got to be close. I feel it."

Just above their heads, the men heard wings flapping, and they looked to see the eagle flying in low. Suddenly, it landed on the ground about 200 feet to the southeast. Without hesitation, they worked their way through thick vegetation in that direction until they halted in the area where the eagle landed.

"What happened to the eagle?" Lorenzo quickly pushed aside numerous branches of young trees that grew close together. "I'm sure he came in here!"

"Keep looking!" Bolt knelt and studied a narrow pathway. "Wait! Did you hear that?"

Lorenzo stopped, listened and pointed to his left, "It's the eagle calling from over there!"

Both men struggled through a thicket that was up to their waist. Finally, they made it to a clearing and discovered the eagle, and it sat protectively beside the little body of Tommy Reed. Lorenzo knelt and observed that the child's-partially-opened-eyelids fluttered. The boy's ears and lips were blue, and he shivered. Alarmed, the medic knew he had to act fast to treat for hypothermia. So, he quickly wrapped the boy in his jacket and held him close.

"Hurry!" Lorenzo nodded to Bolt, "Stand in front of me and hug him!"

Together, they wrapped their arms around Tommy. Gently, the men swayed from side to side, and they gently rubbed the child's body while the eagle watched.

"I've never seen anything like this before. The eagle just stands there," Bolt whispered softly.

"Yeah, it's as though the eagle senses that every second counts." Lorenzo checked the boy's face and worried, "His skin is still blue."

Then, he remembered the power of the Watchman's touch. So, he placed his thumb above Tommy's heart, and immediately he felt a jolt of heated static electricity. The boy gasped, and his eyes widened. Encouraged, he nodded to Bolt, "You feel that flow of energy?"

Bolt smiled peacefully, while he focused on a vibrating sensation that reverberated throughout their bodies. "Yeah, the heat seems to be helping."

After a moment of this, Lorenzo examined the boy's face, and the skin appeared to be pink. Relieved, he grinned and said, "Hello, Tommy."

The boy rubbed his eyes with tiny fingers and whimpered, "I want my Mommy."

Lorenzo chuckled and held him close. "Okay, let's go see your Mommy and Daddy."

When they returned to the campsite, the boy's mother cried out, "My baby!"

While she embraced her child, Lorenzo said, "Tommy is all right." The medic waved to emergency personnel, and they rushed over. "But, let these experts look him over."

"How did you find him?" Sheriff Hamlin patted Lorenzo on the back and chuckled with relief.

"We had help from our own personal trail guide."

A capful of wind caressed Anthony's face when he stepped out of the Jeep near the cabin. "Ah, home sweet home. Man, I'm hungry."

"Uh, oh!" Bolt looked worried. "I'm not sure I turned off the skillet in all that ruckus!"

He leaped out of the vehicle, and, in his hurry, he twisted his right ankle, then stumbled to the ground. "Ow!" Bolt tried to stand up but fell to his side in pain.

Anthony knelt and examined the woodcarver's foot. "I think it's just sprained." The medic put Bolt's arm around his shoulder. "Come on, let's get you inside."

As the men hobbled together, Bolt chuckled over the irony. "How about that? I go on a rescue mission with no problem. Then, I hurt myself in front of my own house."

Inside the cabin, Anthony gently helped Bolt to the couch and lifted his leg on an ottoman. "Okay, rest your foot here." He set a pillow under the ankle to elevate it. "I'll be right back with something to relieve the pain."

Several minutes later, he returned with two ice packs and placed one on each side of the right foot. "This will help to bring down the swelling."

Bolt groaned and sighed. "Did you check the skillet?"

"Here's the good news...you remembered to turn off the stove."

"What's the bad news?" Bolt groaned and grimaced in pain again.

"I had to toss out your pancakes," Anthony handed him two aspirin and a glass of water. "I thought about making us some sandwiches, but I called Sheri and told her what happened. You know how she is in a pinch. She's a real trooper and immediately offered to bring over some roasted chicken soon."

"Perfect! She's a whole lot prettier than you anyway."

"Yep, and she sure knows how to handle you a lot better when you get sick and downright ornery."

Anthony kept busy in the workshop, while Bolt rested his swollen ankle that afternoon. Gradually, he felt restless, and he walked to the mail box at the end of their driveway. He thought about his relationship with Sheri, and a deep love was certain in his heart, but the idea of a long-term commitment scared him. Did he seriously deserve a second chance with anyone, after his tragic mistake with his wife, Amy? Although almost two years had passed, he still could not give himself permission to be truly happy.

"Here's the mail." Anthony handed a small stack to Bolt, "How's the foot?"

Bolt ignored the question, while he opened a letter. He quietly read it, then he grinned and sighed with a look of satisfaction. "Well, after reading this, I reckon I'm feeling pretty good."

"You're taking this fairly well. At least you're not biting my head off like a wounded animal." He glanced at the paper in Bolt's hand, "So, what's in there that makes you happy?"

Bolt smiled and held it up, "This letter is from Mr. Levinson, and he commends you for how well you did handling the delivery of our furniture. Here, see for yourself."

Anthony quickly skimmed it over and handed it back to him. "I'm glad it all worked out." He lifted Bolt's leg higher and added another cushion, "This will help to relieve the pressure."

"I'm proud of you, son. You demonstrated that I can depend on you to look out for my interests."

"Thanks, boss," Anthony continued to examine his mentor's ankle, "That means a lot to me."

"In fact, I don't need an apprentice anymore."

"What?"

"Oh, I know that you still have much to learn about wood working but I think you've progressed enough to become my wingman, you know."

Anthony chuckled at the word, and he could not resist the temptation to tease, "So, you mean you want me to help you pick up women, right?"

His mentor busted out in laughter, "You got me on that one." He winced, as he adjusted his foot on the cushion.

"Well, think of yourself more like my right-hand man, almost like a partner but not quite. Come to think of it, that may come sooner than later, if we keep working together as well as we do, son."

After four days of rest, the woodcarver still had to keep his swollen foot elevated. Meanwhile, Anthony worked on a large oak cabinet in the shop, and he had to be more creative about doing a two-man job. Whenever possible, he used clamps or leaned it against a workbench to hold the pieces together, as he installed the side panels.

For the young vet, he liked nothing better than to work alone or with Bolt in this tranquil refuge away from the world's madness. He was completely focused on each small detail, and this gave him a deep sense of satisfaction. It was his ongoing therapy to heal his tortured mind.

Nothing else mattered. Except, most recently, he thought more about Sheri, and he tried to figure out when or if he should make a commitment of a long-term relationship. Frustrated with his indecision, he paused, then with a loud sigh, he began to pace around the workshop. "Come on, man, get your act together," Anthony spoke loudly, knowing that no one could hear his words. He plopped on a work stool and picked up his carving knife, "What's wrong with, you, man?"

He began to focus on his project again, and gradually he was able to get back into his own peaceful rhythmic groove again. This helped him to relax and not think about the past or future. Now he steadily focused on the present moment, and he was happy.

Hours passed and all was tranquil until, "Clunk!" Startled, Anthony spun around and saw Sheri by the metal door, and he was annoyed to see her entering his sanctuary. Yet, her smile captivated him, so he tried to make the best of it. "Oh…hi. What are you doing here?"

"I have a couple of days off, so I checked on Bolt, and the swelling has gone down a little more." Sheri came over and kissed his cheek, "I'd like to help in whatever way I can. He's so restless, I don't know how long we can keep him inside."

"Yeah, I told him that we need to get crutches before he can move around, but that didn't go over very well."

"Bolt is so stubborn and proud," Sheri paused, "I have an idea. Maybe he'll use a cane instead."

"Hey, I got a better idea. I'll make him a walking stick." Anthony examined some wood on the shelves. "Ah, here's some good, sturdy cedar. When we hike through rough terrain, we make walking sticks out of branches we find along the way. Also, we can easily remove rattle snakes from our paths. This will be more acceptable."

On the sixth day, Bolt had enough rest. "I can't stand it any longer, son. I need to get up and move around." "Okay, let's see how you're doing," Anthony examined his foot and smiled, "It looks much better, but you can't put pressure on it for at least a few more days."

Sheri came in from the kitchen and held up a six-foot-tall piece of cedar wood. "Here, Poppy, Tony made you a walking stick to help you get around."

Bolt examined the inscription of his name and carved details of eagles on the staff. "Nice work, son. Thanks," he grinned with satisfaction, "Now I'm ready to get back to work." Carefully, he tried to hold the stick on his left side and stood up with his right foot off the floor but wobbled a little, then sat back down.

"Take it easy," Anthony held his mentor's arm. "You need to get used to it." He pointed to a five-inch handle at the arm's length of the staff and said, "Hold it here. Now, keep it on the same side as your injured foot."

Sheri reached over and gripped Bolt's arm. "Okay, we'll help you practice around the house first."

Bolt tried it again, and this time he kept his balance, then slowly walked around with a thump, thump of the stick on the floor. As he carefully maneuvered with their help, he grimaced, groaned, sighed and practiced with determination. Finally, he grinned and said, "I reckon I can make it to the workshop now."

By the 10th day, the woodcarver had recovered enough to go without his walking stick. Yet, he admired the personalized designs so much that he used it wherever he walked around the property.

At the café, he strolled in like Moses with his staff in hand and proudly showed off his prized possession to everyone.

"Look, Dan, Anthony made this for me." Bolt held it up and pointed to intricately detailed eagles in flight along the staff. "See, he even carved my name on it."

Dan, a Vietnam veteran with a permanent limp from shrapnel, smiled and studied it carefully. "Wow, man! That looks a whole lot better than this." He glanced at his own VA-issued cane, "Do you think Anthony could make me one?"

Bolt gazed into the wounded vet's eyes, and he was overwhelmed with empathy. He placed a hand on the man's shoulder and felt a warmth of compassion that struck him with an idea. "Of course, I'll get him over here."

Bolt glanced at Anthony, who sat in a corner booth, while he talked with Sheri. The men's eyes met, and the woodcarver waved him to join them.

"You remember Dan?"

Anthony nodded, smiled and shook hands with Dan. "Yeah, we've talked a few times. "How's it going?"

"Fine, but I'm kind of envious of Bolt's walking stick. Any chance you can make me something more personal than this ugly brown thing?" He tapped his cane on the floor.

Without hesitation, Anthony smiled and said, "I would be honored."

Dan sighed and grinned with satisfaction, "How much do you charge to make it?"

"Are you kidding?" Anthony placed a hand on the wounded vet's shoulder, "Dan, you served our country well. It would be a privilege to make one especially designed for you. If you're happy with it, that's all the compensation I need. Let's get a booth and talk about it."

When they sat down, Anthony pulled out a note pad and pencil from his pocket. "Okay, Dan, tell me about yourself."

"I see you carry that around more, lately," Bolt smiled and nodded.

"Yep, I get a lot of ideas in my head, and I like to take notes or sketch whenever I notice things." With his pencil in hand, Anthony looked up at Dan. "Alright, I know you love to go fishing with your 10-year-old son." He drew a boat on the lake. "What else?"

Anthony arrived at the café three days later and presented his finished product. "Here you go, Dan. It has a special hand grip along the side with a unique fit."

"That's perfect," Dan's eyes brightened as he examined the fine details of a boat, a man with a boy holding fishing gear, and their names carved on the staff. Also, three small children stood next to a woman. "I can't wait to show my wife and kids. Thanks, man."

Tom, the truck driver, peeked over from the other booth and enthusiastically said, "Hey, I know a couple of guys at the VA, who might be interested in those customized walking sticks."

Anthony grinned, "That gives me an idea."

"Yep, I'm thinking the same thing."

Anthony scratched his chin, "Do you think it'll work?"

Bolt patted his apprentice on the shoulder and grinned, "Sure, son, anything's possible."

Sheri strolled over with a curious expression. "Okay," she giggled and put her hand on Bolt's shoulder, "What are you two up to now?"

30 Walking Sticks

About 6:00 on Sunday evening, Jenny and Sheri arrived at the woodcarver's cabin, and they all pitched in and prepared the dinner together.

Bolt grilled chicken in a skillet and nodded to Anthony, "You slice the carrots and get the salad ready."

"I'll get the rolls in the oven." Jenny set the tray out and glanced at Sheri, "Check the mashed potatoes for me."

They had met like this almost once a week, and, for Anthony, this was another chance to be with his adopted family. In those moments of sharing a meal, he enjoyed the laughter, story-telling and ongoing jokes.

After dinner, Bolt usually shuffled a deck of cards, but, this time, he took out a sketch pad with a pencil. "Well, ladies, like I mentioned earlier, we discovered a way to help veterans, and we decided to form a non-profit to accomplish our plans. We'd like to enlist you in this family venture." He nodded to Anthony, "Go ahead, son, it's your baby."

"Okay, you all know when I made Bolt's walking stick, I realized that some wounded veterans wanted a personalized staff. I called a few people at the VA the other day, and they're interested in the idea of helping those in need of our free service." He glimpsed Sheri's supportive, loving smile and said, "It's our way of giving back to anyone in need."

Bolt looked up from his pad and held the pencil ready. "To make this work, I'll provide all the wood, and the two of us will carve out the sticks in our spare time. So, let's start with a name for our non-profit foundation. Any suggestions?"

For the next five minutes, it became a lively brainstorming session with everyone participating. Bolt enjoyed the banter, and he enthusiastically wrote down every idea.

Anthony examined the list and said, "While we think about a name, it'll help to come up with a mission statement. Maybe we could say something like we seek to improve the quality of life of wounded veterans, or anyone, who needs support. Our goal is to enrich their sense of dignity and pride with personalized walking sticks."

"How about calling the foundation, Walking Sticks for Life?" Jenny smiled and added, "That fits your vision, doesn't it?"

"Perfect!" Bolt wrote it down.

Anthony nodded in agreement, "Okay, that's settled."

"Now, the next order of business is to think about our level of participation." Bolt tapped his pencil on the pad. "Sheri, I already know that you want to help as much as possible. How about you, Jen?"

"Of course, I saw how excited people were at the café, so it'll be an honor."

Hot, dry Santa Ana wind blew a dust devil in front of Anthony Lorenzo's pickup when he parked near the rescue mission that morning. He carried a personalized walking stick for his friend, Johnny Hobbes. Yet, his war-weary mind was on edge again, and he did not like it. He felt that slight tingling sensation above his heart, and he worriedly looked at Sheri. Deep in his mind, he heard the faint call of the eagle.

"Did you hear that?"

Sheri nodded and gripped his hand tight, "Something's wrong." She glanced around anxiously, leaned closer and clung to his arm for support.

Meanwhile, a middle-aged Vietnamese couple worked in their market around the corner. Refugees from the war, they came to America with dreams of a better life for themselves and their two children. They labored long hours, seven days a week for little money.

Shy about their broken English and unfamiliar with local customs, they had difficulty assimilating in this strange land. Poor, destitute neighbors resented these foreigners. But, as a matter of convenience, they shopped for groceries and other items because this was the only market nearby.

Angry, violent thugs loitered and made drug deals behind the store. The market owners had to pay extortion money to the gang for protection, and it seemed as though nothing could be done to stop them.

As a result, the Vietnamese family lived in constant fear for their lives. In a vain attempt to protect themselves, they kept bars on the windows and a pistol under the counter. Tension was high. Police were understaffed, outgunned, and in some cases, they took way too long to respond in an emergency. It was only a matter of time for this short fuse to ignite in tragedy.

Yet, something was about to happen that would change the neighborhood in a way that no one ever imagined. Unbeknownst to the gang, an undercover agent had infiltrated it's members. After months of planning, 12 well-armed members of an elite task force were poised for the signal to strike.

With a nod, an officer yelled, "Freeze!" Agents swarmed in and quickly disarmed the gang but someone shouted, "Santos is getting away!"

Santos dodged behind a car and ran down the street, while several officers pursued him. In a desperate attempt to get away, he darted around a crowd of people walking along the sidewalk. Just as Santos passed by, Lorenzo swung his walking stick and jabbed it like a sword right between the guy's feet.

This tripped up the gangster, and he fell hard on his face, while his gun slid harmlessly out of his hand. Immediately, the officers retrieved the weapon and made a quick arrest without any further risk to the public.

It was another intrusion to Anthony's peaceful endeavors, and he did not even look back. Instead, he took Sheri's hand and escorted her into the rescue mission. Inside, all he wanted was to completely ignore the constant madness of a city on edge.

"What's going on out there?" Johnny Hobbs greeted him with a handshake.

"Oh, nothing really," Anthony shrugged, "Just little police action."

Sheri chuckled, sighed with relief and joked, "Yeah, every time we come into the city, we seem to notice a lot of nothing."

Rosie hugged her and laughed, "I know what you mean. We had a guy, who came in yesterday, and he shouted that he was Jesus and Buddha all in one. We just ignored him until he started throwing dishes at us. When the police arrested him, he claimed it was all our fault, and he did nothing."

"Well, anyway, I brought you this," Anthony let out a sigh as a way of relieving his tension and handed Johnny the customized walking stick.

Johnny smiled and gladly examined the carved details of his favorite scenes that included sunrises over the mountains and a flock of geese in flight. "This is perfect," he slowly felt his grooved-out name with his fingers, then happily strutted around the hall with his personalized support. "I like the feel of it."

Rosie smiled with delight over the way her husband walked, "Oh, Johnny, you can balance yourself much better."

"It's cool to have my name carved on it, too." He stopped and admired it again, and he said, "Oh, look, honey, it's got a heart carved on it with 'Johnny and Rosie, forever in love.'"

The next day, Bolt smiled and handed Anthony a newspaper, "Here, read this."

Anthony saw the words, "Bystander helps to capture wanted gang leader." He frowned and handed it back to Bolt, "I don't want this kind of publicity, man."

"Well, then, you might want to look at this other article." Bolt held the paper up, "Evidently a reporter tried to find you and wound up talking to Johnny Hobbs."

Anthony read, "Mr. Hobbs said that his friend, Anthony Lorenzo stopped by, just to give him a customized walking stick. He said Lorenzo personally made it to help improve his mobility and give him a sense of dignity. According to witnesses, that same tool was used in tripping up the fugitive."

Bolt patted Anthony on the back and grinned, "Somehow, the reporter tracked you down, and he called while you were out. He plans to do a story on you."

"Forget it! I don't want to be involved!" Anthony handed the newspaper to Sheri and started to walk away.

"Wait, Tony," Sheri held it up and pointed to the front page, "This news could help bring attention to our mission."

Anthony sighed and nodded to the paper, "Yeah, you're right. Okay, I'll give the interview. Maybe the word will get out, so more people with leg injuries can get the personal support they need."

So, the interview took place, and this generated other articles. As a result, more requests came in. Even civilians, who had knee surgeries asked for help, and it did not take long for the fledgling non-profit company to grow.

"This is getting too big for us," Anthony shuffled through mounting orders. "We need help."

Bolt nodded in agreement, "I'll call some of my friends."

About three months later, four woodcarvers around the state had eagerly agreed to make customized walking sticks. Gradually, more artisans signed up as the demand grew.

Anthony and Bolt built a small office in the back of the workshop for Sheri, as she took an administrative role in the operation. In the process, she discovered that it felt natural for her to share their vision with others, and she enjoyed fundraising.

Excited by her recent phone call, Sheri rushed over to Anthony and Bolt. "I just talked with Mr. Levinson," she grinned happily. "He agreed to put on all his advertising that 10% of any purchase of his furniture will go to support our Walking Sticks for Life Foundation!"

Anthony looked up from his work and smiled, "That's great, Sheri!" He paused and enjoyed her presence in his refuge.

"Oh, remember how we talked about looking into ways of helping the homeless to get off the streets?" Sheri grinned and held up some papers.

Anthony put his carving knife down and asked, "Yeah, what did you find out?"

"Well, I just talked with Rosie, and she said that two ministers are planning to meet with Johnny about some of his suggestions. They want us to join them next Tuesday." Sheri glanced at her papers, "We'll be at the mission by noon."

"Perfect!" Anthony smiled, "I heard that more people are interested in trying to make some positive changes downtown since Johnny and Rosie have been working at the mission."

Bolt chuckled at the news, "Just think, it all started by an ankle sprain." He slapped Anthony on the back. "Then you came up with the walking stick to help me. Next thing we knew, more wounded veterans requested it. Now, a lot of people are wanting to make a difference. Wow! Talk about cause and effect!"

Back in the city, Johnny Hobbs felt more at ease and confident, as he strolled with his walking stick near the mission. Without the constant harassment of the local gang, he had many opportunities to talk with the homeless on the streets. Rosie stood beside him when they noticed several families in the park across the street and little children played on swings.

Pleased with the positive changes, Rosie glanced at Johnny's walking stick and smiled, "Not long ago, we were out there struggling to survive. Now, look at the blessings all around us."

Even the Vietnamese couple were aware of the difference. Now, they could freely step outside to empty their trash without fear of retribution. Then, one day, An Dung, the owner of the market stepped out front to clean his storefront windows, and he heard footsteps.

"Hello, neighbor."

Startled, An Dung turned to see a smiling Johnny Hobbs for the first time. It did not take long for the two men to become friends. Local customers noticed a new warmth in the atmosphere, as they shopped with less tension. Instead of shutting themselves off, people greeted each other. They had a fresh air of hope and neighbors spontaneously began to clean up their streets.

While the seeds of hope and renewal were planted, no one knew how long this fragile peace would last. Another gang could take over. Was it possible for the neighborhood to grow and thrive? Only time would tell.

It was a warm sunny afternoon that Tuesday when Anthony and Sheri returned from their meeting with Johnny, Rosie and the two ministers. When they stepped up on the porch and sat down on a swinging bench, Bolt came out of his mountain cabin and asked, "How'd it go?"

Sheri looked up and smiled, "Oh, a lot is happening in the neighborhood around the rescue mission. Now that the drug gang is gone, people are excited about making it a safer place for everyone."

Bolt sat down beside them and sighed, "Well, it's a perfect time to fill the void with something good for a change."

"Yeah," Anthony leaned forward, "Since Johnny Hobbs started visiting people in the streets and their homes, a couple of homeless vets began to go with him. It didn't take long to have about a dozen guys in the area to follow along. Now, they formed their own neighborhood watch, and they call themselves The Peace Walkers."

Sheri chuckled and smiled, "What's really cool is that all the men want to have walking sticks like Johnny's. Now, I have a new order for us to make a dozen more. To top it off, a group of women in one of the churches have volunteered to make bright yellow vests that will have the words, The Peace Walkers with an eagle on the back of each of them."

"This is just the beginning!" Anthony grinned and chuckled, "Church officials are talking about plans to provide temporary shelters, counseling and job training for people who are willing to change their lives."

"It's so amazing," Sheri looked up from her paperwork, "The whole neighborhood is coming together and helping each other."

"Yeah, I've never seen so many people coming together and actually trying to change their community." Anthony grinned happily. "I didn't think it was possible."

"Anything's possible, son," Bolt came alongside and patted his shoulder.

The next day, Sheri rushed into the workshop with a newspaper in hand. "Remember the little boy you rescued a few months ago?"

Anthony looked up from his carving, "Yeah."

"What's up, Kitten?" Bolt stepped away from storage shelves in the back.

Sheri chuckled knowingly, "Oh, you are not going to believe this." She placed the newspaper in front of them and pointed to a headline that said, "Four-year-old boy saves family in burning home."

Bolt suddenly grabbed the paper, "Let me see that. Says here little Tommy Reed woke up his parents and warned them of a fire in the kitchen. The mother, father and three children escaped unharmed. Fire Chief Dan Richards credited the boy for saving his family and their home."

Anthony leaned in and pointed, "The boy was asked how he knew about the fire. He said he had a dream about freezing outside when an eagle landed beside him. Then, it made a bird call, and the boy awoke. Immediately, he got out of bed, saw the flames and told his parents."

"Isn't that amazing?" Sheri giggled with excitement, "This means the eagle somehow reached the boy and five lives were saved."

"Yeah!" Anthony stared at the paper, "So, Tommy Reed actually heard the call of the eagle."

"Wow!" Bolt stood up wide-eyed and smiled at Anthony, "Son, do you realize that if you didn't survive your first blizzard here, none of these events would've happened?"

31 Courtship of Eagles

On a bright morning in June, Anthony zipped up a backpack, tied on a sleeping bag and slung it over his shoulder. "You ready to go, babe?"

Sheri stepped off the porch and adjusted the weight of her hiking gear. "I want to see Pop before we go."

Inside the workshop, the woodcarver busily focused on a statue of an eagle perched on a nest high in a tree. "You two all set for your quest?"

"Yep," Sheri glanced at Anthony, smiled and looked back at the woodcarver, "I got my man, food, water, sleeping bags and change of clothes. What else do I need?"

"Well, Kitten, you both need to travel light, stay in tune with the weather and remember why you are going on this trek."

Anthony spread out a map and studied it. "So, we need to go on the east flank of Eagle Ridge?"

"That's right," Bolt pointed to the location. "I reckon you'll find at least one nesting couple in this area. Your goal is to search for two eagle's feathers and keep one for each of you. Do you both understand why you are doing this?"

Sheri gazed at Anthony and smiled, "Uh, huh."

Anthony smiled back and held her hand. "This is to be our courtship quest. On our journey, we can discover more about each other and learn how to be compatible."

"Good, if you choose to be engaged, you will return with the feathers attached to your left arms with the red scarfs I gave you."

Anthony mischievously grinned and teased, "What if the answer is no?"

Sheri playfully slapped his chest and giggled, "Don't you dare say that."

"You heard her, son," Bolt laughed. "She's already made up her mind. So, if you want to come back alive, you better watch yourself."

"Don't worry about that. I'll be watching her so much, I might forget to come back anyway," Anthony kissed Sheri's forehead and studied the map again. "How long do you think we need for this quest?"

Bolt shrugged, "That's up to you two. I reckon it could take five days, maybe longer. You have enough food for a few days. Then, after that, you'll have to forage for what you need to survive."

Anthony glanced at Sheri with concern, "Isn't it risky? I don't want to put her in any danger."

"If you remember to have faith and follow the eagle, you'll be fine," Bolt grinned and placed hands on each of their shoulders. "Besides, I wouldn't underestimate Sheri's mountain trekking skills. Her father and I taught her well. Right, Kitten?"

"It's been a while, but I think I can still remember a lot of things you taught me."

After more than a half-day's hike, Sheri stopped along the trail, lowered her wide-brimmed hat and looked toward the west. "Must be about 3:00."

Anthony examined his wristwatch and nodded, "Hey, that's pretty good. I got 3:15."

"Thanks," Sheri scanned the base of a hill with her binoculars and pointed, "There, see the jagged boulder that looks like a giant toad?"

Anthony adjusted his lens and spotted the landmark, "Yep."

"The trail forks to the southeast, and, if I remember right, there's a stream and a grassy knoll nearby."

Anthony inhaled the crisp spring air and admired the puffy white clouds that seemed to sail across a blue horizon. "Sounds like a perfect place to camp for the night."

Before dark, they had settled on an outcrop above a nearby stream. Anthony boiled water for chicory on a small fire, then poured a cup for Sheri. "Here you go. Careful, it's hot."

"Thanks," Sheri sipped it slowly and noticed that Anthony sat away from the fire and gazed toward the stream. "Why are you facing in that direction?"

"It's a habit of mine. I can see better in the dark when I don't stare at the flames."

Sheri chuckled and turned around, "Oh, yeah, now I remember how my dad and Bolt did that when I was a kid. They told stories about the pioneers, who stayed alert to the enemy that might come up from behind them. I forgot all about that until this moment."

Anthony leaned back on his rolled-up sleeping bag. "Ah, this is nice. Tis I, who sees flickering gems in a night sky."

Sheri snuggled closer, "Now you sound like a poet. Who said it?"

"I'm pretty sure I just did. Why? Does that turn you on?"

"Yes, it does," Sheri kissed him playfully.

"You taste like the peanut butter sandwiches we ate earlier."

Sheri licked her lips and giggled, "You're right, I'll brush my teeth." She rummaged through her backpack and groaned, "I can't find my toothbrush."

"I told you to double check everything," Anthony glared at her. "Here, you can use mine."

Sheri abruptly grabbed his brush, cleaned, rinsed her teeth and slapped it back in his hand without a word. Then, she plopped in front of the fire in a huff.

"Well, don't get mad at me. It's not my fault you forgot your toothbrush." Anthony dug in his bag and groaned. "I can't find my toothpaste."

"Here!" Sheri threw her tube and it bounced off his chest.

"Hey! What's that for?"

Firelight shined bright red on Sheri's face, as she glared at him, "You're just as forgetful as I am!"

Anthony saw the humor of it all and laughed. "What are we doing?"

Sheri let out a deep sigh. "Oh, Tony!" She hugged him tight and giggled, "Is this what married people do?"

Anthony remembered his brief marriage with Amy, "I'm afraid so." He looked up at the night sky again. "This is reality, babe. If we're going to be soul mates for life, we'll just have to accept each other as we truly are, with all our quirks."

"You are so right," Sheri giggled and teasingly slapped his chest, no one's perfect, especially you." She turned and strutted back to the fire.

"Hey!" Anthony playfully grabbed her hand and chuckled, "Is that any way to talk to your man?"

"My man should treat me like his lady," Sheri pulled away and stood with her back away from him. She crossed her arms and acted as though they were in a classic movie of the 1930's and 40's.

"Well, my lady, how may I assist you?" Anthony bowed and cheerfully played along with her silly acting.

Sheri held out her arm, "You may kiss my hand."

"Very well," Anthony reached, but she pulled back.

"I changed my mind," Sheri puckered up, "You may kiss my lips instead."

"No, I'm sorry," Anthony shook his head, "That would be too forward. I must take this slowly and thoughtfully." He paced back and forth, then snapped his fingers. "I know, the only honorable thing to do is make your bed." Anthony rolled out her sleeping bag and grinned, "There you are, my lady."

Sheri mimicked the look of Scarlet O-hara and held her hand to her forehead. "Oh, my…what shall I do?"

Anthony rolled out his sleeping bag next to hers, then relaxed on his. "Frankly, my dear, I don't give a lamb."

Sheri went along and pretended to cry out, "Oh, Tony, please don't say that! I'll gladly take a burger instead!" She held up her hand and gasped, "I feel faint." She sighed and plopped beside him.

"No! No!" Anthony continued to overact and tried to keep a straight face. "This is unacceptable! I am man! You are woman! This is scandalous!" He rose to his feet and proclaimed, "There's only one thing to do!"

Sheri sat up while in her melodramatic role, "Oh, Tony, what must I do?"

"You must remove yourself, at once."

"Yes, my love," Sheri acted as though she was being obedient to his command and stood.

Immediately, Anthony unzipped both sleeping bags, then joined them together with a zip, zip motion but left one side open. "Well, my lady, would you do me the honor of joining me in a night's rest?"

"Well, if you think this would be the only honorable thing to do, I shall join you, but…" Sheri waved a hand in his face, "You must promise to behave yourself at all times."

"My lady do not worry. My mind is well-disciplined." Suddenly, he tickled her side. "I just have one problem; my hands are completely out of control."

Sheri giggled and they both plopped into the sleeping bag. "Oh no!" She screamed with delight. "I'm being ravaged by Russian hands and roaming fingers!"

The night hours passed quickly until Anthony awoke to sudden movement in the sleeping bag. "Uh, what?"

"Tony, you awake?"

"I am now."

"I have to get up and go pee."

"Okay," Anthony sighed, unzipped his side of the sleeping bag, stood up, stretched, scratched his rear and yawned. In the dark, he heard Sheri ruffling out, while a slight orange glow radiated from a dying fire and shined on her face.

"Where do I go?" Sheri's voice seemed to quiver from either the cold or the need to immediately relieve herself or both.

Anthony turned on his flashlight and felt silly. He should have plotted out a spot for such delicate matters beforehand. "Follow me," he said in a vain attempt to sound like he had it all figured out. He took a step and counted, "one, two, three…" and paced out about 50 feet away from the camp and stream, while she held onto his arm.

Finally, he stopped and scanned the rocky ground. "Okay, this'll do right here."

Sheri quickly squatted, but he shined the light in her direction.

"Hey! Don't look!"

Anthony laughed and turned off the light. "I thought you were a country girl," he teased.

Sheri sighed in the darkness, "Even us country girls need privacy, dimwit!"

Anthony shrugged and grinned, as he walked a dozen paces away and took care of his personal business. Then, he heard a slight gassy sound coming from Sheri, and he could not resist another tease, "Did you just fart?"

"No," Sheri giggled, "There's a frog over here. He did it."

After Anthony added more wood on the fire, the couple settled back in the sleeping bag. For a while, they both stared at millions of twinkling stars in the clear night sky.

Anthony yawned but could not sleep. "There's the big dipper."

"Oh, look! Shooting stars!"

"I see another one!"

Sheri snuggled closer to get warm. "What did you wish for?"

Anthony felt her cheek softly rub along his face and her hair tickled his ear. Yet, flashes of battle memories streamed in and out of his mind, but he forced himself to focus on the moment. "Well, considering that I should have died many times over, I just wish for these happy moments with you to continue. How about you?"

"Oh, I wished that I could get a good night's sleep without you snoring in my ear."

"Hey," Anthony laughed and nudged her, "You snore too, you know."

"I do not," Sheri giggled.

"Yours is a girly snore," Anthony laughed again and teased. "It sounds more like a low puff, and you snort like a horse."

Sheri playfully slapped his chest and giggled again. "Okay," she yawned and rolled over, "Get ready for my girly snore."

"You also fidget a lot."

Sheri turned over and sighed, "What do you mean?"

"You tend to kick your feet while you sleep," Anthony moved to his side and let out gas. "The frog did it."

"You mean like this?"

"Ouch!"

32 Lightning Strikes

On day two of their quest, the couple arrived at a pinnacle that jutted above a ridge like teeth. Sweat dribbled down their backs and gravel crunched under their boots, as they trekked up a steep incline. A bright orange ball glared down like an all-seeing-eye in a azure dome and sunbaked their flesh. Anthony stopped to catch his breath and gave his canteen to Sheri, who took a sip.

"Thanks," Sheri wiped her forehead with a neckerchief, "Phew! I forgot how tough it is up here in the heat." She gave it back to Anthony, and he drank slowly.

"Yep," he sighed, "Doesn't help to have the noon sun beating down on us."

"Won't be long now," Sheri studied the landscape with binoculars. "Bear Meadow should be about an hour's hike over to the east, if I remember right."

Soon, they made it to lush, verdure blanketed in red and yellow spring flowers. "Let's take a break," Sheri removed her backpack and sat next to a fresh, running spring.

"It's much cooler here." Anthony knelt and filled the canteens.

"Oh, look, there's some wild berries." Sheri pulled out a plastic bag and started to collect them from branches.

"How do you know which ones are safe?" Anthony warily studied the fruit.

"My Dad and Bolt taught me a lot."

Anthony picked from the bushes. "We'll need these in another day or two."

"That'll be enough," Sheri grinned with satisfaction and sealed the bag.

Later, they collected acorns, then cracked open the shells and dried them in the sun. The process took several hours of preparation, and by that time, Anthony and Sheri decided to camp on a nearby flat boulder away from the stream.

"It's safer up here," nodded Anthony.

"I know," Sheri spread out the sleeping bags next to drying acorns in the sun, "We used to watch a few bears from here as they came in to eat berries and drink."

Anthony collected small rocks and made a circle for a fire on the granite slab. "I'll get fresh water and boil it." He untied a pot from his backpack and walked over to a nearby stream.

"Okay, I'll get the packets of noodles, and we can have soup with crackers tonight."

Day three started with a stormy deluge that jetted in and raced on. It cleared an hour later but Anthony and Sheri knew the risk of flash flooding in dry gulches. So, they took a switch back up to Eagle Ridge and searched for a nesting pair of eagles near a small stream but saw no activity.

Sheri scanned the terrain with well-used binoculars. "Maybe we should go over to Crystal Lake. There's plenty of fish, and it's a perfect place for eagles to nest."

"A lot of snow melt will be coming down the mountains, so we need to stay alert for possible flooding." Anthony observed water drops puddling along their path from a shimmering white patch on a nearby slope.

"I agree," Sheri focused intently through the lens, "I see an eagle. It's heading over toward the lake now."

It took an hour to cross over numerous small streams until they stopped to search for any sign of nesting. Anthony looked to the west and noticed thunder clouds building up over a jagged peak. "Looks like it could get nasty."

A low rumbling echoed through the mountains. "You're right about that. Pop told me about an old abandoned cabin that was built by settlers about a hundred years ago. Later, hikers fixed it up for a way station. Maybe we can find shelter there."

Another crackling of thunder reverberated through their veins and seemed hauntingly closer. "We'd better move fast!" Anthony felt undulating, static electricity that erected the hairs of his arms and beard.

Sheri looked through her binoculars again and shuddered, "I think I see the cabin. Let's get out of here! I don't like it at all!"

When Anthony and Sheri reached the cabin, they were drenched by relentless raindrops that pummeled the mountains without mercy. Strong winds seemed to whip around them in all directions. Lightning struck a tree, and flames erupted like demons from hell. Then, just as the fire erupted, the downpour extinguished it.

Anthony struggled to push the door, but it did not budge. Sheri frantically dug in her heels to add her weight. Still, it was stuck as though all the forces of nature had no sway.

Bitterly determined, Anthony yelled over the din, "We have to get inside or die out here!" Howling wind deafened his voice.

Anthony stumbled to a small side window, shined his flash light and was surprised to see a chair that blocked their only hope of getting inside. Yet, there was no time to reason why. Nature's velocity battered his weary body. He tried to hold himself steady with whatever weakened energy he could muster.

Fighting to survive, Anthony Lorenzo wildly searched for anything to gain entry. Finally, he spotted a fist-sized rock in a mud puddle nearby, picked it up and broke the glass. Lightning struck again, and another tree caught fire. Instantly, the heavy rain snuffed it out.

He dove in, shoved the chair away, forced the door open and Sheri gushed in with the storm's fury. Immediately, they both struggled to push the door closed and finally secured it. For a split second, it grew silent amidst the cabin walls.

Just as it felt safe, Sheri screamed and pointed at something behind him. The beam of her flashlight shook in her hand.

Startled, Anthony spun around and could not believe what he saw. There, sitting upright was a partially mummified body waiting, as though it had hoped for millennia that someone would come to the rescue. A dirty brown cap was upon its head, and a bony hand rested near a tin mug on the wooden table.

Sheri let out a sigh with the reality of what appeared before her and nervously chuckled, "Okay, this has got to be a morbid joke. Please tell me this is some kind of a prank and I'll believe you."

Thunder clapped and roared so close that Lorenzo briefly forgot he was no longer at war. On high alert, he said nothing. Instead, he curiously examined the body. This was no joke and made no sense. The door was blocked, so no one could have gotten in. Yet, there it was, the remains of someone, who most likely died in the past six months or so.

"Look!" Sheri pointed to the floor, "It's a pistol!"

Lorenzo spotted a semiautomatic revolver, and it appeared as though it had fallen from the victim's fingers. What happened here? Still, Lorenzo said nothing and continued to examine the body. There, just above the temple, a bullet had penetrated through the skull. He studied it closer and found blood-stains on the wall. Could this have been a suicide? But why?

Thunder cracked and rumbled outside. Oppressive winds beat the walls and whistled around the creaky shack. Merciless rain battered the weather-worn roof, leaked through and left numerous puddles in the one-room cabin.

Desperate to hunker down, Lorenzo felt that he was still lost in combat with no way out. He glanced at Sheri's horrified expression, and he knew they were stuck there for the night. So, he grabbed a dust-covered Army blanket from the bed and draped the body.

"Okay, I'll report it to the Sheriff when we get back home." He sighed, looked at the open window and shivered. Cold, damp wind blew in droplets of rain. Yet, fresh air gushed in and helped to neutralize the fetid odor.

"What are we going to do now?" Sheri stood by the filthy bed and glanced around at all the drip, drip of puddles on the floor. "We can't sleep here!"

Anthony saw the worry and confusion on Sheri's face, and he softened back to the present moment. "It's okay, sweetie." He brushed back the hood of her rain coat and stroked her hair. "First, we dry off. Lift up your arms and I'll help with your parka."

Sheri nodded with a look of embarrassment, and she raised her arms, while he removed it. "Sorry, I guess I'm a little rattled."

Lightning flashed, and thunder cracked, then roared menacingly.

"It's alright. We'll get through this." Anthony shook out her parka. He removed his and glanced at the pile of wood near a sooty hearth. "I'll get a fire going."

Moments later, they warmed their hands over a red glow of the fireplace. Anthony glanced at the open window again. Cold wind and rain still blew in, and he knew that something had to be done immediately. He found a box of nails and a hatchet, then with the blunt end, he pounded nails in each corner of the window.

"Careful," Sheri anxiously watched, as he worked so close to the opening. "Maybe you better wait, honey. It's too risky."

Suddenly, lightning struck with a deafening crackle and explosion outside. Startled by the powerful electrical charge that shook the building, Anthony fell to the floor.

Sheri gasped and rushed to his side, "You okay?"

Anthony stood up and shook himself, "I'm fine, I think." Quickly, he grabbed another dusty blanket from the bed and hooked it on the nails.

Sheri pulled out a light-weight six-foot wide emergency tarp from Anthony's pack and had an idea. "Let's make a lean-to with this."

"That's my girl!" Anthony kissed her forehead. "Now, you're back to your feisty country-girl self!" They quickly tacked up a lean-to against the wall, near the fireplace mantel and a chair. "Good job, babe."

Anthony smiled at their accomplishment, "We'll layout our sleeping bags under here for the night. This'll keep us warm and dry."

Sheri reached in her backpack, pulled out a handkerchief, and she took a small bottle of cologne and spritzed it.

Anthony chuckled and asked, "What're you doing with that stuff way out here?"

"You'll see, even a country girl likes to smell nice." She nodded at the covered-up corpse, "Especially around stinky guys. Now give me your handkerchief."

Anthony shrugged and gave it to her. Focused, she sprayed his cloth and handed it back to him. Without a word, Sheri covered her mouth and tied the material behind her head.

As the young vet watched, it dawned on him that this was to help manage the malodor in the room. So, he did the same and sniffed the pleasant aroma of rose. Somewhat relieved, he watched her with more admiration while she looked around the room.

"I'll see if I can rustle up some canned food." Sheri searched through a small cabinet, "It's empty." She spotted a duffel bag on the floor, unzipped it and rummaged around. "There's no food anywhere." She noticed something and paused, "Oh, here's a notebook."

"Let's take a look." Anthony opened it, "Maybe it'll provide a clue to what happened here."

Anthony and Sheri snuggled near the fire and read by flashlight. He pointed to the last entry, "Nov. 28, 1971, Starving! The demons are here! Must end it!"

"That was almost seven months ago!" Saddened by this discovery, Anthony glanced over at the covered-up body and shook his head. "He's been here all this time."

Sheri flipped the pages to the beginning, "May 25, 1969, hospital RC. Doc says I had severe concussion. I remember now. It was May 17, Hamburger Hill. We're pinned down. I'm hit. Ringing in ears. Can't move."

Sheri turned the page. "Oct. 16, 1969, Long Beach. I can't stand it! Demons won't shut up! Can't function at work!"

"Oct. 20, 1969. Fire in kitchen! I didn't mean to! It was an accident! Can't think straight! Dad & Mom tell me to leave!"

"Oct. 25. Found this shack. Nice. Quiet. I'll stay for a while. Need peace."

"Oct. 26. Tried to catch fish in lake. No luck. Try tomorrow."

"Oct. 29. Out of provisions. Caught one small fish. Ate it. Still hungry."

"Nov. 2. Searched for food. Caught another fish. Not enough. Trails are too difficult. Heard enemy fire. Ran back to safety. Hearing voices again. Must hide out!"

Sheri flipped through the pages and sighed, "It's blank until this date." She points to "Nov. 26. Sometimes I catch fish. Not enough! Tried at lake again. No luck. Big man appeared out of nowhere with an eagle on his shoulder. He offered to help. Heard enemy fire! Confused! Scared. Ran for cover!"

"Nov. 27. Big man keeps knocking on door. Offers help again. Voices say, don't answer! Afraid! Could be the VC! I won't let them take me alive! I shoot through door. Man gone."

Crackling, rolling thunder shook the tiny cabin again. Lightning flashed. Anthony ignored the uproar and stared at the page. "So, the Watchman was here."

"Looks like he tried to help this guy," Sheri nodded to the dead man and let out a sigh.

Anthony examined the duffel bag and found discharge papers and a purple heart award. "His name was private Ramon Porrazzo."

Tears dribbled down Sheri's cheeks. "This is so sad," her voice cracked. "We have to let his family know."

Anthony Lorenzo felt his own inner rage and it heated up. "We'll let the Sheriff handle it." He abruptly shoved all the personal items in the duffel bag and zipped it up. "Another casualty of war!" He wanted to shout, but, instead, his voice seemed to fade into a whisper, "I doubt that he will be remembered in the annals of history."

Pin streams of sunlight peeked through several thin cracks in the cabin walls. Anthony glanced at his wristwatch. It was 7:15 a.m. The storm had just passed through and the sky cleared. "You ready to move out sweetie?"

Sheri adjusted her backpack and nodded. Anthony opened the door, and they both stepped out. Cool, clean mountain air filled their nostrils. Left over moisture dribbled off the roof and tear-like droplets splattered sadly to the ground. With a deep sense of mourning for a man he did not know, Lorenzo nailed a small handwritten sign on the door with a gentle tap, tap.

Respectfully, he read the words in silence. "Here lies private Ramon Porrazzo. Combat wounded. Died alone. But not forgotten."

Former Army Medic, Anthony Lorenzo, did a sharp about-face, marched 20 paces, turned and stood at attention in silence. Sheri's eyes reddened when she came alongside her man. Sorrowful tears streamed down her face, and she silently prayed for this lost soldier she had never met. Lorenzo saluted, did another about face and walked away with Sheri beside him.

Sheri held his arm tight and sighed, "He should have a flag."

"He will, sweetie. I'll see to it."

Solemnly, the couple continued on with their courtship quest. Yet, even in their sadness, they felt closer than ever. They watched a pair of eagle mates skimming the surface of Bear Lake. As a sign of their commitment to each other, they continued their search in the wild for two feathers.

An hour later, Sheri glanced at the blue sky, "I see the eagle flying toward the east. Do you think we should follow him?"

"No," Anthony knew their urgent need was to survive, and he worried about his woman, "We've got to find food first." He held her hand tight. While they walked side by side, he glanced at her often. She, in turn, gazed lovingly into his eyes and smiled.

Inspired by her look of love, Anthony stopped and asked, "How are you doing, babe?"

"I'm fine, Tony." She smiled again, "It's okay, we can do this. Like Grammy always says, we need to have faith and not look back."

"You're right, love." Anthony held her close, "Are you ready? "

Sheri kissed his lips. "Yes, I'm ready."

33 Soul Mates

It had been five days since Anthony and Sheri left the comforts of home. Food was scarce and most of the berries and acorns they had gathered were depleted. Bear Lake thrived with trout, and a pair of mating eagles took turns fishing and made it look so easy.

Yet, it was not simple for the wandering couple. Hungry, determined to survive, Anthony made a pole out of a pine branch and attached some line he had brought with him. Sheri, meanwhile, searched under rocks and in crevices for anything to use as bait. Both felt weak and malnourished but were in high spirits.

"I found a couple of grubs, one snail and a beetle!" Sheri smiled and eagerly displayed them in dirty hands.

Anthony glanced at the bait and gazed into Sheri's eyes. Her hair was a mess and she had muddy streaks on her arms and face. "That'll do!" He grinned happily and thought how lovely she looked in her unkempt survivalist way. As he admired her grit, he also worried about her obvious weight loss.

Anthony also noticed that he had tightened his belt a notch. He ignored it and tossed in his line with a grub attached to the hook. "Would you like your fillet sautéed or fried, my lady?"

"I am so hungry; I'll eat it raw if I have to."

Anthony sat on a rock along the lake shore and sighed, "Won't be long now."

Sheri snuggled closer and rested her head on his shoulder while she expected an easy catch. "Oh, look, Tony, there's a big eagle skimming the surface."

Gracefully, its talons caught the fish, and the eagle flew off with such ease that all the couple could do was watch in awe. Minutes passed. Then, an hour went by. Nothing stirred. Even the lake reflected perfect stillness like a mirror.

Sheri leaned closer and examined the fishing pole. "Uh…maybe you need to…"

"Don't say a word!" Anthony interrupted and groaned with increased annoyance at the grumbling sound from his belly. "I know what I'm doing!"

Several agonizing minutes passed. Finally, Anthony jerked up the line and groaned, "What the…? Our baits gone!" He examined it carefully, "Okay, this time, I'll get one."

Frustrated and grumpy from lack of nourishment, Anthony hooked on more bait and repeated the same process. Down to the last grub, he tossed the line back in with a plop of water that rippled in a circle, then waited again.

Sheri searched for more, as she prepared for the long day ahead. After an hour of wading knee-deep and lifting rocks, she finally collected an odd assortment of insects, snails and worms to use for bait. Gradually, she had a stash piled in a dug-out hole along the bank. She sloshed through the water with palms full of wriggling critters for Anthony, but several fell out and plopped, plopped at her feet in the lake.

Suddenly, without warning, a large trout leaped and swallowed a bug whole, then another appeared and did the same amazing stunt. "Did you see that?"

"Well, at least we know they're going after the bait!" Frustrated and hungry, he pulled up his line. "They got this too, and I didn't feel a thing!"

Sheri handed him another snail, "Make sure you hook it on tight this time."

Anthony glared at her, "I'm not stupid, you know!"

"Don't yell at me!" Sheri huffed and crossed her arms, "It's not my fault you don't know how to fish!"

"That does It!" Anthony dropped the pole at his feet, "If you're so smart, you do it!"

"Alright! I will!" Sheri was about to pick it up when something yanked the line and dragged the pole in the lake.

"Hey!" Anthony leaped into frigid water, but the fishing pole disappeared. Cursing and dripping wet, he staggered out, plopped on the muddy bank and groaned, "There goes my line! How could this happen?"

Sheri laughed, sat and crossed her legs next to him. "I don't know, but it did," she shook her head in disbelief.

Anthony picked up a pebble and tossed it in the water. "What's so funny?"

"Oh, I don't know," Sheri giggled. "Maybe it's the way the trout outsmarted us. Or, it might be how crazy mad we got over the whole silly thing."

"You're right," Anthony laughed and sighed. "I'm sorry for the way I acted."

Sheri put her arm on his shoulder and kissed his damp cheek. "I apologize for my silliness, too." She stood up and shook as water dribbled down her arm. "You better take off those wet clothes and dry them out."

"I have a better idea," he sniffed under his arm, "I think I'll go for a swim and do my laundry at the same time." He dove in, spat out fresh water and grinned. "Maybe I'll catch a fish while I'm at it."

"You're crazy." Sheri laughed, "You know, I could use a bath." She grabbed a bar of soap from her backpack, then waded out. "Oh, this is so cold," she giggled and swam in circles, "But, it's just what I need right now."

"Hey, babe," toss the soap to me first. I'll wash, then you take it."

"Why?"

"After I lather up, I'll step out and get a fire going."

Sheri swam over, handed it to him and teased, "Okay, caveman, you make um fire. Me woman. Me catch fish with teeth."

Moments later, Anthony added more wood to a fire encircled in rocks. While Sheri leaned back on a sleeping bag, he checked their clothes on branches. "Maybe they'll dry enough soon." He looked up at a bright noon sun and felt its warmth on his skin.

"You look kind of cute in your underwear," Sheri smiled and winked.

Anthony flexed his muscles and posed, "You like that?"

"Oh, I like," Sheri giggled while she watched from her sunbathing spot on a sleeping bag. "Now, my great hunter, get me some food. I'm hungry."

Anthony knelt and examined Sheri's collection of squirming creatures in the eight-inch hole. "Well, my lady…" He picked up a small stick, then stabbed and impaled a snail. "How about escargot for a meal?" He held it up as its slimy juices dribbled to the ground.

"No thank you, kind sir," Sheri grimaced and rolled to her other side.

Anthony flicked it back into the hole and plopped on the sleeping bag next to her. "Well, we have to do something, or we'll starve out here."

Sheri sighed and sat beside him, "You know…when I was a little girl, Grammy told me that I should always pray and ask God for what I need." She gazed at the limpid blue sky, "I admit that I haven't been very good at it."

"Okay, let's do it," Anthony squeezed her hand and closed his eyes. "Well, God, you know that I'm lousy at this, but we're kind of in a bind down here. I'm asking, not so much for me, but if you could provide food for Sheri, I'd really appreciate it."

For a moment, they sat in silence and observed an eagle over the lake. It dove, skimmed along the surface, scooped up a fish, then, it flew in a straight beeline and dropped a 10-inch flopping trout on Sheri's lap.

"Wow!" Anthony laughed and reached to grab it, but Sheri slapped his hand.

"No, you don't!" Sheri laughed with a smug expression, "That's mine."

"What'd you do that for?" Anthony chuckled and pulled his hand away.

"You didn't ask for one, did you?" Sheri shook her head, "What kind of sanctimonious prayer was that anyway?" She glared, then, with a low mocking voice, she said, "Oh, I'm asking, not so much for me, blah, blah."

"Well, I was just thinking of your needs first."

"Look! Don't be so humble for my sake! If you want something, you ask for it!" Sheri giggled and picked up her wriggling fish. "I'll filet mine while you get your act together," she teased. Sheri spread out her trout on a log and said, "Thank you, fish, for the nourishment of your life."

She wacked its wiggling head with the blunt end of a knife. "And, thank you, God, for this food that I am about to eat," she hit it again with a forceful thud.

Anthony groaned, "Woman! You are driving me crazy!"

"Good!" She laughed, "My mother always said that a woman's purpose is to drive her man crazy!" She giggled and pummeled the fish several more times while its gills moved. "Then, he will melt into your hands."

"Well, I am not melting, woman!" Anthony shook his head and let out a deep sigh of frustration, "I am boiling!"

Sheri chuckled and gutted the fish. "Boil all you want. You still have to ask for yourself."

Anthony groaned again, stood up and held up his hands. "Okay, God! I'm asking you to please give me a fish." Suddenly, he heard the flapping of wings and a large trout dropped directly on his head. "Ouch!" Anthony picked up his fish and moaned, "Alright, alright! You don't have to hit me on the head with it!"

Finally, they lightly cooked their fresh catch over hot rocks in the middle of a fire ring. No one said a word as they happily savored each tender morsel. Nothing else mattered, for they lived fully in the splendor of those precious moments. Even a thought of how they would get their next meal did not enter their minds. Instead, they had learned as a couple to be content with the present.

On the sixth day, Anthony remembered something that Grammy mentioned during their many talks together. When he asked how she managed to do so much around the house, she said God helps those, who help themselves. He thought that was more his way of doing things.

Frankly, he was never much for begging. Yet, even as this came across his mind, he realized how arrogant it could sound if he spoke it out loud. Somehow, though, he felt his maker had a delightful sense of humor and unconditional love, even with his human frailties.

That early morning, Sheri awoke to the chop, chopping of wood and got up. "What are you working on?"

Anthony dragged over some branches near the fire and sliced off small twigs. "I'm making a trap. Maybe I can catch a fish with it." He paused and looked at her sincerely, "This time, I'll pray as I work with my hands."

"Okay, my hunter/lover," Sheri smiled and kissed his cheek, "How can I help?"

"Here, take these two branches and sharpen the ends. We can use them to spear fish." Anthony worked quickly and knew that he burned a lot of calories just to focus his energy on this project.

Sheri eagerly completed her task and stabbed both spears into the ground. "What else can I do?"

"Hold this end." Anthony weaved long thin strips of bark together to build a two-foot long by 10-inch wide trap. He worked quickly to get this flimsy contraption ready with a trap door and a stick that acted as a primitive tripping device. "Okay, babe, just dump the bait at the back end," he tilted it with the open side up.

Sheri filled her hands from her collection in the nearby hole. Then, she plopped the tempting morsels in with a clunk, clunk and asked, "You sure this will work?"

"I'm not sure of anything," Anthony shrugged, picked up the trap and placed it in shallow water close to shore. "All we can do is pray and wait."

An hour passed, and they observed the trout's curious behavior. Several explored around the trap, as though they tried to look for a way to get the bait, but none went directly in.

"I have an idea," Anthony stood up and grabbed his quarter-of-an-inch thick rope.

"What are you going to do?"

"I'll try to scare one in." Anthony tied the rope end around a flat rock and nodded to a spear, "Grab that and stand by as close as you can to the trap." He started to walk away but turned and said, "Take your boots off first. Go very slowly and try not to make a sound. When you get there, stand perfectly still. If you see the fish swim toward you, try to spear one if they don't go into the trap. But, wait for my command, okay?"

Sheri nodded affirmatively. Anthony removed his shirt, took the other spear and quietly strolled to the edge of a narrow inlet where a small stream rushed in near the trap. This natural flow of fresh water provided nutrients and tiny organisms that attracted the fish. He knew it was a long shot, but, with prayer and quick timing, maybe his wild scheme will work.

For several minutes, Anthony silently watched and waited. In the crystal clear, fresh water, he observed a half dozen trout. It was time to act. He looked over at Sheri, who waited about 20 feet away and shouted, "Now!" He tossed the rope out and the flat rock slapped the surface with a loud plunk. Quickly, he dragged it along the bottom and repeated the sequence over and over.

Sheri studied the erratic movement of trout and held her spear ready. Finally, a large one swam in. A trap door slammed shut and it was caught immediately. Another fish swam by. She stabbed but missed it. Anthony slapped the surface to prevent them from fleeing the inlet. Several more swam frantically close and this time she speared a fish, and she deliberately kept it pinned down.

"Got two!"

Anthony spotted a few trout. He stabbed the spear but missed. Then, he remembered his mentor's words, "Breath in, relax, focus, strike." So, he pulled back, watched and waited until the best possible moment. Suddenly, he struck with precision and caught one. Calmly, he brought this to shore and released the wiggling fish on the bank. He tried several more times until he speared another trout with ease.

"That makes four!"

A bright afternoon sun warmed their tired bodies, and fresh food provided relief for the couple. Anthony chewed slowly and gazed at the pristine lake that reflected mountain peaks back into the water. Several fish leaped high, then plopped, plopped and left splashes and ripples on the mirror-like surface. One eagle swooped low, scooped up a wriggling catch and flew over to far off trees on the other side. In their moment of peace and contentment, they savored nature's splendor and quietly nourished themselves.

Sheri sat with her bare legs crossed, and warm sunshine gave her flesh a lustrous caramel sheen that appealed to the young man's visual senses. She took a bite of fish and chewed slowly, as though she had all the time in the world. Anthony sat next to her and admired the graceful, easy-going way that she ate each morsel. It was something that he liked to observe whenever they enjoyed a meal together. This steadily relaxed him, and he allowed himself to slow down his more carnivorous, ravenous eating habits.

After Sheri took a swig of water from her canteen, she sighed and said, "This is so nice here." She turned her head, smiled and kissed his cheek, "I like being with you, Tony."

Anthony rested his arm on her shoulder, and she snuggled closer. "Yeah, I was just thinking the same about you, sweetie."

"Maybe we can come back here someday," she gazed at an eagle that soared above the lake. "This could be our special place," she looked at him. "What do you think, Tony?"

"I'd like that." Even as he said those words, he still struggled to reconcile his painful past. How could he build a future with such a wonderful woman, while being haunted by doubts about his worthiness? Yet, he yearned to start life anew, so he silently prayed that he could live fully with Sheri and not worry about hurting her.

"You deserve another chance, you know," Sheri whispered in his ear, as though she somehow read his mind. "It's time for you to forget the past."

Surprised to hear her words of encouragement, Anthony said, "I want to, sweetie, but it's not easy." He sighed and looked into her eyes, "I need you to help me."

"You can count on me, Tony." Sheri kissed his cheek and rested her warm hand on his upper thigh. "I will always stand by you."

"I know, babe." Anthony liked the way Sheri gazed so lovingly into his eyes, and her smile had a way of melting him. "We make a good team."

Sheri giggled, "It's funny how we work so well together one minute, then the next, we have a silly spat. You know, like the freaky toothpaste incident."

"Well, maybe that's part of learning to get along, honey." Anthony gently rubbed his finger along her lips, and he savored the moment of just admiring her sensuousness. "As long as we apologize and don't hold on to our anger, I think we'll be okay."

Sheri mussed up his hair with her fingers and laughed, "Yeah, it also helps to have a sense of humor. That's for sure. We just don't take ourselves too seriously."

"What humor? I am serious about you, woman. I want to make mad, passionate love to you right now." Anthony leaned her back on the warm sleeping bag.

"Okay, what are you doing?" Sheri gazed into his eyes and smiled.

He playfully nibbled her neck. "I'm turning into a wild man over you."

Sheri giggled, "I confess you do have a certain animal magnetism about you." She rubbed his unkempt hair again. "You look like a shaggy dog. I think you are trying to seduce me."

Anthony whispered in her ear, "Is it working?"

"Well, let me think about this." She paused and gently pulled on his whiskers. "You got dirt in your scruffy beard." She sniffed, "And your breath smells like fish. My, how can I resist the beast in you? Down boy."

34 Eagle's Nest

A breakfast of fresh trout was enough to nourish the couple on their seventh day. While Anthony and Sheri prepared to leave, they were awestruck by a very rare sight. Sunbeams flickered through dew drops on pine needles and translucently bathed their campsite in a rich golden yellow. A mild breeze orchestrated the swoosh in a rhythmic natural dance of sparkling gold twinkling delights in their eyes.

"Makes me want to reach out and swallow each candy-like star," Sheri held out her hand to the magical light and giggled with child-like wonder.

Anthony smiled at the image. "You'll have golden beams shooting out your ears for sure." He adjusted his backpack and glanced at their site, "You ready?"

"Oh, let's stay a little longer," Sheri's voice was like a soft whisper in the breeze. Her face seemed to reflect the gentle glow, while she observed the reverent moment in sheer wonder. Gradually, verdure returned to the pines, and she sighed with pleasure.

Satisfied, she gazed at passing clouds one last time, "Okay, I'm ready now." She pointed toward a southern tree-lined slope, "I think we can get to that bald eagle's nest near the pinnacle just beyond the edge of Bear Lake."

"You're right," Anthony studied the terrain through binoculars. "Most of the activity is up there. Every time an eagle caught a fish, it headed right back to the ridgeline. Maybe they'll lose a feather or two when they go to and from that location. Then, we'll have a better chance to collect what we need at the base of a tree somewhere."

Well-nourished, the couple crossed several streams in search of their courtship prize. During the previous day, they ate the three fish that had been speared. In the morning, they took a captured trout from the trap. Unsure when they would have their next meal, they savored an early breakfast.

An hour later, they made it to a ridge where they had a closer view of an eagle's nest. "Oh, look," Sheri handed the binoculars to Anthony, "There's a breeding pair at the top of that tree just to the east of the lake."

"How do you know which one is the female? They both have similar plumage."

"She's the bigger one on the left." Sheri watched the male, as it flew over the lake and said, "Pop taught me that they usually take turns while they wait for eggs to hatch."

"I see a feather drifting down from the nest." Anthony lowered his binoculars and smiled, "Let's go get it."

Gravelly debris crunched under his boots, and he ran while Sheri followed. At the base of a tree, he stopped, looked around and finally found the eagle feather. Happy with his find, he smiled and stuck it in Sheri's hat. "Here you go, babe."

Sheri looked puzzled and frowned, "I thought you were going to kneel chivalrously and propose to me like my knight in shining armor. I expected you to call me your lady and put this feather on my left arm as a symbol of our engagement."

"I need to find mine first." Anthony felt awkward, as he saw her unsettled expression. He lovingly stroked her hair to reassure her, "I will, sweetie, it's just that I made such a tragic mistake with Amy that I don't want to ever hurt you in anyway." He gave her a quick kiss on the forehead, "Do you understand?"

Sheri nodded and tried to smile, but it was obvious to Anthony that she was not happy with his answer. So, he quickly changed the subject. "Okay, let's go find another one for me, he turned, strolled and examined the surroundings near the eagle's nest.

An hour passed with no sign of a feather anywhere, and this worried him. They were on this quest long enough, and they had too many delays. It was time to get home. Determined to accomplish their objective, Anthony scanned the lake with binoculars and observed a low-flying eagle. "Let's search in that direction." He hiked to the south about several hundred feet and looked around the area.

Moments later, Sheri yelled, "I found one!"

"I'm on my way!" Anthony excitedly ran as fast as he could, and when he got there, he saw her hold up a feather. "Wow! That's a beauty!" He grinned and sighed with relief.

"Okay, here caveman," Sheri's eyes sparkled, and she held it proudly in both hands, "Now, turn into my knight and propose to me." She giggled with satisfaction.

Eagerly, Anthony took the feather and admired the intricate, natural beauty of it. "Oh, I see this has a lot more plumage than yours."

Sheri examined it, "Oh, that must be from the bigger female."

Anthony shrugged, "Yeah, you're probably right."

"That's actually perfect. You can wear the female feather to honor your life-long commitment to your woman." Sheri looked at him with an odd expression. "That would be me, right?"

"Of course."

"Well?" Sheri glared at him impatiently.

"What?"

Sheri frowned and appeared to get increasingly irritated. "Aren't you going to propose and attach a feather on my left arm to signify our engagement?"

Anthony fidgeted and he wanted to follow through, but he also struggled with the haunting memory of the tragedy with his wife, Amy. He loved Sheri deeply. Yet, he still felt undeserving of a second chance. "Uh, yeah, I will. I want to propose in a proper way, so let's wait until we get back home, okay?" As soon as those words came out of his mouth, he knew he was in trouble.

"What!?" Sheri glared at him fiercely, "After all we've been through, you have the nerve to tell me that!"

"Well, I…" Anthony tried to look into her eyes but lowered his gaze. If only she had turned and walked away in a huff, that would have been easier. Yet, there she stood with a raging fire in her stare. "Sorry…I plan to, honey. I just thought, if we waited a little longer, it might be more meaningful."

"Meaningful!" Sheri groaned, "Meaningful!" She let out a deep sigh and shook her head, then glared at him again. "Do you realize that it's been over two years since we've met! I immediately fell madly in love with you! You dummy! I knew I had to wait patiently for you to get over your grief and remorse about your tragedy! Now, after all the adventures we've been through, you can stand there and tell me to wait until it's more meaningful!"

"Ah, honey, please don't take it that way!" Anthony felt hopelessly boxed in. "You know I love you!"

The next couple of hours did not go well. Neither one said a word. They each had their eagle feathers prominently displayed on their hats, but a dark cloud of anger hovered over like a growing thunderstorm. Anthony tried to smooth things over with little gestures, like when he picked a small wild flower and attempted to hand it to her.

Even that did not help, for she immediately turned and walked away. He had seen Sheri pout before, but nothing like this, and he noticed the irony of how they started their day with a sense of magic and wonder.

With that emotional fog came hunger. So, they returned to their original campsite at the nearby inlet in an urgent attempt to find food again. Anthony knew that they had to work together just as they did before, but it was difficult to even communicate while Sheri ignored him. Desperate for something to eat, she took a spear and searched knee-deep in the water, while he focused in the opposite direction.

Meanwhile, a bald eagle circled gracefully above the couple. Silently, it landed and perched on a tree branch and observed the agonizing scene with interest. Anthony noticed it and wondered about the bird of prey, as he had many times before. What role did it play in his world and this grand scheme of the cosmos? Was it truly sent by God as some kind of messenger?

Anthony stood in the water and admired its majestic appearance, and he knew it was more than a coincidence. It had intervened in their lives so many times. Now, he watched, and it looked back in a strange omniscient way.

Another eagle landed next to the first one, and they both stared as though they were keenly aware of the situation. Curiously, he observed how they took turns preening each other.

Were these magnificent eagles sending a message? Was God trying to tell them something? "Sheri! Come here! You need to see this!"

Sheri looked over and saw Anthony pointing to the eagles. Her eyes widened with a sense of wonder and she ran to him. "They are so beautiful," she said breathlessly and smiled in awe.

"Oh, I get it," Anthony turned and gazed into Sheri's eyes.

"What?"

Anthony stroked her unkempt, tangled hair, "Get your hairbrush."

"What for?"

"Come on, sweetie," Anthony smiled, "Just do it, okay?"

Sheri let out a sigh, rolled her eyes, then shrugged and brought it over from her backpack. "What's this all about?"

"Hold still." Anthony slowly brushed her hair. With his complete focus on the task, he said, "Keep an eye on the eagle mates and tell me what they're doing."

"They're watching us," Sheri giggled. "Now the female is preening her mate. Oh, they look so cute together."

"Okay, how do I look?"

Sheri faced him, then examined his beard and sighed again, "You're a mess, you know that?" She grabbed the brush and began to work on the snarls of his facial hair. "You got all sorts of pine needles, dirt, and I have no idea what that is." She picked at something and laughed, "Are you kidding me? It's a piece of fish." She shook her head and gently yanked his beard. "Yep, you're my caveman, alright."

"Hey, speaking of fish, let's see what we can do with our trap." Anthony waded ankle-deep, picked it up and examined it. "Okay, I'll make some adjustments while you collect more bait."

Sheri started her search under a rock and looked at him, "Okay, now I get it. The eagles must be sending a message that we need to act like soul mates and take care of each other. I think they're a lot smarter than we are, Tony."

"Nothing surprises me about these eagles anymore." Anthony set the trap in the water and stepped over to help Sheri. "That's ready. Now, all we need to do is load up the bait."

Just as he turned away, he heard a disturbance in the water. "What was that?" He looked and could not believe the sight before him. There, inside the trap was a large trout. Surprised, Anthony stared in disbelief, "How did that happen?"

Sheri stood with a few snails in her hands and was just as bewildered. "I don't know."

"Wow!" Anthony pointed at the shallow water, "I count one, two, three...uh at least 10 more swimming around." He observed an increased flow from the stream, which entered the lake, "Oh, I see what's going on here. I think the fresh snow melt is attracting them."

Without hesitation, Sheri tossed the bait with a plop, plop that caused ripples in the water. Immediately, she grabbed her spear, made a quick thrust and caught another one. Anthony did the same, and, in minutes, they had a total of six trout.

"This is too easy," Anthony threw their catch on the rocky shoreline. "What happened?"

Sheri spotted the eagles, as they did a wild mating ritual with their aerobatics in the sky. "I think we've just been blessed."

"You're right." Anthony realized how foolish he had been about his hesitation on their engagement and turned to her. "I am so sorry, Sheri." He dropped to his knees and gazed into her eyes. "Will you please marry me?"

Tears streamed down her face. "Yes," she ruffled his hair and teasingly added, "You blockhead."

They embraced, kissed and placed the eagle feathers on their left arms. For the rest of the day, the delighted couple relaxed around the fire. Relieved to finally make their commitment, they worked together to prepare their meals with the fish that was provided. They nourished themselves on four trout over a lunch and dinner, then kept the remaining two live ones in the trap for breakfast the next morning.

With their bodies satiated, Anthony and Sheri felt that they had accomplished their mission. Together, they relaxed on their sleeping bags and planned to journey back home at dawn. All was so quiet, as they observed the stars that glimmered through drifting clouds above them.

"Oh, look, Tony!" Sheri pointed to the sky. "That dim light looks just like you."

"Oh, yeah? Which one is that?"

In her obvious attempt to get back at him for hesitating to propose earlier, she pointed again and laughed, "There! That's Mars! See how dim-witted it looks?"

"Very funny."

"Oh, look!" Sheri teased again, "There's Venus. See how bright she looks. That's me."

Anthony realized that he had to take his punishment. She was not going to let him forget his foolishness. "Okay, babe, what of it?"

"Don't you get it?" Sheri lovingly kissed his cheek. "Men are from Mars. Women are from Venus. You're dimwitted. I am bright. That's why we're so different."

"Oh, yeah," Anthony rolled on top of Sheri and tickled her, "Let me see what's so different about you."

Sheri giggled, and they playfully wrestled until she let out a scream, "Stop it! You'll make me pee!" She gasped and laughed wildly.

Anthony turned on his back. "You are driving me crazy, woman." He caught his over-heated breath and sat up. "Phew! What am I going to do with you?"

"That's something you'll just have to figure out," Sheri giggled and kissed him passionately. Then, she pulled back with a loud smack. "Now, let's get some sleep."

"What? I thought you had to take care of your personal business." He got up and bowed, "I shall not stand in your way. You may proceed to the lavatory, my lady."

"Thank you, sir, but I shall sleep now." She rolled over and swiftly covered herself with the sleeping bag. She ruffled about, patted the material several times, settled in and sighed, "You are excused."

"Well!" Anthony thought she was just play-acting like they had done many times before. So, he scoffed and playfully turned his back. "This is a most unfortunate change of events. Suddenly, it does seem rather chilly this fine evening."

Sheri covered her head and made a muffled giggling sound. "Good, maybe you'll cool off and behave yourself."

Anthony enjoyed his melodramatic acting out and laughed. Then, he placed his fist to his forehead and continued, "Oh, my fair queen." He glanced over to see if she watched his corny performance. Yet, she continued to ignore him.

So, he shrugged, and sighed, "Oh, my heart heats up like a thousand boiling lava flows. How shall I survive a night without a passionate embrace with my betrothed?" Again, he looked and only saw a lump under the sleeping bag. He heard a slight giggle.

"I don't know what you're mumbling about, but I'm pretty sure that wasn't Shakespeare. Now, my dear Prince Dimwit, I must insist that you excuse yourself at once."

"My dear lady, I shall make my leave with a heavy heart. Now, there is only one thing a man must do with such rejection."

He stripped his clothes and said, "I shall drown myself in that very, very cold lake." He looked back to see if Sheri responded, but she continued to lay there. "Okay, I'm going to end it now."

Sheri giggled, but still did not move.

"This is it." Anthony dove in. "Splash!"

"Ouch! Oh! That's so cold!"

35 Heading Home

A loud rumbling noise was heard and the ground shook violently. Lorenzo knew they had to act fast. "Get down!" He pulled Sheri's hand and they dropped to their knees under a slight outcrop, crouched and covered their heads. Suddenly, a landslide of rocks and debris tumbled down on their narrow trail and barely missed them by just a few feet.

"You alright?" Lorenzo stood and helped Sheri up.

"I think so," Sheri coughed and brushed off dust. "That was an earthquake!"

"Yep," Lorenzo looked ahead, "The trail is blocked. I don't see a way around it."

"This is the only trail to get home." Sheri sighed, "Now what?"

Anthony examined the pile of debris and studied the unstable mountainside. "It's too dangerous. We can't climb over it, so we have to go back." He felt an aftershock, balanced himself and held her close. Then, just as abruptly, the tremor stopped. "We have to get off this trail!"

Several smaller rocks tumbled down with a clunk, clunk against his boots, and he quickly grabbed Sheri's hand. "Let's go!" He led her in the direction they just came from, while they felt another tremor. More debris fell along their path, and they dodged more rocks. They ran without looking back.

Finally, after about 20 minutes, they arrived at a stream that had been crossed before. Just as the couple filled their canteens, they felt another powerful jolt, and the ground cracked. Instinctively, Lorenzo wrapped his arm around Sheri's waist, as a two-foot wide fissure opened and slithered for at least 30 feet in front of them.

"Jump!" They leaped over the jagged crack and darted around several trees that quivered while the earth shook.

When they made it to a clearing, well-away from steep cliffs and trees, Lorenzo stopped and looked around. "Okay, we'll be safe here."

Sheri sighed with relief, "Now, how do we get back home?"

He looked at his compass and tried to lighten the mood, "All we have to do is fly northwest, and we'll be there in a few hours."

"Yeah," Sheri laughed and pointed, "Let's ask that eagle for a lift."

"Good idea," he watched the bird of prey through his binoculars and it flew over a nearby hill. "Hey, I didn't notice this before."

"What?"

"Looks like a deer path." Anthony handed the binoculars to Sheri, and he pointed up the ridge, "Here, see for yourself."

Sheri adjusted the lens and focused on the narrow path. "Yeah, maybe we can follow that and find our way back on the trail further up." She gave it back to him and asked, "What do you think, Tony?"

Anthony packed the binoculars in his bag, and he took her hand. "It's worth a try. Okay, stay close to me, babe."

Gradually, after a steep climb, they made it to the top and scanned the terrain again. "Well, the path disappears among these boulders." Anthony glanced at the compass needle, and he pointed to the west, "Maybe if we head in this direction, we can get back on the trail."

Sheri nodded in agreement. "Okay, let's try it out."

A gust of thermal wind blew over, and they reached the top of a ridge. So, they looked down into a deep gorge below. Then, the eagle mates called out, while circling effortlessly high above like compassionate guides in the western sky. Anthony looked up with renewed hope and asked, "Hear that, sweetie?"

"Yes, Tony," Sheri smiled and watched them, "I think we'll be alright now."

"There's the trail." Anthony held Sheri's hand. "We'll go slow and kind of switch-back on the side of this hill until we get to the path. You ready, love?"

Sheri nodded with a trusting smile and sighed, "Uh, huh."

For a moment, he paused and gazed into her eyes. Somehow, the way she always made that breathy expression, it just seemed to melt him. He did not know why, but it did. So, he stroked her hair and kissed her softly, "Okay, sweetie, hold my hand tight and follow me."

Cautiously, they worked their way down a slope until they reached the trail. "Well, that wasn't so bad." Anthony saw that it was clear in the direction they needed to go.

Sheri glanced at the angle of the morning sun and smiled confidently, "Must be about 10:00 or so."

By now, Anthony knew he did not have to confirm the time with his watch. She was always right. So, they quietly trekked northwest in the hope of reaching home before dark. More and more, he felt at ease with their silence, while they hiked in this vast wilderness. As the day wore on, the young couple began to feel the pangs of hunger, but they also knew it was best to keep moving.

By 1:00 p.m., Anthony noticed an increased craving for something to eat, and he stopped to sip water from his canteen. Concerned for his woman's needs, he turned and offered her a drink first. "How are you, love?"

She quenched her thirst and sighed, "I am so hungry." Sheri attempted to smile, but it was obvious that she appeared to be worn out. "Can we call out for pizza now?" She chuckled and lowered her weary gaze slightly.

"That's a great idea," Anthony laughed and looked up to observe the eagles gliding effortlessly in a thermal breeze. "Shall we send them out for delivery?"

While Anthony and Sheri stood together on this lonely wilderness trail, they embraced each other with a trust that only soul mates can fully understand. During their courtship quest, they learned how to lovingly communicate and care for each other. They also discovered the bond of mutual cooperation that is essential for a lasting relationship. Now, completely in tune with each other, they were more willing to compromise and accept each other's quirks with a delightful sense of humor.

Yet, their immediate need was to find enough nourishment to sustain them on their trek back home. This was a major part of the couple's journey of discovery—to creatively provide for their own needs on a moment-by-moment basis. To accomplish this, the couple had to rely on simple faith while following those majestic eagle mates. As God's appointed messengers, these benevolent wonders of nature signaled with various calls and aerobatic gestures to guide the lovers on their way.

Suddenly, the eagles did a rapid nose-dive and flew directly down the trail. "What are they doing?" Anthony glanced at Sheri, "Looks like they want us to follow them."

Just as he spoke, they heard what sounded like someone calling out, so they paused and listened. A woman screamed, "Oh, God! Please help me!"

The medic's training and compassionate instinct kicked in with a renewed jolt of energy, and he grabbed Sheri's hand, "Come on!" They ran toward the cry for help, not knowing what to expect.

When they came around the next bend, they spotted a woman trapped in a low-lying area surrounded by rocks. Although she was only knee-deep in a crevice, and just off the trail, the distressed survivor was frozen in fear. Immediately, Anthony Lorenzo knew the reason, and his eyes widened with the reality of danger.

"Snakes!"

"Help me!" The woman looked up from the gap and reached out her arms in terror.

Stunned by this alarming predicament, Lorenzo tried to keep calm. This was way out of his element. Never had he experienced such a bizarre crisis. He handled bombings and shootings but nothing like a trapped victim with unpredictable rattlesnakes. So, he paused to examine their bizarre behavior. Strange, he thought, with all the commotion, he wondered why they did not strike. He had seen many snakes on hiking trails, and he knew they reacted to vibrations and movements.

Sheri noticed it too, and she boldly stepped closer to the crevice, "It's alright," she said to the woman in a soothing voice. "Keep very still. We'll get you out."

Relieved to see Sheri in control, Lorenzo quickly assessed the situation and observed two aggressive rattle snakes. Both maneuvered in an odd way, and they even intertwined in what appeared to be some kind of dance ritual. Yet, they were very close to the trapped victim's bare legs. She wore thin shorts that must have been torn from her fall. Somehow, he had to distract these poisonous reptiles. But how?

He looked at the woman and smiled to assure her. "You're doing fine. Don't move." While he scanned for anything like a branch, he asked, "What's your name?"

"Linda," Her voice quivered in fear.

Lorenzo spotted a six-foot hiking stick and picked it up. "This yours?"

"Yes, I dropped it when I fell."

"Good, now try to relax. I'm Anthony." He studied the snake's behavior while both rattlers appeared to be more aggressive toward each other but seemed to ignore the lady. "Sheri and I are working on a plan to get you out. So, please keep very still." He gazed steadily into the trapped survivor's eyes. "Okay?"

She nodded nervously.

Sheri curiously observed the snakes, "You know, I remember when Pop and I hiked, he mentioned that two competing males tend to fight it out in what he called a territorial dance."

"Well, love, we may have to do our own dance before this is over."

Sheri chuckled, "Oh, I finally get to do the mongoose dance with you! I'll follow your lead."

"Hurry," whispered the terrified woman. "I just felt something rub against my leg!"

Lorenzo turned slowly, looked at Sheri and nodded, "Okay, babe, step very slowly to your left and pick up several small rocks. When I signal, toss them one at a time at that boulder over there."

Sheri moved cautiously with a keen awareness that these venomous snakes were sensitive to vibrations. Lorenzo watched proudly, as her part-Cherokee instincts guided her one easy step at a time. A slight warm breeze blew strands of raven hair away from her flesh that seemed to glisten to a rich sheen in the sun. The only sound they heard was the call of an eagle overhead. Briefly, Sheri paused, then silently knelt and picked up three small rocks. Gracefully, she straightened herself and stood statuesque and waited for her man's signal.

In that moment, they looked steadily into each other's eyes with a deep sense of understanding. Lorenzo felt a heated sensation on his chest again while Sheri rubbed the spot above her heart and they nodded in recognition. It was time to act.

He turned and looked at the trapped lady and whispered, "Linda, we're going to get you out now. Whatever happens, you must be perfectly still. Do you understand?"

"Yes…please hurry."

The reptiles rattled and slithered near her ankles, and she gasped, "Oh!" she quivered, "I feel them slithering on my skin!"

"It's okay…" Anthony whispered softly, "Just stay completely calm. You'll be alright."

Lorenzo held the hiking stick, stepped carefully to his right, then moved to the edge, just inches from the lady. He looked down and watched the snakes, as they twisted, turned and coiled around each other in silence. Neither one of them rattled their tails. In this strange setting, the medic did not want to harm these creatures, for he knew they served a purpose, but his first priority was to save the terrified woman.

He turned his gaze back to Sheri and spoke softly, "Now!"

Sheri tossed each rock until all three clacked loudly on a boulder. Although the snakes had poor hearing, they immediately responded to the vibration and separated. One quickly slithered in a crevice, while the other snake suddenly coiled dangerously close to the trapped victim and shook its rattle. Immediately, Lorenzo jabbed with the stick and flung the snake to his right. It landed on the trail just several feet from him.

In the chaos, the snake tried to strike, but Lorenzo parried with his stick and held it at bay. Sheri grabbed the woman's hand, pulled her up. They darted in the opposite direction and stopped a safe distance away.

Lorenzo calmly maneuvered with the enraged predator, and, for the first time, he realized the massive size of this snake. He thought of all the snakes he had seen while on hikes with Bolt. This was definitely the biggest.

Its rattle sounded off a menacing warning. It would fight to the death. The big reptile coiled tightly, shook its tail and struck again. Lorenzo dodged to one side and swung back and forth with his stick.

Yet, it continued to block their path home, and this worried the medic. Strangely, he had deep respect and admiration for this creature, and he did not want to kill it.

Still, the snake held its position. Anthony only one choice--end it soon. Hungry, he had to be the predator. That attacking snake would become his meal for the day.

More determined, Lorenzo thought of how he watched a mongoose out-maneuver a cobra and bit its head off, while he served in Vietnam. Both were in a local gambler's cage, and he and his buddies bet on the snake and lost.

Learn from nature, his Vietnamese friend often said, and go with the flow of an attack. So, he positioned himself to a safe advantage on an incline and tapped the stick in front of the snake. Suddenly, it struck, and he parried with his weapon of choice.

"Ah, hah," he whispered softly, "I see your weakness." Lorenzo hypnotically swirled the stick around the snake's head, and he hummed calmly. Then, while the snake swooned, he whacked its head. Immediately, it lowered and coiled tightly in a ball.

Emboldened, Lorenzo stepped closer and prepared to attack. It struck at him again and barely missed his leg by inches, as he jumped back. "Oh, you are fast," he waved the stick at its flicking tongue.

"Be careful, Tony."

"It's alright, love." Anthony kept his focus on his respected enemy and tapped, tapped the ground. It struck again. He chuckled softly, "This is the dance, babe."

So, he moved to a safe distance and looked for another weapon. There, he picked up a flat slab of granite about the length of a football and felt the weight in his right hand. With the stick in his left hand, Lorenzo moved closer and swayed from side to side. A vision of the mongoose kept him loose, as he did a slow dance, while he tapped, tapped the ground and hummed softly.

Cognizant of every move, Lorenzo watched for just the right moment. It prepared to strike. Suddenly he whacked the snake's head. Startled, it recoiled into a defensive circle, and, strangely, it no longer rattled.

"Okay, I don't want to harm you, big fella," he whispered. "So, just back away and let us pass."

It struck again, and Lorenzo jumped to the side. "Alright, you leave me no choice." He grunted, threw the rock and crushed its head. "Sorry, snake, you fought well, and I honor you for it." He pulled out a knife, sliced the body and raised it up. "Thank you, God, for the nourishment we are about to receive."

36 Home at Last

S heri studied the afternoon sun's western direction while they sat around a make-shift stone fire ring on the trail. "Must be around 3:00." She bit into a piece of seared snake.

"Yep," Anthony chewed on his meat and glanced over at Linda, "You sure you don't want to try some."

"I'm not that hungry," Linda grimaced and shook her head with disdain.

"How did you wind up all alone in this crazy situation?" Sheri ate contently but curiously looked at Linda.

"I was hiking with several friends, and we got separated when fog rolled in this morning." Linda crossed her arms and looked pale. "When the earthquake hit, I fell down there." She nodded toward the crevice, "I tried to get out, but when I heard the rattlesnakes, I froze."

"You did the right thing." Anthony reached over with a piece of freshly cooked snake. "Here, you need to eat something."

"No thanks," Linda shook her head again.

"Suit yourself," Anthony shrugged and chewed the tasty morsel himself. "Well," he licked his fingers and sighed, "I'm full." He smiled at Sheri, "How about you, love?"

Sheri grinned happily, "I've had more than enough." She glanced at a foot-long piece of uncooked snake. "What about the leftovers?"

Anthony nodded, "You're right, we can't waste it." He held the fresh kill high above his head and observed an eagle that glided effortlessly along a thermal breeze. Without hesitation the eagle did a nosedive, swooped in, grabbed the meat from his hand and flew off.

Anthony smiled at Linda's wide-eyed bewildered expression. "Ah, it feels good to give something back."

Satisfied with the way their circumstances turned out, he looked down at the fire ring and gently separated the rocks with his boot. Carefully, he scooped dirt in his hands and smothered the cooled-down coals. Since they would be home soon, he poured a little canteen water over it, as a precaution. "Okay, that should do it."

Anthony stood, smiled contently to himself and glanced at Linda. "Let's get you to the ranger station." He turned to Sheri and lovingly kissed her cheek. Then, he grabbed his gear and headed down the trail, while the women followed close behind.

It did not take long for Linda's friends to meet up with them, and Anthony was relieved when her group headed up a northern trail to reach their campsite. While he watched them leave, he smiled at Sheri, "Almost there," he rubbed the back of her neck and felt the warm, stickiness of her flesh. "How are you, love?"

"Happy," Sheri kissed him and smiled, "We're together. That's all I need."

Anthony brushed his fingers through her hair, then gazed into her eyes, "Let's go home, babe."

Finally, after eight days on their courtship quest, the couple arrived at the end of a trail that overlooked Bolt's cabin. Smoke drifted from a chimney in the twilight air. Warm orange light from a window welcomed them back home.

"Well, we made it," Anthony sighed and rested his arm on Sheri's shoulder.

"I am so tired." Sheri looked at the tranquil scene below and smiled, "It's a good tired, though. You know what I mean?"

"Yes, love," he kissed her and tasted the saltiness of her lips, then gazed into her eyes, "I think it's because of how we worked through the challenges together, and we accomplished our quest. Now, our relationship is stronger than ever."

Sheri looked to the western sky, with a red glow of a setting sun behind the silhouette of a peak. "Have you noticed how quiet it's been the past couple of hours before we got here?"

"Now that you mention it, I haven't seen any sign of the eagles."

"Yeah," Sheri looked puzzled, "I wonder what it means?"

"I don't know…" Anthony noticed a sudden chill in the air, "It's strange."

Sheri felt it too, and she leaned closer. "Let's go. I'm cold," she shivered.

When they approached the cabin, a cool wind swooshed in and made them shiver, so they rushed up the porch steps to get warm. Eagerly Anthony opened the cabin door and called out, "Bolt, we're home."

"We're in here," said his mentor.

The couple dropped their gear in the hallway and entered the living room where the woodcarver and Jenny sat together by the fireplace. As usual, they snuggled warmly, while the flames heated up the cozy room, and Bolt rested his arm on her shoulder. "Glad to see you two made it back," he said.

Jenny smiled with a look of relief, while her hand rested on Bolt's knee. "We were just wondering when you might get here."

"We did it, Poppy," Sheri gripped Anthony's hand and smiled. "We're engaged."

For a moment, Anthony and Sheri stood together while they proudly showed off the feathers that were displayed on their left arms. Immediately, Bolt and Jenny leaped to their feet and joyously hugged the couple.

"Congratulations!" Their elders responded in unison as everyone embraced each other in celebration.

Jenny kissed her daughter's forehead and asked, "Did you two set a date yet?"

Sheri glanced at Anthony and smiled, "No, Mom, not yet."

"Yeah, we were kind of busy just surviving out there." Anthony nodded at Jenny and looked back to see a warm red glow of the fire, and it radiated on Sheri's complexion. "We'll figure that out soon, right, sweetie?"

"Uh, huh," Sheri gazed into his eyes with that look of acceptance he grew to love.

There, she did it again, Anthony thought, while he stood admiring her beauty. Every time she made that breathy expression, it felt like she just pushed his hot button. He remembered that other people were in the room and tried to think of something he could say to change the subject. "Um, I…"

"That's alright, you have plenty of time to figure it out." Jenny seemed to sense his clumsiness and wrapped her arms around both of them, "You two look exhausted. Why don't you call it a night, and we can all talk more tomorrow, okay?"

"Thanks, Mom," Sheri hugged her, reached over and embraced Bolt, "Goodnight."

When Anthony dropped Sheri off at her house, he kissed her. "Okay, sweetie, get some rest." He paused and lingered by the closed door.

"Um," Sheri fiddled with her keys, "I guess I should go in now."

"Alright, love..." Anthony gazed into her eyes, "I'll see you tomorrow, and we can talk about setting a date," he warmly kept his palm on her cheek and smiled.

"What date?" Sheri looked up with a mischievous grin and rested her hands on his shoulders.

Anthony saw where this was leading and he laughed, "You know...our..."

"Our, what?" Sheri giggled playfully, "I want to hear you say it, kind sir."

"Okay, my dear lady," Anthony sighed, "Tomorrow we can talk about setting a date for our wedding," he adjusted the feather on her left arm, "Alright, love?"

Sheri giggled again and patted his chest, "Okay, my wonderful knight in smelly clothes, I like the sound of your words." She pecked his cheek, turned and faced the door but hesitated.

"Well, aren't you going to unlock the door?"

"I can't."

"Why not?"

"I don't think I can spend the night without you." Sheri leaned her forehead against the door and sighed, "We've been through so much together these past eight days, that... I just can't go in alone now." Sheri held up her keys without making eye contact, "Here, you unlock it for me."

Anthony reached and their hands touched. Sheri turned, and they just stood there, gazing at each other in silence. After a brief pause, he took the keys and nodded, "Okay, love, I'll unlock it for you." Yet, she was so close that he had to reach around to get the door open. "Now, go on and get some rest. I'll see you tomorrow."

"Goodnight, Tony," Sheri kissed him one more time, then she stepped inside and slowly closed the door.

Anthony sighed, turned, walked to his truck, and each step felt heavy. When he scooted into the driver's seat, he had a strange feeling that something was not quite right.

So, he sat in the dark and stared at the inside house lights being flicked on, and then he realized why he felt this way. Although they were not married yet, Sheri was his woman, and, somehow, she was not supposed to be there. This was not her home. She belonged with him but they still had to wait a little longer before they could have a place of their own.

Sadness drifted in like a thick fog. "What's wrong with you, man," he pounded the steering wheel in frustration. "Go home, get some sleep," he lectured himself, as he felt increased annoyance about his own silly obsession.

Yet, he did not reach for the ignition. Instead, he sat in the darkness like a sick, lonely puppy and stared at the house until all the lights finally went out.

Reluctantly, he started the engine and drove back to Bolt's cabin. "That's it," he groaned, "We can't wait any longer."

Anthony awoke the next morning and sat in the kitchen with Bolt. For a long time, they sipped coffee and talked about the courtship quest and what it all meant for the future.

"Well, one thing is for sure," Anthony looked up from his coffee mug, "I know that Sheri and I are supposed to have a good life together."

"So, I reckon Sheri didn't drive you crazy, is that right?"

Anthony laughed, "Oh, she did, but she also had to put up with my bizarre quirks. I kept getting caught up in my own guilt, and I was afraid of doing more harm by following through with a marriage proposal."

"Don't dwell on the past anymore, son," Bolt patted Anthony on the back and smiled reassuringly, "You've been given a blank slate, and now, you two can write your own life story. So, go ahead, live it to the fullest."

"Yeah, I can see that now," Anthony stood up and brought the coffee pot over. "Do you want some more?"

Bolt nodded, "Yep, thanks." The woodcarver watched, as his apprentice served the both of them. "So, tell me, son, what did you learn out there on your courtship quest?"

"Well…" Anthony returned the pot and sat back down, "I think Sheri and I both discovered that we can work well together through just about anything that gets thrown at us." He smiled, "We sure had our little spats but we always seemed to rebound with a lot of humor."

"Yeah, that's what loving couples do, son," Bolt laughed and stared out the kitchen window like he was in deep thought. "Emma and I had plenty of ups and downs in our relationship but we learned to accept each other's differences. Gradually, we developed an unconditional love, and we tried not to make harsh judgements with toxic words."

"Did you still have a lot of arguments about things?"

"Of course. Nobody's perfect but we worked hard at debating without bitterness and blaming each other. When we got too heated about a problem and said something hurtful, we made it a point to apologize."

"Well," the young man laughed, "I'll be doing a lot of apologizing, then."

"We all make mistakes, son," Bolt leaned forward and smiled, "But, you know…" He paused and seemed to weigh his words carefully, "Emma and I realized that it's best to be forgiving of ourselves and each other. Of course, it was natural for one of us to sulk and pout once in a while but that only made us more miserable."

Anthony laughed and shook his head over his own memory, "Yeah, Sheri and I tried that, and it just added a cloud over us when we didn't speak at all."

"Yep, it's best to not hold grudges, son. Never go to bed angry, and you both will be okay in the long run."

Just as Bolt spoke, Sheri came in through the front door and walked into the kitchen with a picnic basket. "Good morning."

"You're here early, kitten," Bolt hugged her and smiled. "I didn't know you were coming over so soon, considering how tired you both looked last night."

Sheri placed the basket on the counter and kissed Anthony. "Well, like you've said many times, it's best to start early, because we're burning day light. Right, Tony."

Anthony admired her boldness and was delighted with the thought of seeing her so soon. He grinned, "She's got you there, boss." He glanced at the basket and nodded to Sheri. "You're not planning on a picnic after all we've been through, are you?"

"Are you kidding me?" Sheri laughed and took some eggs out. "I'm going to make us some breakfast, and we'll sit on comfortable chairs for a change."

Anthony stretched, rubbed his aching back and sighed, "Good, you had me worried there for a minute."

Sheri clapped her hands twice. "Okay, chop, chop. Let's move it." She spread out tomatoes, mushrooms, bell peppers and cheese on the counter. "Tony, you get the skillet and spatula. We're going to make a big omelet."

"Yes, dear," Anthony teased, laughed and placed everything on the counter.

Sheri grabbed an apron, wrapped it around his waist and tied it. "There, you look so cute."

When Anthony turned around, he noticed that she gazed at him with a lovely smile. In that moment, he realized that her eyes seemed to have more sparkle. "It's so good to be with you this morning, babe." He paused and thought of how nice it would be to see Sheri's lovely face every day.

Sheri patted his chest and smiled, "You might as well get used to it, Tony. I don't think I can be away from you for very long now."

"That's how I feel, love."

Bolt laughed from his kitchen chair, "Well, by the looks of you two, I reckon you had a lot going on out there." He waved a hand to the window.

"Oh, Poppy, you would not believe what we've been through together," Sheri sat beside Bolt and spoke wide-eyed with excitement. "We struggled with thunder storms, an earthquake, near starvation, snakes and a dead guy!"

"Whoa, Whoa!" Bolt let out a deep sigh, "What dead guy?"

"See for yourself," Anthony handed him the dog tags." We found him at that mountain cabin, and he evidently killed himself about seven months ago."

"We left the body there, Poppy."

Bolt examined it thoughtfully and looked up, "Alright, I'll call the Sheriff."

"Thanks, he needs a proper burial." Anthony nodded at the tags, "We wanted to do more but we were too busy trying to survive out there."

"Yes, Poppy, but the eagle and its mate were always there as our guides. They even provided fish for us to eat."

"That's amazing!" Bolt leaned closer and grinned, "I've heard many legends about guiding angels in the shape of eagles and other animals, but nothing like this." He sighed and shook his head with admiration, "You two are truly blessed."

"Yes, we believe that, too." Anthony nodded but added, "What we don't understand is why they disappeared a couple of hours before we got back home."

Sheri put her hand over her heart and looked sad. "Something is different. I don't feel God's presence like I did before."

"I feel the same way," Anthony studied his mentor, as though he wanted some kind of explanation. "What do you think it means?"

His mentor seemed to be in deep thought, while he stood and gazed upon a carving of an eagle on a shelf. The woodcarver picked it up turned to his apprentice.

"Well, son, I reckon I'm not wise enough to say for sure. What I do know is that you have been on a long journey of healing. During this time, you were given a second chance to redeem yourself. Part of that was to go on a quest of discovery with Sheri and find your mutual purpose in life. This meant that you both had to go through many times of uncertainty, and you were lost in your own doubts." Bolt handed Anthony the eagle statue, "What do you think, son?"

The apprentice studied the intricate details of the statue, and he was in deep contemplation for a moment. As he did so, he felt Sheri's hand on his arm. Then, he looked into her eyes and glanced over at Bolt. "Well, what I don't fully understand is the connection between an eagle and the Watchman."

Bolt patted his shoulder and smiled, "The Watchman showed up when you needed him the most." He paused and added, "He's done that for others, and I reckon he could be some kind of an angel like the eagle."

"Yeah, I know I wouldn't be alive if the Watchman didn't intervene to save me."

Sheri leaned closer and sighed, "Then, the Watchman moved on." She looked up at Bolt as she searched for more understanding. "So, the eagles guided us during our courtship quest. Now they're gone. I miss them, Poppy."

"Well, you had a once-in-lifetime mountaintop experience." He took the statue and held it in his hands, as he pondered the matter. "I reckon you're having kind of a spiritual let-down after that natural high you were on."

"I don't understand, Poppy."

"Well, kitten," Bolt let out a breath of air, sat down and patted her resting hand on the table, "The eagle and its mate completed their mission, and now it's up to you two to work out your own destinies together."

Anthony gazed at Sheri and held her hand tight. "But, how do we fill this empty feeling inside?"

The woodcarver shrugged, "I reckon you both will have to live like the rest of us mortals and not depend on your emotions. You've been given a chance at starting your lives out new and fresh. Now, you both can figure out how to manage on your own."

Anthony and Sheri kept their focus on each other and smiled. Without diverting his gaze, the young man asked, "So, what do we do now?"

"Well, I reckon if Grammy Lucille were sitting here with you both right now, she would say it best. Make a good, happy life for yourselves. Take one joyous day at a time. Accept the good and bad. Love each other and God with all your hearts. Laugh a lot. And remember… live by faith, not by sight. This will provide the fulfillment you need to be at peace." With that thought, he stood and said, "I've got work to do."

They watched the woodcarver while he strolled out to the workshop and closed the door. Anthony put dishes in the sink and began to wash quietly. Sheri smiled contently, and she took each plate that her man gave her, then used a towel to dry.

Anthony paused and looked contentedly into her eyes, smiled and asked, "What do you think, babe?"

"We're together, and we love each other. That's what I think."

"Yep, we have a whole new life ahead."

About the Author

Steven S. Foster served in the U.S. Air Force until 1970. Later, he earned a BA degree in communications at Biola College. He wrote numerous magazine articles, and he gave presentations in schools for a nonprofit agency. While he refined the art of studying people and behavior, he settled into a career of customer service. Now retired, he works full-time as an author of fictional stories that inspire and encourage his readers.

www.ingramcontent.com/pod-product-compliance
Lightning Source LLC
Chambersburg PA
CBHW020507260626
47156CB00006B/1902